KING OF THE CROWS

This edition first published 2020 by Fahrenheit Press.

ISBN: 978-1-912526-52-9

10 9 8 7 6 5 4 3 2 1

www.Fahrenheit-Press.com

F 4 E

King Of The Crows

By

Russell Day

Fahrenheit Press

This book is dedicated to William Baginsky.
Because any damn fool can learn, but not everyone can teach.
Thanks.

Chapter 1. The Clocks Have Broken the Key

Extract from the screenplay of Year of the Crow. Lithograph Studios, California (2026)

EXT. EMPTY SHOPPING STREET LONDON – DAY.

An ambulance is lying on its side, one of its blue lights is still flashing; the other is shattered. The siren is not working, and the street is silent apart from the sound of someone running.

Camera draws away from the ambulance and gives us a long shot along the middle of the empty road.

ROBERTSON

(Voice-over)

The smell was the worst thing. Even in the early days, before they began to decay. The smell was always there, in your clothes, in your hair. Once you'd had it in your nostrils you could never forget it. Like standing in a butcher's shop, next to a cesspit. When you caught that smell you ran away. And if you didn't run fast enough, you'd wish you fucking had.

Figure of Robertson enters top of street from the left. He is wearing a grey suit with a white shirt and tie. The suit is crumpled and the tie hangs loose. He pauses and looks around before running toward the camera. As he draws level with the crashed ambulance, shot changes to close-up. He is sweating and breathing hard through gritted teeth. As he passes the ambulance it begins to rock. Shot closes onto the cabin. An obviously dead man is clawing at the windscreen. Robertson stumbles as he skirts the vehicle. He stares briefly at the zombie before he resumes running.

At the top of the street a horde of zombies appear. Sound of gunfire in distance.

INT. HELICOPTER – FLYING – DAY

Close-up on pilot's face, which is largely hidden by his helmet and comms gear. The viewer is not aware of what he is seeing.

PILOT

Christ, look at them, there're thousands. Tell them we got to blow the bridges. Blow them now.

EXT. AERIAL VIEW OF LONDON – DAY

Camera view is from a great height, centre of screen is the River Thames. The camera descends quickly, giving the impression of falling toward the streets to the south of the river. The streets and roads moving toward the river are full of zombies.

ROBERTSON

(Voice-over)

The problem was finding somewhere to run to.

From recording of police interview with Colin Robertson, conducted by the joint agency of the New Metropolitan Police and the Metropolitan Police Department of the District of Columbia (MPDC)
(2nd April 2028)

Winslow - Recording begins at 9.57 a.m. April 2nd, 2028. Present are myself, DC Peter Winslow of the New Metropolitan Police, and Detective Sergeant Miranda Cross of the MPDC.
Cross - Good morning.
Winslow - Being interviewed is Colin Robertson. Would you confirm, for the recording, Mr Robertson, that you have been offered legal representation and have waived the right.
Robertson - That's right.
Winslow - And you are aware that you can change your mind at any point, and request cessation of this interview until you have a legal representative present?
Robertson - Yes, I understand that.
Winslow - Are you aware of why we requested this interview, Mr Robertson?
Robertson - No.
Winslow - The years since the final mutation of the Toxo parasite have been somewhat hectic. The two years of the Outbreak left the government and financial sectors of Europe in disarray which …
Robertson - Do you know who I am?
Winslow - I'm sorry?
Robertson - I said, do you know who I am?
Winslow - Yes, Mr Robertson, of course …
Robertson - Colin Robertson. Miller and Robertson, oh and Maccallan, of course. Hollywood fucking loved Maccallan, didn't they? I was there from the start, you get that? One of the founding fathers of the fight. First wave of the London Take Back. And now I'm the last man standing, so just by default, sonny, I am The King of the Fucking Crows. So, you do not lecture me about the Outbreak. Understand?

Year of the Crow: In Conversation with Colin Robertson. Interview appearing in The Sunday Times Colour Supplement (12/01/2025), conducted by Gail Cinchcross

When I first open the door to Colin Robertson, I realise I'm nervous. Beyond the nervousness I would expect when meeting a national hero. I wonder why this should be, because at first sight Robertson isn't particularly remarkable. He's average height, if broader than many people are these days. The t-shirt he's wearing shows the bulk is muscle, not fat. Rowing against the tide of current fashion (one that he is in no small part responsible for), his head isn't shaved. His fringe, though thin, almost reaches his eyes.

It's those eyes, I decide, that are unsettling. Robertson's forty-three and most of him looks younger, until you see his eyes; they're older, much older, and they never stay still.

Maybe aware of the effect his never-resting gaze is having on me, Robertson smiles charmingly, introduces himself and offers his hand before asking if he can come in. The graciousness of the man dispels the unease and I'm left feeling merely awestruck.

Colin Robertson, the King of the Crows, is coming into my hotel room to give me an interview.

It transpires, there's a condition.

"They weren't zombies," he says, softly. "Don't call them zombies."

It's how the victims of Human Variant-Toxo gondii are referred to in Hollywood's version of the London Lockdown. I don't say this to Robertson of course, but I do ask his opinion of the film. Naturally I want to hear his thoughts on the portrayal of him by Malik Connally, currently Tinseltown's hottest property.

At the mention of Malik, the charming smile reappears, now with a dash of the sardonic.

"Well, he looked better with a shaved head than I ever did."

Malik was the only member from the stellar cast of *Year of the Crow* who ventured across the Atlantic. Agents and producers of the other stars were quick to defend the big names against the tide of criticism provoked by this partisan move. Few of the critics were silenced. The reception the film received across Europe would indicate that feelings are still running high. While the studio was quick to deny rumours that the original cut of the film included a happy ending, such stories continue to circulate.

Ryan Morgan – a previously unknown actor chosen for the part of Rodger Maccallan – maintains that his own reticence to leave the USA was a commercial decision rather than a cautious one.

"You have to understand that over here, many people don't believe the virus has been stopped. A lot of them don't think it's even been contained."

We speak via satellite phone and the quality of the line gives his voice a broken lilt. Something you might not expect, given the heroic timbre he adopted throughout the film.

"People who have travelled outside the US won't admit it anymore, they keep quiet about it. There's still a lot of fear over here. People have been hounded out of their homes. Airline pilots have quit because their neighbours won't talk to them."

For Ryan, 'here' is Utah, one of the landlocked states benefiting from escalating property values as the population shifts inland. Belief across America that the 'virus' (which most Americans still think HV-Tg is) is still active, and possibly waterborne, has resulted in a quiet migration away from the coast. One of the unforeseen effects of the Outbreak has been the decline in surfboard sales.

Given Ryan Morgan's fear of becoming an industry pariah, it's ironic that Malik Connally's role in the film has resulted in his elevation to icon status. Every major studio in the US is currently clamouring for his signature and, European visitor or not, he is regularly swamped by an adoring public. It seems America loves its heroes almost as much as its borders.

From the giddying height he now inhabits, Malik feels able to distance himself from the highest grossing film in over a decade. When interviewed shortly before its London premiere, he was brutally candid.

"It's an insult. An insult to the victims, the dead and the survivors. I'm ashamed to have my name in the credits."

Not, it's been noted, so ashamed that he's asked to have his name taken off them. Or refused his percentage of the box office returns.

Robertson, who has as much right as anyone to be outraged or insulted, is less judgemental. While his eyes continue to check shadows and corners, he smiles that gracious smile again.

"It was what it was, an action film. It wasn't true to life; it wasn't the way it happened. But who'd want to watch that?"

Robertson's name appears on the credits too, as a technical advisor. I suggest it doesn't sound like his role was taken too seriously.

He shrugs.

"I spent a lot of time with Malik. He asked a lot of questions, took a lot of notes. He recorded hours of me rabbiting on. People have told me he got my voice down to a tee … I can't hear it, personally. I spent an hour or so talking with the story consultant. Over the phone, of course. He wanted chapter and verse. Same with the guy who played Miller."

It is the portrayal of Miller in *Year of the Crow* that has most angered survivors of the London Lockdown. Again, Robertson, widely recognised as Miller's closest lieutenant, is more sanguine.

"There's an idea that Miller was this charismatic leader of the lost, some sort of messiah. There was something about him, but it wasn't charm or charisma. It's hard to describe. He was a force of nature. I'm not trying to detract from what he was, but it was less about him leading and more about everyone else following. I think if he'd taken a left and the rest of us had headed right, he wouldn't have even noticed. He wasn't someone they'd want to put on the big screen. He wasn't a film star."

When I asked what he was, Robertson's answer is instant. It's not something he has to think about.

"He was driven, a driven killer. And at that time, that was what we all needed. That's why I don't like it when people talk about zombies. That would have been easy, special effects and make-up coming at you. It wasn't like that. The Gonzos were victims of a sickness, they weren't dead already, we had to kill them. And they felt pain. They felt. But Miller understood, Miller knew they had to be killed."

As he's spoken his eyes have finally settled, although it's clear whatever they're focused on is visible only to Robertson himself.

From Kings of Crows: Life on the Wrong Side of the Lockdown, by Colin Robertson with Michael J. Ritchie, Celsius Press (2025)

Anosmia. Lack of the sense of smell. I don't know if there's a special word for midlife-crisis-induced-lack-of-smell, but that's the kind I have. My midlife crisis came at age thirty-seven. Young, I know, and possibly the only time in my life I'd been ahead of the game. My parents always said I was a late developer.

At thirty-seven my gut was climbing the waist of my trousers and I'd started to count, obsessively, the number of hairs I'd leave in the comb each morning. The accepted solution in those days was to join a gym you'd never go to or pay an arm and a leg to have a personal trainer shout at you. I couldn't afford either. I signed up to a local karate club; thinking I'd get fit, build confidence and learn self-defence. That was what the poster on the leisure centre wall offered. As well as the sales pitch, there was a photo of someone performing a head height kick.

In my third lesson, I walked straight into such a kick and was taken to A & E to have my nose realigned and my consciousness assessed. The waiting room was full. The staff were trying to avoid eye contact, so they could pretend not to see the latest arrivals. The doctor who finally saw me was jittering with caffeine and grey with fatigue. She looked me over, decided I wasn't about to switch off and dismissed the security guard. I think that was the week they started issuing ambulance crews with sidearms.

She did something to my nose that resulted in a white flash of agony and a loud cracking sound. Then she told me it was likely I'd sheared my ethmoid plate in two and severed the olfactory nerves. At least my nose was straight again.

That's why I don't talk about the smell.

Most people have something to say about the smell. The way it'd cling to them, following them and how they could never get it out of their noses. I missed all that. I don't imagine it was anything good. End stage of the disease, just before the infection took over, or killed them, body functions began to erode. Bowels, bladder, stomach: they'd usually empty.

I've read accounts of victims speaking tongues, uttering the ten thousand names of god, issuing prophecies. Whatever they may have said, they said it from in a puddle of shit. I never heard anything other than gibberish. Some of them would lock onto a phrase or a line that they'd repeat constantly. I think that's where the spiel about prophecies came from.

If you were part of it, caught up in the fighting, you'll know what I mean. I got separated from the group one time. I don't know how it happened, but I got left behind in a building we'd been stripping. I was on the second floor, in a room at the end of a long corridor. I realised it was getting late and I made to leave before it got dark. As I got ready, I heard all hell break loose on the road outside. The group had moved out of the building and into the street. I found out later they'd been caught in a crowd of Gonzos. Fresh ones. It looked like another group of survivors had got infected and switched-off. They were still strong.

Our group was good; we'd had a lot of experience by then, but these were fresh and took a lot of killing. We lost people, I feel guilty about that; maybe if I'd been there it would have made a difference.

When I heard the battle kick off, I made to run out and help. As I left the room, at the other end of the corridor six or seven Gonzos appeared. Most of them were quiet, not all the victims babbled. One of them, though, had locked into a phrase.

He was shouting, "Tick-tock, the clocks have broken the key."

Shouting it again and again.

The pack saw me or heard me and ran forward. I was alone and unarmed, I'd left my axe somewhere and anyway there wasn't the space in the corridor to swing it properly, and there was nowhere to run if I missed. I ducked back into the room and slammed the door behind me, piled desks and filing cabinets against it. Then waited.

I was stuck there until the next morning. They didn't let up for a minute. The entire night they hammered at that door. I was lucky, it was a heavy-duty fire door and thank God it opened outwards, so it held. The sound of the hammering changed the longer they carried on beating against the wood. The pounding began to sound wet, then became a sharp clacking noise and finally turned to scratching. They hammered at the door until their fists turned to pulp, carried on until the bones were poking out of them. It went on so long, they didn't have enough left to punch with and they just scratched away with their stumps.

Sometimes they'd scream, cry even. Those were the really unlucky ones. The disease left enough of their brains intact to register the pain.

There was none of that on that night. But all the time I was listening to them trying to break through the door, the chanting one kept it up: Tick-tock, the clocks have broken the key. Tick-tock, the clocks have broken the key.

Sit in a world where nothing makes sense anymore. Sit in the dark for nine or ten hours listening to someone beating themselves into jelly and bellowing one string of sounds.

People crave order, something to believe in. If there's no order your mind tries its damnedest to find some.

The group found me the next morning. When they'd got to a safe place, they counted who was lost and, soon as it was light, went back to account for people. When they didn't find my body, they went back into the last building I'd been seen in and followed the sound of the Gonzos trying to break down the door.

I had that bloody phrase going around and around my head for days. I kept on trying to decipher it. What had it meant, what was the poor bastard trying to say?

It meant nothing, but I can see why people cling to the idea that the Gonzos were trying to tell us something. Something's out there trying to get a message through: there's a plan. Compared to the idea that it was all just chance, it's a comfort of a type. Chance doesn't care and can't be appeased and can't be reasoned with. Chance means it could all happen again.

**WE CAME, WE SAW, WE FUCKED THEM UP!
AREA CLEARED. WELCOME.**

Medium: Oil-based white paint on brick, applied by brush.
Date: Unknown.
Location: Side of domestic dwelling in Tooting. Located on the end of a terrace, the wall overlooks a patch of vacant ground that is thought to have served as a fire pit.

From The Writing on the Wall: The Story of the Lockdown told in Graffiti, by T.L. Kimble, Oxford Press (2026)

April 2nd, 2028

"There." Winslow put the book on the monstrosity of a desk and tapped on the open page. He didn't stop tapping even when I'd turned to look. "That is what I:m talking about."

Tap, tap. Tap, tap. Tap, tap.

I turned back to the transcript of Robertson's interview.

"What is?"

I was clearly meant to pick up the copy of Kings of Crows, so he could come closer and direct me to the right passage. Possibly with one hand resting inoffensively on my shoulder. It was obvious that a showdown needed to happen between us, but I wasn't in the mood. Also, I was curious to see how long he would keep up the staccato finger jabbing. Winslow had a selection of mannerisms for claiming attention. I'd wished, more than once, that he'd simply develop a nervous tick, a quiet one.

Tap, tap. Tap, tap. Tap, tap.

When I waited for him to explain, and made no move to pick up the paperback, his expression wavered between confused and exasperated. It's an expression I've found often accompanies a sense of entitlement. In the same way a sense of entitlement accompanies a promotion, particularly one that hasn't been earned.

The breath he drew sounded as if he wanted to sigh, and served to inflate his chest, allowing his unbuttoned jacket to frame his torso properly. He was a good-looking man, I had to concede that. He hadn't missed many meals.

"He says here about being cut off from the others. He claims he doesn't know how it happens. To me that doesn't ring true. When my group went in, we made damn sure we stayed close together. Getting cut off could mean …" He clicked his fingers. "I find it hard to believe a man with Robertson's experience would let that happen, and he sure as hell wouldn't forget about it. That bit bothers me."

He began tapping the page again. I waved the gesture away and sat up straight, putting more distance between us. I knew the passage of the book he was referring to and, for different reasons, it bothered me as well. Assuming it bothered Winslow at all, that was. Anything that could be segued into a mention of his combat history tended to 'bother' him.

"How many times did you have contact?" I watched Winslow over the expanse of the leather-topped desk. The question pleased him. He sat back, cocking one arm over the back of his chair, to think about it. I bet myself another mouthful of coffee that he'd take his jacket off before the telling was over.

"Eight, maybe nine, times."

"And you never forget those times?"

"No, never." He adjusted his position and I swigged most of my coffee ration for the day. "You see things like that, survive them …"

He left the sentence to hang.

"Eight or nine times?" Winslow nodded and looked away into the middle distance, was about to say something, then felt the quality of the silence and looked back at me. "Robertson and Miller were close enough to London Bridge to see individuals jumping into the water when the army opened fire. Wrong side of the Lockdown and with nowhere to run when the hordes were forming. Less than a month after that, half of London was dead or insane. Robertson most likely had contact eight or nine times a day for damn near two years. I'd be surprised if he remembers every time he was near-killed, never mind every time something went wrong. And put your jacket back on, it's cold in here."

The noise level picked up when I stopped speaking. Clearly, we'd had an audience. Winslow unpursed his lips, but I interrupted him before he started.

"For the record, Constable, I don't trust him either."

I don't imagine he appreciated it, but it was the kinder way to pull rank. I could have reminded him why I was sitting in a freezing asshole of an office with its left-over luxury desks and its wet-behind-the-ears staff. Why I wasn't three and a half thousand miles away with my family.

I'm lying. It wasn't kindness. I didn't give a shit about Winslow's male ego. I just didn't want to tell him about being in France when the cats started to die.

Harley TD, et al., From Bad Kitty and Cat's Eye to The Rapture Bell and Captain Z: Nomenclature and Common Perception of Human Variant-Toxoplasma gondii. New England Journal of Psychology 2025;9: 699-702

Prophecies weren't the only religious overtones tagged onto the back story of the Breakout. HV-Tg has been labelled the Judgement Virus, St Peter's Call, The Rapture Bell and a dozen others. Those of us fortunate enough to live in regions still afforded full internet access can spend days cataloguing them. Between 2020 and 2021 there was a tenfold increase in the number of internet sites promoting the belief that the HV-Tg pandemic was a divine judgement. The proliferation of such sites has slowed, but it has certainly not stopped. The question is whether such material is simply a symptom of the fear and blame culture, prevalent in post-Toxo society, or a root cause of it.

If you'd rather pseudo-science to quasi-religion, you'll need better software. The geeks and the conspiracy theorists have teamed up and taken their brand of misinformation into the pits of the dark web.

HV-Tg will usually be referred to, with almost friendly familiarity, as 'Gonzo' and frequently be categorised by a number supposedly derived from the number of mutations it had been through. Most contributors to these sites simply use one to four (and beyond should they subscribe to the belief that HV-Tg is still ascending numerically). Some refer to one, two, three and Tee. Tee, standing for Terminal. The real show-boaters will write of primary, secondary, tertiary and terminal stages.

The idea that Toxoplasma gondii made the leap from a widespread, though largely innocuous, disease into the pandemic killer league in three neat steps is as laughable as the judgement from above scenario. One thing that lends fuel to the already flaming pyres of delusion is the speed of the spread.

The earliest references to the France Cat Flu plague were recorded in November 2019. By the summer of 2021 conservative estimates maintain that thirty-three percent of the population of France were dead with a further ten percent subject to the psychotic phase of the illness, "switched-off" in the common parlance.

Even with adjustment to the number of refugees who fled into Germany and Spain, the death toll was in excess of twenty million. There are, at the time of writing, no reliable figures allowing separation of those who met their death via the natural course of HV-Tg and those who died at the hands of those suffering infection-induced psychosis. When the almost inevitable cholera epidemics swept through affected cities, the death toll rose still further.

Chapter 2. Marcia and Steve

Dirty Kitty (Runny Cat, Shitty Kitty)

Reference to behavioural changes displayed by cats infected with mutated Toxoplasma gondii. Owners reported domestic cats unlearning their house training and defecating indoors. It was observed that feral cats would no longer bury their faecal matter, instead choosing to defecate in exposed (populated) areas.

The A to Z of Gondii Names By William Patrick, Starsland Press (2026)

October 12th, 2020
(Six weeks before the first officially recognised case of HV-Tg induced psychosis)

Sixteen, seventeen, eighteen.

Robertson flushed the strands of hair away. He'd counted twenty the day before. Pulled each one from the comb and dropped it into the toilet pan. Two fewer; was that good or bad? Was he losing less or was there just less to lose? And he'd nicked himself shaving. Hadn't felt it at the time, but as he looked in the mirror a tiny bead of blood gained enough weight to drop free of his jaw and land on the collar of his shirt. Red on white. Great. He could picture Maccallan rolling his eyes. There wasn't time to change it now, he was already running late.

The alarm had failed to wake him, and he'd overslept, though it would be truer to say underslept. Steve and Marcia had been arguing again. The noise hadn't been the issue, they were nowhere near as loud as the alarm he'd successfully ignored. But since he and Janet had broken up, he'd become addicted to the dramas, played out two or three time a week, in the flat below.

The night before they'd started in the living room, not loud enough for him to hear the dialogue but the stamping footfalls traced the discord as it moved back and forth. The volume increased steadily, punctuating the couple's bedtime rituals, until Robertson could make out the words. The missing cat figured in the argument, and something about abusive phone calls. Blame was being apportioned by Steve.

The layout of the downstairs flat differed to Robertson's. The neighbours' bedroom was directly below his living room and he delayed going to bed to listen in on their fight. It was something he'd have not done before Janet left. When he'd first caught himself eavesdropping, he thought the bitter pleasure it gave him was knowing that he was spared such exchanges.

Surely solitude was preferable to that.

Now he wasn't so sure, perhaps it was envy. Maybe something baser. The fights invariably ended in a bout of carnal arbitration and, lately, he'd stopped pretending to be annoyed at being able to hear.

He pulled his raincoat on as he left his flat, swore when the collar caught the nick on his jaw. Marcia was in the downstairs hall. Steve had already left, presumably for work, but Robertson could only guess. He only knew the couple's names because they shared a front door and communal doormat where the morning post landed. It struck him as odd that he knew nothing about the woman other than her name and the sound she made climaxing. And that her cat was missing. The thought popped into his head just as Marcia said good morning and he nodded in reply, embarrassed.

Her eyes were red, and he assumed she'd been crying again. Not dressed for going out, she was holding a half-filled black rubbish bag. He offered to drop it in the bin for her, felt himself blushing as he took it from her. She probably thought he was some desperate sad-act who curled up every time he spoke to a woman.

The black bag had been scrunched closed in her fist rather than tied. When he dropped it into the shared waste bins by the front door, it flopped open. A collection of cat toys fell out, along with one of those Day-Glo cat-coats they sold to mark pets out from ferals.

The office was busy but sparsely populated. Maccallan had his tie pulled down, showing his top button was open and revealing an inch of his tan. It was his way of looking active and on-top-of-things. He rolled his eyes at the blood spot on Robertson's collar.

"Jerome's called in sick. Reckons it's this Frog Flu, if you could take some of his load. He was already covering for Susan."

He gave Robertson a matey pat on the shoulder, said thanks 'Collie' and, before he could say anything in response, headed back to his office. As he waited for his computer to wake up, he watched the younger man over the top of the screen. Behind the glass wall of his office he stood and looked out over the half dozen desks. Technically the day didn't start for another ten minutes, but people were already tapping keyboards or talking earnestly into phones. Only three of the desks were occupied. Like Maccallan's trick with his tie, masking his lack of any real input, the staff sickness was masking the lack of work currently passing through the office.

"Two," said Rich, from the desk next to Robertson's. He didn't look up as he spoke and his fingers on the keyboard didn't slow down.

"Already?"

Rich made a sound in the back of his throat, amusement and contempt in equal measure.

"First thing he said when he got in, 'sunrise over the Thames, wonderful'." He imitated Maccallan's voice quite well, exaggerating the tone of fake modesty. "Then the usual gripe about the cost of parking permits that close to Central London."

“My heart bleeds,” Robertson said and put two ticks on a clear patch of the desk blotter. The words came out sounding harsher than he’d intended.

Rich had been the one who’d come up with the ‘Chateau Maccallan lottery’. That had been months before and it had become another part of the daily routine. At the start of the day they’d each estimate how many times Maccallan would casually mention the location of his ‘apartment’; it had never been a flat. Closest number won and the loser made the drinks in the afternoon coffee break.

“You okay?”

The rapid typing hadn’t stopped, but it had missed a beat. He could feel Rich looking at him.

“Yeah, I just get sick of that supercilious little twat.” He was about to say more but realised something about Rich’s manner had changed. He’d become tense, as if he was bracing himself; here we go again, his posture shouted. Robertson managed to push the tirade into a mental corner. “I’m fine,” he told Rich.

The day had ground on, like every other day. The only bright spot had been winning Rich’s silly game and having a mug of instant coffee delivered to his desk. It had left a brown ring on the cheap veneer.

As they’d packed up for the day and got ready to leave, he’d asked Rich if he fancied going for a drink. He’d decided he’d invite Hannah, sitting at the third desk, to come along too. If Rich said yes. Rich didn’t. He demurred on the suggestion casually; he had a previous booking. A friend’s leaving drinks, somewhere in Camden, there was no extended invite to Robertson. Hannah shrugged into her coat and sailed past him on her way to the door. Robertson had an unpleasant sensation of being invisible, as if she were as unaware of his presence in her work life as Marcia was unaware of his overhearing her home life. As he locked the office door behind him, he saw Hannah walking with Rich, towards his car.

The glass panelling at the back of the bus shelter had been shattered but was held in place by eight or nine posters. Most of them were official health notices but a pair of them were homemade flyers with home-printer photos of cats. Phone numbers, MISSING announcements, offers of rewards. The web of cracks spanning the glass emanated from behind the dented picture of a mean-eyed tabby.

It started to rain as the bus arrived and the windows were beginning to mist with condensation. The lower deck was less than half full, but he chose to stand in the area earmarked for prams and wheelchairs. In the seat next to the double-width exit door, a man probably no older than Robertson dabbed alternatively at his nose and his eyes with the same handkerchief. He'd shed his overcoat and moons of sweat soaked through the material of his shirt. At each stop he'd breathe a sigh of relief when the doors hissed open and let cold air wash in. When he caught Robertson's scrutiny and met his gaze, his eyes were wet and blood shot. He smiled, as if embarrassed at being seen in public.

"Frog Flu," he offered in defence. "I felt fine this morning. Bloody Kitty Lickers, eh?" He tried to laugh but ended coughing into the sodden handkerchief.

The rain didn't ease up and the walk from the bus stop left him drenched. A young woman scuttled passed him, shoulders hunched, head bowed. A few paces ahead she stumbled, regained her footing and kicked out at something. A black cat sprinted across his path and scrambled up a fence into a hedge. Robertson overtook the woman as she stood at the edge of the pavement, scraping her shoe on the edge of the curb and muttering.

It was quiet downstairs and he turned the TV on to fill the silence. Dinner was frozen sausages. At the last minute he decided it wasn't worth putting the remains of the packet back into the freezer and cooked all of them. He distributed them across three sandwiches. He was starting on the third when Steve knocked on his door.

The communal hallway was cold; the front door was badly fitted and exchanged heat for cold draughts. Steve was in jogging bottoms, stripped to the waist and showing off a torso that he'd obviously built in a gym. For a panicked moment Robertson imagined the man knew he'd been listening to his sex life and had come down to warn him away.

"Sorry to bother you, I was just wondering if you had any aspirin or something? Something for a headache." He sounded embarrassed. "For Marcia."

"I might have. Come in, I'll have a look."

Steve glanced behind him before stepping into the hall. The gesture grated on Robertson. Was he worried he'd be seen? He came into the flat just far enough to let him pull the door to behind him; he didn't push it fully closed.

Robertson wanted to say something, make a comment on what he regarded as a slight. He couldn't think of anything. There was half a box of no-brand paracetamol at the back of the bathroom cabinet, a reminder of Janet's presence. He handed them to Steve. The thanks were genuine and the way he hurried back to Marcia made Robertson think he'd misjudged his body language. The man didn't want to be away from his unwell partner.

"If you need anything, give me a shout," he'd called from the doorway as Steve went down the stairs two at a time.

The flat beneath was quiet that evening, the only sounds were regular footfalls to what must have been the kitchen and the water pipe's tell-tale knocking when a tap was run. The public information posters all agreed that copious liquids were more beneficial than antibiotics.

As he was coming down the stairs next morning, he met Steve the way he'd met Marcia the day before: exiting their flat holding a plastic bag. This bag was smaller, a carrier bag. Steve was holding it away from him, caught between fingertips. He was still stripped to the waist and the delicate positioning of his hand seemed comical. The effect was compounded by his pinched expression. When he looked up, Robertson saw it wasn't a prissy expression of distaste, Steve was squinting. His eyes were tearing badly and the skin around them was puffed and red.

When Robertson offered to take the bag to the bins for him, he shook his head.

"No, this is full of cat shit, I can go back in and wash me hands."

Robertson held the door open for him.

"You've found the cat then?" he said.

Steve was struggling with the bin lid.

"Nah, it never come back. Just shat under the sofa before it left. I reached under it looking for something and …"

He pulled a face rather than elaborate further. Despite the cold he was shiny with sweat.

When he got back to the flat after work there were ribbons of yellow and black tape strung across the road and a collection of police vehicles ensuring they held. The crowd gathered at the cordon was mainly other commuters. People like him who'd come home from work to find their street was a crime scene.

There was a pair of uniform police, armed with clipboards and expressionless faces, listening indifferently to the tide of whining complaints. It was cold and damp and everyone wanted to be indoors, and everyone lived just over there. The tension in the crowd was being steadily ratcheted up with each denial of every request to cross the line.

Matters weren't helped by a squawk of feedback from a megaphone, and an announcement from inside the cordon.

"There is a siege situation underway and …"

And the rest of the message was lost in the chorus of dismay and low-level panic. At the other end of the street there was a flurry of movement as a police car dressed in reflective tape was ushered in. Someone used the words 'armed response team', and Robertson felt the air around him tighten.

The message about the siege situation was repeated. After "and …" came the warning to stay indoors. It was easier to hear this time; the outraged cries and complaints had stopped as people grabbed the lifeline of mobile phones.

The faces in the crowd around him were lit either in the come-and-go washes of blue light from the police cars, or the sickly green glow of phone screens. Everyone looked ill. Later Robertson would wonder if he'd seen that only in hindsight.

The megaphone told the crowd to disperse. A few drifted away, non-residents with no investment in the street to keep them there in the rain. The remainder stayed put or shuffled a few steps back, showing no real indication of moving on. When the phone calls and texts started getting answered, people were able to connect their family's fear and worries to the rest of the crowd and they began to press towards the tape again.

Robertson held back. He didn't have loved ones on the other side of the line, just neighbours grieving for a lost cat, and an empty flat. When police started to appear at the cordon, getting ready to repel boarders, he made motions towards leaving.

That's when he heard the gun shots. Three of them. Bang, pause, then bang-bang.

The gunshots were another thing he'd think about later. He'd heard gunfire before, played back on the news, or over some muppet's web page, #LONDON SHOOTING. They always sounded flat and dull. Something that could easily be put in a box labelled nothing to worry about. Put that same noise in the street you live on and things changed. Or was that hindsight too?

There were two directions that night. People moved towards the situation, or away from it. Robertson chose: away.

The situation was over and done with surprising speed. Most people were allowed back to their homes before the night was done and got to sleep in their own beds. Even Robertson was allowed back to his flat after twenty-four hours.

Steve and Marcia's door was sealed with the legend: CRIME SCENE DO NOT CROSS. Black letters against yellow tape. A bored PC guarded the door for a further day, while groups of officials drifted back and forth. A reporter asked Robertson for an interview, but lost interest when she realised how little he knew.

Then it was over.

The news reports were low on details. The coverage jostled for prominence with the ongoing stories coming in from the continent

Extract from the screenplay of Year of the Crow. Lithograph Studios, California (2026)

INT. ROBERTSON'S LIVING ROOM – LATE EVENING

The room is plainly decorated and sparsely furnished. A small TV sits against the wall. In front of it there is a sofa; this is where Robertson is sitting wearing only boxer shorts. On the TV screen a news report of a violent stabbing is playing. Robertson is blank faced and obviously bored. He's startled by an urgent hammering on his front door.

ROBERTSON

(Rising from the sofa)
Alright, keep your hair on.

INT. ROBERTSON'S HALLWAY

Viewed from close to the front door. The hammering is louder from this vantage point. Robertson is seen coming out of his front room and walking to the front door. He looks annoyed. The hammering is becoming increasingly frantic.

ROBERTSON

(Pulling the door open)
I said, keep your …

As he opens the door Marcia, wearing a nightdress, stumbles inside. She is crying and has blood splashed over her face. Robertson catches her.

MARCIA

Something's wrong with Steve. I can't get him to wake up, I think he's … I think he's dead.

ROBERTSON

(Seeing the blood on her face)
Are you hurt, are you bleeding?

MARCIA
No, it's Steve's.

Marcia is yanking on Robertson's arm, trying to pull him out of the flat.

Please. You've got to help me, please.

ROBERTSON
(Tense, but calm)
Is there someone in the flat, did someone attack you and Steve?

MARCIA
No, he's been ill. Please.

Robertson nods and goes down the stairs to Steve and Marcia's flat. Marcia starts to follow him but stops halfway down. Her nerve has failed her, and she is too scared to go back into the flat. The front door is half open and as Robertson makes his way through, the POV changes and we see his face from the interior of the flat. He grimaces. We freeze.

ROBERTSON
(Voice-over)
And there it was. For the first time. That fucking smell. They say you never forget your first time. Maybe they're right.

INT. STEVE AND MARCIA'S FLAT
The door opens onto the living room. It is bigger than Robertson's living room and looks more lived in. The space is dominated by a huge TV screen. The same news report that Robertson was watching upstairs is playing, but the sound has been muted. In front of the TV is a low table and a three-seat sofa. The sofa has been made up to act as a bed;

there are pillows at one end of it and a tangled duvet. The table is littered with medicines and the remains of a half-finished meal. The camera pauses briefly on a cat litter tray that is sitting in the corner. The litter has been disturbed and a lot of it is laying on the floor. It is very quiet, and the lighting is quite low.

ROBERTSON
(voice-over)
Because, the first time you go in, into that smell, you're an innocent, a babe in arms, a virginal bride who doesn't know she's married a monster.

Robertson moves across the room toward the bathroom. The bathroom is connected to the living room via a short hallway. There is an ironing board near the entrance to the hallway; a pile of white shirts is waiting to be pressed. As he reaches the door, Robertson grimaces again and, as the door swings wide, he recoils. The room contains a bath, toilet and sink which are all white, as are the tiled walls. The space is very brightly lit. Steve is on his knees, hunched over the toilet bowl. He's making noises that could be vomiting or choking. There is a lot of blood on the floor.

ROBERTSON
Steve, you okay?

Cut to close-up of Robertson's face, obviously aware that he is asking a stupid question. He moves slowly into the bathroom, realising he has stepped in a puddle of blood. Shot closes in onto the back of Steve's head. Volume of noises he is making increases, the vomiting sounds resolve into loud chewing.

ROBERTSON
Steve?

Robertson puts a hand on Steve's shoulder, Steve's head whips round. The lower half of his face is covered with blood and his mouth is full of raw meat. His eyes are pale and vacant.

ROBERTSON
Jesus Christ!

Robertson jumps back and Steve lurches to his feet. In the process of getting up, he lets go of something he is holding, and it lands on the toilet seat. A fast cut-away shot to the toilet seat reveals the front half of Marcia's pet cat.

Steve throws himself at Robertson. Robertson, moving backward in the narrow hallway, stumbles and falls onto his back. As he falls, he reaches out and grabs the ironing board, bringing it down with him. Steve, roaring, drops on top of him. Robertson manages to get his forearm under Steve's chin and is just able to keep him away from his face.

Close shot of the two men's faces. Steve is snapping his jaws open and shut, trying to bite Robertson, chunks of cat flesh falling from his mouth. Robertson begins punching Steve in the side of head. He punches hard and repeatedly, but Steve doesn't register the blows. Robertson, thrashing his head from side to side, sees the plug from the iron. With much twisting and straining he manages to grab it and, using the flex, pulls the iron within reach. He smashes the iron into the top of Steve's head until Steve goes limp and stops snapping his jaws.

Seemingly in a panic, Robertson pushes the dead man off him and rolls him onto his back. He straddles Steve's chest. Panting hard, he is unable to take his eyes from the bloodied corpse and raises the iron, unsure whether to strike again. Shot moves to living room. Marcia is framed in the doorway. She starts to scream.

ROBERTSON

He was trying to kill me. I … I …

Robertson realises Marcia isn’t looking at him or the body of her husband. He turns to look behind him. Cut to doorway of bathroom. Marcia’s cat is crawling out of the bathroom, entrails dragging behind it.

THE MILLER CREW LONDON TOUR 2021!
BALHAM SW12!
JUNE CLEARANCE SALE!

Medium: Red spray paint
Location: Frontage of Balham East Rail Station. The station building was the site of a communal dwelling/shelter during the early months of the Lockdown. The words 'thank you' appear below this piece along with a list of names, twenty-seven in all. Various mediums and styles have been used to compile this list.
Date: June 2021

From The Writing on the Wall: The Story of the Lockdown told in Graffiti

From Kings of Crows: Life on the Wrong Side of the Lockdown

Months later I met up with this woman, Jenny. We hadn't recognised each other at first. It wasn't surprising. We'd all lost weight, I'd shaved my head – almost everyone did; hair meant lice – and of course we were all pretty grubby by then. We only started talking about Steve and Marcia because she thought she knew me from before. When we compared notes, it turned out we'd been neighbours.

She was holed up in Balham when our group moved through and cleared it. She'd been caught up in the Lockdown too but had gone in the opposite direction to Miller and the rest of us. There was some family connection with Balham, so she'd headed straight there. I don't know much about how she got from one point to another. We didn't really share war stories much in those days. Back then, it was just business as usual. If you told someone the things you'd seen or done, the most likely response would have been, 'So what?'.

Thinking back, I wonder if we weren't all a lot closer to losing the plot than we realised. We dealt with whatever we had to, then just put it aside. If we talked at all, we talked about what we'd been before the Outbreak. Or what we were going to do once things got back to normal.

We never allowed ourselves to think that things were going to stay how they were. Never.

I don't suppose anyone will ever know for sure what happened in the flat. The people involved are dead by now.

According to the papers, the police answered a call from concerned neighbours reporting a violent disturbance. The first policeman on the scene went in and found Marcia trying to drag her screaming partner across the floor. The second cop ran in and the situation got worse. The long and the short of it was one of the cops wound up barricaded in the bedroom with Steve, the other barely escaped alive and called for back-up.

After two hours of pointless negotiating Marcia burst out the flat with a kitchen knife in each hand, ran at the police and got shot. When the first bullet didn't slow her down, two more took the top of her head off.

By Jenny's telling, the police had a floodlight on the front door and men in flak jackets running left, right and centre. After an hour of calling through the windows and trying to get someone to talk to them, they were getting ready to storm the place. Before that could happen, Marcia burst out, naked and covered in blood, shit and vomit. The usual switcher thing. Jenny said she'd had a knife in each hand but hadn't had time to run at the police before someone put a hole in her chest. And that was when she ran at the police. There was a pause when everyone froze and took on board that a gun had been discharged, and that it hadn't worked. Two head shots quickly followed.

The guys in flak jackets swarmed into the building. The 'hostage' was led out supported between two uniforms. Steve was carried out ten minutes later in a body bag.

That may have been one of the last police negotiating sessions in Europe. Not long after that it was assumed all siege-type situations were a switch-off and negotiation was carried out by a sniper. There were stories about dog handlers sending in attack-trained German Shepherds, and the dogs never making it out alive.

Chapter 3. Cheats, Liars and Cat Shit

Kitty Fuckers (Kitty Lickers)

Racist term, popular in British far-right circles and separatist groups during the early stages of the Outbreak, although the political wings of such organisations distanced themselves from its use. The term was a reference to the belief that the spread of HV-Tg could be traced to poor hygiene and perverse sexual practices. Used mainly in respect of the French, the term was often tailored to which hate group was appropriate, as in, 'it's all down to those Jew-boy Kitty Lickers in Paris'.

Note: In the southern states of America the term Cat Back has replaced the use of Wet Back, as the favoured reference to Mexican migrants. It has suited the agenda of both the new-right and ultra-orthodox church to believe, or at least to propagate the belief, that HV-Tg is rife in South America.

The A to Z of Gondii Names

April 4th, 2028

I showered at the station before heading back to the flat. I'd been stranded in London for nearly three years, for two years in France before that, yet I still referred to the places I'd lived as the flat or the house or the room.

Home had been America. Not strictly speaking the country, certainly not the country it had become since its borders had closed. Or closed to everything except wealth. Money was still allowed in. The memory of America, or at least the memory of what I'd left there, was what I'd once considered home.

It wasn't there anymore, not really. With the chaos of the Outbreak and collapse of Europe, the new-right hadn't even needed to push its separatist agenda. Human Variant-Toxoplasma gondii had handed the victory to them.

If gondii had waited six months before jumping ship from feline to Homo sapien nervous systems, then the presidential elections may have gone a different way. As it was, footage of French police machinegunning hospital entrances and German freight trains carrying the dead to mass fire pits provided a shaky, phone-footage backdrop to a fear-induced landslide. Millions of patriots supported the US economy, using their 'Merickan dollas to buy 'Merickan guns, convinced the second amendment was going to keep them safe from the plague. Gondii was a redneck campaign wet dream. The perfect excuse to bolt the doors against intruders, and the perfect scapegoat for the ensuing poverty. The world's banks had fallen, the money in your pocket was worth less now, but in Europe it was just plain worthless.

I showered at work from habit. It was a general rule of thumb that official buildings would have reliable running water, hot water. The private sector was more hit and miss.

The flat was in fact an official housing placement. One of the impossibly spacious and luxurious dwellings abandoned in the rush of the Lockdown. Or later, if the original owners weren't lucky enough to get over the bridges to the relative safety offered north of the Thames. However the flat had come to be empty, no viable claim had been made on it and so it became civil property.

It was nine in the evening when I got in. That meant an hour before the window of phone use was, arbitrarily, closed until five the next morning. I busied myself with getting the place warm and pretended that I wasn't delaying the call. The main living room was a huge space with twin aspect sash windows and an intimidatingly high ceiling. Victorian, I'd been assured by one of the moving crew when I'd commented on it. The crew had consisted of two men. Stupidly young, as so many people seem to be these days, and at least fifty percent overstaffed. I had very little to move. Files, some IT equipment and my clothes. Not, by any measure, an extensive wardrobe. During the time I'd been in Paris, haute couture hadn't been a priority.

We carried two boxes each up the stairs and I was in situ. Furniture came with the flat. Along with a slight smell of mould. When I took it over, one of the sash windows wore a cataract of plyboard. Left bare, the plyboard's only decoration was the stencilled HMG ACQUISITION symbol. Even that had been truncated when the board was cut to size. At some point during its abandonment the window had been smashed. Other than the furniture, which was expensively tasteful to the point of being almost invisible, the suggestion of some act of violence to the window was the flat's only personal touch. When I was tired or, just as commonly, when I was trying to keep my mind from other things, I would study the areas around the plyboard, trying to build a picture of what had happened.

Somebody trying to get in or somebody trying to escape?

Or was it just a random fact of the Lockdown?

A stray bullet or stone? Storm damage?

That thought made me smile. It was all storm damage of one kind or another. Whatever had put the window out or in, I'd never know. Like so much of London, the flat had dealt with it's history as if it was a hostile witness.

The smell was from the carpet which I had yet to dry out. The flat's main heat source was a gas fire and the on-off supply situation, and the cost, made the carpet a long-term project. Someone, possibly from the same department that had supplied my moving crew, had made a form's-sake attempt at cleaning away the tendrils of black mould around the edges of the frame. The effort had achieved little more than spreading the spores more uniformly across the eggshell walls.

After I'd put the fire on and arranged the contents of the kitchen into something that, at least in the dim lighting, looked like a meal, I checked for other outstanding tasks.

It was nine twenty-five. My fairly new career in policing had ingrained the habit of taking time checks at every juncture. Allow five minutes securing a connection, ten if there was any problem, another five minutes to verify the Bitcoin transfer. Less than twenty-five minutes of talk time.

The less-than-twenty-five minutes yawned before me like a crevasse. I wasted another two minutes doing nothing other than dreading the call.

The furniture in the flat was self-consciously modern. Probably bought to contrast with the Victorian cornices and ornate door surrounds, its pastel pale upholstery and unobtrusive lines made it look timid. Like Oliver Twist asking if there was any more. Maybe that was my mood speaking as I sunk into the armchair. Maybe it was an American lack of Victorian imagery to draw on.

The phone rang six times before David answered it. It was one of the few changes I could map in a marriage taking place across an ocean. There was a time, and not long ago, when David always, always, answered within two rings. The sound of an incoming call triggered some Pavlovian response in him that sent him madly routing through layers to get to the right pocket. Carefully tailored jackets or delicately set outfits could be reduced to an unmade bed by a single wrong number.

Now it took six rings. I tried not to picture him with the phone in his hand, recognising the number and needing to brace himself before pressing the green button.

"Hi, you." His voice was carefully light. Face to face I'd have probably been able to hear the effort that casual tone was taking, but the echoing mobile made the pretence easier.

"Hi, yourself." The echo on the line whispered my reply back to me. I listened to it carefully. "Just checking in."

"Yeah, good. Good."

I looked around the flat and wondered, not for the first time, if Miller and Robertson had camped out in places like this. Had they had officers' quarters while the grunts lay on the floor? Had they been equal?

I'd spent too long in Paris to believe in heroes anymore.

The silence on the phone was dragging on too long. I couldn't remember my next line. Did I ask about his day, his job? Was it too earlier to ask about Maria?

Some longer forgotten designer had built the impression of comfort into the chair I sat on. It was a sculpture of gentle arcs and supportive contours, on a plinth of chromed steel solidity. A chair where you could relax, in the certainty of your place in someone else's life. I stood up and took the phone call over to the plyboard window. If I'd headed for the intact one, I could have enjoyed what view London had to offer. The streetlamps wouldn't go off for another hour. Habits, old and new, die hard. I'm happier approaching windows with the view of not being seen.

"How's work?" David asked, beating me to the punch.

"Oh … you know."

There was another pause. In it I could hear slightly more than the slow drift of people separated too long.

Finally, "No, I don't know."

The quality of the phone connection made it hard to read his tone. But there was something in it, exasperation or impatience. The perpetual call of the misunderstood male. Part of me, a big part, wanted to slap the comment down, but I didn't. That he didn't know how my days went was no more his fault than mine. And, perpetual call of the put-upon female, I had to be the bigger party and submit.

I'd left JFK, as it still was back then, two days after Maria's fifth birthday. She had folded a piece of cake into a foil-wrapped napkin and slipped it to me at the front door. In another life, where I was back home a week later, it was the sort of cutesy behaviour I'd have committed to a laden memory and in later years, wouldn't even know I'd forgotten. Forgotten in the same way that you forget the first words you wait for with bated breath. You forget because a million others quickly follow and blur the view.

In the five years since I'd seen my daughter, that slice of cake, given with a secret 'just between us girls' expression, had taken on more importance than either of us would have believed possible. My stomach still knotted with guilt at the memory of casting it into a trash later.

I hadn't made it back in a week.

The auditing division of the bank had put a strict cap on my expenses tab. My tour of Paris wasn't going to encompass any five-star hotels. Third day of the trip, someone at the branch I was vetting suggested a guest house their sister-in-law ran.

Nods of understanding were exchanged and a miniature bank fraud was agreed on. Events, big and small, at some level will pivot on a pinhead-sized fulcrum. For the sake of making fifty dollars on a crooked expense claim my life was turned inside out.

The boarding house, I think, was nice enough. I don't trust my memory to provide a clear picture of my feelings about it at the time. History has painted over them with a lot of ill will. One memory I do trust is the landlady's cat escaping the entryway when she opened the door to me. It was twilight and the animal lit out for the night life of Montmartre followed by a stream of Parisian curses.

There were signs on every corner, black on yellow, warning that stray cats would be caught and held. Chipping your animal was the only way to guarantee its return. I'd seen a stray despatched by baton-wielding gendarmes on the cab ride from the bank. The animal had been bagged in bright yellow plastic and thrown into the back of a Peugeot, along with what appeared to be a dozen more. The cab driver seemed to find it faintly amusing that the police were now contrôle des parasites; pest control. He stopped sucking on his cigarette long enough to make a loud drawn-out mewing sound as he edged the car past them. He mentioned that there was a ten-euro reward for each dead stray that was presented at a police station. He thought that was funny too. I wondered how civilians were supposed to know a chipped cat from a stray.

I thought my landlady had a cold or was upset about the almost certain loss of her pet. She'd chased it along the street for some way before giving up and returning to show me to my room. We had to climb three flights of stairs. There was a lift, running up the centre of the building with the stairs spiralling around it, but it was currently out of bounds. Before his dash for freedom, Felix had registered a dirty protest and shit in it, copiously, as she was at pains to explain. She could have saved her breath. The stairway stank. Felix evidently hadn't been a well cat.

The landlady dutifully made out a receipt for more than the agreed price, so my expenses claim would tally, and bid me good night. By five a.m. she was grieving the death of her son and I was in a quarantine zone.

I took more interest in European news than many Americans, but even before the borders closed tight that wasn't much to boast about. If I'm honest, the superior grin I wore for my knowledge of affairs that didn't end at US soil wasn't really deserved. I followed the financial news. The dip in the strength of the euro with an attention to detail that stopped at the border of headlines. The term 'relative quantitative easing' was on the periphery of my interest. I knew the euro was losing value because there were now fewer Europeans and overseas tourists to spend them.

The central economies weren't printing more. There were more relative to the population. That was as much as I needed to know. Europe, and by extension Britain, was undergoing a massive population reduction. That it affected my bank was relevant. That it could affect me was unthinkable.

Unless you took the trouble to think about it.

I didn't.

There was a problem with French cats. Why should I change my travel plans? David and Maria had waved me off at the end of the drive, Maria on her daddy's shoulders. She was big for her age and every time she climbed up for a ride David warned her, only half joking, that this might be the last time.

There was talk about the dangers of traveling to Europe, but there nearly always was. We'd laughed about our neighbours who'd cancelled a trip to London because they saw a report on a riot in Berlin. Of course, we were far too sophisticated for knee-jerk panic reactions like that. So I blew the obligatory kisses and let the cab carry me to JFK. In my memory they waved until the cab turned left at the end of our street. They probably did but, in reality, I'm making an assumption. Once the driver pulled away from the curb, I had my phone out and was lost in correspondence.

So, no; David didn't know what my work was like. The last time he'd seen me I was an auditor in an international bank and now I was a member of the overseas branch of the Washington Police Department. Chasing money with a warrant card instead of an expenses account.

"It's work, David. I do it because I have to, and it means I get paid and can afford phone bills and lawyers to chase my 'fitness to return papers'. And I hate it."

I tried to keep the edge out of my voice, but I didn't do it very well. Even to my ears they were the words of a scold. David, who had always had an economy with words, didn't speak for a few moments. The tiny silence had a lot to say. It said I had no idea what it was like living the US anymore, I'd never been a single parent family and, of course, I wasn't there. Unfair and, because it went unsaid, impossible to refute. David would have been better in an interrogation room than I'd ever be.

"Well if you don't want to talk about work, what shall we talk about?"

"How's Maria? Is she home from school yet?" I knew the answer to that and hated myself for asking. It was a cheap ploy to gain … what? Pity? The moral high ground by virtue of being the more miserable?

The five-hour time difference meant it was a little before four at … home. Maria wouldn't be back from school yet. I'd only get to speak to her at weekends. I'd tried calling during my lunch breaks, catching her just before she left for school. But interfering with her, and David's, morning ritual had been disruptive. And I was always left in a bad mood, certain that I could handle the morning prep for school with less drama and rush. The goodbyes had been hurried and awkward, not something to savour, not the way I wanted it to be. So, I'd stopped, restricted myself to weekends and holidays.

David told me Maria wouldn't be home from school for another hour. She had cheerleading practice. His tone implied I should have known. Tuesday afternoon was cheerleading practice, of course. It rankled but I let it pass.

"Is she coming home on the bus?"

Domestic details, keeping the illusion of family life alive and thin. David paused before answering and I changed my assessment of his ability to operate in an interview room. It was the cheater's pause. My hasty training by video link to Washington had covered it, but being official they'd had another name for it, lumped it under some title along the lines of, Involuntary Body Language in Stressed Individuals or Subconscious Signs of Deceptive Speech Patterns. It didn't really matter what they called it, with me the title amounted to Teach Your Granny to Suck Eggs.

I'd spent years combing bank records looking for cheaters, fraudsters, thieves. Again, the name didn't matter. People trying to pull a scam. Sometimes I'd interview people, ask them to explain a discrepancy, or more often ask them to explain to me what this meant. The cheaters tended to be men. And men, no matter what your authority or your background or your knowledge, see you as a woman first and mentally assume a superior stance. Especially men sitting behind big desks. I never simpered and pretended a delicate femininity; I didn't need to. Nature had given me ovaries and that was all it took. Superior men in power breathed a sigh of relief that head office had only sent a woman to look into matters, and they began to talk away the problems.

They'd pause first.

Cheaters always do, a last-second blink-and-you'll-miss moment of thought. A pre-flight check of the bullshit that's about to get launched.

David. Cheater's pause. Then, "Joanna's collecting her."

Even over the echoing line, the innocence his answer radiated was palpable.

"Joanna? Should I be jealous?"

"No," he said, laughing.

After a slight pause.

To get away from the minefield I'd just stepped into I blurted out that I'd met Colin Robertson that morning. It wasn't the liar's pause this time. It was the genuine article.

Finally, "Wow. Really? *The* Colin Robertson. The King of the Crows?"

The King of the Fucking Crows.

"That's what he said."

And so we talked about work until the line was cut at ten o'clock GMT.

The streetlights went out at ten and the bedroom darkened another notch. I checked the battery life on my laptop. The icon claimed I had another hour, which was optimistic, if electronic devices can be said to be optimistic. I called up the transcript o the interview with Robertson and read it through again.

I hadn't told David that I hadn't warmed to his hero. I had disavowed any belief he had that Robertson might be an American. It was the type of low-grade conspiracy nonsense that filtered down to the masses without most people realising.

The barely plausible and the completely insane could be seen as they crossed the horizon. Government funded biochemical weapons labs, the hand of God, Allah, Satan, HaShem, delete as appropriate. Extra Terrestrials, naturally. People rejected or embraced as they saw fit. It was the little details and snippets of misinformation that slid in unnoticed. That ridiculous film hadn't made the waters any clearer.

I let David be star-struck by proxy, but, national hero or not, I didn't trust Robertson as far as I could throw him.

Chapter 4. Trust

Am I the only one who can see that Gonzo was an orchestrated black ops mission? It was an attack ON THE WEST'S WAY OF LIFE! Anyone who can't see that is a moron or a traytor.
Username:KillerKitty

****

If it was an 'orchestrated' attack on the west's freedom to use upper case letters and ignore spellcheck, why wasn't the prime target the US of A?
FYI: Disagreeing with an idea doesn't automatically make someone a moron or a 'traytor'.
Username:BobCat

****

Fuck you BobCat!!!!!!!!!!!!!!!
Username:Magnum

****

BobCat, a couple of facts for you.
1. The United States was the primary target zone. The only reason Europe was the location of the initial disease breakout was ease of deployment. The liberal leftist president of France made his country an easy target in the way our own country would not have been.
2. Gonzo infection was meant to reach our shores via contaminated illegal immigrants fleeing the Outbreaks in Europe.
3. The United States was able to keep itself safe by proper policing of its borders. Again, this is something the weak leadership of France was unable to do. All the bleeding-heart liberals can thank President Drumph for that.
4. The United States STILL IS THE PRIMARY TARGET ZONE. Sorry if the caps upset you, BobCat, but I think it's worth reminding people this situation is on-going.
Before posting sanctimonious replies to other people's comments perhaps you should take the trouble to check

your facts.
Username:Solider-of-Truth

****

Yeeeeh! FUCKING-A SOLIDER-OF-TRUTH.

SECOND AMENDANMENT KEPT US SAFE!!!!!!!!!!!!!!!
Username:Magnum

****

Magnum,
Exactly how many people do you know who protected the US of A from Gonzo, using a gun?
I'm guessing none (exactly the same as the rest of us). Also, capital letters and exclamation marks do not turn random phrases into a point of view.
Solider-of-Truth,
Exactly where do you get your 'facts' from?
You'd do better to buy a dictionary and learn the difference between fact and supposition.
Gonzo and subsequent pathologies resulted in the death, directly and indirectly, of between 35 to 47 percent of Europe and the UK (these figures are from the World Health Organisation). Most of Africa was left untouched, as were Russia and India.
Australia has remained free of Gonzo by employing a simple screening method. Drumph hasn't saved America, despite what he claims. All he has done is pursue an isolationist agenda. Something that ignorance and fearmongering gave him the power to do.
America has fared no better than any other nation in the economic fallout of the European collapse. Thanks to the short-sighted policies of Drumph, and his ilk, it is likely to fare considerably worse over the coming years.
Username:BobCat

****

FUCK YOU BOBCUNT!!!!!!!!!!!!

THE ONLY RESAON I DON'T SHOVE MY .357 MAGNUM UP YOUR FAG ASS IS BECAUSE YOU'D PROBABLY LOVE IT!!!!!!!!
Username:Magnum

****

Russia wasn't effected?
Of course it wasn't effected. They had the cure all along because they released the virus.
Username:TeeSouthWR

****

Gonzo isn't a virus.
Username:BobCat

****

Australia is a ticking bomb, their government is putting their own people at risk. When the dead start to rise they'll be crying to the USA to bail them out.
Username:Zom-B-hunter

****

their will be NO HELP and NO MERCY for communists in russia and the mooslims in africa.
The RAPTURE BELL will TOLL and only the just will BE SAVED.

"AND LIGHT WILL BE NO MORE. THEY WILL NEED NO LIGHT OF LAMP OR SUN, FOR THE LORD GOD WILL BE THERE LIGHT, AND WILL RAIN FOREVER AND EVER" Revelation 22:5
Username:SON_OF_GOD1334

From Kings of Crows: Life on the Wrong Side of the Lockdown

For me, what evokes that first day of the Lockdown – running along the curve of the Thames trying to get to a bridge before the detonations started – isn't the smell, it's the car alarms. I know there were other sounds. All the sounds you'd expect with mass panic. Gunfire too, the army boys caught south of the river were desperate to get over those bridges. It's the car alarms that stick in my mind, though. Even now I sweat if I hear one.

Most of the roads were impassable. The army and police had road-blocked the major routes out of the city, but people kept trying. As the side streets choked up, people abandoned their cars and ran. I guess setting the alarms was reflex; maybe some of them thought they'd be coming back for them in a few days. We were scared then, scared for our lives, but we didn't know the scale of it. Think about that; we honestly thought if we got to a bridge before it blew up, the army were going to let us cross. We thought that getting to the river was going to make a difference.

So, people locked their cars and set the alarms. The cars didn't care what bumped into them, healthy or infected, they went off.

I met up with Miller early on. Really early on. Just after the explosion on Tower Bridge. The roads were solid and so was the panic. People had started to run and that was never going to go well. Someone fell, others fell on them. People got trampled. The noise was enough to drive you mad. If a sound could be made by a human being, then it was being made that day. Yelling, shouting, screaming and crying. I swear at one point I heard singing. And all the while those car alarms.

It didn't make any difference. Run, scream or sing, there was nowhere to go.

There were helicopters with tannoys hovering all along the river. They kept repeating the same thing: Stay calm and move away from the river, stay calm, there is no need for panic. I remember the message being cut off midstream and a klaxon sounding instead. It gave six long blasts then stopped. It's strange, but it annoyed me that they gave six blasts, something about that was disjointed somehow. Three blasts would have been fine, or maybe five, not six. Then a new message: Demolition of the bridges will take place in sixty seconds, if you have not cleared the bridges do so now. Then the countdown.

The bridge was heaving. Nobody could have got off it in a minute. I saw at least one person jump over the side; whether they were trying to escape the explosion or the crush of bodies, I couldn't say.

When the countdown ended, and there was no explosion, some people cheered. I might have been one of them. For a moment, there was a faint hope that the Lockdown had been cancelled. Then the other bridges went. The sound rumbled along the Thames and the dust cloud that had been London Bridge appeared to the west just before Tower Bridge erupted.

Someone in the Royal Engineers fouled up. When the charges went, they only took a chunk out of one of the supports. It did the job, except the bridge didn't blow, it folded. It was slow. People started jumping en masse. One of the helicopters dipped down low over the river. For a second, I thought it was to pick up the people who'd wound up in the water. We still had our minds set to normal – expecting officials to help. Or at least to make a show of helping. Then the machine-gunning started.

I'm not angry. It was bad at ground level. I mean, we could see the crowds trying to get to the river, we could feel the panic. But the guys in the air had been looking over the city. They'd seen what was coming. Not a couple of them heading towards us but hundreds. They saw what was happening, what was left in their wake. We were spared that at least.

People didn't know where to run once the helicopters started firing. Mostly they ran into each other.

I was lucky, I'd been pushed into some sort of recess. It was the size of a doorway but ended in a wall. Quirky old London building. Me and this shortish man who turned out to be Miller. The doorway, which wasn't a doorway, was close to a corner and the way the crowds were moving meant we had some kind of protection. Like a rock in a river, the water flows around it and leaves a patch just behind that's almost calm. We were like that. Not that I was calm, but I avoided the worst of the current.

Swiss Brain (Swiss Grey, Swiss Matter)

A reference to the multiple cysts found in the brains of individuals affected by HV-Tg Induced Psychosis.
e.g. 'That Gondy's grey matter's got more holes than a Swiss Cheese'

The A to Z of Gondii Names

June 19th, 2021

"Check. Oh, damn."

Sol tried to right the knight he'd just knocked over and succeeded in knocking Johnno's rook off the edge of the board. He swore softly and apologised.

"Christ on a bike, Sol, watch what you're doing."

Johnno had been from Liverpool; his accent had a nasal quality that made it carry. The comment raised a hissing tide of shushing noises. Feeling around the upturned crate, he acknowledged them with an impatient gesture. When he found the rook and sat upright again, Sol repeated his apology. He held out his open hand in mitigation. Even in the dim light the tremor was visible.

"It's bad tonight."

Johnno nodded his understanding and made to put the rook back into play.

"Was it here?"

Sol shook his head, "On the white square."

"You sure?"

"White square, diagonal to your bishop."

Sol seemed certain. Johnno set the rook back on the table and turned his attention to the check he was in. He moved his king into a square at the edge of the board.

Sol took the uncovered bishop with his knight.

"Ow ay."

The outburst earned Johnno another chorus of shushing.

"You might as well pay up now," Robertson said.

The voice came from behind Johnno and made him start.

"No way, it ain't over till the fat bird sings."

Robertson moved to the side of the improvised table. He squatted on his haunches, using the fireman's axe as a prop to steady himself.

"He's going to nail you. Five moves, tops," he said.

"Three," Sol said.

Johnno's hand hovered over the board, moving from piece to piece, as if waiting for one of them to signal that they'd had an idea. When no strategic advice was offered, he flicked his king over, conceding the game. He pulled a nylon rucksack onto his lap and withdrew an opened carton of cigarettes that he held out to Sol. The old man pulled two packets out and they vanished into a pocket of the quilted parka he was wearing.

"I tell you what, you old bastard, if we were playing for real money, I'd be fookin' skint." He addressed the remark as much to the crouched figure of Robertson as to the old man.

Sol adjusted the flaps of his pocket, securing his winnings.

"It is real money," he said. His voice was quiet, but the tone had an edge to it.

Robertson shifted his weight slightly; angling himself towards Johnno, who was busy packing the remaining cigarettes away. He'd picked up on the edge in the old man's voice as well.

"So, how'd you work that out? I've never seen the Queen's head on any bifta I've ever smoked."

Sol made a snorting noise.

"By that logic the Japanese yen isn't money, nor is the dollar, the rupee or the rand."

"Yeah? Well try spending any of those in Liverpool and see how far it gets you. I'm talking about legal currency."

His voice had become more strident and somewhere in the shadows of the storehouse someone hushed him again. As Johnno turned to respond, Robertson said, "Keep it down."

The big Liverpudlian lifted one hand in a gesture of submission.

"Why do you think a piece of paper with some fancy printing on it is money?" Sol demanded. "The cigarette packets you just put in your bag have pretty pictures on them too."

Johnno didn't reply.

"Answer the question," Robertson said.

Johnno looked at him. His mouth twitched with a response, but he bit back whatever he'd been intending to say and mumbled, "I don't know."

Sol's face was hard to read in the dim light. The warehousing space they'd occupied for the last two weeks was rich in supplies and shelter, but hard to secure. Five entrance points, only three of them small enough to barricade efficiently, and the ground outside the main entrances was easy to cross. And the days were getting shorter. It wasn't a good place or time to be showing lights. To illustrate the point someone stumbled and swore in one of the corners. The shusher, who seemed to have found his role in life, let out a sibilant hiss.

The old man felt inside his coat, fumbling his way ponderously through the folds. When his hand reappeared, there was a slip of paper in it. It shook in harmony with his grip. When he moved his hand into the smudge of light from the LED lamp, illuminating the chess board, the Queen's head stared up at them.

"There you are, Johnno, Her Majesty Queen Elizabeth, promising to pay the bearer fifty pounds, no less." Sol angled his wrist; the gesture made it appear that he was offering the note to Johnno. "I'll pay you fifty pounds for another packet of cigarettes."

The big man laughed.

"Fookin' money's no use to me now, is it?"

"So, it has no value?"

"Not now it ain't."

Sol's trembling fingers folded the note in half and slipped it back into his coat. "But packets of cigarettes do?"

"Yeah."

"Which makes them money. My fifty-pound note hasn't changed since it was printed, same ink, paper and clever little serial number. Yet, I can't use it to buy a packet of cigarettes and I don't even smoke. The economy has changed."

"That don't make biftas proper money, does it? They're not legal tender, are they?"

"Ahhh," Sol highlighted the sound by lifting a finger. "Legality, now there you have a point. Money can only truly work with the rule of law."

Extract from the screenplay of Year of the Crow. Lithograph Studios, California (2026)

INT. WAREHOUSE – NIGHT.
Panning shot shows a handful of small fires with groups of people huddled around them. There are about thirty people in all. Most of them are sleeping, a few are upright and watchful, and several are cleaning guns.

Robertson is walking quietly around the groups. He stops now and then with his head cocked, listening. He pauses and his attention is drawn to a trio of men sitting around a blanket which is serving as a card table. One of them, Chan, has evidently just won a hand and is pulling a pile of items toward him: cigarette packets, bars of chocolate, two bottles of spirit. He is oriental and clearly very old. His clothing is bulky as he is wearing many layers. The two men he is playing against are both heavily built.

CHAN
(Exaggerating his accent and talking in pidgin English)
It great pleasure play with you, gentlemen. Always great pleasure.

CARDPLAYER ONE
You slant-eyed fuck.

CARDPLAYER TWO
Nah, forget this shit. All bets cancelled, you ain't having my bloody Scotch.

Cardplayer Two reaches over and tries to grab one of the bottles. With startling speed, Chan snatches the bottle and clutches it to his chest.

CHAN
No your Scotch. I win. You lose. Fair square.

Cardplayer Two leans closer; his hand closes round the neck of the bottle. Close-up on his face as he grins menacingly.

CARDPLAYER TWO
So, what you going to do, Chinky? Call the police?

ROBERTSON
(Out of shot)
How about we call Miller over?

Shot changes to show all three cardplayers plus Robertson, who is standing directly behind Cardplayer Two. Cardplayer Two, until now unaware that Robertson was at his back, freezes at the mention of Miller's name. He doesn't let go of the bottle, but he doesn't try to pull it from Chan's grip.

CARDPLAYER TWO
We're out there risking our necks to bring back supplies. This old bastard sits on his ass all day and I'm now supposed to give him my fucking Scotch?

Robertson moves around the three men and stops beside Chan. He stares levelly at Cardplayer Two.

ROBERTSON
You ain't giving him anything. You lost; you're paying your debts. You want to live by the laws of the jungle? Then you can fuck off and tell those things out there what you think they owe you.

Cardplayer Two obviously doesn't like this but he lets the bottle go. He stands and tries to give Robertson the hard-eye treatment. Robertson doesn't back down and Cardplayer Two turns away. Before he can walk off Robertson grabs his arm.

ROBERTSON

(Speaking softly)

If we don't look out for each other, if we just strong-arm people to get what we want, we're no better than those … things.

June 19th, 2021

"Money," Sol said. His voice was harsh, there was tension in his words. "All money, be it coins, notes or cigarettes, depends on two things: trust and the rule of law. If you don't trust my fifty-pound notes to be of value, then they have no value. So, my banknote is just a sheet of elaborate markings. But you trust cigarettes. Cigarettes you can swap for food, drink … sex even, given the right set of circumstances. But" – he held up a trembling finger – "but, trust in the money means nothing if there's no rule of law to hold people to account for their agreements. Or if the money can be picked up for nothing. Free money doesn't work, it destroys economies."

Slowly and with great concentration, he began setting the chess pieces on the board, ready for another match. Johnno shook his head.

"Yeah, that just proves my point. Those biftas can't be money, can they? 'Cos there's no bizzies around to lay down the law. So, I can just take 'em."

He reached over the chess board and grabbed the side of Sol's coat. The old man didn't react; Johnno pulled the at the Velcro flap of a bulging pocket and pulled out the packets of cigarettes. He stood, towering over the old man and waving the packet back and forth like a hypnotist.

"No law. So how are these–"

Without rising from his haunches, Robertson turned the axe over and rammed the shaft into Johnno's crotch. As the man doubled over, Robertson stood and grabbed the back of his collar. He brought the head of the axe up to Johnno's neck, the edge tucked under the man's chin. For a few seconds he didn't speak. The silence of the warehouse was broken only by Johnno, gasping for breath.

"This is the law Johnno. I'm holding it against your fucking neck. You want to make a phone call, lodge a complaint?"

Robertson waited for a response; other than a ragged whine of pain, none came. He took the axe away from the man's throat but didn't let go of his collar; held him bent double. Sol watched impassively for a while, then returned to setting up the chess board.

"I was only joking, Sol. Take the bloody fags, take 'em."

Robertson jerked the man upright. Still holding his collar, he pulled him close, their faces separated by inches.

"Next time we have this conversation, I won't be using the blunt end. You get that?"

"Yeah, yeah, I get you Rob, I get you."

Robertson released his grip and pushed him away. Johnno took a step back; he was still crouched slightly. He nodded, though it wasn't clear who to, or why. In the shadows, someone cleared their throat and asked someone else to pass them the water. Someone else, over in one of the corners, laughed. It was shrill and sounded loud against the silence. The self-appointed noise monitor issued an urgent 'shhh'.

Robertson leaned over and set Johnno's upturned crate back on its side. He sat and regarded the chess pieces. Sol had already made an opening move.

"So, what was all that about?"

"I give the boy a lesson in economics, he takes offence." The old man hunched his shoulders in a parody of innocence.

"I'm not talking about your financial advice." Robertson moved a pawn and tapped it pointedly on the board before setting it in place. "When John Boy put his rook back on the board, you told him it had been on the white square. So it left his bishop uncovered."

Sol laughed softly and patted the pocket where the cigarettes were stowed.

"I wanted his money."

"I mean, why did you cheat? You'd have won anyway."

"There was a film, years ago, I can't remember the title, but there was this one line in it that really struck me. Money won tastes better than money earned." He leaned closer to Robertson. His voice was low, little more than a whisper, but Robertson could hear the smile in it. "I'll let you into a secret. Cheated money, stolen money, tastes better than both."

Chapter 5. Economies of Fail

From Kings of Crows: Life on the Wrong Side of the Lockdown

If the money had still worked, I think we'd have ridden it out. That sounds harsh, but I believe it. One of the Crows, with the group almost from the start, used to lecture about economics. According to him, the biggest problem the country faced was the collapse of the economy. The example he used was the hospitals.

They were overrun. They just couldn't cope with the amount of HV-Tg coming through the doors. Even when the government ran endless TV ads, telling people not to go to A & E with gondii symptoms, people just poured in. Nurses got sick; doctors got sick. If the disease didn't get them exhaustion would and then the switcher attacks really picked up. Still nurses and doctors turned up for their shifts. Until the money stopped working. People will risk their lives for money, but they won't work for free.

It wasn't something people liked being told. They wanted to blame the government, or just hate the victims. To think it had all collapsed because, basically, people didn't turn up to work? That was too much.

I don't know how right he was in saying that; there were a lot of factors. But there's no question, the economy was one of them.

The violence was probably the tipping point but on its own it wouldn't have been enough. Gondii eroded everything first. The infrastructure began to fail. Money lost value quicker than people could supply goods. By the time cheques had cleared they weren't worth the things they were buying.

The disease itself put unbearable pressure on the medical services, the loss of life devalued the money so what goods and services were left were too expensive to buy. Then the police and army and even the civil service were understaffed and stretched to breaking point.

Then the disease changed, at just the wrong time, and instead of dying, victims turned into monsters.

All the conspiracy theorists – spouting all their fantasies about Porton Down weaponising cat-scratch fever or some new world order flooding Europe with infected cats – I can see where they were coming from. Taking a long back view, it all seems too precise to have been chance.

That was part of the reason for doubling back and heading east along the river. In retrospect it seems crazy, but everything was crazy back then. We were killing dozens, sometimes hundreds, of people each day. Getting weaker by the hour. Someone said if the government, any government, was going to try to put it back together, they'd start with the money.

So, we headed towards the banking sector. In fairness, crazy or not, it made as much sense as anything else we did back then.

April 5th, 2028

Tap, tap. Tap, tap. Tap, tap.

I promised myself, I'd break Winslow's fingers the first chance I got.

"His meaning's not very clear there."

Tap, tap. Tap, tap. Tap, tap.

"Where?"

"There."

Tap, tap. Tap, tap. Tap, tap.

We'd moved out of the office with the massive dark wood desk. The team, all eight of them, had been shunted up a floor. Below us, unhealthy looking men and women with face masks and steam cleaners chased mice, and their droppings, out of the lower levels. The water supply wasn't matching the demands of the cleaners and sounds of complaint drifted up the stairwells. Along with clouds of steam.

Too cold to open windows we all worked in the over-moist air, cursing the paranoia that made chemical warfare on mouse shit a mandatory requirement.

Winslow carried on his self-important tapping. Sitting at a stiff recline and regarding the page in front of him like a mandarin glaring at a peasant.

We were facing each other across the expanse of another ego-boosting piece of office furniture. I hadn't taken enough interest in the building to find out who'd owned it before the Lockdown. If pressed to make a guess, I'd have said a mid-range investment house. We weren't billeted near enough to the centre of London for it to have been a major player's nest, but there had certainly been big money involved. A lot of that money had gone into dressing the boardrooms and meeting spaces. I'd have bet a ticket home against a penny that the furniture had been picked, from a glossy catalogue, by a man with a big expense account and erectile dysfunction. The whole place screamed testosterone with an insistence that belied true confidence.

Winslow loved the place.

Tap, tap. Tap, tap. Tap, tap.

I made a noise to let him know I was willing to listen but bent my head back to the block of printouts I was reading. I was aware that the other five or six people working at the same table were watching the exchange. More accurately, the lack of exchange. Annoyed at my own pettiness as much as Winslow's habits, I kept my head down and ignored him.

It took him a surprisingly long time to realise he was being ignored. By then he was trapped in the inertia of his actions. Aware that his little attention-seeking device had been spotted for what it was, he tried to disguise the finger tapping as an unconscious gesture of deep thought. Adding a syncopated rhythm fooled no one.

I heard his weight shift as he leaned across the table to bring what was bothering him into my range. When I looked up, a uniformed PC caught my eye and smirked. I frowned but he just looked away, still grinning. There was too much inexperience in the room. Too much youth, I corrected.

I was no more experienced than the rest of them. Sworn in as a member of the Washington State Police (overseas representation), under a hastily thrown-together set of legislation. I'd been stationed in London barely three years. Doing real police work for considerably less.

I'd become a cop in one of the whirlwind bursts of panic-driven energy that the US Government gave off between barren stretches of complacency. In the normal world I'd have been sitting in a training academy listening to grey-haired veterans talking about arrest warrants and restraint techniques.

I corrected myself again. This was the normal world.

"That line there."

Winslow tapped the page again, caught himself doing it and stopped abruptly.

It was Robertson's book, again. His account, probably ghostwritten, of the Outbreak of HV-Tg on British soil and his fight, alongside Miller, to lead a group of survivors across London. A quiet voice, that sounded in my head alone, made another correction: not Robertson's account, Robertson's version.

"One of the Crows, with the group almost from the start, used to lecture about economics?" I looked up again, and Winslow nodded. I waited for him to explain and it became a minor battle of nerves that left us both looking stupid. The fact we had an audience was emphasised when the smirking PC spoke up.

"What's the problem with that?"

Winslow, magnanimous in his plain clothes, was pleased to explain to the uniform.

"It's not clear if this man he's referring to was in the habit of lecturing Robertson's group of survivors, or if he had been some sort of lecturer before the Outbreak." He leaned his weight back into his chair again. Looked distant and thoughtful. "Little details like that worry me sometimes, they get in here."

He put his thumbs against his temples and made tiny circular motions.

I wondered if he practiced the routine in the mirror. Convinced himself that he was an experienced detective with a dozen files under his belt, all marked solved. He was working too hard at looking troubled to notice the PC was fighting the urge to laugh.

I surprised myself by throwing his sinking credibility a lifeline.

"That paragraph seemed odd to me as well."

Too dense or too vain to be grateful, Winslow stopped trying to tunnel into his frontal lobes using his thumbs and managed to give the impression I'd derailed his train of thought.

"Why?"

"Nearly everyone he mentions in this book, he has a story about. Even when it's someone he obviously doesn't like, like Maccallan, he doesn't pass them over. If they're stuck in his mind for some reason, they get a part in his narrative. Not this guy, not the economics lecturer. One line, no name, then he's out of it. Odd."

"Maybe he was edited out," PC Smirk suggested. "Saving paper and all that."

He illustrated his point, badly, by holding up a thick wad of paperwork. Paper hadn't been rationed, yet, but it hadn't got cheaper either.

"But," Winslow chimed in, "he describes him as 'one of the Crows, almost there from the start', but he doesn't name him. That is odd."

His face became slightly pinched, real thought replacing the posing of thinking. Seeing he'd lost his brief moment with the cool kids, PC Smirk went back to whatever he was doing. I didn't have much of an idea what that might have been. Police work was still largely a closed book to me. I'd been drafted into the Washington force as a stray American caught on the wrong side of the Atlantic when the borders closed. A stray with a good working knowledge of how money worked. Used to work. How it walked and talked and made its moves. Then I'd been given to the Met as a liaison.

Then I'd been promoted. Because, if the US Government was going to liaise, it was going to make good and sure its liaison officer could pull rank.

Winslow had forgotten the other thing about Robertson's account that had bothered him. His sojourn in an office, barricaded behind a heavy-duty door while a Gonzo beat itself to pulp trying to get in, chanting the keys have broken the clock.

It still bothered me. I wanted to know what was in an office that warranted investigating. An office with an armoured door.

Chapter 6. The Stuff of Legends

Cups of the daughter lost free to be sung

(Annotated in the medical records of: ████████ DOB: ██████
HOSPITAL: St Demlings Hospital, Essex, England.)

Cups = Vessels, items capable of holding or carrying / Women
Daughter = St Mary / Virgin Mary / Women
Lost = Lost / Damned / Forsaken
Free = …of sin / Cleansed / Forgiven
Sung = Praised / Prayer

This is clearly a reference to Judgement Day. Those deemed cleansed (Free) shall be taken unto the Lord to sing his praises (Sung). The mention of 'Cups of the daughter' could mean this property was directed at fallen (Lost) women, as a warning to them to seek redemption and forgiveness (Free). It also serves as an example of the fate awaiting sinners should they choose not to hear the call. Cups, having two meanings, refers both to women and vessels in the literal sense. A reference therefore to The Rapture when the righteous shall be carried bodily unto heaven.

Warnings from the Damned: Prophecies of the Undead Explained, Texas Evangelical Press (2026)

"The stories about Miller being a priest are just that, stories. The idea's taken hold since the film came out. I think they ramped up the religious angle for American audiences. Miller didn't give sermons, and if he prayed, I never saw him do it. I know the stories about him being a priest were floating around even before they turned the whole thing into a Hollywood fantasy, but that was just people trying to lay claim to a slice of the legend. I've had people telling me he was a rabbi, an imam, a Buddhist monk. Same thing with the race angle; he was Irish, Scottish, Welsh. Half-American was the last one I heard. People want a hero; if he's one of the home team, so much the better.

"Malik told me, when they were casting for someone to play me, there was talk of using a Chinese guy. It tied in better with all those dopey kung fu fights they filmed. "

When I ask Robertson if he finds the idea offensive he laughs, and it isn't entirely convincing. At the same time his watchful eye comes to a halt. Once more, I have the feeling that the room we're in isn't as real to him as the memories interviews like this rekindle.

"The movie was a fantasy. It sold tickets and made money." He laughs again. "Maybe that's the way it should be. At the time, when we were living it, it didn't seem real. It all happened so fast. We went from normal life to madness, in less than six months. I remember people protesting the feral culling, it caused enough of a stink to make headlines. People were up in arms, because council workers were being paid to kill cats. Three months later, those same people were beating their neighbours to death with hammers, because they thought they'd switched-off, gone Gonzo."

Cubits (Q-Bitches, Q-Bits, Q-Men)

Members of the joint police and military forces in France (especially Paris) assembled during the three months following the official recognition of the Outbreak. The Brigade de Prévention des Risques Biologique (GPRB) quickly gained a reputation for violence and incompetence. It is possibly noteworthy that the slang terms and nicknames given to them are in English. It has frequently been reported that the GPRB employed increased levels of brutality when dealing with foreign national and ethnic minorities.

The A to Z of Gondii Names

Donna's Story

The madness that destroyed Paris never had raised the interest that Robertson and Miller's grind across London had. Partly, no doubt, it was the language barrier. English, always the translation of choice, was always going to sell more legends than French. And Paris had been dealing with gondii longer and so had longer to make mistakes.

If the early cat culling and lock-up hospitals had worked, the government would have simply been voted out in the next election – by an ungrateful and largely untouched population. It would have been left to history to thank it for its foresight.

As it was, the measures failed and the French became the nation of violent brutes that shot patients in their beds and sent the army into hospitals, while HV-Tg was left to run rampant.

The stories from Paris, had anyone wanted to hear, weren't vastly different from those of London, Berlin, Madrid or any other densely populated area that found half its citizens dead or psychotic.

The quarantine patrol around my Parisian boarding house was armed. Guns held awkwardly, tight against flak jackets hastily striped with yellow chevrons of spray paint.

The GPRB hadn't been in existence for more than six weeks. The ink on their firearm licences was probably as new as the paint on their hastily assembled uniforms. I found this out months later. If I'd been as aware of European news feeds as I liked to think I was I'd have known, and I'd have stayed home. I wasn't the only American caught there. Tourism had petered out; Europeans were, for the time being, staying home, doing as their embassies advised. The eastern contingent of visitors had found their visa being refused or 'lost' months before.

My credentials as a seasoned traveller meant I was too sophisticated to keep anything but euros in my purse. I quickly found out the error of my ways. The yellow-striped Quarantine-men refused bribes in European currencies. When I tried wire transfers, I found my accounts stopped at international borders. Changing euros to dollars was pointless.

The boarding house was almost dead centre in a terrace. Every building in it was sealed with an official self-adhesive notice in French and English. I don't remember the exact wording and internet searching has drawn a blank, one of the many 'holes' in the world wide web that appear around government issues post-gondii, but the gist was, "Stay calm, stay indoors, do what we say". Like a lot of French officialdom, it was styled to look reasonable but policed with an iron fist. Unless someone waved enough dollars under the right nose.

I suspect most of Europe was already running on bribes and panic by then. The way most of the world still is.

The street must have been a dream assignment for the newly appointed, and frankly terrified, Q-bits. I saw four people slipping from doorways and scampering through the temporary wire fencing at the ends of the street. When I tried it, waving a fistful of euros, I was guided, gently, back to my boarding house. Gently but with the added incentive of being shown the gun.

When I doubled the number of euros I was waving, the surgically-masked face succeeded in looking sympathetic. Slowly, maybe for dramatic effect or possibly trying not to scare me, the Q-man pulled a sheath of notes from somewhere behind the bulk of his flak jacket.

It was beginning to get dark, but there was still enough light for me to make out the notes he was showing me. 500-euro bills. About forty of them.

"One week's wages," he told me.

I'd tried to bribe him with three hundred.

The first twenty-four hours we'd been quarantined weren't significantly different from the twenty-four hours before. The residents of the street, guesthouse lodgers like myself, or natives, took the enforced day off with a mix of annoyance and resignation. Most people stayed indoors, though I did spot one or two dog walkers exercising their right to spread animal excrement across the sidewalks.

I worked from my laptop and made phone calls. I remember making waspish remarks to myself about the number of people taking time off sick. Blaming the laid-back French attitude and pairing it with the lax social habits of the dog walkers.

On the second night, one of the guests was taken sick. Then the quarantine felt different. Dangerous rather than inconvenient.

The building I was staying in was directly opposite the house with the sickness. It was a shorter building and much newer. I'd wondered if it wasn't a replacement for property destroyed in the war. At some point in the small hours the Q-bits stationed an armed officer on the front door.

I'd been on the laptop, still in my business clothes – professional habit, even when sitting at a computer in an anonymous room watching the banks collapse.

I had our Hong Kong branch online. Half nine in their morning, half two in mine.

I was possibly the last person to work with Jim McGregor. One of the final communiques the bank issued started with the set phrase, "It is with deepest regret …" and ended with the normal platitudes about, "a much-loved family man", who, "served the bank for years", "in the Hong Kong office", and would be, "sorely missed".

I never did find out how he died. Gondii's a fair bet; it didn't make it as far as mainland China, but Hong Kong effectively ceased to exist. The last plane out didn't make it off the end of the runway.

Gondii or suicide. Bankers are big on suicide during financial meltdowns.

Day three the numbers of GPRB had decreased and a handful of regular police had filled the gaps. We were told to stay indoors, not to even stray into the confines of the street. Come mid-afternoon one of the dog walkers made a noisy protest and shouldered past the Q-man who tried to herd him back inside.

I didn't witness the altercation; I just heard the shots. Juan, who lived in the house next door and watched events from an upstairs window, told me discussions had quickly got heated. The owner began shouting about dogs needing their exercise and, again, made to push his way past the Q-man. The dog, an old spaniel with bald patches, began to strain at its leash. There was a burst of fire from a machine pistol and the animal vanished in a mist of gore.

The Q-man was obviously shocked at what he'd done. It was likely the first time he'd used the gun outside of a shooting range. He bellowed something about how the dog didn't need a walk now, so get back in the house. Juan wasn't clear on what happened next. The dog owner either went for the Q-man or made some panicked move that looked like he was going to. There was another burst of fire. Then silence.

I ran out of my room and made it to the top of the stairs before freezing. In my memory, something I know better than to trust implicitly, I leapt from the edge of my bed at the sound of the first burst of fire and made it to the landing when I heard the second. Then I froze.

The timing sounds plausible, but my room was at the front of the house and the sound of gunfire would have been audible from my bed. I'm not sure, standing at the top of the stairs in the building's central column, that I would have heard the second shots being unleashed. I think in some strange way I've made it more romantic in the self-telling. Lone woman bravely running towards the sounds of unjust lawman, given pause only after the second round reminds her she's unarmed.

It's more likely I made a terrified dash away from the street when the Q-man turned his macho fantasies into a blood-soaked reality. I reached the stairs and realised if I went down them, I'd be heading towards the danger.

I don't know how long I waited at the top of the stairs. In my memory it was a long time, but I doubt it was. As I've said, memory isn't always trustworthy. When I unfroze, my legs began to shake. Not a tremor, not the kind of thing I'd get after an hour in the gym. My legs rattled and then folded when I let go of the handrail. I almost fell forward and went headfirst down the stairs. Somewhere on the floor below a door opened and then slammed shut. I heard a bolt being snapped into place. It seemed very loud and I realised I could hear my heart beating.

I tested my legs on the stairs and managed to get six steps closer to the street before common sense turned me around and set me to locking my own door. There was more gunfire. A single shot this time. Later Juan, who'd still been at his window, told me it was a senior gendarme unleashing a single shot into the air. The two or three front doors that had opened banged shut.

At the time, the element of control behind the firing of a single shot only added to the fear. My imagination added a human target to the scene, but it wasn't needed. I couldn't have been more scared.

Europeans like to think Americans are weaned on the sound of gunfire. It's a misconception. Along with the permanent good weather and universal wealth. The people most likely to shout about their second amendment rights are least likely to be the ones hearing shots in anger. What most Americans think is the sound of gunfire is the sanitised, danger-free crack of practice rounds on the range. Put most of the good ol' boys in a saloon, with a six-shooter for a sense of honour, and they'd gladly swap the second amendment for a safe house and a police force. So, I sat in my room listening and trembling.

I didn't put the call through to David until it was dark. Only half an hour before my regular call time. It's something I want to remember as an act of control and consideration. But in my low points, wondering who Joanna is and how she fits into the life I left behind in the US, it seems like the first crack in the façade. A definite point of realisation where I had to accept David and I wouldn't be there for each other.

I told him, carefully, about the shooting and he issued a few expletives and a lot of futile advice. I listened to all the pat warnings to lock my door and not to confront anyone. I told him he should contact the French Embassy in Washington; I would get hold of the American Consulate in the morning. As I said it, I kicked myself for not doing it the moment I heard gunfire.

My mind was racing at that point. I was picturing an Army Hummer loaded with a precious cargo of US citizens plucked from the Parisian streets. Official French thuggery cowering under the glare of grim-faced GIs. That bubble burst against the awkward silence coming across the Atlantic.

"What?" my voice echoed back at me, filling the time lag of the connection.

"You've not been watching the news?"

"The police are fucking shooting people in the street here. So, no I haven't been fucking watching the news."

More silence.

"They closed the US Embassy today, French and German, Spanish too. Navy choppers lifted all the personnel out. There's nothing we can do. We've just got to wait it out."

We?

Neither of us really said anything more that evening. David let out a shuddering sigh and worked at holding back tears. When he failed and began weeping down the phone line, I joined in. I didn't feel like crying, it was something ticked off my to-do list already, but I managed to draw some tears from somewhere.

In hindsight, and this is one memory I trust fully, it was the last thing we did as a couple.

The news became important. More truthfully, the act of watching became important. Briefly it turned into a ritual because, if I was watching the news, I was being proactive. The broadcasts themselves weren't worth the effort. Information was scarce. I allowed myself a day of delusion and took comfort in the banal presentations. Heroic doctors working hard in the face of increasing workloads. The recall of Médecins Sans Frontières staff from disasters abroad. Heroes returning to the motherland in her hour of need. There were staged shots of serious-looking people disembarking from airplanes while carefully corralled crowds cheered them home.

If you didn't look too closely you didn't see how thin the crowd really was. Now and then a cameraman would pull back too far, and you'd see the swathes of empty tarmac at the edges of the corralled welcoming committee.

Two days after the shooting, another resident of the boarding house knocked on my door asking if I wanted coffee; she had coffee if I had sugar. Neither of us had milk.

It was the first time I'd spoken to another resident. Michelle reminded me of a child who'd hurt themselves and was pretending they hadn't. Her overly bright eyes weren't disguised by the stiff smile she presented. She made an elaborate fuss over putting a coffee maker on a cooker top and launched into a rapid monologue. A string of sounds made from snippets of good news, gleaned from the France24 channel. She put great faith in the movie star homecoming of the MSF personnel. It was all going to be fine. They'd get everyone vaccinated against grippe de chat, and normalcy would be returned.

As she repeated the official line she bounced around the tiny flat, setting cups out, smoothing the covers on the bed. Being normal. The façade flickered when she straightened the curtains and avoided looking through the windows.

I drank my coffee. I want to remember struggling to get away and leaving Michelle with her fantasy of safety, but I know I didn't. We made the coffee last, rationing it without ever admitting to each other that we knew we had to.

Michelle had that easy glamour that French women were renowned for. Even when she was ready to come apart at the seams. We talked clothes; she gracefully gave me advice on better ways to wear a suit and softened the comments with praise for the quality of my French. I offered to help with IT problems.

I'm a cop now, even if poorly trained and roped in to fill the gaps left by gondii. Now, I'd down the coffee in one and leave the clueless civilian to her quivering delusion. Back then I was a bank auditor, a mother, someone's wife and I was scared. It was late when I left Michelle, and even then it was only because the Q-bits were hammering on the door.

Extract from the screenplay of Year of the Crow. Lithograph Studios, California (2026)

EXT. DESERTED PEDESTRIAN SHOPPING SQUARE – DAY

The square is a large flat area paved with dull grey slabs and hemmed in on three sides by low-fronted shops. Most of the shopfronts have been smashed and looted. A slow panning shot takes in the scene. The camera comes to rest on the shattered window of a clothes store. The wrecked display comprises several life-sized mannequins and long drifts of white statin; these are blowing through the shattered window and trailing on the sidewalk. The door of the shop is fronted with mirrored glass, which has a crack running diagonally across it. A zombie is crouched in the remains of the window display.

Close-up on the zombie. It is trying to bite the face of a mannequin. The hard plastic is scratched and gouged; the zombie has obviously been working at it for some time. There is a gunshot and the zombie's head bursts.

Shot changes to show Miller standing at the head of his group of survivors. He is shouldering a rifle.

MILLER

Wait.

Close behind Miller there is a group of eight or nine people. Two of them are the men who we've seen playing cards with Chan. It is them he is addressing. The two card players exchange glances and roll their eyes, but they stay where they are. Miller is staring at the headless zombie. Behind him people begin to shuffle their feet and look impatient.

CARD PLAYER ONE
What's your issue? It's just another dead Grip, man.

MILLER
And this is just another row of empty shops. Nothing worth running after. Let's wait a minute.

CARD PLAYER TWO
Enough already, it's dead.

Both the card players walk past Miller and advance on the store front. Miller unslings his rifle and appears to draw a bead on them. The people behind him are uncomfortable with this. Robertson, who has been to one side watching events, steps closer to Miller. Robertson has his fireman's axe resting on one shoulder.

ROBERTSON
Problem?

MILLER
(Still sighting along the rife)
Something's not right.

As he speaks the card players reach the store front. One of them kicks the headless zombie and mimes a surprised reaction when it doesn't move. Both men laugh. Neither is aware of Miller pointing the rifle in their direction. The other card player slings his own gun across his back and moves to open the door of the store. As he reaches for the handle, the glass of the door shatters and a zombie falls through it. Others follow it, they stumble over the first one which is then trampled underfoot. The card player, walking backward while trying to unsling his rifle, tangles his feet in a length of the cloth trailing from the window display. He falls onto his back and screams as he lands.

Camera angle changes. Viewer sees from Miller's POV. As the card player falls, Miller - his line of sight now clear - pulls the trigger and fells the zombie nearest to the fallen man. He shoots two more before the other card player, in attempting to help his friend, blocks his aim. Close-up on Miller.

MILLER
Oh, sweet Jesus.

Robertson and Miller both run toward the store. Miller has replaced the rifle with a revolver; Robertson is now holding the axe across his body. He arrives at the storefront ahead of Miller. He meets the first zombie he encounters with a sweeping karate kick that flips it onto its back. He swings the axe, splitting its skull open. More zombies are coming through the door. Robertson continues fighting at the door while Miller and the card player cover the window. Zombies have begun to come through it. They are being slowed by the tangles of cloth, but there are a great number of them.

Close-up of card player, still on the ground on his back, his face is contorted with pain.

Camera pulls up into a gradual aerial shot, slowly revealing the scene. The man on the ground is badly injured; a shard of glass has pierced his leg and he is losing blood. From the bird's eye POV we can see a second group of zombies is on the move. It has separated Miller and Robertson from the main group who now have their own battle to fight.

MILLER
Take this, I'll get him.

Miller hands his revolver to the uninjured card player, who is struggling with his bulky rifle. Miller picks up the injured man by his shirt front and, despite his screams, puts him across his shoulder.

MILLER
(Shouting)
Come on, we gotta move.

ROBERTSON
Go, get him out of here, I'm right behind you.

Miller leaves with the injured man over his shoulder. The other card player follows, walking backward and shooting into the window where the bulk of the zombies are now coming from. From the POV of the retreating men we see that Robertson is about to be overwhelmed. Miller, struggling under the weight he is carrying doesn't realise he's leaving his friend in trouble until it is too late. The second wave of zombies is now between him and Robertson.

Jump cut to Robertson. He has his back against a narrow section of brickwork and a zombie is snapping at his face. Robertson has the shaft of the axe across the neck of his attacker and is straining to keep it at bay. Another zombie stumbles against the first, arms flaying and clawing at Robertson. The first zombie prevents it from reaching its target, but the additional weight is too much, and Robertson's arms begin to give way.

Camera moves in on Robertson and the zombie until they fill the whole screen. Viewed side on, their faces are only inches apart. We freeze.

ROBERTSON
(Voice-over)
I was always told, when you get this close to death, your life flashes before your eyes. Like some kind of home movie that only you get to see. Everything

you ever did. Or didn't do. Everyone you ever knew, or ever lost.

The picture advances, a frame at a time. There is no sound at this point. We see the zombie, teeth snapping, inching closer to Robertson. Robertson turns his face to the side, still trying to get away.

ROBERTSON
(Voice-over)
And you watch your own little film show, knowing you'll never see any of these people again. Unless of course one of them fucking turns up.

The frame by frame motion continues. When the zombie is almost on Robertson's face, a blurred image appears at the side of its neck. The next three or four frames are enough to show the creature's head moving away from Robertson. Full speed resumes along with the sound. We hear a blade moving swiftly through bone.

Now, from Robertson's POV, we see the face of Maccallan. He hasn't shaved his head and his hair is wrapped in a brightly coloured bandanna. Before spinning and killing another zombie with the machete he's holding, he acknowledges Robertson with a nod. The coat he is wearing is a long duster and it swirls around him as he moves.

ROBERTSON
Maccallan? Jesus Christ, I thought you were dead.

(Voice-over)
What I meant to say was: I thought I was fucking dead.

Chapter 7. London, Paris, Lincoln

From Kings of Crows: Life on the Wrong Side of the Lockdown

I don't know how many I killed. The first of us, the first to fight, didn't keep score. There wasn't time. After the army withdrew — and no one would work in the hospitals anymore — the first packs started to appear. A lot of people think they had some instinct that drew them together, but I've never bought into that idea.

The lowest estimates say thirty-six percent of Western Europe died in the first year of the Outbreak. If the figures were the same for London, that's a lot of infected people to deal with. There were a lot of barricades and roadblocks thrown up, a lot of fires too. People, infected or not, could end up being channelled. If you weren't careful, or your luck ran out, you could end up with no place to go. If the Gonzos saw you, heard you … whatever … if they knew a live one was about, they'd shuffle around for days. Others would get caught up in the pack. Eventually they might move on. By then there might be dozens of them. Then they'd get channelled into another pack.

Take on a pack and you don't have time to keep score. You sure as hell don't worry about carving notches. I saw people doing that. The latecomers, the guys that came out of hiding once all the hard work had been done. By then there might be ten of us going in to deal with a dozen of the things. We'd clear a street, check the buildings were empty. More than once I saw some muppet filing a tally mark on the handle of an axe or a baseball bat.

November 2nd, 2020

"I'd like a word. In my office."

The office was a self-important chunk of space, walled off from the open-plan floor by glass panelling and a set of venetian blinds. Rich joked; they were the hardest working blinds in London. Maccallan lowered or raised them a dozen times a day.

Maccallan didn't wait for a reply. Once he'd spoken, he turned and went back to his desk. The glass door was left open, indicating Robertson should follow. Rich gave Robertson a tight-lipped smile that was fifty percent sympathy and fifty percent embarrassment. The phrase, survivor guilt came to mind, but it was uncomfortable. Robertson shook the thought away.

In the two weeks since Marcia's shooting, four other residents of the street had died. Although less dramatically. Four that he knew of. Dark coloured vans with hastily-lettered signs reading, Private Ambulance, would pull up and remove sheet-wrapped bundles. The last one he'd seen had morbidly decorative stains left by escaping body fluids. The attendants wore latex gloves and paper surgical masks. He chanced to glance into the rear of their van. Other sheet-wrapped passengers were already in place.

Of the four removals he'd witnessed, only once had somebody followed the deceased from the house. Screaming and red-eyed, a widow, maybe a mother, scurried beside the stretcher. She alternated curses that they were taking the body away, with yowling complaints that they had taken so long to do it.

A lot of houses in the street were dark, abandoned or with occupants beyond the need of light.

Maccallan was behind his desk. He didn't immediately look up as Robertson came in. He was staring at his computer monitor and was slow to take his eyes off the screen when he finally did turn round.

"Ah, Collie," he said, then made a quiet hissing sound, drawing air across his teeth. "Sit, please."

He pointed at the chair. The name Collie had always pissed Robertson off; it made him sound like a dog. He'd never mentioned it, assuming Maccallan would only consider it a point scored if he knew it bothered him. Maccallan was the only one to use it.

Robertson sat and waited for him to continue. Maccallan gave him a smile, not dissimilar to the one he'd been given by Rich. The addition of capped teeth and a built-in gym-healthy glow stole any sincerity from the gesture. He gave off the impression that he thought he should be embarrassed and was doing his best to play the part.

"This is very awkward." Maccallan rested his forearms on the desk and tilted his body towards Robertson. He hadn't blinked, and Robertson found his own eyes starting to itch in sympathy. "The housing and letting market is incredibly slow at the present time. Stagnant, in fact."

He picked up a pen and began to fiddle with it, making a show of being involved. The length of the performance made Robertson suspect Maccallan was enjoying himself, or at least enjoying the confirmation of his position of boss-man.

"So, I'm getting the sack, yeah?" He wanted to sound confrontational, but his voice sound flat, even to him.

Maccallan reacted with pitch-perfect sympathy and a disclaimer.

"My hands are tied. This decision came down from head office. We can give you a month's salary." He glanced to one side, across to Rich's desk, then he leaned towards Robertson. There was a pause while he waited for him to lean in too, and complete the image of collusion. Robertson nearly did but stopped himself. If Maccallan wanted to play out some personal big boss fantasy, he could do it without a straight man.

"If you want, I'll give you that in cash." He drew the last syllable into a gentle sibilance.

To save himself the need to thank the man, Robertson told him he'd take a cheque.

From Kings of Crows: Life on the Wrong Side of the Lockdown

I was probably one of the last men in London to be given formal notice. Which I suppose makes Maccallan one of the last men in London to dismiss someone. He did it well, give him his due. Put it down to natural talent, if you like. I was given a month's salary, in a cheque that by the time it cleared was worth less than the paper it was printed on. Clearing my desk took less than five minutes, and four of those were spent exchanging phone numbers and email addresses with Rich.

We did the thing you always do with people you get on with at work, but who aren't really friends; we told each other we'd meet up for a drink, both knowing we'd never see the other again. Having said that, after the army came back in – dragging the police and the government with them – and some form of order was restored, I did try to find out if Rich had made it through. I couldn't find any record of him. Not surprising really, so much was lost in the first weeks just after the Lockdown.

One estimate puts the loss of infrastructure at fifteen percent – so many buildings burned down. All those hospitals that were torched, taking the records with them. So many died. That last day, when Maccallan fired me, Rich wasn't looking well, red eyes, the usual. The TV, radio, billboards, everything told people to stay home if they felt ill, don't go to work. But people did; maybe it was a form of denial. I've got a cold, hay fever, I'm not sick with it, not me. But the other factor, and we're back to money again, was the amount of businesses that folded. People were scared of losing their jobs. People wanted to look like good employees.

As I said, by the time my redundancy pay had cleared in the bank it was worthless. Not long after I left the office for the last time, it all became academic.

The Lockdown came.

Robertson is remarkably sanguine about the government's decision to relocate to the Scottish Parliament building in Holyrood. He doesn't claim any knowledge of the thought processes behind the decision.

"Everything in the south went to hell. And it happened so fast. The illness," Robertson snaps his fingers to mark his points – "the economy, the NHS collapsing. Then the victims switching off en masse." He spreads his hands in a gesture of helplessness. "Nobody could have got it right, nobody."

Critics of the then government, both opposition and back benchers, point out that China had verified cases of HV-Tg. In the case of Shanxi the numbers ran into thousands. The Chinese response was fast and decisive, and the country now claims to have been largely untouched by the strife that destroyed much of Europe. When I put this to Robertson, he shakes his head and there is, improbably, the trace of a smile.

"If you believe that you'll believe anything. They probably kept the Gonzos under control the same way the French did, by machine-gunning whole hospital wards."

Unconfirmed reports, the only sort that come out of China, other than official news bulletins, back up Robertson's belief. It is widely believed that however many lives may have been saved during the Outbreak, a comparable number have subsequently been lost to famine. Within days of verifying the connection between domestic cats and the spread of HV-Tg, the Chinese government instigated a massive culling programme; a move dubbed genocide by animal rights organisations.

Since the removal of their main predator, bird and rodent populations have thrived. The loss of crop yield to the increased pest population has been huge. There is also speculation that many waterways are riddled with Weil's disease due to the increased number of rats.

There has been talk in Britain of changes in the law that would, in effect, prevent survivors or their families from bringing legal action against the government. There is concern within the military that this will mean a mass of lawsuits being brought directly to the army and against individual soldiers. American lawyers are reportedly offering their services to British law firms, on a no-win-no-fee basis. It would appear they have nothing to fear from Robertson.

"I never blamed the soldiers for what happened on the bridge," he says. "Everyone, everything was wrong that day. But no one knew what to do, everyone was terrified. The attacks had been getting more common. At first people would put it down to stress. The victims were scared. Gondii was one hundred percent lethal. If you caught it, it killed you, one way or another. It was that simple. That's almost unheard of, even the worst pandemics and conditions in history have left a few infected survivors in their wake. Not gondii. As diseases go it was almost perfect."

During the transition of government from Westminster to Holyrood the chain of command became blurred. Records of names and dates were not always kept in accordance with best practice. What records there are have been declared official secrets and won't be due for public release until 2071. It may never be known who planned or rubber-stamped the blockading of London's bridges.

At midnight, on 2 March 2021 the British army closed all access to routes across the Thames. The disruption was huge. The scheduled London-wide newscast, telling people of the action and advising them not to travel, went out more than seven hours late on TV and radio. The inclusion of the message on most internet sources and social media sites was largely ineffective. The result was that most Londoners didn't hear about the emergency measures until eight a.m. By that time traffic had gridlocked and panic had taken hold. Requests to avoid crossing the Thames were ignored and a mini exodus took place. The checkpoints on the bridges, where army doctors attempted to check all people crossing from south to north for signs of HV-Tg, were quickly overwhelmed.

As the hours passed, panic grew and rumours spread.

Who it was that gave the order to fire on civilians has been a matter of ongoing and, to date, fruitless investigation. Ironically, one of the few positive comments to be found in the critical review of *Year of the Crow*, is for its re-creation of that event. The scene, early in the film, shows a young solider firing into the air to bring the surging crowd to order. The sound is mistaken as an opening volley and what ensues is history.

It was the only scene shot under the directorship of Antoni Kowal. He was dismissed by Lithograph Studios when it became apparent that his vision for film was radically different from that of the studio's investors. He is currently chasing investors to fund an independent docudrama about the Lockdown.

The Lockdown was a calculated move. It led to the first mass attack on British soil. The same thing had been tried in France with the same result. The Illuminati knew the results they'd be getting. It was all done for a reason.
Username:Seeker_of_Truth

****

The Lockdown was just business has usual. The Fat Cats screwed up and the ordinary man (and woman) in the street paid the price.
Username:4KneeKate

****

And, as usual, they got away with it because most people refuse to see the truth.

Fat Cats = Money = Government = Power = ILLUMINATI
Username:Seeker_of_Truth

****

As usual, they got away with it?
What did they get away with? In effect, once the Government moved to Scotland, they were forced to form an emergency committee with the opposition parties, just to make up the numbers. They were losing power, not gaining it.
Every time the Lockdown comes up online, one of you conspiracy dickheads starts spouting shite about the Illuminati. There's never any evidence to back up what you're raving about and you can never tell anyone why this Illuminati wanted to spread plague and kill half of Europe.
Username:EchoFlood

****

It was a JEWISH ZIONIST conspiracy!!
The ILLUMINATI used SATANIC rituals to POSSESS people &

turn them into ZOMBIES to do there bidding!!
That mass attack in London was PLANNED. The ZOMBIES were being controlled by ZIONIST OCCULTISTS!!!
Username:Warrior_4_GOD

****

Mister EchoFlood,
You said it yourself, albeit unknowingly:
FAT CATS.
The real Fat Cats are the Illuminati. Everything that has happened in the last six years was for a reason and the reason was, as ever it was, MONEY!
The real reason millions of people died was so the Illuminati could get their money.
Most of the dead died without leaving a will. Even if they did, the people they left their money to were also dead. All the extra money went to the Government.
Username:Seeker_of_Truth

****

Mister Seeker,
You're using childish ideas to make sense of the sad little fantasy world you're living in.
The deaths of all those people didn't make anyone rich.
Yes, I'll concede that a lot of people died intestate and I'll accept that for those who didn't, the intended beneficiaries may have well died too. The fact remains though, the massive depopulation caused by gondii, created a massive devaluation of currency, not an increase in wealth.
I live in the north of England. I was one of the lucky ones who was largely untouched by the Outbreak and the ensuing violence. Less than six months after the first reports of violence coming up from London, I was a multi-millionaire. It didn't make me rich it just meant I was holding on to a lot of near worthless money.
Username:EchoFlood

****
EchoFlood you are one DUMB FUCK!!!!!!!!!!!!!
I was a multi-millionaire but I wasn't rich????????
EchoFlood = DUMB ASS!!!!!!!!!!!!
Username:Magnum

****
Mr EchoFlood,
Not all wealth is tied up in paper money. The dead left property behind as well. How many streets are now empty and 'owned' by your government, instead of by the people who would have rightfully owned them but for gondii?
Also, you might want to ask yourself this: where did all the gold reserves go?
Username:Seeker_of_Truth

From recording of police interview with Colin Robertson.
(2nd April 2028)

Winslow - Who made the decisions?
Robertson - I can't remember. It wasn't like we were having board meetings and taking minutes.
Winslow - So how did you decide things?
Robertson - There was a hard core of people, mostly the ones who'd been at London Bridge and made it through the horde.
Winslow - The King Crows?
Robertson - Not in that way.
Winslow - But you were the leaders, this hard core were the Kings of the Crows.
Robertson - No, everyone thinks that. In the early days, right at the start of the Takeback, the group wasn't the Crows, all that nonsense came later. I'm pretty sure that bullshit drifted in with Maccallan and his bloody machete. He probably thought he was on some kind of team-building exercise. Anyway, the Kings of the Crows was the whole group. Someone, this old boy, pointed out that wherever the group went it was trailed by a flock of crows. Crows and magpies mostly, but someone said they'd seen buzzards once in a while. Crows were the most common. Someone started saying we were the Kings of the Crows. It sort of stuck, people started saying the damn things were lucky. One fucker used to be on edge until he'd seen the first crow of the day, said they were a good omen.
Winslow - Did you believe it?
Robertson - Believe what?
Winslow - That your group was being followed by crows.
Robertson - It wasn't a matter of believing it. It was fact, the crows travelled with us.
Winslow - Why would birds be following you?
Robertson - You can't guess?
Cross - Crows eat carrion.
Winslow - And?
Robertson - We put a lot a work their way … oh, for fuck's sake. We killed Gonzos, some days we'd kill hundreds of them. Crows are intelligent birds, they figured out that where we went there'd be bodies to be picked over.
Winslow - And you were okay with that? Leaving corpses in the street for the crows?
Cross - You didn't get a choice.
Winslow - We never left the dead to rot in the street.

Cross - You were out in the sticks. You don't know what it was like in the big cities.

Winslow - I wasn't in the sticks, I was in Lincoln. Pre-Outbreak, we had a population of nearly a hundred thousand. We had our share of Gonzo attacks.

Cross - No, you didn't. Not like London or Paris.

Winslow - The French screwed it up from the start.

Robertson - Oh, for fuck's sake. Look, if you two are playing good cop, bad cop save your fucking breath and stop wasting my bloody time.

Winslow - Interview suspended at 11.16 a.m. Sergeant Cross, would you mind …

(Recording paused)

April 2nd, 2028

"Interview suspended at eleven sixteen a.m. Sergeant Cross, would you mind stepping outside with me for a minute."

Winslow left the interview room, a hastily-converted side office, without turning to see if I intended following. As I stood to go, I saw something pass quickly over Robertson's face. I couldn't place it; it wasn't a smirk, something closer to a wince. The sort of expression you flash up unknowingly if you see a child fall over.

Once he'd pulled the door shut behind me, and put Robertson out of the picture, Winslow gripped me round the bicep and dragged me around so he could lean into my space. I took hold of his hand, fingertips pressed hard into the joint of his thumb, the juncture where the bones link, just above the sensitive webbing of flesh. The initial jolt of pain made him let go. I kept the momentum of the reaction going and bent his wrist down and back. I stopped at the point of pain but met his eyes with silence, so we were both on the same page.

"You like being in plain clothes?" I used my pulling-rank voice. It was something I'd had down to a fine art long before signing up to the police. Bank auditor, detective sergeant. It was all the same to the person one down in the chain. When Winslow didn't answer I repeated the question. He nodded his head, short jerking movements. "Then you'd do well to remember who the senior officer is here. If you ever lay a hand on me again, I will personally make sure you spend the rest of your career walking a beat. Are we clear on this?"

More resentful nodding.

It wasn't the speech I wanted to make. The one I wanted to make didn't have any words in it. It involved pressing my full body weight through the bones of Winslow's wrist until they snapped, then putting him on his back and kicking his balls until they split open.

In those parts of the world, Lincoln for example, where there hadn't been enough violence and pain to go around – or at least not enough of the type of violence that wasn't wholly one-sided – men had held on to their dominant place in the market. Winslow was shocked as much by my reaction as by its efficiency. In his experience women didn't do things like that. At least no women that hadn't switched.

My verbal response was part battlefield diplomacy – one of Juan's turns of phrase that had amused me at one time – part expediency. I needed the job, the position. Beating subordinates to a pulp would lose me at least one and possibly both. The special relationship wasn't what it once was.

"Now," I said after Winslow had adjusted his clothing and started to convince himself he'd given into authority, not a woman, "what's your problem? Why the break?"

"I'm not the one with the problem." He flexed his fingers. Trying to make it look as if he was having trouble keeping his hands from going to DEFCON 3 on my throat. In reality he wanted to wince and rub at the soreness. My nails were short, but I'd still left three crescents of angry redness along the back of his thumb.

"Then why interrupt the interview?"

"You're undermining me, undermining the investigation."

"Why do you say that?"

"I fought too. I wasn't in London. I wasn't one of the Kings. But I had to go out and deal with those bloody things. I've seen enough blood and guts to last me a lifetime. And I stand by what I said – we didn't leave victims of a plague to rot in the street and get picked over by crows. No matter how good a film title it made."

By day eleven, no one knew why the quarantine was still in place. The regular police and the GPRB were as scared as we were. If you looked south, three pillars of black smoke were stamped against the horizon. The day was clear and still, the smoke wasn't moving with any speed. The distance made them appear solid. Juan said they reminded him of sculptures by someone or other, I forget who.

We had no idea what was burning or why. I'm sure, at the time, we were panicked and desperate for information. Now, it's just another detail, something in the scheme of things that doesn't matter.

News blackouts, internet and phone shut downs, they were new concepts to us, the children of the information age. It was surprising how quickly we adapted to the idea of never knowing.

The orders to stay in our "homes" had been rescinded to a series of curfews. People grumbled but didn't argue. Two more residents of the street had been shot. At least nine had been declared infectious and were hustled into what we, Juan and I, had dubbed "Chez Merde".

Chez Merde was the first building in the street where someone had died of gondii. Assuming you discounted the one I was bunking in. The landlady's son, as I'd learned from Michelle, had been lying in his sick bed for a week. On my first night in the house, as I slept, he'd had a psychotic episode and ran at his mother screaming gibberish. Terrified, she'd run out into the street. The car that swerved to avoid her hit her son. He continued to scream gibberish and sank his teeth into someone who went to his aid. It was the sirens that finally woke me up.

The ambulance that attended was a military vehicle. Bright yellow diagonals had been roughly sprayed across its drab camo body and "GPRB" stencilled on the doors. The son, long since dead, was bundled into a body bag by medical orderlies in fatigues and gas masks. His mother and the would-be good Samaritan, with only slightly more compassion, were also put in the ambulance. They weren't marched in at gun point, but it was clear they had no choice. I don't know what happened to them. The street was quarantined less than an hour later.

The first death at Chez Merde, two days later, was less spectacular. The property was another guest house and the demise of its owner left it unoccupied. Whatever residents had been lodging there were gone. I assumed they'd been caught on the other side of the quarantine barricades or had had sufficient foreign currency to bribe their way out.

The ambulance that arrived to take that body away was a repurposed delivery truck, the beer logo on the sides bisected with the yellow stripes of the GPRB. The two men who entered the house were both armed and gas masked.

People with symptoms of gondii were asked to report to Chez Merde. For treatment and the safety of others. Visitors were not allowed. A guard was posted at the door, usually a dedicated Q-man, but sometimes a regular gendarme. Always armed.

It only struck me later how bizarre it was to see people lining up at the steps of the sagging house. It was something Robertson mentioned in his book. A period of transition where people were watching the world fall apart around them and weren't quite ready to give it up. People still wanted to think it was going to be okay. The sickness would pass. Normalcy would be restored.

Men and women in fatigues entered the house on a daily basis. They went in with a guard and the requisite breathing filters, but they wore white coats over the camo patterns. I told myself they were doctors. Six residents that I knew of knocked on the door and were ushered inside. Within the week various "ambulances" had come and gone and removed five body bags. After that, people were less willing to approach the place. When that happened the Q-men started to monitor us more closely. If someone didn't leave their home when it was permitted, it was assumed there was something to hide.

Infection began to be suspected rather than declared.

The number of personnel in the street steadily declined. More regular police had been brought in to boost the Q-men numbers, but they were thinning too.

Dog Boy – as we named the Q-man who'd machine-gunned the decrepit spaniel and its owner – had been given a field promotion. The attrition of the older hands and the influx of new ones had left him senior by default. Privileges of rank didn't extend very far. Endlessly at the call of the military radio he wore on a lanyard, he was maturing fast and obviously not enjoying the process.

I found myself feeling sorry for him. Juan, who'd lived opposite the murdered dog owner, had no such feelings.

"Dog Boy's inspecting his troops again," he said.

I turned from watching the smoke towers on the horizon and looked where Juan's gaze was fixed. He was glaring down the length of the street. We were standing, together with most of the remaining residents, at the far perimeter of the quarantine zone, as far from Chez Merde as possible. A chain-link fence marked the border, running across the road. At one side it was jammed into the recess formed by a doorway; at the other it was secured with zip-ties, wound round a streetlight. There was a single strand of barbed wire threaded through the upper reaches. The real barrier was the police car on the other side. The man at the steering wheel chain-smoked and bleeped his car horn at us if anyone shook the chain-link fencing. The one time somebody had persisted he held a machine pistol in view. The fence shaker withdrew; the cop put the gun away and shrugged like he was saying, I know, but what can I do?

Dog Boy, oblivious to Juan's scrutiny, was talking to one of the regular police who was drifting aimlessly. Too far away to hear the conversation, we were left with telegraphed body language to interpret. It was hard to follow the chain of command. I'd assumed the Q-men, thrown together under hurried emergency powers would be subordinate to the established gendarmerie. I wondered if I'd been wrong, or if the depletion of both forces had left power vacuums that filled too quickly to have true authority. The regular cop managed, with a lexicon of gestures only available to native Parisians, to display, with every civility, an utter contempt for Dog Boy.

Dog Boy was the bigger man, by a good six inches. Even with most of the street between us I could see the pressure building up in him. Beside me Juan blew out a staccato jet of smoke.

"Ah, the burdens of leadership," he said.

As he said it the regular cop pointed directly at us. When Dog Boy didn't react immediately the cop energised his pointing by shaking his arm.

"What's that about?" I said.

Juan flashed me a glance and I assumed my attempt to sound casual hadn't worked. He pulled hard on the cigarette and cursed when it burnt down too far and scorched his lip. Dog Boy was moving towards us. If he'd been a soldier, I'd have thought he was marching; his movements were sharp and angular. Tension ends in motion.

"You have symptoms?" Juan wanted to know.

I shook my head.

"You?"

"Non."

Nervousness reverting to its mother tongue.

The other resident, closest to us, drifted away. Not far, but enough to demarcate a separate area. Symptoms or Dog Boy; either was something to avoid being aligned with.

Dog Boy wasn't out of breath when he got to us, or rather Juan; he was young and fit. It struck me again, how young. He was part of the full-time guard. They'd now moved into one the empty buildings. The first few nights had been loud, the soundtrack to a frat house rather than an army camp. It hadn't lasted long. Personnel changed over or vanished too quickly for any real esprit de corps to develop.

I saw him every day and closely enough to know he hadn't shaved in four days. His stubble was peach fuzz, and barely that. Juan's cheeks were steel blue in comparison.

"Madame, Monsieur."

The formal greeting threw me slightly. Perhaps my contempt had bred familiarity. Juan didn't answer, beyond a sharp nod. Although he'd just ground a cigarette under his heel, he took out his last half packet and inserted one at the corner of his mouth. He turned bodily to offer them to me, although he knew I didn't smoke. Before realising he wasn't included, Dog Boy had half raised a hand to accept one.

"One of my men seems to think you have been spending your nights at the lady's apartment?"

The accusation, phrased as an inquiry, was delivered in French. Rapidly spoken and with his attention unwaveringly on Juan. He broke eye contact with him only to flash me an apologetic smile. He knew I spoke fluent French; I'd spared us both the halting tedium of his English many times already.

"And you imagine in some way this is any business of yours?" Juan answered in English, spoken so fast it took me a moment to understand what he'd said.

"We are concerned with people's health."

Again, Dog Boy snapped out a smile in my direction. We made eye contact for a split second and he quickly looked back to Juan.

Juan was slowly opening his arms and arranging his features into an expression of mock horror. Still in English, but slower now, the way you'd speak to an imbecile, he said, "Oh no, we are gathered together. It is terrible. We are doomed."

The small crowd who'd moved away from us were watching the scene while moving farther away. Juan knew he had an audience. To his credit, he stopped hamming it up and carried on smoking his cigarette without speaking.

Dog Boy took a breath and his right hand, which had been restless since being refused a cigarette, came to rest on the butt of the pistol hanging from his belt. The crowd edged back another foot and what small conversation there was petered out.

"Monsieur," Dog Boy switched to his halting English, "the illness is not fully understood. The doctors say it is ..." English failed him, and he switched back to French to tell us, "it is most easily spread by the exchange of body fluids."

This was all directed to Juan, but as he finished speaking he turned to me. I believe he was about to offer me a tongue-tied apology. He didn't get the chance.

I saw Juan make a sudden lunge. Before I had the time to fear for his life, I was gagging on the taste of second-hand smoke. Juan's nicotine-coated tongue thrashed widely in my mouth. He broke the embrace so quickly I almost lost my balance.

"There, we've exchanged body fluids. What she has I have. Now, are there any more questions?"

This was thrown out in French, heavily accented French; Juan projecting his Parisian bloodline at the bumpkin. There was a moment, a fraction of a moment, when I thought the bumpkin was about to level all cultural divides with a burst of gunfire. It was over when the flat of my hand connected with Juan's face. That's not quite right. It was over when the crowd burst out laughing and someone even applauded.

Juan was rocked by the blow and stared at me, eyes and mouth wide. I might have laughed at that face myself in different conditions, but I was too occupied with stalking back to 'the lady's apartment'.

Dog Boy caught up with me as I reached the front door.

"Merci, Madam," he said as he passed.

At the perimeter people were still laughing. It wasn't a good sound.

By nightfall the next day, nearly all those people would be dead.

Chapter 8. Bacon and Eggs

From recording of police interview with Colin Robertson.
(2nd April 2028)

Winslow - Interview resumed at 11.27 a.m. Present are DC Winslow, DS Cross and Colin Robertson.
Robertson - You two kissed and made up?
Cross - You headed south initially, is that right?
Robertson - What do you mean "initially"?
Cross - The first few days of the Lockdown. After the bridges were decommissioned.
Robertson - Decommissioned? You mean after the Royal Engineers blew them sky high, along with every poor fucker who was on them?
Cross - You headed south, is that right?
Robertson - We didn't head anywhere. We stayed alive, and that involved moving.
Cross - So, the decision to move south was random?
Robertson - It wasn't a decision. It just was. The bridges went up in smoke sometime around midday.
Winslow - The official report says it was 2.26 p.m.
Robertson - Really? Well, while the likes of you were making official reports and giving people decent burials, I was watching people die and trying to stay alive.
Cross - My understanding was the influx was coming in from the south.
Robertson - It was, overall. But the fact is, down on the ground there wasn't any direction. You went where you saw an opening.
Cross - How many do you think there were?
Robertson - How many Gonzos, you mean? Impossible to say. Maybe not that many but everywhere was choked, the roads were all blocked solid. When word spread that the South East had been declared a disaster zone people tried to get out. London gridlocked and panic did the rest. I saw as many people trampled to death as I did attacked. People tried running when they saw a Gonzo. Then they'd come up against a crush of people coming the other way, a Gonzo in a packed crowd would do a lot of damage.
Cross - How long did it take you to get organised?
Robertson - To get properly organised, you're talking a couple of months; I mean before we were running a tight ship. In terms of taking control, taking the offensive … hours. By the time it got dark we were getting the hang of killing them.
Winslow - Practice made perfect.
Robertson - Not even that. The people who'd wasted their time flapping about

or trying to reason with them were already dead. Dead or infected.
Cross - The survivors floated to the top.
Robertson - What?
Cross - Something a man I knew in Paris used to say: the survivors floated to the top.
Robertson - I heard Paris was bad.
Cross - It was. So, by the time it was dark, you'd sorted the wheat from the chaff. You knew what you needed to do to stay alive. But you carried on going south until you reached …
Winslow - Streatham.
Robertson - It was still early days. We were organised, in as much as we knew how to stay alive, but it was day to day. We didn't have any kind of plan, we were drifting.
Winslow - That drift just happened to take you closer to the epicentre of the UK Outbreak?
Robertson - I was following Miller. He wasn't a tactician.
Cross - Then why were you following him?
Robertson - Because he was floating to the top quicker than anyone else.

From Kings of Crows: Life on the Wrong Side of the Lockdown

Standing next to Miller on a barricade one time, I saw him tilt his head slightly and sniff. It was the late watch and almost dark, so I couldn't see his expression. This would have been early May and by then we'd learned not to show lights.

"One's close."

The words were flat. For all the emotion in his voice he might have been talking about boiling a kettle.

I listened but couldn't hear anything. When I said as much, he asked if I couldn't smell it. I told him about my ruined nose, and he told me I wasn't missing much. It was a long speech by his standards, and I was eager to keep the conversation going.

Hero worship?

Maybe, though this was before Miller was really Miller, if you get my meaning. But even then you could tell there was something about him, so I wanted him to talk to me. I asked him what the smell was like.

"Ever used oil-based pastels, you know, like soft crayons?" I hadn't, I didn't have a clue what he was talking about, but I nodded and said yes. "They smell like that, only worse."

Then I heard it, that funny brushing sound like someone sweeping a stair carpet. Swish, pause, swish, pause. One step at a time, dead limbs being dragged along. Miller was off the barricade and running to meet it before I'd picked up my axe. It took me a long time to get the hang of swinging an axe.

I don't know if he was armed that night, it was too dark to make out. The stories about him always fighting unarmed are rubbish. Everyone carried weapons, you had to. But I did see him go hand to hand more than once. I think he did that night.

Later, I asked someone about the oil-based pastels. She said they smelled faintly of excrement.

Extract from the screenplay of Year of the Crow. Lithograph Studios, California (2026)

EXT. IMPROVISED BARRICADE – TWILIGHT

The barricade is a construction of burnt-out cars and building materials. It is approx. ten feet above street level. Enter Miller. He approaches Robertson and Chan who are on watch, although Chan appears to be sleeping.

MILLER

You eaten yet?

He offers Robertson a can of soup which has already been opened and is visibly steaming. Robertson wrinkles his nose.

ROBERTSON

I'll get something later. You should get some sleep.

MILLER

Tried already, it wasn't happening.

Robertson exchanges a look with Chan who has woken up and taken the soup. From somewhere in his multi-layered outfit he withdraws a spoon.

CHAN

Boss man sleep. No good you him die exhaustion. Sleeeeeep. (Makes loud snoring noises.) Is good night for sleep, mister Grippy, he no here. Nice and quiiiiiet.

MILLER

That's the problem. I can't sleep when it's too quiet. I drift off and almost forget what's happened. The quiet, the peace … it feels real again. Normal. Then I remember and … I'm wide awake.

It's as if some part of me is always out there, always caught up in it and another part is back there, back before it all went to hell. As one part lets its guard down to rest, the other shakes it awake, to remind it what's really happening.

As he's been talking Miller has moved away, farther along the walkway of the barricade. He doesn't appear to be talking to the other men at all. Robertson opens his mouth as if about to speak, but Chan waves him to silence and joins Miller. Close-up shot on Chan's profile. The grin he always wears is gone and his jaw is jutting forward. In this shot his age is apparent, his face his heavily lined and his hair is very thin, yet his posture suggests great strength. He isn't looking at Miller. Both men are staring out across the barren aspect of a looted shopping plaza. The only movement is a stick-thin dog cautiously investigating an empty shopfront.

CHAN
(Chan drops the pidgin English. His voice is quiet and measured and his diction is flawless.)
It isn't happening, it has happened. Now, we wait for the next thing to happen. The world is always between different states. This will pass and something new will come in its place. Something better, because it is the time for something better. For now, this is your time, men like you and Robertson and Maccallan. You are what the people need, you keep everyone alive, keep everyone going. When this time passes, then you'll find the different parts of your soul and put them back together.

Just visible to the side of Chan, we see Miller nod his head. Shot cuts to close-up of Robertson staring at Chan in astonishment.

ROBERTSON
You've been able to speak proper English all this fucking time?

Before Chan can reply there is a piercing series of yelps. In the dim light we see the stray dog is in the grip of a zombie. The yelping stops suddenly as the zombie bites into the creature's neck. A second zombie lumbers into view.

MILLER
Damn it.

Miller vaults over the barricade, quickly followed by Robertson.

From recording of police interview with Colin Robertson.
(3rd April 2028)

Cross - You more or less followed Miller because he was good at killing Gonzos?

Robertson - Yeah. You were in Paris, right? Set up camp and got a shower block organised? Nah, course you didn't. You killed Gonzos, dozens and dozens of the poor bastards. That's why you're alive.

Winslow - You followed a man, who you're making sound like a near psychopath, aimlessly across an infected city. No plan, no sense of purpose. Then you turn round, on a sort of group whim, and head back towards the Thames. Going through all the same shit over again.

Robertson - We were heading towards the light.

Cross - Hallelujah.

Robertson - Where did you head? What was your great plan?

Cross - I didn't really have one. After a week of drifting I decided to try for the coast. Get to England.

Robertson - Well, there you go.

Cross - Who was Chan?

Robertson - You what?

I saw a thread on another message board, claiming Miller was Chinese.
Has anyone else heard these rumours?
username: YanCee
rank: NEWBIE
number of posts: 3

****

I have seen similar threads on a number of boards. As far as I know there's no evidence to support it.
username: Gripped
rank: VETERAN
number of posts: 86

****

In his book Robertson doesn't make any reference to Miller's ethnicity. I think if Miller had been anything other than another white male there would have been a mention of it.
username: Millofile
rank: VETERAN
number of posts: 203

****

Typical white man's arrogance. Default setting of the hero is another white male. Do you think all the Grippers were black?
Racist.
username: Don_X
rank: REGULAR
number of posts: 47

****

I envy you your computer, Don_X. It must be some state-of-the-art shit if it can tell you my colour and gender from reading one post!
FYI, I am white but I'm actually a woman. My assumption

that Miller was a white male is based on the fact Robertson – himself white – doesn't think to mention Miller's colour. To me that implies he wasn't seeing Miller as in any way 'other'.
And no, I don't think all the victims of HV-TG induced psychosis were black.
username: Millofile
rank: VETERAN
number of posts: 204

****
Or it could be Robertson didn't mention Miller's colour because Robertson doesn't regard someone as 'other' because of the color of their skin.
username: Don_X
rank: REGULAR
number of posts: 48

****
You are twisting my words.
Robertson, a white male, would be unlikely to describe someone of his own ethnicity in terms of his colour. No more than a native of Japan would write a book about Tokyo making endless references to encounters with Orientals.
username: Millofile
rank: VETERAN
number of posts: 205

****
Millofile, I get your point, but I have read Kings of Crows over 20 times and I can't recall Robertson stating anybody's race, creed or color.
By your argument, for the whole of the Lockdown, almost two years, Robertson only interacted with white Britains.
username: Kimble23
rank: NEWBIE

number of posts: 17

****
Kimble23,
Thank you.
Millofile you're just projecting your own racist views onto Robertson's account.
There is nothing in Kings of Crows to say Miller was or wasn't white, black or Asian.
You're assuming he was white because that is all your narrow world view can accept.
Miller led his people across hell, fighting all the way, to lead them to safety. The way Moses led his people.
Like Moses, he was played by a white actor in the movie.
THAT DOESN'T MAKE IT THE TRUTH!
History is a constant whitewash!
YOU! ARE! A! RACIST!
username: Don_X
rank: REGULAR
number of posts: 49

****
Okay everyone, chill.
This thread is going off topic.
Don_X, check your inbox, I've sent you a Personal Message.
username: GymBad
rank: SITE MODERATOR
number of posts: 1098

****
MILLOFILE=RACIST
username: Don_X
rank: Regular
number of posts: 50

****
User, Don_X, has been removed from the list of board

members and will no-longer be able to post comments on this site.
username: GymBad
rank: SITE MODERATOR
number of posts: 1099

****

I think Miller might have been a Chinese. I think the character of the old Chinese guy, Chan, in the movie, was a hidden reference to it. A kinda in-joke. Chan doesn't appear in the book.
username: Kimble23
rank: NEWBIE
number of posts: 18

****

I met a guy who went to the same school as Miller and Robertson. He sez they were both white London boyz.
username: Crowman
rank: NEWBIE
number of posts: 10

****

Miller and Robertson must have gone to the world's biggest fucking school. The amount of arseholes who claim they sat next to them.
They didn't even meet until the Lockdown.
Tell your friend he's full of shit.
username: Gary_Blaire
rank: Regular
number of posts: 38

From recording of police interview with Colin Robertson.
(3rd April 2028)

Cross - Chan, who was he?
Robertson - He didn't exist. The scriptwriters made him up for the movie.
Cross - I mean, who was he based on?
Robertson - You'd have to ask the scriptwriter about that.
Winslow - The film was based on your book, but you don't know who Chan was meant to be?
Robertson - The film was based on my name, not even that, it was based on Miller's name. Ticket sales. They were just making a zombie film dressed up as a piece of social history. Tacking, based on the book of Miller's right-hand man, onto it was good for book office.
Cross - I think you're being a bit harsh on it. Yeah, it's all jazzed up and they've gone for beefcake actors in a big way, but the gist of it's the same. Going south, then turning round and cutting back towards the Thames. They shuffled the cast around a bit but the story's the same.
Winslow - Nothing to say to that?
Robertson - Like I said, talk to the scriptwriters. Chan's something they came up with. Maybe they thought it'd be better for the story if it looked like we had a thinker on board. Wise old Chan, directing everyone with his wisdom and humanity.
Cross - And you're saying there was no one like that?
Robertson - I told you, we weren't really planning; Miller wasn't someone who made plans.
Winslow - But there was a hard core of Crows deciding things by committee?
Cross - And this amorphous mass decided out of the blue to double back and cross one of the most dangerous areas in England.
Robertson - We saw the light. Hallelujah.
Winslow - Here's the thing; we spoke to the engineers at Waltham Cross. The way they explained it, when they switched on sections of the grid, they didn't have a huge amount of control. They were doing this at the end of June 2021. Things had calmed down by then, but they weren't over. They couldn't pick and choose, couldn't light a certain street for instance. They lit up a big chunk of London. So, you'd have seen a lot of lights.
Robertson - What we saw was light, warmth, heating enough water to wash properly, cooking food so it was actually cooked instead of burnt or raw. Civilisation.
Cross - DC Winslow, remind me: which part of civilisation did this ad hoc steering committee head for?

Winslow - They went for the financial sector.
Cross - Vast tracts of London had the power back on, and you headed towards the banks?
Robertson - Civilisation is money.
Winslow - Is that a quote?
Robertson - One of the guys used to say it.
Winslow - Is that the lecturer?
Robertson - Now what are you talking about?
Winslow - Your little book. You mention one of the Crows, one of the first to join your group. You say he used to lecture on economics. Civilisation is money; is that from one of his lectures?
Robertson - I bet you were bullied at school.
Winslow - It's not me we're talking about here.
Robertson - No, and it never has been, has it? There was a top dog at your school, there's one in every school. Top marks in class, or captain of some fucking sports team, or maybe he just punched harder than anyone else. Whatever. Top dog, but that wasn't you, was it? You were one of the tag-alongs, following him around. Two steps behind and just out of sight. And you've been there ever since, haven't you?
Winslow - Like you with Miller, you mean?
Robertson - Oh, nice comeback. You know, if she'd said that it might have stung.
Cross - What's that supposed to mean?
Robertson - Something else this lecturer character said one time: if you have an egg for breakfast, a chicken was involved; if you had bacon, a pig was committed. You and me, Detective Sergeant Cross, we were the bacon. We were committed, up to our knees in blood and shit every fucking day. Some people, Detective Constable Winslow, some people sat in their coops for a couple of years laying eggs.
Winslow - Interview suspended at 11.49 a.m.
Robertson - Now, there's a man who knows how to make an exit. You're not going to run after him, hold his hand?
Cross - I don't think that's necessary.
Robertson - I wouldn't be so sure. I think he might need his nose wiping.
Cross - Have you always been intimidated by authority?
Robertson - Oh Christ, what is it with you sceptics and all the psychobabble? You think I'm intimidated by the likes of Winslow, seriously?
Cross - Then what is your problem?
Robertson - Probably the same as yours.
Cross - That sounds like psychobabble.

Robertson - I get a dozen letters a week, all from the States, all from therapists, all offering me free counselling. I know the catch phrases by now.
Cross - Okay, what's this problem you think we share?
Robertson - Some people lost everything in the Outbreak, family, home, money … everything. Other people gained. Muppets like your little friend out there. If the Outbreak hadn't taken out a third of the country where do you think he'd be right now? I'll tell you, walking around Lincoln with a blue tit on his head pulling people over for not having lights on their bicycle. As it is, he's a big shot detective in the Smoke. And he gets to throw his weight around because the Emergency Measures Act is still in place. How long do you think you'd be able to keep me here if I had a fucking lawyer?
Cross - It isn't going to get you anywhere, you know, goading us.
Robertson - Goading, us? You and Winslow don't qualify as an 'us', and for the record, I don't know where I'm supposed to be going. I still don't know why I'm here.
Cross - Officially, Maccallan. Was he bacon or egg? Nothing to say to that?
Robertson - Unofficially?
Cross - We want to know who made the decision to head towards the banking sector, and why?
Robertson - I thought the interview had been suspended.
Cross - Interview suspended at 11.51 a.m.

Chapter 9. Nasty Work

April 3rd, 2028

I left Robertson alone in the makeshift interview room. Which broke a score of regulations, but the Emergency Measures Act was known to forgive sins. At least ones made by officials.

He'd had his chair tilted so it rested on its back legs. The angle allowed him to sit back with his fingers laced together across his stomach. A vein in his right temple contradicted his air of boredom with its own beat.

Winslow hadn't gone far. After slamming the door behind him he'd got no further than the opposite side of the corridor. He was facing the wall, leaning with his weight supported on his forearms. A study in anguished solitude. I bit down the ripple of annoyance for his obvious showmanship. And Robertson's assumption that I shared his dislike of the man.

His comments about psychobabble had touched a nerve. Low start-up costs and a ready supply of trauma victims to prey on meant psychotherapy was one of America's few growth industries. High-profile survivors, like Robertson, were the gold ring. The analyst that could boast of treating the King of the Crows could print their own money. Or code their own blockchain.

"You alright?"

He nodded stoically, then levered himself away from the wall. I tried not to wonder how long he'd have waited for me to come out before moving.

"He's a nasty piece of work," Winslow said.

I agreed with him but again there was a ripple of unease. Winslow shouldn't have been surprised, shouldn't have expected a Hollywood legend and then been disappointed to meet a human being. It was what I'd come to expect from David, safe at home in NY, watching events on a TV screen and jealous that I'd get to interview a legend while he had to raise our daughter.

Bacon and eggs.

I shook the thought away and realised I'd shaken my head at the same time. Winslow gave me a funny look.

"You ready to go back in?" I asked him, pinching the bridge of my nose to feign tiredness.

"Yeah," he said, but made no move to go back to Robertson.

I thought for a second he was going to ask if I was alright, and the feeling brought with it something like panic. I didn't want sympathy. When he spoke again it was in a whispered rush and I couldn't tell if he was angry or embarrassed.

"You're wrong about Lincoln. The pair of you, you and your friend in there." He glanced at the room where Robertson was waiting. "It was worse in London, sure, but we weren't sitting around drinking tea and waiting for someone to wave a magic wand. I was there when the riots broke out and they tried to burn down the hospitals. I was there when people were getting beaten to death by their neighbours 'cos they had a fucking cold. So, don't tell me I had it easy. Alright, just fucking don't."

It was his cue to spin round and stamp back into the interview. He didn't, and the lack of theatrical timing lent his speech some sincerity. I was expected to reply.

"Robertson isn't my friend. Now we've got a job to do, so if you've finished being offended, I'd suggest we get back to it."

"Come on then."

He did the Hollywood bit, span round and slammed the door open with the palm of his hand. All one fluid motion. I could picture him practising his moves in front of a mirror.

"Interview resumed at twelve-oh-four p.m."

He sat and regarded the slumped figure of Robertson, who hadn't changed his pose of indifference.

"Back again so soon?"

"So, Chan didn't exist," I said, "and he wasn't based on this 'lecturer' character?"

The men broke away from their staring contest to look at me.

"As I keep saying, you need to ask the scriptwriter about Chan."

"I might just do that."

He still didn't move but the vein in his temple took it up a level.

Although there were bigger battles and problems to come, for me, the first week after the Lockdown was the worst. That was the time when I had to face the reality of the situation. Seeing the bridges collapse, seeing the army machine-gun its own people, that was surreal.

From British citizens to outcasts, in the space of five minutes.

It was too big a leap to make in one go. Then the first of the horde caught up with us. There was no time to think about what was happening, no adjustment. That numbness didn't last long. It was a luxury item.

We were on the move constantly: fighting, looting. People don't like that word, but it's a fact. We needed things: food, clothing, weapons. When we'd get to a shop that someone had been in first, we'd sometimes find an IOU tucked into the till or a letter of apology. Nearly always with a name and address. In one shop I saw, someone had written on the wall, SORRY, I HAVE TO FEED MY CHILDREN.

In the days immediately after the Lockdown, I slept a lot. Partly it was sheer exhaustion, but I'm sure it was also my mind protecting itself.

I don't recall dreaming at all. Head down, eyes closed and bang. I'd be out of it until someone woke me up. It was like I'd shut down rather than try to deal with it.

The people who couldn't sleep, they didn't tend to make it. When you were awake you had to be on your toes, but it was more than that. When you were awake you had to be 'there'. Totally there. And when you were there, it was inescapable.

But the thing is, the human mind isn't built to work that way. Humans are strivers. That's why we're top of the food chain. I don't think the Buddhists got it right. We don't settle for the moment. Humans want the next thing and the next after that.

Easy to mistake that for a sense of purpose.

That was the gift Miller gave us. Purpose. His sole purpose was killing Gonzos, but at least it was a reason to wake up. Once we'd settled into a routine, worked out how to stay alive and stay ahead, then there were other people's ideas to get behind. But to start with, Miller was all it took.

That's what got me through that first couple of weeks. I'll always be grateful to Miller for that. Always.

If you were in a place that escaped the worst of the Outbreak you can only imagine the way it flipped people's lives around. It was a massive culture shock, maybe the biggest one mankind's had to date.

In less than six months, Europe went from a westernised, technological culture to a wasteland.

It wouldn't be right to say the first week was the hardest. There were harder times coming. Bigger battles to be fought and untold trouble getting food and water. Water would become one of the main issues. In the first few days the water supply was easy. Taps still worked and even when the pipes ran dry there were still plenty of properties with water tanks and shops with bottled water. It didn't last nearly as long as we'd all imagined it would. If any of us were imagining it, of course. I don't think it's doing anyone a disservice to say that for the first month we were living moment to moment. We had a lot to learn.

All that said, for me at least, the first week of the Lockdown was the worst.

Knowing it had happened to me. I hadn't escaped, I wasn't one of the lucky ones. Lucky to be safe or lucky to be dead. Take your pick. I was neither.

June 19th, 2021

Sol's hands were trembling badly. Robertson wasn't surprised when three of the pieces were knocked off the board.

As Sol reset the game, Robertson asked him, "You ever heard of John Campbell?" Sol shook his head. "Blues singer. He wrote a song called Wiseblood."

Sol affected a look of confusion.

"You tell me this, why?"

"The opening line went, 'I got wiseblood baby, I can see through your lies.'" Robertson sang the line. A few people looked up, surprised.

"Very nice. Poetic, even. It's relevant, how?"

"That bishop of yours wasn't covered. My king was one square over."

Sol smiled and returned Robertson's pieces to their original positions.

"I'll still beat you."

"Then why do you keep trying it on, you old bastard?"

"It'll take more moves this way. Playing fair only delays things." He gestured to the board, waiting for Robertson to signal his satisfaction. When he nodded, Sol chuckled, "All this adhesion to rules will do for you is prolong the agony."

Robertson considered the board. Sol was still amused.

"You think you're going to win this time, given your unbroken string of defeats?"

"You got any razors?" Sol didn't speak, but in answer patted one his coat's many pockets. "Good ones?"

Sol rolled his eyes and shrugged, exaggerating the motions in the dim light.

"I'll guarantee that what I'm holding is better than what you've got. You win, I'll give you two razors."

Robertson began softly singing again, "I can see through your lies …" Sol shook his head, overacting the look of disappointment. He reached into his layers and pulled out a plastic bag of cheap disposable razors.

"Those things are shite. I win, you give me five."

"If you win. But when you don't?"

"Chocolate?"

Sol dismissed the bet with a flick of his hand.

"Rum?"

"Life's not hard enough without hangovers and tooth decay?"

"What do you want then?"

Sol glanced around them and moved in a little closer. He flicked his attention briefly to the gathering of people who had gravitated to Miller. He said, softly, "Influence."

"Meaning?"

"Where the glorious Mr Miller goes, others follow."

"Is this conversation going to take long?"

"Why, you have a pressing engagement?"

"I want to hurry up and collect my razors so I can have a shave."

"Such optimism. This group is drifting, it lacks purpose, it needs a leader."

Miller was sharpening one of his knives. He was running a steel down the edge of the blade with slow deliberate sweeps. In the quiet of the disused classroom the sound was loud. Someone followed his lead and started honing the edge of a bayonet. Then another joined them.

"Like you said, we're following Miller."

"Leading is not the same as being followed. Direction, purpose. The Buddhists have it wrong, all that malarkey about mindfulness and living in the moment, pah. Humans don't work that way, we need the next thing and then the next thing after that. Direction, purpose. Without that we're no more than apes, picking lice out of our fur and throwing dreck at each other."

"That's where you come in, is it?"

Sol chuckled again, "Me? Do I look fit to lead the people to the promised land?" He held up one of his hands, so they could both watch the tremor. His hands had been steadier while he spoke. Now the tremors were more pronounced. "No. It's where you come in. You're possibly the closest thing that man over there has to a friend. You have his ear, you could be his council."

"And what makes you think I've got any more idea about what's next?"

"Ah, that's where I come in."

"You want me relaying your plans to Miller?"

"I want you to influence Miller."

"Why not talk to him yourself?"

In the corner, Miller had moved on to his next knife, one of the butcher's knives. In the shadows, the people gathered around had the appearance of supplicants. Those sharpening their own knives were matching his rhythm of steel against edge.

Sol didn't answer his question. Instead he indicated the chessboard.

"Make your move. Maybe you'll win and this conversation will be academic.

Hurry up, then you can have a shave. Maybe you'll stop scratching."

Robertson moved a knight, capturing one of Sol's pawns. Maybe prompted by the old man's taunt, his chin began to itch. He rubbed it with the palm of his hand. He'd become overly cautious about scratching, the risk of breaking his skin. Sol ignored the loss of his pawn and put him in check, pinning his queen.

"Oh, you bastard."

"Shall we talk some more about influence?"

Sol didn't want to talk inside. After he'd stowed the chess set away, he and Robertson eased one of the external doors open. The door opened onto a flat roof. The space wasn't much larger than a smallish back garden but at some point it had been used as a break area. There was a pair of shoddy wooden benches and the obligatory planter, filled with a neglected shrub and a layer of cigarette ends. Many of them were fresh.

"We should be going that way," Sol said.

In the dregs of the day's light, Robertson couldn't see more than the slope of the old man's arm, pointing somewhere roughly north east. Their elevation wasn't high but the sky in the direction Sol pointed had a luminous quality.

"Back to the Thames?"

"Over the Thames."

"Last time I tried going to North London I got shot at."

"That was months ago. The border will have moved, if there still is a border."

"Says you."

Sol stepped away from the waist-high barrier running the roof's perimeter. He sat stiffly on the one of the benches. Robertson stayed close to the edge of the roof; his head was cocked. He could hear footsteps below, on the road that had run behind the one-time school. Without being fully aware he was doing it, he separated the sounds of the footfalls and counted bodies.

Three.

He tilted his head trying to hear more. One of the three was crying, the sobs mechanical and lacking humanity. Another was caught on a single word, maybe not even that, two syllables on a loop: scree, scree, scree. Like the sobbing, the pitch and the rhythm were robotic. The word was drifting away, fading as it shuffled along the road. Robertson strained his ears.

"What are you listening to?" Sol asked.

His voice seemed loud and Robertson started, hand tightening on the shaft of his axe. He made himself relax and was about to apologise, but realised Sol wouldn't have seen the movement in the dim light.

"Nothing," he said. "Couple of Gonzos."

Sol didn't answer immediately, and when he did he sounded annoyed.

"They've got nothing to say. You keep eavesdropping, trying to work it out; you'll end up as worthless as they are."

Robertson saw Sol's head jerk in the gloom. It was impossible to say if he was indicating the Gonzos in the street below or the rest of the group, huddled in the building they'd just exited.

Robertson moved along the barrier, trying to blot out the sounds from the street.

"Why do you want to head to the river?"

"There are lights."

"We're segregated from the light. That was the point of the Lockdown. Containment."

Sol snorted.

"You really think a stench of water will do the job? Trust me, other side of that river … dead, dying and switched. Same as this side.

"Plus the army."

"Army, he says. If there was still an army, there wouldn't have been a Lockdown."

"And how do you work that out?"

"How many people died on the bridges you reckon?"

When Robertson didn't answer Sol repeated the question.

"I don't know. Hundreds?"

"Meh, who knows. My point is, in a matter of minutes a handful of armed men wiped out whole swathes of the population. Yet our government abandons the capital and heads north because a pack of drifting psychos are coming. Why not send the army in, armed to the teeth and spitting vengeance?"

"You sound like you know."

"Same reason we're losing people day after day. Lack of common sense."

As if to illustrate Sol's words the door behind him burst open and a figure was briefly framed in the weak backlight. Before the door slammed shut the figure, tall and wide, Robertson guessed a man, began to cough convulsively. He bent at the waist, holding onto his knees to support his weight. After a full thirty seconds he hawked up a wad of mucus and spat it onto the ground between his feet.

Panting for breath and trembling from the spasm, he eased himself upright, then searched through layers of clothing. There was the flare of a match and a bright point of light as he sucked on a cigarette, unaware of being watched. Sol addressed Robertson.

"You see my point? We've got people dying every day. We lose more to dysentery and chest infections than to the Gonzos, and this genius is spitting on the floor."

The figure with the cigarette, still panting, took a step towards Sol.

"Hey, fuck you, you old …"

Robertson stepped into his path and jabbed the blunt end of his axe into his chest. It was little more than a tap, but the shock of the blow caused the man to stagger back and fall.

"Hey," he said again, and began to get to his feet.

"Fucking stay down, or I'll take your head off."

The smoker recognised Robertson's voice and froze. Remarkably the cigarette was still pinned at the corner of his mouth. He sucked in desperately and started coughing again … Robertson backed away two or three steps.

"You fucking ill?"

The tip of the cigarette zigzagged frantically in the dark as he shook his head.

It took him three goes to say, "Bit of a cough. My eyes are fine. It's not Frog Flu."

Behind him, Robertson heard Sol make some remark. He sounded tired, but angry tired. Not old.

"Get over to that side of the roof and fucking stay there." Robertson gestured with his axe to the edge of the roof, farthest from the door and the benches where Sol sat. As the man scrabbled away, trying to control his cough, Robertson said, "I see you going back through that door tonight, I'll throw you over the side. You got that?"

Sol had left the bench. Robertson had heard his knees click as he'd stood, then he'd listened to the shuffling steps. When he was happy the coughing man was at the far side of the roof, he followed.

The old man was looking at the glow of lights to the north.

"The army was probably decimated before the Lockdown. When the domestic situation became critical, they pulled the military away from active service abroad."

Robertson nodded. It had been one of the last major news stories he'd seen before the emergency measures had reduced the media to propaganda and public information films.

The influx of service personnel had been massive. Serious-faced politicians had told upbeat press conferences that the exercise marked the biggest mobilisation of British forces since the Second World War. Sincerely grinning spin doctors had given interviews at the edge of airfields. Battalions of men were herded from specially-chartered commercial jets to be packed into coaches and army lorries.

The cameras zoomed in, looking for smiling squaddies to back up the official take.

The film of a dozen men being stretchered off the flights by red-eyed medical orderlies was cut halfway through transmission. It was one of the last pieces of uploaded video to go viral.

"Drag hundreds of men across Europe, pack them into planes, trains, boats. When they get off, stuff them into overcrowded barracks." Sol sighed heavily. "The people in charge, they never learn."

"Yeah, well I guess they didn't have much of a precedent for Gondii, did they?"

"You ever heard of Spanish flu?"

"Rings a bell."

"It's actually a misnomer, it originated in Kansas and was taken to Europe on troop carriers. Thousands and thousands of men heading out to World War One, crammed into the holds like so many sheep. Coughing and sneezing and incubating. The men who survived the war got put back on the same ships and took the epidemic back home. America lost more troops to Spanish flu than enemy fire. By nineteen eighteen, worldwide, the death toll was over fifty million."

Robertson muttered, "Christ."

Sol surprised him by laughing.

"Compared to this, fifty million barely warrants a mention."

"You think?"

Another laugh, "Who needs to think? Look around you. What do you see?"

Other than the glowing skyline to the north east, London was in darkness. Robertson felt something in his stomach, the feeling he remembered as a child: flying down the slope of a big dipper, unanchored from the world for a split second. It wasn't a feeling he'd ever enjoyed.

He had to make a second attempt before he could answer.

"I see the end of fucking days, Sol. Game over."

Sol patted him on the shoulder. He expected, wanted, some consoling statement.

"Maybe. Maybe not. In America, during the Spanish flu epidemic, in some cities they had carts going around the streets collecting the dead. They couldn't print death certificates fast enough to meet demand." He fell silent and turned again to the glowing horizon. "In the middle of all that, do you know what the undertakers did?"

"What?"

Sol laughed again, "They put their prices up."

"Bastards … ow!"

Robertson put his hand to his temple. Sol had clipped him with his knuckles, and he could feel the old man glaring at him.

"No. No, they weren't. They were the keepers of the faith. While people like you were wringing their hands and volunteering to carry slabs of meat out of the hospital beds, they kept the market running."

The silence the speech earned him didn't quell him. He made to rap his knuckles against Robertson's head again. Robertson swatted his arm away.

"You're pushing your fucking luck."

Sol muttered a curse and pointed north again.

"That is where they are keeping the faith." The words were slow and careful. As if he were talking to a particularly slow animal that couldn't master house training. "Money. Economics. That is civilisation. Now, we can wring our hands and weep and wail about the end of days, or we can keep the faith and prepare for what happens next." His tone softened and he lifted a hand slowly. Despite the lack of light, his fingers found Robertson's chin and held it. "If we don't take action, we're just going to do the same thing day after day. Sitting in a circle, watching the tribal chieftain sharpen his knives until the knives have all turned to rust. Or we can head that way and do something worthwhile."

Robertson brushed the old man's fingers from his jaw.

"You think that's what happening there? The government's back? They're rebuilding?"

Sol's laugh was close to fatherly.

"That way is Threadneedle Street. Someone has decided, of all of London, the place they need to keep the lights on is the financial sector."

"And you think heading there is our best chance?"

"It is if we're going to rob a bank."

Chapter 10. Screams and Bite Marks

Is there any more information on the Zeta-Presentations?
Member:(Board ID withheld)

****

There was an article posted recently on the X ABOUT ZEE site. There is a short video clip with it that shows a male Zeta-Presentation in US army fatigues being taught to shoot a gun. It appears that the disease has mutated again and the subjects being infected are now closer to the Alpha-Presentations seen in Paris.
Member:N_CRYPT

****

I've seen that posting. It's a hoax. That video clip has been pulled from an old army recruiting advertisement and been doctored to make it look grainy.
Member:Skull_E

****

Hey, look guys, a Fed.
Yeah, sure … it's all a hoax.
Go back to sleep America.
Member:N_CRYPT

****

Fuck off Fed
Member:(Board ID withheld)

Juan didn't come over to my apartment that evening. I didn't know if he was weary of being witnessed or pissed at me for slapping him. Whatever the reason, I found I was relieved. The first time he'd stayed the night in my flat I'd been glad of the company. Loneliness, because of the distance my job put between me and home, had never been a problem before. Technology shrank the miles. Phone calls, video links, texting. Sometimes the relentless contact had felt like a chore. I'd listen to reports of Maria's day at school and David's routine and have the luxury of being impatient to get back to work. Now, with the phone and internet so unreliable, conversations had become bursts of gabbling. Desperate attempts to communicate between breakdowns.

The nights were the worst, even before the power supplies began to fail. During the days there were things to feel resentful about. Routines dictated by the police or the Q-bits. The lack of fresh meat or vegetables. There wasn't a shortage of food, that would be months away, but the rations were bland or ill-chosen.

But once the curfew was reached and we were corralled into our lodgings, time weighed heavy and there was nothing to do but worry.

I didn't sleep with Juan. The first few nights were purely for company and frankly anybody would have been preferable to solitude. My neighbour on the floor below, after her initial visit to share coffee, had become reclusive and only left her flat when called out in the mornings. The moment the medics had carried out their checks she would vanish back inside. I'd taken to leaving tins of food outside her door.

I don't recall if Juan had asked to accompany me back to my lodgings or if I'd suggested it. It might have been a silent decision, but for me there wasn't any other agenda. I'd assumed that was understood.

The therapy generation, currently inhabiting the American dream, may have a list of reasons for Juan equating being scared to foreplay. The most likely assessment, in my opinion; that's just the way men think.

In total he spent three nights in my room, dozing in the armchair that took up an eighth of the floor space. Kissing me in front of Dog Boy had been the first physical contact we'd had. Though, with hindsight, it was inevitable. Given a few more nights and little more finesse it might have been a successful seduction. Those were trying times.

I tried my phone and the closest I came to a connection was a 'no service available' message. My computer cheerfully displayed the Google search box but was unable to connect to any web pages. I scrolled through the modest collection of personal photos I stored on the hard drive. All that did was bring my state of dislocation into stark relief. After a few minutes the images of David and Maria playing in the garden or pulling faces at Thanksgiving began to feel like mockery. When I shut the computer down, I had to stop myself throwing it at the wall.

Outside, disturbing sounds competed for my attention. The echoes of distant gunshots had become routine with startling speed. What had come to worry me more was the lack of sirens. In the first days following the street's quarantine, the pulse of sirens was constant. It had slowed and some nights I'd only hear one or two. I told myself it was a positive sign.

On the nights Juan had stayed we would sit, usually in the dark, and talk until one of us drifted into sleep. I don't remember what we talked about. Probably the small annoyances of life under martial law. I'm sure neither of us looked out of the windows. My apartment was at the front of the building and the view looked over a reasonable spread of Paris. At some point I'd taken to avoiding the window; it had started unconsciously but quickly became an article of faith. If I couldn't see what was outside of my street, it was business as usual for the rest of city. Having someone to talk with meant I could ignore the sounds also.

Three shots somewhere in the distance, the deep rumble of people en masse. Like the noise outside a football stadium. Without Juan's presence, the sounds invaded my head. Not watching the window began to feel like it was watching me.

The view was at a far enough remove not to be terrifying, but I could feel my stomach knotting. At least a third of the city visible from my window was in darkness. The darkness wasn't complete; the shimmering glow of fires was scattered throughout. The idea that the sounds I could hear were like a sporting event became darker, and I remembered sport was basically a civilised form of combat. And if you removed the civility from it …

The need for company became absolute. I left the apartment and for a while, just glad to be away from the window, I stood in the hallway not sure what to do. The curfew was on. I couldn't fool myself anymore that this was a quirky story to tell everyone once I was back in my home. I decided to go down to my neighbour and try to invade her self-imposed isolation.

The lights on the landing of the boarding house were bright. They robbed the spiralling staircase of any charm it could have laid claim to, but I was glad of the bulbs that night. The lack of shadows was comforting. Michelle's door was shut tight and the pile of tins I'd left there that morning were still waiting for collection. I made myself jump by knocking on her door. The sound seemed louder than was possible, the quiet of the building's interior as frightening as the noise.

There was no answer.

I knocked again, harder this time. Then again. I could hear movement behind the door.

"Michelle, it's me, Donna from upstairs."

The movement on the other side of the door stopped as if I'd flicked a switch. I called her name again, the pitch of my voice higher than usual, levered into the point where the door abutted the frame. The way you'd call to a child who'd shut themselves in their room.

"I'm … alright," Michelle's reply was too loud. Something she must have realised because when repeated it she spoke too quietly.

"Can I come in? I've got some coffee left, upstairs."

Silence from behind the door again. I was about to give it up and return to my room when the rattle of a door chain startled me into taking a backward step. The door cracked open; its movement brought short by the security chain.

Half of Michelle's face stared out at me. The bright light from the hall might have made her look paler than she was, but even by my kindest estimate she looked terrible. I expect I looked about as good. Fear is draining. Pressed close to the gap as she was, I could only see her right eye. I had to hope the red streaming puffiness was the result of crying.

"No, thank you. And thank you for leaving the food. But I don't want to come out. Sorry."

She began pushing the door closed.

"We're the only ones left in the building," I told her. It hadn't struck me until that point, but that was the case. The landlady, her son, the other guests were all gone. We two were left. It felt important. It also felt wrong. "We need to get out of here."

I can't know what she might have said to that if the gunfire hadn't broken out. Maybe she'd have had an epiphany and we'd have struck out across Paris together; maybe she'd have slammed the door in my face anyway.

It was automatic fire, muffled but close, definitely in 'our' street. Two bursts, something shouted in French, then a third burst. And the screaming started.

I almost ran up, back to my room, but Michelle's desperation to hide from it made me do otherwise. I wish I could say it was something noble and human. A brave decision to take charge, or some such. It was contempt that drove me to go down the stairs. I didn't want to be one of the people who hid under the bedcovers and waited for their fate.

Most of what happened in the street that night, the part from when I opened the door and looked out, is a confused blur of snapshot memories. Dog Boy dragging an injured Q-man behind a blazing police car. Juan breaking a police baton across the face of a ragged figure that stank of shit. The ragged figure falling then, incredibly, rising again and launching itself randomly at another resident of the street. Screams and bite marks. And most of all a man putting a bullet through his own head because he'd been bitten.

We didn't know the term Gonzo at that point. Naming and recording events wasn't a priority. Later into the Outbreak the infected who developed HV-Tg psychosis 'switched', as the Brits had it, became less functional. The disease mutated several times. Something that possibly saved the human race from extinction. In the early days the attacks in Paris and London, and I assume the rest of Europe, were where most of the damage was done. The first Gonzos, the Alpha-Presentation as some call them, were more 'human' than the next. They were capable of acting in groups, possibly even planning. I've read reports of houses or blockaded streets being laid siege to. I take most of the reports with a pinch of salt.

One of the things not always spoken of is the mob mentality that took hold in the early days. That night in the quarantined street, I saw the break in the fence at the end of the road where the infected had gotten in; a car had been driven through it. Even then, in what I realise was the beginning, I never encountered a Gonzo that had maintained enough cognitive function to drive.

And it was quickly apparent that shooting a Gonzo and shooting a normal human produced different results. A lot of the gunfire that night found its way into people who weren't suffering HV-Tg psychosis.

My neighbour's decision to hide in her flat was as effective as any suicide bid. As effective as the petrol bombs that were being deployed. I don't know how many died that night. I've also never been able to find out which side was lighting the fires. Only the fire in Chez Merde was ever traced to a definite cause.

Five of us that made it out of the street crammed into a repurposed Citroën with yellow Q-bit markings: Juan, Dog Boy, me, an older member of the regular police who'd been assigned to the street and a horrible young man with eyes the size of dinner plates.

The policeman was bleeding from a huge wound on the side of his face. His head was shaved tough-guy close, in the traditional way of French officialdom. The lack of cover made it easy to see that most of his right ear was missing. Presumably the same teeth that had claimed his ear had also left their mark high on his cheekbone. He kept his eye screwed shut. The blood was running down his neck and shoulder. In the morning when we had light, we could see the gearshift was coated with it. We would have likely thrown him out of the car had he not been driving.

The Citroën had careened down the street, away from the inferno of Chez Merde. A group of men, none of them Gonzo, something I'd be willing to swear, hurled stones and bottles at it. They scattered when it mounted the sidewalk and drove straight at them. Juan, myself and a third resident were pinned into some doorway. We'd been trying to escape one of the mobs. Whatever coherency might have existed between infected and healthy had clearly broken down. I want to think that at some level the uninfected – we quickly began to think of them as the 'humans' – had some agenda, a mission of some form, however misguided. The alternative is that the veneer of civilisation is so thin all it takes to take break through it is the opportunity.

By the time the marauding mob had melted into just a mob, the street had been laid waste. Some of the Q-men and police may have escaped in the confusion but I doubt it. The barricades at either end of the street, erected to contain the residents, worked as well to contain the warders. That Juan and I survived was chance, nothing more. He didn't scour the darkness hunting for me, and I didn't rush around looking windswept and in need of rescue.

When I rushed from my boarding house, Q-men and police were firing bursts of automatic fire into an advancing crowd. People fell screaming. Some took bullets with barely a break in momentum; others just fell. The crowd kept coming forward carried by infection psychosis or group madness, it didn't matter.

Beyond not staying in the building, my planning hadn't progressed. Getting past the crowd wasn't an option so I sprinted ahead of it, trusting, because there was no choice, the gunfire to buy me some time.

Time was metered out in fractions of a second. Planning was anything beyond the next minute. Seeing the sunrise would mean I'd played the long game. I sprinted from the door, moving left. I was aware of the sound of gunfire ahead of and behind me.

Despite their arms the Q-men were on the losing side. It was a numbers game and the numbers were against them. When the gunfire to my back stopped and all I could hear was screaming I didn't look round. I kept running.

I saw Dog Boy, shouting, moving around, firing his gun. A resident I'd never spoken to ran past me, in the opposite direction. I heard him scream a moment after he left my sight. I didn't turn. One of the few buildings not on fire or blocked by fighting was a café. Its doorway was a strange point of dark calm and I threw myself into it. Pressed against a section of brickwork I took a full second to breathe. It felt like a luxury.

Like all luxury, it was fleeting. The next breath I heard drawn wasn't mine. Choked with phlegm it was closer to a death rattle than a breath. Except the force of it was too great. It was a sound I'd get accustomed to. The sound of a body working far beyond the limits of normal endurance.

The smell hit me. I still don't know how I'd missed it until then. Fear of more immediate dangers, or maybe it was masked by the smell of arson and gasoline. Once my nose had admitted it though, there was no escape. Shit, blood, vomit and urine, plus any other fluid a human body can produce.

There's still a lot of talk of zombies. For those of us that lived it, the comparison doesn't work. Actors in latex masks, shuffling comically around, ignoring the fact they're dead. The gondii victims weren't dead. They should have been, but they weren't. Their lacerated brains had switched from the normal functions of life and, by association, death. The disease drove them on.

Who or what the Gonzo I encountered in that doorway had been I can never know. I can't even say if it was a man or woman. It was another moment where the choice was act or join the victims. As the Gonzo lunged I threw my arm across its face, in a tight arc. I remember, very clearly, the blow connecting high on its face. I hadn't moved with any thoughts on where to strike or what to avoid, but as chance would have it my first desperate attack was the correct one. Later I would see people, more often men, sign their own death warrants with an instinctive punch to the jaw or a brawler's headbutt into the nose. More often than not they broke their own skin against infected teeth. Headbutts broke the noses of opponents that didn't react to the pain but produced rivers of infected blood. It was cold comfort to know they won the fight as they developed symptoms a few days later.

The jolt of the impact travelled up my arm and into my shoulder. For a split second the pain eclipsed the fear. I'd caught the Gonzo at eye level. The bony ridge of my forearm connecting with the fragile bone on the outside edge of its eye socket. The blow would have probably felled it had it not been for the infection driving it on. I don't remember the rest of the fight. I've heard other survivors give similar accounts. The details become blurs, the fact they survived being all they are left with.

And what's the point of recalling it in detail? That night was no different in reality than a hundred that were to follow it. We fought. Some people lived and others died. The difference could be as narrow as a lucky blow or an untimely stumble. I lived. Juan lived. Dog Boy lived. Two others made it out of the street.

Another doorway, this time beside Juan, still holding the splintered stub of a broken police baton. The Citroën pulling up, and Dog Boy regarding both of us down the barrel of his gun.

"Contaminated?"

Juan, frantic, nodding his head and shouting, "Non, non."

Then barrelling out through the mob. The last escape pod, with all its seats taken.

Chapter 11. Snapshots

French Cat Flu (Frog Flu)

Misleading references to HV-Tg. The misnomer originated in the Saint-Denis region of Paris where an increase of Toxoplasmosis gondii in cats was missed due to habitual misdiagnosis. The mistake was compounded by British vets who, by convention, regularly used the term Cat Flu to describe a variety of pathogenic infections.

The A to Z of Gondii Names

I don't know how our government can even think about issuing passports to the French. It was their incompetence that spread the cat flu virus.
username: Pairiot-and-Proud21
rank: REGULAR
number of posts: 95

****

Who said the Government is thinking about issuing passports to the French? I haven't heard about this.
username: Zippy
rank: Newbie
number of posts: 3

****

What do you mean by our government? Are you talking about the American government?
username: Fax2Know
rank: CONTRIBUTOR
number of posts: 1000+

****

Of course the US government, OUR GOVERNMENT. THIS IS AMERICA!
username: Pairiot-and-Proud21
rank: REGULAR
number of posts: 96

****

Okay, Pairiot-and-Proud21, a couple of points you need to take on board
1. This is not America. This is the internet. You may well be accessing it from a location in the USA, but other users reading your posts could be anywhere.
2.The American Government cannot issue passports to the French. Governments, American or otherwise, can only issue passports to their own citizens.
I assume you are referring to the recent CNN report,

concerning a democrat member of the House of Representatives who suggested easing the non-domestic travel restrictions. Is that the case?
username: Fax2Know
rank: CONTRIBUTOR
number of posts: 1000+

****
All I know is the government is talking about letting diseased kitty fuckers into my backyard!
You better tell them I'm cleaning my guns and checking the sights!
username: Pairiot-and-Proud21
rank: REGULAR
number of posts: 97

****
FUCKING-A PARIRIOT!!!!!!!!!!!!!!!!!!!!!
Those cat humping disease bags ain't bringing there stinking virous here.
AMERICAN SOIL FOR AMERICAN SONS!!!!!!!!!!!!
username: Magnum
rank: REGULAR
number of posts: 106

****
The government is not talking about letting diseased people from anywhere onto US soil. All that has happened is a bill has been put forward that travel restrictions are revised for healthy individuals.
As to the sentiment, American Soil for American Sons; many of those seeking entry into the US are American citizens who were caught in Europe during the Outbreak. These people are now being denied the right to return home.
And (once again) HV-Tg is not a virus.
username: Fax2Know
rank: CONTRIBUTOR

number of posts: 1000+

****
Why should we let the damn Cat Fuckers in any way? Who gives a shit if it's a virus or not?
The clues in the name * FRENCH * Cat Flu.
And If the SOBs had kept it to themselves Europe wouldn't have gone all to hell.
username: Jawcreek
rank: TROOPER
number of posts: 204

****
The term French Cat Flu is misleading. It was employed widely by the British tabloid press during the early stages of the human variant Toxoplasma gondii (HV-TG) pandemic.
HV-Tg is not a virus, it is a mutated form of a microscopic parasite most commonly spread by cats. The cats themselves were not harmed by the parasite but served to pass it on to other mammals. Exposure to the parasite could lead to the development of the condition Toxoplasmosis. When the parasite mutated, felines began to develop a highly aggressive form of Toxoplasmosis. In Britain, where the name French Cat Flu was coined, the more general term cat flu doesn't necessarily mean a cat has influenza. Vets in the UK use cat flu as a general term to describe the clinical signs that cats often get with upper respiratory infections. This caused misleading reports in the media that were never corrected.
Toxoplasma gondii, in its original form, was already widely spread throughout the developed world. The first verifiable incidents of the mutated versions have since been traced to Spain. France was the first nation to realize the threat posed to humans and instigate a plan of action. Because of this the French have been unfairly blamed for the rapid spread of the disease.

username: MidwestVet
rank: CONTRIBUTOR
number of posts: 568

****

All I know is I won’t be letting any Kitty Licker on my property.
AMERICAN SOIL FOR AMERICAN SONS
username: Lone_Star
rank: TROOPER
number of posts: 201

Becoming Maccallan. Interview with Ryan Morgan appearing in Stars and Sounds Magazine (#37 July 2025), conducted by Sarah Feldman

Ryan Morgan's Utah home is pleasant, if modest. Not unlike the man himself. When I suggest his future might include more luxurious accommodation he smiles and tells me he's happy where he is.

Financially, he could be happier. Cast in the part of Rodger Maccallan, the relatively unknown actor was offered a flat fee for his services. Leading man Malik Connally allegedly negotiated five percent of the box office for playing the role of Colin Robertson. Malik has since become one of the film's most vocal critics, decrying *Year of the Crow* as, "symptomatic of Hollywood's toxic nature." He has implied that he may quit the movie industry completely. Receiving five percent of one the biggest grossing films in history means he can afford to.

Ryan is more respectful of the film that has made him a household name. The closest he has come to public criticism was to say the portrayal of events wasn't intended to be realistic. Something he repeats when I raise the subject of the film's sanitised account of the London Lockdown.

"We were making something people would want to see. If we had made it true to life, made it like a documentary, it would have been too intense." He pauses and then adds, "No one really wants to see what it was like."

Ryan didn't visit the UK before filming started. He wasn't unusual in this. The only member of the cast to do so was Malik Connally. The film itself was made entirely on location in Boston, MA. The set designers and prop-crews – who turned the self-consciously 'English' tourist areas into a replica of London during the Outbreak – were the only members of the production team to receive any critical acclaim. The make-up teams were rounded upon for producing an army of text-book zombies, and the decision of the CGI team to place Big Ben on the south side of the river Thames is likely to go down in movie history.

I ask Ryan how he prepared for the part.

"Hours and hours of phone calls, Skype calls, emailing. And, of course, the studio had access to Maccallan's flat."

The studio in fact owns Rodger Maccallan's flat. Like many victims of the pandemic, Maccallan died without making a will. Like most of the empty property in what remains of London, its ownership passed to the state. When Lithograph Studios heard the flat was still awaiting clearance, they bought it for an undisclosed sum. It's another record for the studio, being the first Transatlantic property deal carried out since the US banks closed all dealings with Europe. It is also possible it was the first real-estate deal carried out using cryptocurrency.

Ryan produces a thick file containing hundreds of photographs of the flat's interior. It appears to be exactly as it was on the day Maccallan left it. There are several close-ups of a small coffee table. On it are an open book, a fine china beaker with the word COFFEE printed on it and a bowl. The beaker and the bowl both have a coating of mould.

"The rest of the flat is clean," Ryan tells me. "Packed with a lot of stuff, but clean. It looks like he heard Miller and Robertson and just left. No turning back, didn't even finish his coffee. Just gone … boom."

Another photo of the table is a close-up of the base of the mug. There are two opened sugar sachets resting next to it. The next photo is an extreme close-up of the sachets.

"One of them's half full," Ryan says, drawing my attention to the detail. "From that I worked out he took one and half sugars in his coffee."

It's an attention to detail few actors can boast.

Scenes from a Crow's Nest: A Photographic Essay of The Flat of Rodger Maccallan, by Gordon Price, Pullman (2026)

Introduction

History expects more of its heroes than simple endurance. Taken in isolation, the innate human desire to survive is unlikely to secure anyone a place among the legends. If it did, a contemporary history of Europe – or even a census – would be corpulent with the weight of heroes.

Something more is required. What that something is, is unspecific. It might be a degree of selflessness, although the history books have never been short of individuals whose selfishness is described as indomitable will and is subsequently veneered with admiration. Novelty alone is often the factor separating those who were merely in the count and those who actually counted. The keepers of order seldom rise above the mundane, and history is liable to file them away in dusty archives and dry reference texts.

By those somewhat fickle standards this volume may never be classed as a documentation of heroism. The following 451 photographs (reproduced with the kind permission of Lithograph Studios) are, in the main, no different to a collection of interior shots randomly pulled from an estate agent's window. It is of course the knowledge of whose interior they depict that gives them an emotional resonance.

Some of them, like the view of the abandoned breakfast (#3.57 Contents of coffee table, p32) hint at the story of the man who left the flat never to return. Others such as the cataloguing of the supplies (#4.03–#4.68 Contents of kitchen, pp54–73) hold, at least in retrospect, a stark poignancy. It was the well-ordered dwelling of a survivor who'd made plans to weather the storm. The fact that the flat and its contents endure, largely undisturbed, shows the quality and accuracy of its planning. Maccallan's decision to leave the security of his home could in some lights be classed as an error, even foolhardiness. For while the flat has survived its owner has not.

It is, however, the decision to leave that secured Rodger Maccallan an entry onto the roll of heroes. In his exit from his carefully prepared shelter, he achieved the transition from man surviving to man with a purpose. The very first photograph in this collection (#0.01 Unsecured entrance way, p3) is some indication of how he left the building that day. When he heard the call of Miller and Robertson, and doubtless the cawing of the following crows, he ran towards a purpose with no thought of turning back.

While many of the pictures you will see here have a story to tell, some will simply present questions that will never be answered. The images of

Maccallan's bedroom are deeply disturbing and not solely because the act of viewing them feels overly intimate. The content of photos #2.02 to #2.11 particularly reveal an intensity of feeling that few could match. The bizarre nature of the pictures can only remove knowledge of the man, not add to it.

Why would a man of Maccallan's obvious intelligence waste valuable fuel making printouts from his laptop? Why would he stockpile printer ink cartridges and carpet the floor with pages of accounts? Of course, we will never know.

In some ways that is the great tragedy of Gordon Price's pictorial record. Extensive and meticulous though it is, it can never be more than a demonstration of one more thing that is forever lost to our generation.

Prof. K.M. Laurel
Head of Post-Pandemic History
Magdalen College
Oxford

#3.09 Long shot of east wall. Bookshelves.

The photo shows a set of floor-to-ceiling shelves comprising ten levels in all. The top and bottom levels have been designed to accept volumes slightly larger than A4. The levels between are smaller and capable of holding nothing larger than a standard format hardback. In this picture few of the titles can be read and the books appear to have been randomly placed. At a conservative estimate there are at least a thousand books in the picture.

#3.10 Closer focus shot of east wall. Upper left section of bookshelves. Reading L. to R.: first sixth of upper three shelves.

Closer focus reveals details of book spines. The contents of the uppermost shelf are mostly large format coffee-table books. The titles are eclectic, and books appear to have no obvious connection to their neighbours. The first book on the shelf is titled *Architects' Sketchbooks*; the last title visible on the shelf is *Infographic Guide to the Movies*. The books have been arranged in alphabetical order by title. The second shelf contains a mixture of hardback and paperback books. These are also an eclectic collection of titles and genres, both fiction and non-fiction. Some of the spines are pristine while others are creased. On this shelf the books have been ordered alphabetically by the name of the author. The choice of titles appears to be almost random but there is a preference for factual works of finance and computing.

None of the books in photos #3.10 to #3.28 have visible book markers in them.

#3.57 Contents of coffee table.

Close focus on round, glass-top coffee table, taken from above at an angle of approximately 60 degrees. The table has been identified as being 90cm in width. The floor of the flat is visible at the edges of this photograph. It appears to be hard wood. On the table are resting a fine china beaker with the word 'coffee' printed on it, a matching bowl and a matching milk jug. All three items are coated with a thick layer of mould. Alongside the crockery are three stacks of copper coins and two opened sachets of sugar. Beyond the crockery, placed as if to be read while eating, is a large-format book. It is lying open, displaying a double page picture of a Lamborghini Aventador S Roadster.

#3.61 Contents of coffee table. Close-up of coins.

The coins have been sorted into separate denominations and stacked into individual towers. The tower on the far left of the picture consists of two-pence pieces and contains twenty-four coins. To the right of the two-pence pieces, central in the arrangement of towers, is a tower consisting of nineteen one-pence pieces. The tower at the far right of the picture is made up of half-pence pieces. There are eleven coins in this tower. The half-pence piece was demonetised in the UK in December 1984.

#4.00 Bedroom floor. View on entering bedroom.

The floor is hardwood. It is covered with documents. Most of these are A4 printouts. Interspersed with the printouts are A5 sheets and what appear to be various receipts.

#4.64 Contents of wardrobe. Right-hand side.

This photograph shows a fitted wardrobe with sliding doors. The right-hand door has been pushed aside revealing the right half of the wardrobe's interior. Hanging in the far left of the space are three suit-cover bags. To their right are seven pale blue shirts in clear plastic covers. The bottom of the wardrobe contains a shoe rack with two pairs of Oxford shoes and forty-eight 500ml bottles of mineral water. The top shelf of the wardrobe contains five unmarked file boxes and a canvass backpack. There is an empty space at the far right of the shelf.

#4.68 Contents of wardrobe in detail. Backpack.

The backpack has been placed on the bed. A pair of one-metre rulers has been placed beside and beneath it allowing the size to be gauged. The backpack is approximately 40cm in height and 20cm in width. The zip securing the pack's closure has been opened allowing the contents of the backpack to be displayed. The angle of the photograph makes it impossible to accurately assess their number, but the pack appears to be at least three-quarter filled with rolls of banknotes.

#4.75 Detail of bedroom floor. East wall, space in front of right-hand door of wardrobe.
The picture shows a Dell laptop computer; it is partially open. The screen is shattered. Five of the keys have come away from the keyboard and are lying on the floor.

Chapter 12. Old Friends

April 3rd, 2028

Winslow seemed not to notice the room was gradually getting quieter. Or maybe he did. He may have known all eyes were turning to him and mistaken the lull in activities for bated breath. He carried on tapping the copy of *Scenes from a Crow's Nest.* The illustration he was repeatedly indicating showed Maccallan's broken laptop, lying on the floor of his flat.

The book was thick and heavy, two hundred and fifty glossy pages of indexed and catalogued tedium. It was a big seller in Japan and America. Both nations – untouched by the gondii pandemic – were far enough removed from the visceral trivia of survival that heroism was allowed to become a cult. The pretentious foreword from an Oxford don lent the trivia an academic sheen. Readers could pretend they were fascinated rather than voyeuristic.

I'd seen the book myself. Everybody in the investigation had looked it over. Almost everybody working in the building had drifted by at some point to see it. At least all the men. The price in Europe, where paper stock prices refused to fall, had set the purchase of the tome beyond the reach of most. My decision to request a copy from the publishers for official use in the investigation had bought me a short spell in the limelight.

The copy we'd been sent was a second. The spine was broken and there was no dust jacket. The page with the edition number had been torn out; title page and cover were scored through with permanent marker. There'd be no resale value there.

Tap, tap. Tap, tap. Tap, tap.

"Would you like me to get you a rattle?"

Winslow focused on me for a second and then looked around the room. More than one person's eye quickly dipped back to their desktop. The level of noise picked up again and the room suddenly felt noisy.

"Rattle?"

"Rattles." I didn't want to have to say any more. Explaining would turn a sarcastic comment into something petty and spiteful. Winslow was quietly waiting. "Noisy little things babies shake around to get attention."

"Really? My understanding was babies shook them around because it made them laugh."

More quiet waiting. I tried to lighten the sudden mood, "Obviously a man without children."

"Not since the hospital in Lincoln burnt down, no. You wanted something?"

The last was addressed to a uniformed PC who'd watched the exchange from the corner of his eye. He responded to Winslow's question with a flurry of frantic inputting on his computer. For a moment his embarrassment eclipsed mine. Before I could say anything more, Winslow span the copy of *Scenes from a Crow's Nest* around and pushed it across to my side of the table. The page he'd been tapping ripped almost clear of the spine.

"Page on your right," he said.

With no book to tap he drummed his fingers.

"The broken computer?" I didn't get an answer other than the drumming. "What about it?"

Winslow leaned forward, resting the weight of his upper body on his elbows. I'd expected him to pull a staring contest, but he practically ignored me. Instead he was looking at the picture of the damaged laptop.

"I've gone through that book page by page. There are only three places in that flat where there's any kind of mess. There's a single dead mouse in one of the traps he'd set in the kitchen, and that flat was empty for almost a year. One mouse in a year. Maccallan had that place in order. I don't know about you, but I spend my life emptying traps and cleaning up mouse shit. Maccallan had everything set up so well even the mice didn't know how to get at his food."

I drew the open book closer to me and flipped the pages until I found the photos dedicated to the kitchen. There was tinned and dried food in abundance. All sealed tight and all packed with precision. One picture showed cans of soup stacked in a cupboard. The labels all faced the same way. I didn't notice, but Winslow pointed out they were in alphabetical order. Chicken to Windsor, via mushroom and tomato. It took me a while to find the dead mouse. The only sign of disorder in the kitchen, it had warranted a full half page.

"I assume item two is the coffee cup?"

I didn't hunt for the photo of Maccallan's abandoned breakfast. It was an image I already knew; everyone did. It had been one of the photos used on the movie posters and had caught people's imagination for some reason. One of the few true-to-life parts of the movie had been the faithfully reproduced interior of Maccallan's living room. Its appearance in the film had been fleeting. Maccallan, filmed from behind so as not to ruin the reveal in the rescue scene, hears screams and gunfire. Instantly he abandons his breakfast, grabs his machete and runs to embrace celluloid immortality. The camera lingers poignantly on the half-finished coffee and cereal.

It was the point where I'd left the cinema. Robertson, one of the few public figures to defend the film, had maintained Hollywood was right to turn the truth into a fantasy. I know what he meant. The brief glimpse of authenticity I'd had was enough to turn a distraction into a flashback.

"You noticed the coins, of course?"

"Is that a comment of some sort?"

"Rattled?"

"Yes, I noticed the coins. What about them?"

Winslow wasn't quick to answer, and I braced myself for more point scoring.

"Well, Detective Sergeant Cross, you're the banker. No matter what it says on your ID about Washington State Police you're just a reworked numbers cruncher. So, why don't you tell me about the coins?"

Rather than get into a pissing contest about rank, I went to the book's index and found the listing for the close-up on the coins.

"Three piles of decimal coins with a face value of about," I estimated the number of coins, "eighty to ninety pence."

I was floundering and didn't like it. If Winslow, at that point, had gone for another round of dick-waving I'd have pushed the copy of *Crow's Nest* down his throat. He nodded, but I couldn't tell if it was at me or at the other people in the room.

"Face value. What's their real value?"

"Now? I doubt they've even got scrap value."

"Because the Treasury decommissioned them, yeah?"

"Demonetised them, but yes, they're not 'money' anymore."

Winslow eased himself forward a little and did his tap-tap thing on the open book.

"That pile is made up of half-penny bits. Those were taken out of circulation before I was even born. So even at the most hopeful estimate, even on the first day Maccallan barricaded that stairwell, all those coins represent less than seventy pence. And if Robertson's telling the truth about when Maccallan made contact, he'd have been living in there for nine or ten months. Those coins were already worthless. Same as all that paper money in his rucksack."

"Maccallan might not have known that. Most people don't understand money. He could have thought all he had to do was keep his head down and wait it out. When someone found a cure, he'd crawl out a rich man."

The smile Winslow produced missed being condescending by a hair.

"What does his bedroom floor look like to you?"

I answered the question by nodding at the wall directly behind him. I'd hoped he'd turn to look and, in the process, hurt his neck. The wall at Winslow's back, had been covered with a skin of cork boards. Notes and interconnected reports showed the workings of three separate investigations. One of them ours.

Winslow didn't bother to turn.

"A crime wall? Yeah, that's what I thought of at first. But then I'm a copper, not a banker."

"Enough, Detective. I used to be a banker, then the world went to shit. Now I'm six thousand miles away from home and I'm a police officer. And at this table, I'm the commanding police officer."

"Yes, Sergeant." Winslow pinched a block of the book's pages together and flipped them over. The estimate was pretty good, and he only had to flick over three more to get to the photograph he wanted. A shot of Maccallan's bedroom floor, layered with carefully set out documents.

Tap, tap. Tap, tap. Tap, tap.

"Let's pretend the world didn't go to shit, shall we? You were never separated from your family, mine were never burnt to death and you're still a banker." Tap, tap. Tap, tap. Tap, tap. "Now, what does that look like to you?"

The penny had dropped, no pun intended, before he'd finished his speech. The only thing missing from the photograph was a calculator.

"It looks like an audit."

From Kings of Crows: Life on the Wrong Side of the Lockdown

The group got bigger, but looser towards the end of the first year. To start with the hardcore, what people would later call "The Kings of the Crows", had probably numbered no more than twenty. People are surprised that I didn't know each and every one of them. But it wasn't really that type of situation. In truth there wasn't much of a common bond across the group. No one signed up to join the good fight. We were just hanging together because it gave us the best chance of staying alive.

Of the original twenty or so we lost seven in the first month. That time was horrendous. Gonzos were increasing then. Most of the people who gathered at the river on the first day of the Lockdown were healthy, or at least infection free. But there were still huge numbers of victims in their houses. As the arson attacks on hospitals and doctors' surgeries became more common people hid when they got sick.

As the switch-off phase of the disease became more common, every street we encountered was a risk. And of course, the disease was still spreading among the survivors. It's what stopped massive groups forming. Or at least surviving. Overcrowding led to infection spread. Spring was the worst time because it was warm but there was still a lot of rain. Moist and warm equals disease. On occasion we'd run into packs of fifty or sixty Gonzos. I think some of those were communities of survivors that had packed themselves in too tight.

You had to clear up as you went. Leaving people with infections behind was asking for trouble.

There was a point where the numbers of people in a group became unmanageable. This is like the looting. Now that it's more or less over, nobody wants to admit they were involved, or they want to put a spin on it, so they come out looking like heroes. No one likes to admit they turned people away. But the fact is, it had to be done. I've met with other people who made it through the Lockdown. Without exception they've said the same thing: they turned people away or they drove them away. The communities that tried to make room for everyone ended up creating graveyards.

Fifty to sixty people is manageable. With those kinds of numbers there were enough of you to set up watches, patrols. Enough people to take out any Gonzos that might happen along. But the number is small enough to feed, and to spread out.

It's easy to be wise after the smoke's cleared, but I'm still amazed at some of the stupid things we did at the start. When it got dark on the first night, we all packed ourselves into a single house. As I say there were around twenty of us then. Someone woke me up in the small hours to take a turn watching the door.

I stood at the foot of the stairs for two hours. The whole time I was there I could hear this constant coughing: somebody in the front room, where six or seven people where bedded down. We did the same the next night and the next. On the fourth day, some fella lost a piece of his hand when he was bitten. His wife and brother-in-law insisted on looking after him. In the end, all three of them died. Infected another two, that brought the toll to five. We got a bit smarter after that, but it took longer than it should have.

By the start of the winter we were organised. People would be assigned to a pack of four. We might extend that for families. Those four would work together, bed down together. If they got sick, they did that together too. Survivors would be isolated for a month at least.

If we were on the move and couldn't find a big space to spend the night, we'd take over a street rather than just one house. Those types of rules did more to keep us alive than anything else. That and boiling the water. Never mind gondii, there was plenty of run-of-the-mill stuff that could kill you. Cholera and dysentery took a lot of people out. Not many of ours; we learned our lessons.

On the day Maccallan appeared, we numbered between fifty or sixty. We were running at max. That same morning we'd turned away a three-man team who'd offered to buy their way in with a load of supplies.

I was the first to see Maccallan. He'd been quietly pacing us for a while before he made contact. He'd recognised me from when we worked together. Or thought he had. I guess he wanted to be sure before he put his head above the parapet. The last time we'd spoken he was firing me. Awkward at the best of times.

When he finally called over and I stopped he held his hands up. Not right up like he was surrendering, just away from his body. Showing us he wasn't armed. It wasn't necessary; he obviously wasn't dangerous. His clothes were clean and the only thing he carried was one of those over-the-shoulder satchels that were big with all the hipsters and bright young things just before it all fell apart. Even his boots were clean.

He obviously had a bolthole somewhere. A lot of people had tried to wait it out. I don't blame them for going that route. It's what I'd have done if I'd had the choice.

For me the opportunity didn't present itself. I was caught at the river when the bridges were blown and thrown in at deep end. It's something I need to be grateful for; I went to back to my street and most of it was rubble and ashes.

Once the rioting and burnings stopped the upmarket tower blocks were fairly easy to defend. The high-density stuff, down the rough end of the manor, was little more than a collection of vertical Petri dishes, and once there were a handful of switched-off residents wandering the communal areas …

I remember Maccallan talking about his flat a lot. He'd never say precisely where it was, but he liked to imply it was riverside property. We'd worked in letting, we could both make studio apartment sound like penthouse. Instead of bedsit.

I don't know why he came out of hiding just then. Later he told me it was because he'd seen me from his flat and recognised me. I don't know if that's true. We hadn't been close before the Lockdown, but I suppose if you've sat alone in your flat listening to the world go to hell, anything from the good old days is going to look like a step up.

I don't know why I let him in. Not after we'd turned down three other men bringing a damn sight more to the party. Was it a bad decision? In retrospect: yes. He could have waited it out another nine, ten months and come out when they started setting things back to rights. That way he'd be alive today. There was a bit of grumbling from the team I was with, comments about another mouth to feed. It was obvious he'd been hiding. Maybe I was more nostalgic than I thought.

February 12th, 2021

"Hey. Hey."

"Look, pal, take the hint an' fook off, alright?" Johnno's voice was high, his Liverpool accent becoming more pronounced as he got angry. He shoved the man who been following them in the chest for the second time. The man staggered back but managed to stay on his feet.

"Okay, okay. Let me talk to that man, there. We know each other, he'll vouch for me."

Johnno was bringing up the rear, along with Miller. They'd taken to moving from street to street in teams. A team of those too young or too old to fight and a team of fighters, forming a loose quad formation around them. Robertson, at the front, turned to watch the big Liverpudlian heft the baseball bat. He'd stopped speaking and Robertson knew the situation was about to tip over into violence.

He thought of the silence before a fight as part of the new order. Displays of aggression and anger didn't impress Gonzos. The group had quickly learned that battle cries did little more than increase the odds of attracting extra trouble. Those that hadn't learned; hadn't learned the hard way. They'd lost a complete team that had decided football chants were due a revival.

The man took a step back, then another and held his hands away from his sides, showing they were empty. There was a machete tucked into his belt. Like the clothes he wore, it was very clean. No coat, no backpack, just a fabric satchel slung across his chest. Johnno tested the weight of his baseball bat again, slapping it into the palm of his hand.

Miller had his head angled, listening, but not to them. Robertson wasn't sure he was even aware of the situation developing a few metres away from him. He was registering normal human beings less and less.

"Your friend over there will vouch for me, just ask him." The unarmed man was wary of Johnno's bat, but he wasn't backing off. He was gesticulating at Robertson.

The team in the middle of the quad comprised two girls barely in their teens who wouldn't be parted, and Sol. They watched Robertson as he moved towards the trouble. The man made a move towards him and Johnno brought the baseball bat down in a lazy arc, blocking the way.

Maccallan smiled and let out a theatrically loud sigh of relief when Robertson stood in front of him.

"I thought it was you. I saw you when …" He didn't finish the sentence, turning instead to point along the route the two teams had just taken. "My place is up there. When I saw you …" Again he left the end of the statement unsaid. He continued jabbing a finger at a block of flats with expanses of smoked glass and balconies dressed with exotic planters. His breathing was fast. The encounter with Johnno had shaken him.

"You do know him?" Johnno asked, and lowered the bat when Robertson nodded. "Sorry about that, Boss. I didn't know, did I?"

Robertson waved the apology away.

"We got all the people we need, Maccallan. Fuck off and crawl back into your hidey-hole."

Miller still had his head to one side, ignoring the exchange. On the edge of his vision Robertson saw him slip one of the butcher's knives from the webbing around his leg. Maccallan was working hard at getting his breathing under control. He shook his head.

"Look … look, Collie–"

Without warning, Robertson punched him in the solar plexus. Maccallan folded with a hollow whooping sound and keeled over as his knees buckled. No one moved, except for Miller who was drifting towards a fire-gutted shopfront. Robertson watched, expressionless, as Maccallan gasped for air and then vomited noisily.

When he was quiet again, Robertson, avoiding the smears of bile, rested the head of his axe against the side of Maccallan's face.

"I'm not a dog. So, don't call me collie."

He'd intended turning away and leaving Maccallan where he'd collapsed. But Maccallan nodded and pulled himself into a sitting position.

It took him two attempts to speak. "Okay. Okay, understood. I can help."

To Robertson's left, Johnno laughed. The way his voice got higher when he was angry, his laugh got higher when he was relieved. Off to the right, things were happening in the shopfront. Robertson didn't take his eyes off Maccallan.

"Help with what? IT problems?"

Taking it as a cue, Johnno laughed again. Maccallan nodded, answering Robertson's question.

"Yes, exactly. I've got mining programs. You're heading across the river, aren't you? I've got the software. I just need the power."

More noises from wherever Miller was. Still not looking away from

Maccallan, Robertson waved Johnno towards the shopfront.

"Go and check Miller's alright."

Johnno ran towards the fight without hesitation.

"Why do you think the power's on?" Maccallan was sounding desperate. "They're trying to keep the hard drives running." His attention flickered away from Robertson's face. Sol had appeared at Robertson's shoulder.

"Smart boy," Sol said. The words were low, only for Robertson's ears.

"Maybe."

Over in the shopfront Miller was hacking at a Gonzo. There were three of them; the biggest was a woman. She was moving quickly and didn't look as if she'd been switched long. She'd been young. Maybe twenty, hair short and roughly cropped. At a guess she'd been part of another group.

The other two were older and it was hard to tell gender or guess their ages. Without the infection driving them, they'd have long since lain down and died. Slower, less awake than the one Miller was worrying at, they were shuffling towards Johnno who was waving his arms to get their attention and draw them away.

Robertson clinked the axe head against the machete Maccallan had in his belt and jerked his head in the direction of the fight.

"Go and make yourself useful." Then louder, shouting to Johnno, "You can back off. The cavalry's here."

April 4th, 2028

We agreed I'd go into the interview room without Winslow and talk to Robertson without the tape running. Winslow had suggested it. I'd asked why and he carefully set his face into a blank.

"He thinks you're a kindred spirit, remember? You two fought the odds while I was raking in the good fortune. While you and the King of the Fucking Crows were cutting a swathe across Europe and making the world a better place, I was being a run-of-the-mill copper in a Lincoln police station. Where one of the countless luxuries I enjoyed was a soundproofed interview room."

That Winslow had heard – through the wall – Robertson's little analogy, about bacon and eggs and the difference between the committed and the involved, shouldn't have mattered. He had access to the interview recording and, as ranking officer, I would have passed them to him for transcription anyway. But, hearing the comments drifting through the wall had added another layer of resentment to whatever it was bubbling between us.

A uniform brought Robertson up to the 'holding cells', a repurposed suite of rooms that had been used for records storage. Solid doors, good locks and no windows. Robertson had spent three nights down there. He looked ready to spend another three and another three after that. As he was walked down the corridor, I heard him joking with the uniform.

I was waiting at the table next to an empty seat where Winslow would have sat. Robertson settled himself across the table from me and winked at the uniform who nodded back. As he pulled the door closed behind him, I caught his expression. I didn't know what he was thinking, but I painted my own interpretation onto his face and read it as disapproval.

"Looks as through you've made a friend," I said, before remembering our voices would carry in the corridor the uniform had just entered. Robertson gave me a contrived look of puzzlement. "Your star-struck escort."

Robertson ignored the remark, "Where's Big Boy?"

I pretended not to know who he meant. He made a show of studying his nails and drew his mouth into something the shape of a smile.

"You're wrong about Detective Constable Winslow." He faked another look of puzzlement. "He's been through the mill."

"Don't tell me, he lost his parents to cholera or he saw a Gonzo put the bite on his wife. Everyone's got a sob story. Everyone. There wasn't anybody in Miller's group that didn't go through the mill. Not everyone got to come out of it ahead of the game."

"From where I'm sitting you don't seem too badly set. You think everyone in the holding cells gets to laugh and joke with the PCs?"

Robertson had been leaning back in his seat, as close to relaxed as was possible in the plastic stack-a-chair. Now he brought himself forward and rested his arms on the tabletop. With deliberate slowness he turned to look at the audio equipment that I hadn't yet switched on.

"What did you do before it all went tits up?"

He wasn't smiling now. As the words left his mouth his lip sealed into a hard line.

I debated whether I should answer or not. Would it build rapport or show my hand? What would a real officer of the law do? Interviewing methods were part of my sketchy police training that I'd largely ignored.

Instruction was delivered by an ageing Met officer who'd been pulled from retirement in a bid to fill some of the gaps left in the force. What enthusiasm he'd ever held for his job had long since faded away. He looked like anyone of a thousand others, someone who'd lived through the gravest threat humanity had ever faced and come out the other end wondering why they'd bothered.

Aside from his sonorous voice and lack of interest, my own arrogance had helped me dismiss the lecture with little more than a passing nod. I'd been an auditor with one of the world's biggest banks, I'd been flown into Europe ensuring the good and wholesome 'Merickan-dolla was where it should be. Wheedling facts from double-entry cookery books and divining truth from the accounts of the unaccountably affluent.

And, embodiment of the American dream that I was, I couldn't believe the stakes could have gotten any higher than money.

Robertson was waiting on my answer. I told him I was in banking. He tilted his head, as though listening to a voice I wasn't hearing. I had the sensation that he'd filed the piece of information away, and I regretted giving it to him.

"Nice. Status, respect. Big house in somewhere like …?" I copied his head-tilt motion rather than fill in the blanks. The other question, the one he wasn't asking, played across his face; why was an ex-banker with an American mandate interested in him?

Abruptly he pushed himself away from the table and leaned back into the stack-a-chair again. The liar's smile was given another airing.

"Do you know what I was before it all fell down?"

"I understood you were in real estate. That was where you met Rodger Maccallan."

"Real estate?" For a moment his smile looked genuine, but it still lacked any humour. "I worked in a letting agency. I went and sat at the same poxy little desk five days a week for four years. And no bugger knew I was there. I'd sit watching my life tick away and all I'd get was the chance to come back the next day and do it all over again. Go home on the bus, sit in a shit-hole of a flat watching the box and listen to the couple next door having rows. I barely existed. And now I'm a somebody. Just like your friend Big Boy out there."

He jerked his head in the direction of the door, then snapped forward in his seat again, putting his elbows on the table. The movement was sudden and caught me by surprise. I flinched and Robertson saw it. I expected him to regard it as a victory, but he appeared to have startled himself as much as me. He didn't try to lounge in his seat again, but he inched away from the table, moving out of my space.

"Yeah." He pulled in a slow breath. "Me and Big Boy have both moved up the ladder a bit. Now, when we tell our sob stories people listen, 'cos we're the cool kids. But I'll tell you the difference. Big Boy's loving it, living the dream and believing people when they salute."

"You'd sooner be back in your shit-hole flat with your old job?"

Robertson barked out a laugh.

"I'm not saying that." He did the head tilting thing again, not taking his eyes off me. Having appeared to make some decision he settled himself into the angle of the stack-a-chair again. "There used to be this magazine, before the Outbreak, it had some stupid name, People's Lives or True Lives. You ever hear of it?"

"Can't say I have."

He nodded, and I had the impression again that he'd filed something away.

"You haven't missed much. It was just sob stories, back to back: my stepdad abused me, stabbed on my honeymoon. Shit like that, pages and pages of it. Used to find it in doctors' waiting rooms. I saw an article in it once about this poor cow, had something wrong with her face. Born with it. The quacks couldn't operate to correct it until she'd finished growing. So, she grows up getting bullied and teased and pointed at."

"Children can be cruel," I said, "especially girls."

"Yeh, but when the time came to have the plastic surgery, she turned it down. According to the article she wanted people to accept her as she was."

"Sounds like a brave girl."

"I think that's what the article was going for, plucky victim of circumstance battling on and not letting it get her down. All very uplifting." He said it in a sneering tone.

"You have a different take on it?"

"You could say that. I'll be honest with you, when I read that article my reaction was, stupid bitch. I couldn't imagine why she'd do that to herself. She had the chance to come in from the cold, to fit in and she turned it down. But …"

"But?"

"But she'd lived her life seeing what people are like. And she'd always know that. She wasn't being brave, she just didn't want to put herself through surgery for the chance to join the human race."

I glanced at the door without meaning to. Robertson saw the movement.

"Am I boring you?"

"I'm wondering where this is going."

"Your little friend Winslow's where he is because the world fell apart and made a space for him. And he's wagging his tail and strutting his stuff. The Outbreak made him, gave him a place. Me, I was made by my life before it. I wasn't offered a place, I had to cut one out with a fucking axe. And don't give me that blank look, you know what I'm talking about."

Winslow chose that point to come in. He didn't make eye contact with me and avoided looking at Robertson. If Robertson hadn't already guessed our conversation was being listened to, I suspected Winslow's entrance let him in on the secret.

Winslow started the recording gear and announced the time, date and those present.

"Mr Robertson, would you care to tell us when Rodger Maccallan joined your group of survivors?"

Chapter 13. Burning Issues

In the Grip (Gripped, Gripper, Grippy)

Term meaning to suffer HV-Tg induced psychosis. Most commonly used in America and Canada. Derived from the French: grippe de chat (cat flu). The term was popularised by its use in the film *Year of the Crow*.

The A to Z of Gondii Names

EURO PSYCHOS SET TO INVADE BRITAIN!

Headline from The Sun newspaper (02/05/2021)

UK OPEN TO IMMIGRANT 'ZOMBIES' AT DOVER

Headline from The Daily Mail newspaper (05/05/2021)

From Storyless People: Failures of Humanity During the HV-Tg Pandemic, Dr R.T. Baranski, Warwick Press (2027)

Survivor guilt has long been recognised as a verifiable condition (Piorkowski, 1983; Williams, 1988) and many psychologists now believe its prevalence in Western Europe is eclipsed only by PTSD (Pinkerton, 2026; Richardson et al., 2027). Most sufferers of the condition are regarded with bafflement by 'outsiders'. People not exposed to the traumas of living through the worst of the Outbreak find it hard to comprehend the self-loathing sometimes experienced by those who did. "Why should you have guilt?" they ask, "you did nothing wrong." Stories of selfishness or acts of brutality that made the difference between life and death usually fail to dent this assertion.

It is rare, however, to find understanding or sympathy extended to anyone involved in burning hospitals.

Many of the narratives recorded in this book have been told anonymously, but most were told in the first person by those involved. I have recorded hundreds of hours of accounts – far more than the scope of this work could contain. I have catalogued accounts of bloody street fights, looting, theft, murders, sexual assaults. The stories, for all that they are intensely personal to those involved, seldom stand out as anything other than examples of their genre. The following is, in my experience, unique.

Subject X was not alone in his actions in the early days of the Outbreak. However, he was the only individual I encountered who gave a personal account of being part of the mob violence that led to the destruction of thirty-two hospitals across the UK.

At the time of the interview X gave his age as thirty-seven, although in common with many who lived through the London Lockdown, he looked older. His natural height was hidden by a pronounced stoop and he was painfully thin. When he smoked, which he did almost constantly, his hands trembled and by the end of our interview the floor between his feet was scattered with ash. The only time I saw him smile was when I asked him if he was sleeping rough. For some reason he found the question comical.

Note: Although recorded in both audio and video, X insisted the camera was set at an angle that would not capture his face. Any references to facial expressions, therefore, have been removed from notes made at the time.

Transcript of X's story (transcription starts two minutes fifteen seconds into recording)

... Lisa had needed to see a doctor. Nothing to do with Toxo, she'd spilled a pan of hot milk

down her leg. She was in a lot of pain, but didn't want to risk the local A & E. The news was full of stories about zombies and how you shouldn't go to hospital unless you had no choice. I told her to get in the shower and I ran cold water on her legs and dosed her up with paracetamol. We didn't have any bandages in the house, so we wrapped a pillow case over the burn.

Next morning, the pillowcase was stuck to her leg. The burn had wept into the material and … set. We got her back in the shower and spent half an hour soaking it off. All the skin came away with it. By lunchtime she was desperate. I called a cab, but the driver refused to take us to the hospital. He dropped us off two streets away. Lisa couldn't put any weight on her foot. I half carried her.

*The A & E was packed. Even with all the warnings people kept turning up. There were two security guards at the entrance, wearing face masks. One of them had one of those American-style truncheons, a what-do-you-call-it, a Billy Club? The other one asked why we were there. I was pissed off by then, Lisa was in tears and getting hysterical. We were both panting for breath. I yelled at the guy, 'Look at her f**king leg. What do you think we're here for?' He looked at me without speaking, then took half a step forward. It was only then that I saw he had a taser gun.*

He showed me the taser and once he was sure I'd got the point, he asked us again what we were there for. This time I just said, 'My girlfriend burnt her leg'. He asked us other stuff then: if either of us had a fever, running nose, double vision? Did we own a cat? He was asking both of us. We kept saying, 'No, no, no'.

Finally, they let us in. The one with the Billy Club pointed down a corridor, told us to go to the end of it and turn left. He said it two or three times, like it was very important. I was helping Lisa up the stairs and the guy with the taser took another step towards me. He told me to keep a lid on it, said I wouldn't get a warning in there. He said it very softly, I thought he was playing the hard man. Maybe he was being nice.

(X swallows and takes a massive pull on his cigarette. He is blinking back tears.)

Every day, I wonder what would have happened if he'd just shoved the gun in my neck and fritzed me out. I wish he had.

The corridor we walked down was covered with signs and posters. All about Toxo. There was one that was a close-up of a pair of eyes. You've probably seen it. The eyes were all puffy and red, they looked like someone had sandpapered them. Above the eyes it said, 'IF YOU THINK YOU'VE GOT HV-TG DON'T VISIT'. That poster was everywhere, all along the walls. It was like being watched.

There were more guards at the reception desk and a sign with 'AGGRESSIVE BEHAVIOUR WILL NOT BE TOLERATED'. It wasn't an official sign. It had been written on a sheet with marker pen.

We answered the questions about Toxo all over again, then sat and waited. It was so quiet *it was spooky. Some people were talking but they were doing it in whispers. No one was getting lairy or kicking off about not getting seen. And there were no children. Anytime I'd waited in a queue before, before Toxo, there'd always been a baby crying. It was like it was the f**king law. But not then. No one wanted to bring their kids to a hospital and risk getting them infected.*

Somewhere in the building it was noisy. It was low but I could hear this rumbling sound the whole time. Once in a while there'd be a crash, or someone would shout. We couldn't see where it was coming from. Once there was a scream and everyone jumped. The two guards at the reception desk both tensed. Three people stood up and walked out. Didn't say a word … they just left.

When Lisa finally saw a doctor, it took less than two minutes. I can't remember anything about him apart from the smell. Bleach and body odour. He wrote us a script for painkillers and antibiotics and rushed us out. There was an armed guard with him the whole time.

Lisa got sick two days later. I don't honestly know if she caught it in that place. All I know is she died. I stayed with her for the first night, waiting on the sofa. Half scared, half worried. She convinced me it was just normal flu, not cat flu. Told me to go home so I wouldn't catch it and miss work. It was early on and we were still worrying about things like that. So, I went home.

I felt like shit. I wanted to go, wanted to be safe. I told myself I'd have stayed with her if she'd asked me to, but I don't know if I would. I might have made excuses for myself and left her anyway. I rang her from work, three or four times. When I called her in the evening, just before I left the office, she sounded really ill. I had to strain to make out what she was saying. She said she just wanted to sleep. I got home and collected some clothes together. Ready to stay at her place, you know?

(X stops talking, and I almost ask him if he wants to take a break. Before I can he closes his eyes and his jaw clenches. He doesn't open his eyes again until he has finished his account.)

*But I didn't want to go and stay with her. I didn't want to risk it. I was scared. I knew she had Toxo by then. I couldn't admit it, couldn't let myself know how scared I was. I rang her again. Her mobile went straight to voicemail. Lisa was the only person I knew, under sixty, who still had a landline. She was into all that retro s**t. It rang and rang and went to answerphone. It was one of those old-fashioned things that had a tape in it. I left a message telling her to pick up, so I'd know she was alright. Then I rang again, and again. Pretending I was worried.*

She picked up the landline on the fifth go. Snapped at me for waking her up. That was what I'd wanted of course. I snapped back and we had an almighty row. She slammed the phone down and I stayed home, kidding myself I was the injured party. I didn't ring her the next day. My conscience finally got the better of me the day after. By then she wasn't answering the phone.

I never saw her again. Someone in her family, don't know who, called me a week later and told me she was dead. They warned me that she'd had the 'disease'. Told me I needed to be sure I was clear.

*I went out drinking. I'd just left Lisa to die alone because I was scared of getting infected, but I went and sat in this trendy pub, packed to the rafters with w****rs. Sat crying into my drink.*

*I don't know how it started, and that's the truth, but someone was complaining about the hospitals being packed with 'that f**king* Frog *Flu'. Someone else started bitching about it too, some sob story about being thrown out of A & E.*

I don't know what version of my story I told. Not sure I told it at all. But it didn't matter. For me it was like getting religion, I'd seen the light. It wasn't my fault. It was all because of the hospital. The news reports the next day said it had happened at ten o'clock. I can't have even been that drunk, not by ten.

I don't remember leaving the pub, don't remember details. Just the feeling really. All the fear, guilt, anger. It was the hospital's fault. In my mind, we were about to do something noble.

We didn't go to the hospital I'd taken Lisa to. There was another one closer. Someone had made petrol bombs, it might even have been me. I remember throwing one. Shouting, 'This is for Lisa'.

The next morning, I forced myself to believe we'd done a good thing. Struck a blow and fought back. I was so convinced; I did the same thing the next two nights.

(X stands and walks out. Tape ends.)

Can someone explain to me, why there are enough police on the streets to pull me over to check my road tax (like the roads are worth paying tax for), but not enough to trace the scum that torched the hospitals?
JawDee: Contributor
Posts: 54
Location: Norfolk

****

If you were pulled over for a tax check it wasn't the police, it was the Inland Revenue. Like all official bodies the police are massively understaffed now, and they must prioritise. It's likely that many, if not most, of the individuals involved in the attacks on hospitals are dead. Investigating events that took place over four years ago would be hugely expensive in both monetary terms and man-hours.
The sad fact is that those responsible for the atrocities may never be found.
Ken03: NewB
Posts: 12
Location: Swansea

****

Collecting tax is more important to the government than tracking down murderers?
This government is fucked up.
JawDee: Contributor
Posts: 55
Location: Norfolk

****

At the moment, the country needs money more than it needs justice. So, yes, collecting revenue is more important. Investigating historical crimes won't put money into the treasury.
Ken03: NewB
Posts: 13

Location: Swansea

****

I thought it was only in France that people attacked hospitals. Did it really happen in Great Britain also?
MillerSan99: Poster
Posts: 101
Location: Nagoya, Japan

****

Yeah. My sister was killed in one of the fires. She'd been in a car crash and was bedbound. We'd seen stories on the internet about hospitals being attacked, but we didn't know whether to believe them or not. There were so many rumours flying about. Me and my father were talking about collecting her the next morning and caring for her at home, to be on the safe side.
Anyway, that night the mobile networks shut off at about six o'clock. That had been happening a lot. Then the BBC reported there had been fire at my sister's hospital. We hammered over there, but there was nothing we could do. The building was burnt out.
The mobile networks kicked in again the next morning. They're saying now that when the authorities heard about the attacks, they shut the system down to stop the word spreading and adding to the chaos.
My brother-in-law died that night too. He'd been staying with my sister in case there was trouble.
PeteS32: NewB
Posts: 05
Location: London

****

Sorry for your loss Pete.
Wax_E: Poster
Posts: 114
Location: Luton

****

Yes, Pete, sorry for your loss.
I don't understand, why were people attacking the hospitals?
MillerSan99: Poster
Posts: 102
Location: Nagoya, Japan

****

People had started to switch-off. The newspapers were full of stories about Paris being overrun with zombies. One of the tabloids ran a big story about mortuary staff Britain in being issued with guns. Once there were a few cases of switching over here, people panicked. They thought the hospitals were full of Toxo patients that were about to go Gonzo and run amuck.
Everyone was terrified.
NotRich: Poster
Posts: 121
Location: Not stated

****

Everyone was terrified.
Not everyone set light to buildings and murdered innocent people.
A friend of mine was a nurse in St Georges. She told me people were pelted with stones and bottles as they tried to get out of the buildings.
I don't care how terrified they were. Anyone involved with burning the hospitals is gutless scum.
Ken03: NewB
Posts: 14
Location: Swansea

****

I'm not trying to justify what happened. All I'm saying is nobody was thinking straight. People were scared senseless and did things they wouldn't do normally.

I’m sure anyone involved back then is full of remorse now.
NotRich: Poster
Posts: 122
Location: Not stated

****
Gutless scum.
I don’t care if they are full of remorse, hanging’s too good for the bastards. And fuck you if you think otherwise.
Ken03: NewB
Posts: 15
Location: UK

****
Yeah. Why ain’t the police pulling them in, instead of doing me for road tax?
JawDee: Contributor
Posts: 56
Location: Norfolk

Alcoholics Anonymous meeting, 4th April 2028

- Hello. Erm … my name is Richard, Richard York. I … I've been told I have to attend these meetings. It's part of this suspended sentence thing. What?
- We ask all new members to state their problem. It's the same for everyone.
- I was arrested for breaking and entering.
- I meant the nature of your problems with alcohol and substance abuse. I know it can be embarrassing, Rich, but everybody here is in the same boat.
- Okay, my name is Richard York, Richard, not Rich, and I drink too much, and I've experimented with drugs.
- Richard. Every one of us here tonight is an alcoholic or an addict. A crucial part of allowing ourselves to get beyond that is to admit, to ourselves and others, that we have a problem.
- I told you, I'm here because it's one of the conditions of staying out of prison.
- Okay. Let's move on. Richard, would you care to tell the group a little about yourself?
- Like what?
- Perhaps you could tell us why you think you drink too much.
- What else is there to do? I've got nothing else. No job. My girlfriend died of Toxo in the first wave. My family were based on the South Coast, I've got no idea if they're alive.
- You drink to blot it out?
- I guess.
- And get high?
- What else is there to do?
- Were you stealing to fund your habit?
- Fuck this.
- Richard, you should know under the conditions of your suspension you're required to attend these meetings. If you walk out now, I'll have to report – Richard. Richard, please, don't make me do this …

Official Police Statement, 6th April 2028

I am PC 394 Asher attached to Wilson Street Temporary Policing Station. On Monday (5/4/2028) I was on duty in full uniform in Rowan Rd, E1.

At 22:30hrs approximately I heard a female voice. It was loud and sounded distressed. I heard the female shouting, "Help, I'm being robbed." I then heard a male reply, "It's alright I'm leaving, I'm leaving. Just shut up." I knocked on the front door of the residence the voices were coming from and shouted, "Police officer." The woman called out again, "Help me, I'm being robbed." I was on the footway directly outside the front door and could hear the voices through an open window to the left of the door, which had the number 31 stencilled on it in white paint.

Fearing for the safety of the female occupant, I tried the front door, but it was locked. Using my power of entry under the Overarching Emergency Measures Act 2021, I forced entry by breaking a glass panel in the door with my baton and reaching inside for the latch. I entered the residence and made my way to the source of the disturbance. The woman's cries were getting louder and more agitated.

I was alone and fearing for my safety and that of the female. I radioed in for back-up. I decided not to wait for back-up to arrive before intervening. A woman I now know to be Susan Boid (WF, DOB 3/5/1990) and a man I now know to be Richard York (WM, DOB 8/11/1979) were struggling in the front room. She was using both her hands to hold onto his right arm and using her body weight to keep him from getting away. He was struggling to free himself and flailing his left arm. There was a red mark on her left cheek. He was slurring his words and his eyes were red and glazed. He was drunk.

I said, "What's going on here?". When they saw me they stopped struggling and Richard sighed. I asked what was happening and Susan Boid told me.

She had been dozing on the sofa with the lights off when she was woken by the sound of breaking glass.

She had remained on the sofa as she was afraid to investigate the source of the noise and was unable to call the police as the 22:00hrs blackout of mobile phone systems was in effect.

Richard entered the room and began searching.

She saw him put several objects into his pockets.

On turning to leave the room he caught sight of Susan and she screamed.

Richard attempted to leave the room, she tried to stop him, and he punched her in the face.

I asked her if she knew Richard and she said no, she had not seen Richard York before tonight.

Richard York had remained silent throughout. I cautioned him and said, "Is that right?" He was now seated, and he said:

He had been drinking and had mistakenly thought the house was his.

When he found his key would not fit the lock, he had broken a pane of glass to effect entry.

He realised his mistake when he was confronted by Susan.

On being confronted by Susan he panicked and tried to run from the house.

As they had struggled, he accidentally struck her in the face.

He denied 'punching' her.

I told Richard I was going to search him. I requested he stood and kept his hands out by his side. He complied. He was wearing loose-fitting denim jeans and an oversized dark green parka with a number of large external pockets. As no male colleague was on hand to conduct the search, I told Richard that he was to slowly empty each pocket on my request. As he did this, I had my baton drawn and I held behind my right leg, hidden from his view. I was on my own and faced with a potential suspect who according to the victim had already used violence. If he were to produce a weapon from his pocket or his demeanour changed then I needed to be in a position to react quickly.

Richard complied with my request to empty his pockets. His pockets contained:

A wallet with an old-style driving licence and a Grade II standard-type ration book. These were taken from his inside right coat pocket.

A key ring with two keys and a standard Bank of England USB token. Taken from the left hip pocket of his jeans.

A small digital camera with the letters S B written on it. Taken from the left lower pocket of his coat.

Two figurines of Buddha made from a gold-coloured metal, both taken from the right lower pocket of his coat.

An ornate paperweight made from a silver-coloured metal. Taken from the upper right external pocket of his coat.

I asked Susan if she recognised any of the items Richard had produced from his pockets. Susan said the camera, the figurines of Buddha and the paperweight belonged to her.

I told Richard he was under arrest for burglary and assault. He offered no resistance and complied when I told him I would need to handcuff him. I placed standard issue handcuffs on him, securing his hands behind his back.

I radioed for transport and PC 209 Darren Bolton arrived at 22:41hrs. Bolton and I put Richard into the car and drove him to the Wilson Street Temporary Policing Station designated for holding prisoners. During the journey Richard became agitated and stated repeatedly that he had "Friends with influence". When Bolton asked him who, he replied "I'm a good friend of Colin Robertson. I'm buddies with the King of the Crows".

I made these notes when reasonably practicable after the event.

Chapter 14. Staying Clean

February 12th, 2021

Maccallan made a lot of noise as he dealt with the two Gonzos. At first it was a series of grunts and panicky yelps but, as he realised he was winning, the sounds became more exultant. Johnno watched him impassively. He only commented when Maccallan turned away from the bodies and lifted the machete above his head, signalling his victory.

"Keep that fookin' blade low you twat," Johnno bellowed at him.

Maccallan's arm snapped down in front of him, blood arced from the machete leaving a line of drops along the pavement. Johnno glanced at Robertson before moving closer to Maccallan. Maccallan nodded.

"What's that on the fookin' pavement?"

He pointed at the witness mark, brightly red against the pale concrete.

"Blood," Maccallan said, confused.

"That's right soft lad. Blood from a fookin' Gonzo, blood infected with fookin' Toxo. You don't wave it around your fookin' head. Couple drops of that in your eye and that's it, over and fookin' out." He turned to look at Robertson. "We keeping this daft bastard?"

"Yeah. Show him how to clean that blade without getting himself killed. And keep the noise down."

Without appearing to notice the exchange going on behind him, Miller carried on methodically working the Gonzo he'd killed. When he finished with the torso, he changed knives and cut the tattered trousers away.

They'd stopped while there was still about an hour of daylight left. The lead party had found a supermarket. A large group had inhabited it for a time. The shelves had mostly been stripped bare. A corner, of what had been the clothing section, still held the smell of frightened people massing together. A pair of sleeping bags too stained to keep lay in a detritus of empty food wrappers and tins.

The dead had clouds of flies for markers. Robertson took Maccallan with him to investigate. The man's voice was getting on his nerves, but he offset it against the satisfaction of ignoring him.

At the end of the retail floor, farthest from the remains of the sleeping area, a room had been formed by draping bed linen across the entrances to one of the aisles.

Robertson used his axe to hook the top edge of one of the sheets and pull it down. He peered cautiously into the gloomy space. There were four bodies. Three of them had been covered: two with opened-out sleeping bags and the third, the size indicating a child, with a fleece blanket. A cartoon character grinned up from the bundle, most of its features blurred with dark mould. The last body was uncovered and curled into a corner formed at the junction of two shelving racks. Rats had found it. Maccallan had to turn away. He finally stopped talking but the respite was short-lived.

"Toxo?" he asked, as Robertson walked away from the scene without comment.

"Could have been anything. That," – he jerked his head in the direction of the bodies and the makeshift room – "looks like a sickbay. Dysentery, cholera, bad case of flu." He shrugged. "At a guess, I'd say people started getting sick so they put them over here."

"Is it safe to stay here?"

"Yeah. These people were stupid. If they ain't dead already they soon will be."

"Maybe they were just unlucky."

Robertson grunted and gestured with his axe down the aisle; it was lined with freezers. The food packets were gone but the empty cabinets had been used as bins. Bottles filled the spaces.

"Whoever they were, they sat in here shit scared and got drunk. Find the booze aisle. I'll bet you anything you like it's empty. The bleach, the disinfectant, the stuff that might have stopped that kind of shit," – he jerked his head back the way they'd come – "they didn't have the sense to take."

"If it's safe why did they leave?"

"My guess is more of them started getting ill. They panicked and split up."

"Rather than getting busy with the bleach?"

"Infection control. Toxo ain't the only thing waiting to kill you." Robertson hefted the axe and brought its head into the fading light. "You remember that."

"I will." Maccallan eyed the axe head. "Col … Colin, I want to help."

"Then find some bleach."

"I meant …"

"I know what you fucking meant. Now find the bleach. I'll see what Sol has to say about anything else."

"I thought Miller was in charge."

"Miller's who they follow. Sol's the brains."

Robertson took the axe blade away from Maccallan's face and held his gaze.
Maccallan hesitated, then asked, "And you?"
"I'm the man who says who lives or dies."

Once we'd left the quarantined street and the riot behind us, Juan began cursing the two policemen. First, in general terms under the umbrella of the government and the uniformed thuggery they employed. The sergeant, white-knuckled hands tight on the wheel, ignored him as he guided the Citroën through the dark city. Dog Boy spared him a glance, but little more. He was worrying at the radio he carried.

I may have been in shock, or just too tired to be scared any longer. The interior of the car felt as if it was a long way away. The scenes playing across the cracked windshield were no more important than the last reel of a film I'd missed. Random sights flashing up in the flicker of the car's remaining headlight. Shattered shopfront. Wreckage of a van buried in a house front. Body hanging from a streetlamp. None of it was real at that point.

The sergeant coasted the car to a halt when we reached a street where the lights were still on. Without a word he put the parking brake on and climbed out of the car. The young man, who'd already been in the back seat when Juan and I clambered in, threw his door open and bolted into the darkness. I never saw him again and no one mentioned his flight. It joined the huge gallery of random images I was too tired to be concerned with.

The engine was still running. In the middle of the road, the sergeant stripped off the heavy stab-vest he'd been wearing and put it neatly on the hood, then he took his pistol and put the end of the barrel in his mouth. Juan, at last, stopped cursing and my feeling of being separate from everything around me clicked off as if someone had thrown a switch.

The sergeant trembled, his head and his shoulders quivering. It was only then I saw the wound on his arm. His shirt sleeve had soaked up the blood, but as he lifted the gun to his face the torn material fell away showing the flap of muscle torn or bitten away. None of us in the car moved. The trembling became shaking and he dropped the gun and fell to his knees. I thought he was sobbing. After a while, it might have been seconds or hours, I realised he was praying.

I don't know if that's something my memory has fitted onto the scene or if it really happened. Either way, I knew what I was watching.

Dog Boy climbed slowly from the passenger side of the car and went to the man. There was a brief exchange of words. Then Dog Boy nodded, drew his own pistol and put two bullets into the top of the sergeant's head.

When he got back in the car, he handed me the stab-vest.

"He wanted you to have this."

The gun he handed to Juan. Juan gave it to me the next day. He had no idea how to shoot.

I don't know what to say about the journey across Paris. I've heard accounts of people from other European cities. People who sat and waited it out, others that broke for the border only to find the grass on the other side wasn't greener, just infected. Some people keep their silence and others trumpet their history. Most of mine seems lost. It isn't a blank, I wish it was, but there isn't a narrative to it. Robertson's remarks about the early days of the London Lockdown and the drive to just stay alive struck a chord with me. But it was a tuneless chord.

The staying alive part was almost easy. Rather than a desperate scrabble for supplies or brutal wars waged for a quart of drinking water, a flat to-do list of horrors became the norm. Kill a dozen infected to get to a grocery store. Tick. Pillage a bookshop for kindling. Tick. Cut our hair off and listen to the lice burst when we throw the snippings into the fire. Tick. Watch a man request his own execution rather than go down with Toxo. Tick.

In my memory, which I know better than to trust, by the time Dog Boy had driven the little Citroën out of the street, we'd shed all our tears. The sergeant's body was just another part of a count no one was keeping.

I don't have a chronology for my time. I don't know if we set out for Calais on the first night or if we decided it after a month or six. Given that I was in a France for over a year it seems unlikely that my decision to head to the coast was taken early on. The distances weren't that great.

Despite having been back and forth to France on the bank's behest for years, I knew little of the country other than the language and the manner of its bankers. At least its crooked ones.

Juan wanted to take charge, but he'd so carefully set himself up to be Dog Boy's superior that he dare not risk making decisions that might prove to be wrong. Taking the reins fell to Dog Boy.

I don't know how long it took. In books they'd say it happened over night; maybe it did. But Dog Boy went from being a young cop, out of his depth and afraid, to being an old man before our eyes. Juan's jibes about the pressures of leadership became too obviously real to be even remotely funny. He didn't stop them. They too became part of the surreal routine we fell into.

Our model of survival was different to Robertson and Miller's. Maybe lacking a mass unified start point, like the bombing of the bridges, we became a three-person guerrilla unit. Reliant on ourselves and responsible for only ourselves.

Juan referred to us as bandits, though it might have been one of the attempts to rile Dog Boy. Whereas Robertson's group forged its way across London, like locusts, we kept a low profile. Depending on your mindset, we avoided the worst of the violence and maintained our humanity, or we lived like rats.

By the time I reached Calais there was something like hope in the air. By then hope had begun to taste toxic.

Extract from the screenplay of Year of the Crow. Lithograph Studios, California (2026)

Ext. BLUE COLLAR HOUSING DEVELOPMENT – DAY

Silence. The sky is grey and overcast. There are flashes of lightning on the horizon. We see Robertson standing at the end of the street. Camera pans down to ground level. Robertson's POV. The street is choked with abandoned cars. Zombies are milling aimlessly between them. For a few seconds the silence is unbroken, apart from the thud of their bodies as they bump against the rusting hulks. Jump cut to close-up of an air horn. The viewer barely has time to register what the camera is showing them before the air horn is activated. Camera pulls back, moving in from behind Robertson, we see Miller leading his group of followers into the street. Maccallan is at his side, also holding an air horn. This too is activated. The sound is incredible. Alerted by the noise, the zombies shuffle more purposefully toward the group. At first their movements are stiff, but they steadily gain speed.

Cut to close-up of Miller, then Maccallan. Neither man speaks. Camera returns to Robertson. He grimaces and throws the air horn aside.

ROBERTSON

Come on then, you fuckers.

The three men simultaneously break into a run and charge at the approaching horde of zombies. POV changes to an elevated shot. Behind Robertson, Miller and Maccallan, the rest of the group is readying itself to fight. As they move forward the camera pans along them. The group is far bigger than the last time we saw it. As it advances doors open and people leave the safety of their homes to join the fight.

ROBERTSON

(Voice-over)

And without even realising it, we started the Takeback. We cut them down and maybe we showed the way, or just provided a glimmer of hope. Whatever we did, and why ever people followed us, we grew stronger and started taking our world back.

From Kings of Crows: Life on the Wrong Side of the Lockdown

I don't know when people started keeping count of their kills. I think it started when Maccallan joined. At least he was the first person I noticed doing it. It never became the norm as such, but a lot of the latecomers were taken with the idea. People who started coming out of hiding towards the end of the second summer. People who'd been fighting from the start. Most of our group didn't bother. If you'd been on the riverbank on the first day of the Lockdown, you'd already lost count. If some of us had put notches into our weapons every time we'd taken a Gonzo out, we'd have had nothing left to fight with.

I remember one guy with a baseball bat that he'd cut twenty little nicks out of. Twenty. He was so proud. He didn't make it. A few weeks before the army began deploying again, he was playing silly buggers with a Gonzo he'd found in a doorway. The thing was on its last legs, barely able to stand. Mr Twenty was poking it and jumping away when it tried to lunge at him. He did it about a dozen times. When he finally killed it, he made a big show of winding-up with his bat to hit it. By that stage we were encountering more and more Gonzos that were rotting away in front of us. This one was covered in open sores and its skin was hanging off it. When the bat connected with its skull, it practically exploded. Mr Twenty got sprayed with blood and Christ knows what else. He ran around like a headless chicken spitting and screaming.

We made him walk on his own. Mobile quarantine we called it. It was a formality really. One of the guys told me it was the rebirth of civilisation. We couldn't afford to spend time on the dead wood. He spent three days assuring us he was fine, he wasn't infected. By the fourth day he was coughing and rubbing his eyes. I can't remember who put him out of his misery.

I saw a lot of people die. Not just victims of Toxo, or people infected by the Gonzos. Some were careless, like Mr Twenty; others were just flat-out unlucky. It didn't take much to tip the scales back then. A broken leg and you were pretty well done. Tiny things that wouldn't have mattered in the normal world could destroy you. Cuts and grazes would turn septic if you weren't careful. The best investment you could make back then was bleach and that hand-gel with the alcohol in it. We lost people because they needed medication that they couldn't find. Chemists were looted early on. People panicked and cleared shelves of every drug they could find.

When the latecomers died, it always made me angry. They'd nearly made it. If they'd waited it out just a little longer, they'd have probably survived.

I don't believe in anything, no higher power, no wheel of fate. It's all meaningless.

Chapter 15. The Work/Life Balance

PUBLIC TOILET.
OFFICIAL OPENING AUGUST '21
MILLER CREW CIVIC WORKS DEPT.

Medium: Yellow spray paint
Location: Frontage of a bank occupying a corner location of Epsom High Street (CE8). The script is accompanied by an arrow indicating the fire-damaged commercial property immediately to the right of the bank. It is the only fire-damaged property in that section of the street.
Date: August 2021
Note: This is the last known example of graffiti to use the identifier Miller Crew. Hereafter, all pieces applied by Miller's group of survivors were credited to Miller's Crows or, more commonly, Crow Nation.

From The Writing on the Wall

April 6th, 2028

Winslow had his back to the rest of the room, me included. The collection of notes he'd tacked to the wall held his attention. At least that was the look he was going for. Pre-Outbreak – when paper was cheap and police departments had real budgets – he'd have likely filled the wall with photographs and printouts.

"Does the name Richard York mean anything to you?" I asked the back of Winslow's head.

He kept his hair short. Through the dark bristle I could make out two crescents of scar tissue. They looked like the result of blunt trauma rather than sharp edges. He didn't turn round. Since our last session with Robertson, he'd avoided looking directly at me. I couldn't tell if he was embarrassed by the ex-Crow's low opinion of him or angry at the perceived connection between us. I wasn't expending energy worrying about either option.

His head tilted to one side; an indication that he had heard.

"In relation to this, you mean?"

He waved a hand at the mess of notes.

"Of course."

There was a pause, during which I sat down and began booting up an ageing desktop. The system was full of glitches and annoying layers of security. It required three usernames and passwords to allow me to log on. Getting a printer to work could eat half the morning.

"Robertson mentions a Rich early in his book. I don't think he gives his second name," Winslow said.

He didn't volunteer any more. Or bother asking me why it might be important. The copy of Robertson's book was buried in the debris littering Winslow's desk. I began scanning the early pages, hoping the name Rich would jump out at me. It was a trick I'd found I could pull with errant figures – sometimes – when I was on the audit trail. I found him in the first chapter. As Robertson was leaving work for the last time. His comment was that they exchanged email addresses and told each other they'd meet up for a drink, both knowing they'd never see the other again.

"Bolton brought a Richard York in last night, burglary with assault. In the car on the way back to the station he was shouting the odds about being friends with the King of the Crows."

Winslow finally swung round. He still didn't look at me; instead he frowned at the book. Just to annoy him I did the little double tap on the page.

Tap, tap. Tap, tap.

Ignoring the sarcasm, he pulled the book towards him and, without urgency, read the page.

"Let's see if there's any connection," he said, finally.

Bolton was one of those people who saw the funny side of everything and probably thought he was the life and soul of every party. He'd told me about Richard York's arrest as I'd come into the office that morning, laughing as he recounted the petty thug with the big-talk about our celebrity.

He was less amused when I told him to retrieve the paperwork and bring it to my desk before he ended his shift. We'd met as he'd been heading out of the door after a night-duty. I hoped the laugh he'd given himself was worth it.

The report, when he put it in front of me without a word, surprised me with its completeness. I'd expected something sloppy, but PC Bolton was evidently a better copper than I'd given him credit for.

Richard York's story wasn't that different to any number that came attached to humans who'd survived by turning into animals. Having watched any number of people die and losing everything he cared about, he came out the other end wondering what he'd stayed alive for.

Post-Traumatic Stress Disorder, survivor guilt, shell shock, pick a label you like the sound of. Naming it and living it are different things.

The new world he'd survived the birth of didn't offer comfort. No job, no family, society redrawn in ways that would take another generation to understand. His decline was almost inevitable. Substance abuse, drinking, crime. The spiral too well known to escape.

York was in one of the hastily-converted storerooms. Home comforts amounted to a mattress on the floor and a chemical toilet. Prisoners thought likely to kick off got a mattress and a bucket.

The auxiliary WPC in charge of the 'cells' tutted as she tried to read the details of York's admission. Whoever had written up his arrival had the handwriting of a six-year-old.

"He's being kept here until Monday," she finally said, after deciphering the mess of ink. "He was already on a suspended sentence."

"So, what happens Monday?" I asked.

"Transport to Wayland. He's going to be looking at two years of 'voluntary work',” she laughed. “That should put some muscle on him at least.”

Voluntary work crews amounted to good old-fashioned chain gangs. He wasn't going to pass Go or collect two hundred dollars. York was going straight to jail. It might keep him off the meth a while longer, maybe it would straighten him out, but I doubted it. The jibe about York needing to build some muscle wasn't without a basis. Typical tweeker build; I could have circled his biceps with my finger and thumb.

York was collapsed on the mattress. Home comfort didn't extend to a pillow, so he'd rolled his coat into a tube and put it at the head of his 'bed'. When he'd lain down, he'd missed it and his head had lolled to one side. He wasn't asleep; his eyelids were at half-mast. Withdrawal fatigue.

The auxiliary tapped the side of her boot against York's ankle. She used more force than was needed.

“York. Wake up, you've got company.” She found this funny and barked out a harsh laugh. “Come on, wake up.”

York stirred, lifted his head; it seemed to take a huge effort. The auxiliary kicked him again.

“On your feet.”

“We've got it from here Constable,” Winslow told her, putting an edge on the words.

She looked disappointed but left the room without saying anything. I rolled my eyes as she left but Winslow either didn't see or chose not to react. I wondered if he'd put me in the same category as the auxiliary: uppity civilian playing at being a real copper.

York was making puffing noises, the way weightlifters do before snatching the barbells off the mat. His exertions provided enough power to pull himself into a sitting position. His breathing was still heavy as he regarded us both staring down at him.

Winslow surprised me by lowering himself onto his haunches, putting his face at the same level as York's. I didn't envy him the proximity. York's teeth were a collection of blackened ruins, the beginnings of meth mouth. I could see how bad his breath would smell without needing to inhale it.

“You Richard York?” Winslow asked.

“Yeah.”

“You know how much trouble you're in?” York shrugged and looked ready to flop onto his back again. “Assault, burglary. Not good my friend, not good at all.”

“It was an accident. I was pissed as a fart and went into the wrong house.”

Winslow laughed and forgot himself enough to cast me a glance to show we were both in on the joke. The gesture could have been for York's benefit.

York didn't have a house to be mistaken about. He didn't even have a front door to call his own. He'd been registered at the Bantam Road Community Shelter. Officially that was the only title it laid claim to. Off the record, at least the record that was printed on headed government paper, it was a C-rated dwelling. Commonly known as a third-class ticket. It was where troublemakers and hopeless cases were housed. People the over-stretched police force would need to get hold of sooner or later.

York had been picked up for breaking and entering three months earlier. He avoided a custodial sentence by being bound over, on the condition that he attended substance abuse counselling sessions.

He'd had just enough sense to know that, after blowing off the meetings, returning to a government-run shelter was a bad move. Staying out of trouble had been beyond him.

"What do you want? I'm tired. I want to go to sleep."

Winslow's laughter appeared to have touched a nerve. York had straightened his posture as he spoke. With the flash of dignity, it was possible to see the man he'd once been. There was a hint of someone handsome under the loose skin and ruined teeth. There was the ghost of intelligence there too.

"When they pulled you in, you were mouthing off about knowing the King of the Crows."

"What about it?"

And just like that the good looks and intelligence were gone, buried under a dirty layer of need and cunning.

"Is it true?"

"What if it is?"

Winslow didn't answer immediately. He pursed his lips slightly and looked the wreck of a man up and down with open contempt.

"Have you ever been on a voluntary work team, a prison team?" York didn't say anything, but he did seem to shrink. It was all the answer we needed. "They feed you. And if you can stand at the end of the day, you'll be allowed a shower. That's about as much as I can promise you."

"I haven't done anything I–"

"–was drunk and walked into the wrong house. We heard you the first time." Winslow, still crouching, began tapping out a rapid rhythm against his knee. "What did you mean you knew the King of the Crows?"

York lacked the energy or maybe the will to lift his head, and he addressed the patch of floor between his feet. The shoes he was wearing looked as if they'd once had a sought-after label. Something that told the world you were an up-and-coming player. The left one had a length of blue nylon string instead of a lace.

"Colin Robertson. We used to work together."

"Really?"

Even without looking up, Winslow's smile was obvious.

The ghost of dignity-lost reared its head again. "Fuck you if you don't believe me."

Still without looking at Winslow he dropped onto his back again and closed his eyes.

"Easy enough to check. He's upstairs now, in the canteen. Perks of celebrity, he gets to eat the same rubbish we do. It's still a damn sight better than the slop you'll be getting in Wayland."

"What do you want?"

"Did you know any of the other Crows?"

"I knew Maccallan."

"You were in with all the movers and shakers, weren't you? And yet you're sitting in a cell waiting for a minivan to run you along to Wayland."

"Maccallan was my boss, Colin's too. We all worked together in this shitty little letting agency. Maccallan was the regional manager. Cunt that he was."

"You didn't get on?"

York rolled over onto his side, facing the wall and made as if he was going to sleep.

"Listen, Richard." Winslow moved nearer to the figure on the mattress. He didn't get up and achieved the moment with a bizarre, knees-bent waddle. I had to fight the urge to laugh. "You have fucked up one time too many. Now, doing a stint in a prison work party is likely to finish you off. I've seen what it does to a man. Guys twice the size of you and three times tougher get ground into dust. Do yourself a favour and play nice. I give you my word I'll do what I can to get you back on the program. You go back to the Bantam Road shelter, attend your meetings and tell them what they want to hear – I'm an addict but with your help I can be a saint."

York didn't move, didn't answer.

"Or you can lie there," I said, "waiting for the bus to Wayland. Meanwhile, your good buddy Colin can finish his lunch and wait for his ticket to the US."

York began to weep.

We put York in an interview room and gave him a solid meal. Which was one of the things he needed, if not what he wanted. I could tell by the way York pushed the food around his plate and chewed it, blank-faced, that he wasn't tasting it. The dignity and self-respect he kidded himself he still had didn't extend to asking if he could use a shower or have a toothbrush.

I'd read some dreary article a few days before about the long-reaching effects of the HV-Tg pandemic. The writers adopted the standard doom-laden tone, foretelling of wasted generations and long-term psychological impact on the mass of the population. Winslow's take was less understanding. He delivered his judgement just before we went in to start question time.

"He needs to pull himself together."

I thought he had a point but wouldn't give him the satisfaction of agreeing with him.

"He's been traumatised. He's still quite young. He was little more than a boy when it all started."

Winslow snorted.

"He's alive, he cared enough about himself to survive the world breakdown. Now it's building up again and what does he do? Wait for someone else to look after him."

I let it go. I'd be arguing about something I didn't really care about. York was the last of my worries. The article I'd read had also touched on the subject of compassion fatigue.

When he'd finished eating, I put a cup of tea in front of him and started the tape rolling. Winslow, for the benefit of the tape – one of his favourite phrases – explained to York that he wasn't being interviewed in relation to anything involving his arrest, and that the conversation we were having could not be used against him at any future time. The last was complete fiction. York nodded and we prompted him to speak for the benefit of the tape.

"You worked with Maccallan and Robertson?" I asked him.

"Yeah, before the disease. Is it alright if I smoke?"

"Go ahead."

York began checking his vast collection of pockets, while Winslow and I watched him. Later, when I played the interview tape back, I timed the performance. There's a two-minute blank in the recording; the only thing to be heard is York patting his empty pockets.

He made a play of looking embarrassed and there was a flash of that misplaced dignity before he accepted that no one was about to provide him with tobacco. I took a moment to wonder at the strange variant of pride that stopped a man asking for a smoke, but allowed him to break into someone's home and steal their things. It's a trait that seems to be exclusively male, even in junkies.

"What was the nature of your work?" Winslow asked him.

"It was a letting agency. The company was an offshoot of a big, high street estate agents. We handled high-end leases and rentals, luxury end of the market. The clients we dealt with didn't want to be associated with anything as common as a high street name."

"And you worked with Robertson and Maccallan for how long?"

York gave the question a lot of thought before saying, "Three years, about."

"Just the three of you?" Winslow asked.

"There were two others. They both went down with Toxo."

"Who did what?"

"Maccallan was the manager; he ran the office or branch, whatever you want to call it. Me and Colin were front of house, doing the phones. We'd deal with people looking to let property or looking for a place to live."

"Maccallan was senior then. Had he been there the longest?"

"Nah. He joined up the same time I did. Robertson was there before either of us."

"Then why was Maccallan made manager?"

From recording of police interview with Richard York.
(6th April 2028)

Winslow - Then why was Maccallan made manager?
York - He came in as a manager. He said he had a degree in business studies.
Cross - And did he?
Cross - For the benefit of the tape, Mr York has shrugged. Could you tell us what you mean by that gesture, Mr York?
York - I don't know if it was true or not. He was a real prick, always full of himself.
Winslow - You didn't like him?
York - I didn't have to like him, I had a job to do.
Winslow - What about Robertson?
York - We got on alright, he was okay.
Cross - How did Robertson get along with Maccallan?
York - He couldn't stand him, but like I said Maccallan was a prick. He gave Col a hard time.
Winslow - In what way?
York - He was always finding things to pull him up on. He was delighted when he finally got to sack him.
Cross - Why was he sacked?
York - Toxo. The south was a hot spot, people didn't want to live there. Prices dived and the lettings game dived with it. Col came in one morning with a pair of black eyes and Maccallan put him on three weeks unpaid leave, 'cos he couldn't appear front of house like that. By the time three weeks was up the business was dying on its arse. It was easy to get rid of him then.
Cross - Why didn't Maccallan like Robertson?
York - I think Colin frightened him.
Cross - Was Robertson violent?
York - Not frightened of him that way. Colin was a clever bastard. He could have done Maccallan's job stood on his head.
Winslow - But Maccallan was put in charge, not him?
York - The business was all about image. We were basically offering places the size of rabbit hutches to knobheads with more money than sense. Some of those dickheads would pay thousands and thousands of pounds a month for a bedsit the size of that cell you put me in. All because it came with a Central London postcode. Wankers.
Cross - You mean Robertson's face didn't fit?
York - I guess. I think Maccallan might have been told to get rid of him. He asked me a few times if I thought Robertson was on the fiddle.

Winslow - Was he?
York - I don't know. I don't. If he was, he'd have been too good at it to get caught by me or Maccallan. Like I said he was a smart cookie.
Winslow - How did he take being sacked?
York - He was pissed off, but he'd been fired, how was he meant to feel?
Winslow - Did he say anything about it to you?
York - Said something like, "That prick's just fired me", and cleared his desk.
Winslow - Did he make any threats; say he'd get him back. Anything like that?
York - No. He told him to fuck off before he left. Maccallan came out of his little office as Col was leaving. He held his hand out to shake. Col told him to fuck off and walked out.
Winslow - What did Maccallan do?
York - He put on his serious face and told me it always made him sad to have to let someone go. He tried to make it sound like he was the head of Microsoft. Wanker. You could tell he was loving it. It made him feel important, plus he was relieved to see the back of Col.

Chapter 16. Birth of a Nation

Chinese Pest Control (See also Cat's Coffin)

Wok. Reference to racial slur, dating back to the nineteen seventies, that maintained meat served in Chinese restaurants was often cat. The term became common again after China instigated a cat-culling programme.

The A to Z of Gondii Names

Big in Japan: Talking with Hamish McDonald. Interview appearing in the Sunday Times Colour Supplement (09/02/2025), conducted by Louie Berger

Hamish McDonald has a strong Canadian accent and an even stronger laugh. He's also huge. He describes himself as, "An unholy mix of Canadian lumberjack stock and Japanese refinement". We're speaking in a vegan café, situated somewhat uneasily across the street from a cheerless brick-built building with blacked-out windows and a 'members only' sign on the door.

The uninviting building is Temur's Gym, known in martial arts circles as 'The Bear Pit'. Once the Holy Grail for cage-fighters hoping for stardom, it's an invite-only establishment. This is where Hamish has just come from, and he has the bruises to prove it (Canada has yet to adopt America's touch-averse sensibilities). His massive forearms are mottled, and his knuckles are thick with callouses.

I ask him if he's expecting trouble and he laughs.

"No, I've been into contact sports for years, since I was a teenager. That's how I got into acting, bit parts in low-budget Kung-Fu flicks. But for the part of Chan I had to slim down. Now I'm trying to get the muscle back." He laughs again, "It gets harder as you get older."

Hamish turned sixty last year, though you wouldn't think it to look at him now. To appear older, for the role of Chan, he shed almost thirty pounds and shaved his head. Make-up and clever camera work did the rest. Acting did the rest. Meeting him, in the flesh and out of character, it's possible to appreciate the quality of his performance in *Year of the Crow* .

It's a performance he's received little praise for. The movie goers that made the film a commercial success were dazzled by the special effects and Malik Connally's portrayal of Colin Robertson. Hamish's transformation into Chan went largely unnoticed. For many of the film's critics, however, the character of Chan became the focus of their strongest condemnation.

Chan's pidgin English, used for comic effect, aroused claims of racism and cultural stereotyping. The decision to cast a Japanese actor to play a Chinese man upset many in the Chinese community. When it became more widely known that Hamish was mixed race, another faction of outraged social-medialites began shouting whitewash.

Only in Japan, where the film has a massive following, has Hamish escaped vilification. In fact, he has gained a cult following. There have been suggestions in the press that an invitation has even been extended to him. When asked to confirm this he nods.

"I've been sent the official paperwork to allow me to enter Japan. At least one film company has sent me a script with a promise of the starring role."

Is he tempted?

"Not really, it's flattering, but I don't speak the language. I've never set foot in the country. If I go there and it doesn't work out there's no guarantee I'd be allowed back into Canada. My family's here, my friends."

When I ask him how he feels about the criticism of his part in the movie, his good humour fades.

"It's upsetting. People don't realise how much of a film, any film, is made in the editing suite. When I was playing Chan and doing the velly solly, Ching-Chang-Chinaman routine I didn't know it was going to be a gag reel type thing. When I was talking to Peter Hunt, who wrote the original script, he told me Chan was a hustler. All the scenes with the pidgin English were meant to be about him playing with the prejudices of other people. He was meant to be incredibly smart. That version of Chan was left on the cutting-room floor."

Was much of his performance lost?

"Oh, a huge amount. Hours of dialogue. I'd argue the best parts of the script, but the producers wanted maximum screen time for the main characters. People who'd read the book wanted to see Robertson, Maccallan and Miller. A make-believe like Chan was never going to be the focus."

Perhaps it's a tribute to Hamish's performance that so much of the discussion among detractors and lovers of the film alike has concerned the validity of Chan. Claims and counterclaims rebound around internet chat rooms. Was Chan a composite figure, a genuine member of Miller's group, or just fiction made up for cheap laughs?

Extremes exist in all camps. The message board AS4AS (American Soil for America's Sons) currently has over twenty threads lamenting the inclusion of the 'fabricated character'. The postings are from patriots, outraged at the media's attempt to inject PC values into the story of the pandemic.

Was Chan based on a real person? Hamish isn't much wiser than anyone else.

"Pete told me he'd sort of built Chan to hold all the things he'd talked about with Robertson, when he was getting background info. When they exchanged emails, Robertson was very factual. Pete showed me one of the things he'd been sent. It was three pages on the best way to secure a building for a temporary stop. Tiny details, like how to check if there were rats and how to collect rain water. It was a survival guide. But when they spoke on the phone or on a video link, Robertson would relax and talk about the people more. Pete got the impression Robertson was lonely. He also said a lot of stories had the same feel to them," Hamish laughs, "whatever that means. I guess when he put those stories together, he came up with Chan."

The effort to get anything done was immense. Looking at it on a map, the distance we crossed was nothing. But it took us months. Of course, we were on foot; cars and vans were a waste of time. Even when we were a small group, we would have needed a fleet of working motors to carry us all. And the roads were nearly always blocked.

Things had been getting bad before the Lockdown; there was a lot of panic and pointless fighting. We found several streets that had been barricaded: cars pulled across the road, usually burnt out. To move something like that we'd have needed a tow truck or bulldozer. It was easier to walk.

We couldn't just get up and go, then stop when we were tired. Dozens of people, they all needed food, water and shelter. And we had to keep clean, not clean as in groomed, clean as free from infections. And there were the Gonzos to deal with.

In the first nine or ten months, the disease was everywhere. The number of victims that switched, as opposed to died, was terrifying. Maybe they were reacting to the stress as well, or maybe the disease progressed more quickly when everything broke down and there were no treatments available.

It amazes me, looking back, how few people in the group cracked up. It happened early on, people would withdraw, go silent. Two or three just vanished, walked away and left everything behind them. Like Scott of the Antarctic. Another couple topped themselves.

We had to be careful about people acting up. It wasn't a party; we weren't expecting people to jump around grinning and laughing, but if people started bellyaching too much, they had to be straightened out. It was another type of infection.

Extract from the screenplay of Year of the Crow. Lithograph Studios, California (2026)

INT. LIVING ROOM OF ABANDONED HOUSE - NIGHT.
The room is furnished in an outdated style and shows signs that it has been ransacked at some point. A fire has been set in the grate and a pan of water set to boil. Robertson and Maccallan are sat side by side on a couch, Miller is standing to one side of the fireplace. Chan enters the room followed by Josh. Josh's shoulders are slumped and he's staring at the floor. Chan leads him to an armchair that is leaking stuffing.

MILLER
Have a seat, Josh.

Josh flops limply into the chair. He looks briefly toward the figure of Miller but then returns to looking at the floor.

ROBERTSON
Here, have some of this.

Robertson reaches into his jacket and pulls out a bottle of bourbon. Josh hesitates, Robertson unscrews the cap and jiggles the bottle so it makes a sloshing sound.

ROBERTSON
Go on. It's the good stuff.

MILLER
I'd take him up on it. Last time I saw him get a round in was 2003.

Josh nods, takes a sip from the bottle and grimaces. He makes to hand it back to Robertson but Chan intercepts it.

MILLER
You having a bad time, Josh?

Josh, still hunched over, nods and sighs before sucking in a deep breath and flinging his head back. He starts to speak but appears to be addressing the ceiling. POV lifts and revolves until we are seeing Josh from above. His head is at the bottom of the screen.

JOSH
It never ends. Wake up, stay alive, sleep, repeat. Even when I'm asleep I see grippies. I can't take it anymore. What's the point? Seriously, what is the point?

Josh falls silent, still staring at the ceiling. POV cuts so we are looking at Miller. For a few seconds the room is quiet and still, then Miller pushes himself away from the wall and turns to face the fire. He shifts the burning pieces of wood around with the toe of his boot before moving over to Josh and putting a hand on his shoulder.

MILLER
We carry on for whatever comes next, whoever comes next. If we don't fight, those things out there win. If we have one breath left in us, we need to use it to take this world back.

The room is quiet again. In the corner of the shot Chan can be seen happily drinking Robertson's bourbon.

MACCALLAN
And anyway, we can't stop now; Robbo here needs to replenish his booze supply.

February 14th, 2021

There were three delivery vans still parked up at the back of the supermarket. Robertson commandeered one and threw his sleeping bag and backpack into a corner of its box-body. The roof was made of translucent plastic and it cast the interior with a sickly milk-coloured light. The effect was like being submerged in water. For some reason he liked that.

At the far end of the loading bay, crows were beginning to gather. The four bodies from the makeshift sickbay they'd found had been moved there. Even wrapped in layers of black bin liners the birds knew what they were. They strutted around the crumpled forms, pecking, then stepping away as if waiting for a reaction.

The team that had carried the bodies away and cleaned up the aisle they died in were huddled together watching the crows work. They'd folded the dead into shopping trolleys to move them. It wasn't the first time they'd done that, or similar. The gallows humour that had accompanied the first two or three times had stopped. Too routine to be shocking, it had become just another thing to deal with. The control of booze within the group was often suspended for those on cleaning duties. Four bodies wasn't a big deal in the course of things but the inclusion of a child made things worse. The crow watchers passed a selection of bottles around. They drank in silence.

"Intelligent creatures," Sol said.

Robertson jumped. The old man had appeared at the rear of the delivery truck without warning. He was holding a bottle of lemonade, using both hands in a bid to keep it steady.

"The crows?" Sol had the bottle to his lips but managed to make an affirmative sound. "They're scavengers," Robertson said.

"And we're not?"

As they watched, a huge bird half flew, half hopped onto one of the bundles. It began to pick at the layers of plastic shrouding. Robertson looked away. In the sky directly above more crows circled.

"We don't pick skin off dead bodies."

Sol laughed, "No, we just pick over the corpse of a dead city."

The big crow flicked scraps of torn plastic aside, then its beak began to glisten wetly.

"I'd shoot the fucking things, if I had a gun."

Sol took another sip of the lemonade and gave him a quizzical look.

"That might not be the wisest of moves, from a political standpoint."

Robertson grunted in agreement and retreated into the back of the van. Some distance from the group of people passing the bottles around, Miller was sitting with his collection of knives spread in front of him. They were arranged in strict order of size. He was honing the edge of one of his machetes. His hands ran the whetstone along the metal automatically. His attention was set on the crows. The knot of twenty or so survivors that gathered around him, hanging on his every move, also studied the birds as they fed. Some of them threw scraps of extra food towards them. The crows were the only ones not observing silence at the meal.

"What's the matter? You don't like to watch people at worship?" Sol said, following Robertson's gaze.

He lowered himself slowly to the floor, wincing. His knees made a soft grating sound as they flexed. Robertson, ignoring Sol's comment, busied himself setting up camp. He was unsure if Sol was referring to Miller's ring of admirers, or Miller's admiration of the crows.

Sol wanted to push his point, "You've seen what he does with the infected?"

"Yeah. I'm trying to keep that quiet. I've told Johnno not to go yapping about it."

Sol laughed; a short burst of sound more related to contempt than humour.

"The man thinks he can keep it quiet. Maybe tomorrow you stop the sun coming up?"

"And what would you suggest?"

Sol waved the question away, "Nothing to do, everyone who wants to hear the story already has, and if they haven't, they've made their own story up. Anyway, is all for the good. The world's gone mad, you want it should have a sane messiah?"

"Messiah?"

"His people think he's leading them to the Promised Land."

"That was Moses. He was a prophet, not the messiah."

"That suits me. Miller's flock can believe they're going to the Promised Land. Meanwhile, you and I can follow the profit."

Despite himself, Robertson laughed.

"If either of you are right."

Sol dismissed the statement with another wave.

"Your friend Maccallan seems to be thinking along the same lines."

"I used to work with him. We're not friends."

Sol was about to laugh but caught Robertson's expression.

"So, you wouldn't say you trust him?"

"I don't need to trust him."

He tapped the shaft of the fireman's axe that he had laid beside the sleeping bag.

Chapter 17. In the Dark

From The Outbreak in Europe, by Adele Bisset (Translation by Edward Simpson), L'Equipe (2027)

The Tunnel of Tears sounds almost romantic, like the Bridge of Sighs. The reality was far from romantic. The chain of events that led to the huge loss of life in the dark recesses of Paris's super-périphérique, Europe's longest underground roadway, may never be known.

Wreckage at the north entrance of the tunnel suggests a major road accident took place. The number of vehicles involved varies depending on which source is used. Even the records kept by the engineers of the French army, who were tasked with clearing Parisian roads, do not provide a definitive answer. Reports have placed the number as low as six and as high as eighteen. It is probably of importance only to obsessive information addicts.

To those more concerned with the human history of the Outbreak, it is enough to know that the north to south carriageway of the A86 road tunnel was blocked early on.

The duplex design of the tunnel, with two entirely independent lanes of traffic, meant the southbound carriageway of the tunnel formed a clear path to Calais. For the waves of people fleeing to the coast it seemed an obvious way to avoid the chaos in Paris. It was on the face of it a logical assumption.

However, it has been pointed out by many historians, logic was one of the first casualties of the Outbreak.

April 7th, 2028

It surprised me how long it had taken to get the warrant for the search of Robertson's flat. The Emergency Measures Act of 2021 had reached far and wide across the British legal system. Its implementation had been fast, but its retraction was slow. Officialdom cited lack of personnel to research the legal and procedural implications, the time constraints on the sitting government, and, of course, lack of funds. Jailhouse lawyers and bar-room politicians tended to the view that Big Government wasn't hurrying to loosen its grip on the population.

One of the few things to be rewritten had been the rules on property ownership. The idea that an Englishman's home was his castle was hardwired into the national mindset. And the government, on both sides of the coalition, was made up of people with enough funds to actually own property.

The warrant, when it had finally arrived, had been pushed through via Washington. Unfortunately, neither Washington's reach nor the 'special relationship' could magically produce the personnel to staff a full search unit. Luckily for Winslow and me there was almost nothing to search.

I'd expected something quietly luxurious. Nothing I'd seen of Robertson led me to expect a home built for entertaining, but I'd have thought he'd have left austerity behind him. He was a high-profile figure and I'd assumed his biography and connection to the film would have afforded him a generous portion of life's comforts.

"Delightful," Winslow said.

I didn't like the snide tone, but I could see his point. Not that I intended admitting it.

"I think you'll find a lot of people living in places like this."

"Really? I think you'll find very few of them do it by choice."

Robertson's home was in an end-of-terrace house. One of four cramped apartments, it had a view of a burned-out street from the front and a concrete yard from the rear. The whole was watched over by the ruins of a business estate. Occasionally a truck crawled out onto the broken roads, but most of the units were empty shells.

The three other apartments were unoccupied. As was the house next door. The building was largely intact, but the bottom floor had been gutted by fire. It was the only one on that side of the street to have been torched.

It was a large house, at least by the standards of Central London. The ceilings were high and melted pleasingly into the walls via ornate plaster coving. Despite the violence that had visited the street, the building was in reasonable shape. The window in the bedroom was boarded over. Not with officially stamped plyboard, as featured in my government supply accommodation. Instead six floorboards had been nailed across the gap. It looked as though Robertson had repaired it himself. The wallpaper had peeled away, but the black mould that usually accompanied such damage had been scoured away in a tide of bleach. Robertson's favourite air freshener. The roof of my mouth felt raw in the relentless alkaline odour.

The mattress and bed frame were a mismatched pair. The base a large double, with a single-size mattress dumped on top. There was a clean base sheet and a sleeping bag on it. The wardrobe held an unremarkable collection of clothes and a fireman's axe. Presumably the fireman's axe mentioned in the book and made into legend via the film. Next to it was a machete, with a collection of notches filed onto its back.

And the bottled water of course.

I had the same stash. Most people did, along with a huge collection of purifying tablets, if they could get them. Water supplies had been among the first things to be restored but some lessons run deep.

The kitchen was stocked but not impressively so. I didn't doubt Robertson had funds to buy on the thriving black market, and the lack of evidence only made me more suspicious.

"An upright and law-abiding citizen," Winslow said, examining the collection of officially rationed tins. We shared a glance that by our standards could be classed as friendly. We'd finally reached the same page without the semaphore of tapping.

What there was to be turned upside-down, we duly did. Nothing. At least nothing we knew the significance of. We had no idea what we were looking for. We locked the door behind us, and Winslow muttered, "After you" at the top of the stairs. I could hear his knuckles rapping on the banister as he followed me down.

I struggled with the front door. Robertson, or someone equally unskilled, had hung a new door at some point and the fit wasn't good. I realised Winslow wasn't behind me once I was outside.

Tap, tap. Tap, tap. Tap, tap.

I debated going back to the car we'd been allowed use of for the morning, but suspected I'd blink first.

Winslow was carefully not looking my way as he beat out his thought pattern on the door of the lower-floor flat.

"What?"

Winslow still didn't look at me, and he waited a few seconds before speaking.

"Why is this unoccupied?"

He flicked a light switch and a bare bulb unleashed its thirty watts of glory onto the hallway. The street was on the working grid. It was even hardwired into the broadband. Winslow had noted the fibre optic junction box at the end of the road. Its orange paint was the brightest spot against the smoke-stained buildings. Empty buildings that could be broken into were ten a penny. Intact, fit for human habitation, on a working part of the grid, hooked to the net? That was a different story.

The plank nailed horizontally across the frame looked like another floorboard, culled from the same batch that had fixed the broken window in Robertson's bedroom. The padlock and hasp looked new.

"What does it say on the warrant?"

I pulled it from the bottom of my hip pocket. It entitled us to search number seven Baxter Road. There was no distinction between sub-dwellings. In short, we had the nod to search the downstairs flat.

We used the wheel wrench from the car to break the hasp away. Winslow dipped under the board nailed across the doorframe and fell forward in a cloud of curses.

The floor had been pulled up directly inside the door. Winslow pulled himself upright and continued the round of swearing.

The lower floor windows were all shuttered and the front room was accordingly dark. I stared into the gloom until my eyes adjusted to the lack of light. Winslow was slapping at the wall around the doorframe. He snapped, "Got you," and there was the click of another light switch. He clicked it on and off three or four times before accepting it wasn't making any difference.

We used the torches on our mobiles to scan the room. It told a story familiar to many properties in the affected cities. In the corner furthest from the door was an old mattress. The obligatory litter of food wrappers and plastic water bottles had migrated to the edges of the room. It didn't look as if the occupancy had ended well. The mattress was murky with stains. Toxo infection, when allowed to run its course, normally ended in a puddle of shit, blood and urine. The condition of the mattress suggested they'd at least been spared the indignity of HV-Tg psychosis. The room should have stunk of human functions. Instead the air crawled with alkaline fumes. Winslow, tap-tapping his free hand against the side of his leg, directed his light to the foot of the stained 'bed'. Four empty bleach bottles had been dropped there. There was another smell too, something chemical that seemed to be under the floor. I couldn't place it; it was somewhere between oil and vomit.

The internal door leading to the next room was locked. No single plank and hasp this time. There was no visible hardware on our side, but the door was fixed tight. The doorknob had been removed, smashed off if the tale the splinters told was true. Getting a grasp on the featureless plain of timber wasn't made any easier by the holes in the flooring. As at the front door, the boards had been wrenched away.

"Look at this."

Winslow held his mobile closer to the frame, more splinters. Screws, or nails powered into the frame from the other side.

"Siege?" I suggested.

It wasn't unheard of for people to seal a room around them and try to wait it out. Many died in the attempt. There was a new breed of urban myth on the rise. Stories of what had been found by clean-up crews or army units when they broke down the barricades on somebody's safe place: single bloated corpses surrounded by a family of bones; homes full of dismembered bodies with the wasting remains of a Gonzo surveying its work. There may have been a grain of truth in some of them. I never troubled to dig too deeply into the tales; I had bad dreams enough for one lifetime.

One of the reports that had been confirmed more than once was the story of the booby trap.

"We ought to get one of the cleansers out to look at this," Winslow said.

He reverted to form and made a face like a man deep in thought.

"I don't believe the cleansers came here, took a corpse out and left without checking the room next door." Some things, even with personnel and budget restrictions, were being done properly. Clearing the dead before letting the living return was one of them. Since cleansing, the room had been sealed from the inside. "Robertson's been here."

"And you'd stake your life on it?" Winslow asked.

"If we go back to the station and ask for a cleansing team you know what'll happen. They'll check the records to see if this street has been done. That'll take a month, at least. Then they'll come back to us and say it's been declared safe. Then we'll have to put in a request to the army to have it checked. That'll take another month."

Winslow trained the light from his torch onto the floor. He began making his way back to the front door, being prissily careful. Stepping over the holes where the boards had been removed as much to make a point as to make his way.

"Who do you think pulled these boards away?" he said. I didn't answer. "I'd guess your friend Robertson. I nearly broke my damn neck."

"Well, doesn't that prove my point?" I trained the beam from my mobile on the sealed door. "That's his work."

"I agree." He stepped back into the hallway. "But what makes you think he wouldn't booby-trap it after he'd sealed it?"

He waited for me to answer, knowing he'd won the point but needing me to admit it.

We went round the rear of the house and kicked a section of fencing away to get into the backyard. The concreted area was littered with a collection of tins. They made it difficult to reach the back of the building without making a noise. Many of the tins were new, bearing the government rationing labels, all pale brown utility and lacklustre contents. From the rear, the building was shuttered closed. More repurposed floorboarding. The oily-sick smell lingered there too.

"He's not getting in there this way."

I snapped back at the pointless comment, "I can see that. He might just be hording black market supplies."

Winslow smiled in a way that made me want to punch him.

"People who do that don't stop. They keep adding to their stores. They don't seal them shut. There'll be a way in."

Having proved his point about the wisdom of forcing the door, Winslow conceded my point about the time delay on calling an official cleansing unit. He tapped out his thought processes on the bannister again as we went back to Robertson's flat.

"He likes pulling up floorboards," he said.

The flooring in Robertson's bedroom looked like an exercise in tie-dying and was infused with his signature bleach perfume. Winslow knelt to tug at the edge of the ruined carpet. His trousers, torn when he'd fallen in the flat below, ripped completely across the knee. He didn't waste any more curses, just sighed heavily and rolled the carpet back.

I found a screwdriver in a kitchen drawer and Winslow produced a thick-bladed knife. We levered at the joins between the boards around the bed. Four came up, revealing a hole smashed into the ceiling below and the top rung of a ladder.

We listened for sounds of life and heard nothing. The feeble light from the phones was swallowed by the room below.

"You alright?"

Winslow's question made me jump. I'd been staring into the hole in the floor for too long. I told him I was letting my eyes adjust.

I lowered my feet onto the rungs of the ladder.

We'd abandoned the Citroën within an hour. Roads were blocked with abandoned cars or piles of debris. Dog Boy and Juan had debated the decision by shouting at each other. They'd started arguing as we'd driven away from the body of the sergeant. A pattern developed quickly and became entrenched into a routine. Dog Boy would say "left," Juan would say "right," then they'd shout at each other. Juan didn't have the grace to listen to what Dog Boy said and Dog Boy didn't have the sense to ignore the griping. In short, they behaved like men.

After the first few days I didn't even pretend to take an interest in the exchanges. Juan, for all his confrontational posturing, always came short of taking charge. Whatever the subject in contention, the ending was always the same; Dog Boy would finally throw his hands up in despair and simply do whatever he'd suggested in the first place. He'd tell Juan he was free to take his own course. Juan never would. Neither would I.

I didn't pretend anymore that I had any real connection with either of my traveling companions. Being in a group, even a small one, increased my chances of staying alive, and maybe getting back home. Standing still wasn't an option, and Dog Boy and Juan weren't about to set up house together.

At the mouth of the A86 tunnel the obvious argument was, should we go through or round? The burnt-out remains of a tanker were angled across the road, a dozen smaller vehicles were arranged around the hulk. The wrecks had started to rust. Clearly the tunnel had been blocked for some time.

I took myself out of earshot as the two men wound themselves up for another set-to. The performances had quickly ceased to interest me, and I'd taken to waiting them out.

They argued in whispers, the fear of attracting attention reducing the tension to hissing sibilance. The volume was beginning to climb, but I'd become adept at reading the tone without bothering to hear the content. They were winding down. When Dog Boy made his theatrical psssshh and threw his hands in the air, I knew it was over. I joined them beside the burnt hulk they were using as a map table. The road map had been one of the things we'd taken from the

Citroën.

As the light began to fade Juan clicked on a small torch he'd found in the last gas station we'd looted. He played its beam over the map. Sections of it had been scored through with a marker pen. Areas we already found impassable. They formed a roughly-shaped crescent, with the mouth of the A86 tunnel at its apex.

"The big cheese here has decided to end it all and invites us to join him," Juan said.

He tapped the mouth of the tunnel, then pointed over his shoulder at the real thing.

Dog Boy was already shouldering his backpack and getting ready to leave.

"You want us to go through that?"

Dog Boy nodded. Whatever reserves of patience he'd had, had been spent on Juan. When I asked him why, he leaned over the map and traced the arc of the crescent with his finger.

"All this to the east is tight-packed streets. If we go that way we'll never make it through the city. If we don't get killed in the rioting the disease will take us." He pointed at the markings he'd made on the west side, "Same here."

It was getting steadily darker. The power was out everywhere by then. The only lights in the city were fires or torches. Headlights of cars were getting few and far between. Somewhere far off to the north somebody shouted, then screamed. Or maybe somebody else screamed.

"I'm not taking her through there," Juan announced.

He stood straight, arms crossed high on his chest, feet set shoulder width apart.

"You're not taking me anywhere," I snapped and shouldered my own pack, settling it squarely on my back and tightening the straps. I marched past him and towards the tunnel. With hindsight, it must have looked as if I was walking towards Dog Boy. Together we got to the very edge of the opening.

I'm sure the way I remember it, the picture of it I carry in my mind, is more ominous than it actually was that night. But, the memory is what you live with. I'd argue that point with David on the phone – while he'd sit safely in the US and tell me I needed to live in the here-and-now and put the past behind me. There is no past, not really. Not as long the human brain brings back the memories, be they accurate or rose-tinted nightmares. The past is what you live with and that makes it the present. If the past exists, it's in purely relative terms.

The mouth of the tunnel sucked the light from the setting sun. Dog Boy shone his heavy-duty torch into it and the darkness swallowed it whole.

"Are you sure about this?"

Dog Boy laughed at the question. It was a bitter sound that made me turn to him.

"You and him, Juan, all the time … all the time." I couldn't see his face, the sunset was behind us casting him into a silhouette, but I saw he was shaking his head. "Why would I be sure? If I was sure, would it make you feel better?"

He played the light from his torch over my torso with an impatient jitter. It took me a moment to see he was telling me to put my own torch on.

"I'm not sure. But I'm sure the streets around here are dangerous and the route above ground alternates housing estates with kilometres of woodland. I think, think, the tunnel will be quicker."

With that he stepped forward. I looked behind me, waiting for Juan to follow. I couldn't see the glow of his torch. I hurried in the tunnel and caught up with Dog Boy.

"Juan's gone," I said.

Dog Boy's surprise caused him to break stride. He quickly regained it and the collection of creaking sounds from his pack made me think he shrugged.

"His choice. If you want to go and look for him, go. I'm going this way."

I hesitated long enough to make myself think I was worried about Juan, then I followed Dog Boy with his plan and his gun.

The room below had the same oily-sickness smell I'd encountered at the rear of the house. It was familiar but at the same time unsettling. The light of my phone was just sufficient to cast more shadows. After I'd performed a trio of rapid, limb-jerking spin-arounds, I admitted to myself I was spooked and forced myself to listen to the space around me. Nothing.

It was a trick I'd learned early on, even before I'd jumped into the Citroën and escaped the burning remnants of the quarantined street. The fear was too big to be denied and the darkness so deep it swallowed any attempt to whistle in it. Admitting I was scared, letting go of the denial, freed up whatever internal resources I had left.

I was crying as I looked for the light switch. I didn't waste energy trying to stop it or trying to pull myself together. Once I'd found it and the room came into view, I scrubbed my face with my hands.

The room I was in was the same dimensions as the one upstairs. Again, there was the base of a bed pushed against one wall. In place of a mattress there were a dozen desktop computers. At least three of them looked brand new. Coaxial cables bled from the machines and traced their way to memory blocks and routers. The power cables clumped together into a collection of extension cords that snuck along the bleach-scoured baseboard and into the adjacent room. There were no LEDs blinking back at my stare; all the screens were dark.

Behind me, Winslow climbed down the ladder, then tapped a rhythm out on it. I waited him out, rather than interrupt the concert.

"What is that smell?" he finally asked.

I had one of those moments where two thoughts cross-referenced. I'd asked the same question after Dog Boy and I had shuffled through the first half mile of the A86 tunnel. It was the same smell – stale exhaust fumes that had wormed their way into the structure of the walls.

Chapter 18. The Iconic Butcher

Miller's Meat (Miller's Mince)

A reference to John Miller's proficiency at close quarters combat. As in 'Miller makes mincemeat out of Gonzos'.

The A to Z of Gondii Names

February 14th, 2021

A Gonzo had drifted in from somewhere. Miller had run across the loading yards panicking the crows, so they took off in a clattering mass, cawing their displeasure. His entourage of followers had run at his heels but drawn short as he neared the shuffling form. A man, elderly, missing an arm and kept alive by the Toxo.

Robertson watched the crowd forming a loose circle. No one spoke or called out, but he could feel the excitement radiating from them. Their reserve lent the scene a religious feel: mob made congregation; Miller made icon. The silence ended with the wet clang of a butcher's knife. When that noise stopped the crowd didn't disperse; they stayed to watch Miller work. The crows circled, waiting for their turn.

Maccallan wasn't part of the crowd. Robertson had spotted him, standing away from the spectacle of Miller's kill. He watched as intently as anyone, but his focus was on the crowd, not the performance. As though he'd felt Robertson's scrutiny, he looked up sharply and made eye contact. Robertson gestured for him to come over, then turned and went back into the delivery van.

Sol was still sitting with his back against the wall of the van. He was staring at the fingertips of his right hand as they trembled. When Robertson lowered himself on to the sleeping bag he'd laid out, the old man drew his hand into a fist, then looked away from it. He swallowed and blinked rapidly before speaking.

"Miller's getting worse."

"Does it matter? They still follow him."

Sol nodded. His expression was sour.

"And if he's so far gone you can't steer him?"

"There's half a dozen people who'd split off if I gave the word."

Sol made a sound that might have been a curse or just a groan.

"Half a dozen? There were sixty-four of us two days ago. This morning there's sixty-one."

Robertson dismissed the statement with a flick of his hand.

"Idiots who didn't have the brains to clean up after themselves. Half a dozen people we can trust is all we need."

"And yet you don't break away from the main group."

Sol and Robertson both turned sharply in the direction of the voice.

Maccallan had appeared at the back of the van. Robertson didn't respond to the comment other than to stare levelly at his old boss. He didn't speak until the other man started shuffling his feet and glanced over to Sol. It made him look as if he were seeking an ally.

"Get in here and pull the door to," Robertson told him.

Maccallan struggled with the van's doors. When he'd closed them in, he stood and glanced between Robertson and Sol, uncertain what he should do.

"You get to thinking you're cock-of-the-fucking-walk around here, Maccallan, and trust me, you'll be cut down to size. You got that?"

"I got it, I got it. You're in charge. You say who's in or out."

Again, he looked uncertainly into a wall of silence. Robertson uncurled himself from the floor and walked to the rear of the van. He had the axe in his hand.

"Forget in or out, I say who lives and fucking dies. Get that?"

"Yes. I get it. You're the boss, you're the boss. Understood."

"You reckon you got something we need?" Rather than speak, Maccallan nodded. Robertson hadn't blinked, hadn't taken his eyes from him. "Go talk to Sol."

Sol had his hands tightly clasped in his lap. He motioned Maccallan to sit by inclining his head. Robertson didn't step aside and Maccallan had to step round him. He regained some of his poise when he sat opposite the old man.

Robertson remembered the body language from the days in the office. It was Maccallan's about-to-strike-a-deal stance. The flash of confidence vanished when he saw Robertson was still eyeballing him.

"So, talk," Sol told him.

"I think I know what you're trying to do." Sol didn't answer and Maccallan glanced at Robertson. "You're heading to the banking sector. You want the money."

Sol laughed, "What money? You honestly think they reduced all the bridges to rubble trying to stop a plague? The fat cats and the bankers and the politicians bought themselves a little time. And what do you think they did with it? Opened a few hospitals, fed some orphans? Those vaults were stripped months ago. Even if they weren't, the question still stands: what money? This?" His hands betrayed him when he tried to yank something from a pocket. He cursed and with slow, methodical movements took a wad of fifty-pound notes out. "This isn't money any more. This isn't even good for wiping up shit." He lifted the notes into the air and let them fall. "I'm an old man. I'm living in a nightmare and you're talking about money." He clasped his hands into stillness again. "What good's money now?"

"I'm not talking about notes. I'm talking about money. If I'm wrong about this, fine. I'll doss down for the night and when it's light I'll just head back to my apartment and wait it out, but I think I know the lay of the land here. Colin and I were workmates for some time."

He smiled and leaned forward, obviously having more to say. Robertson remembered that look from the office as well. The smile Maccallan used when he had some snippet of information to impart. In the know and just short of patronising.

Robertson lifted his axe and took a lazy swing.

Maccallan yelped and threw himself to one side. The head of the axe was set in the plyboard floor. It was a foot from where he'd been sat, but he was gasping like a fish flicked onto the riverbank.

"You better get to the point real fast, Maccallan. These ain't the good old days and we weren't any kind of fucking 'mates'. We worked in the same shit-hole. Difference was you were top dog then."

Robertson pulled the axe free and made a show of examining the edge on the blade. Sol chuckled and the sound made Robertson jump.

"I've seen your sort before, Mr Maccallan. Entrepreneurs were the last name they had for your breed. Before that it was yuppies, before that you were just wide boys. My father, God rest his soul, would have called you a spiv." He pursed his lips and spat. "You always think you're in the know, always think you're one step ahead of everyone else. Maybe you were … once, but it's a different world now. It's my understanding that when you were Mr Robertson's boss you fired him. So, if I was you, I'd make the sales pitch of my life. And when you've done that I'll consult with Mr Robertson regarding your future."

"If you want to go back and look, in my apartment there's over a hundred and fifty k, all in cash. Every shred of it worthless. I'm sorry I fired you, alright. But I had to. If main branch had found out what you were doing, there'd have been a full-on audit. And that would have fucked up what I was doing. But if we go at this together, we can start over, fuck sterling, we go mining."

Extract from the screenplay of Year of the Crow. Lithograph Studios, California (2026)

INT. GLASS-FRONTED RECEPTION AREA OF LARGE OFFICE BLOCK - NIGHT.

POV is outside looking in. The reception is set in a luxurious atrium clad with cream marble. The lights are working and the space is amazingly bright. The front of the reception area is plate glass with a revolving door set in it. Robertson, Maccallan and seven other members of the group are moving around inside. It is hard to make out what they are saying, but it is possible to hear them laughing. The lights go out, then come back on, then off again and back on. There is more laughter and someone cheers.

ROBERTSON

(Voice-over)

It was like turning on the Christmas tree lights when you're a kid. Click, and there you go; twenty-five little bulbs come on and you're in Wonderland.

As the narration ends the soundtrack switches from the laughter and high spirits inside the building to the sound of ragged breathing outside. POV begins to move toward the reception area.

ROBERTSON

(Voice-over)

Then a bulb would blow and everything would go dark, and you felt like Christmas had been fucking cancelled.

POV switches from outside looking in to inside looking out. The camera is positioned at the rear of the reception area, so the group of survivors is visible in the foreground with the expanse of plate glass behind them. With the lights on, the glass acts like a mirror obscuring the view out into the street. Everyone has their backs to the glass, watching Robertson and Maccallan. One of the survivors is fiddling with a CD player. The Bee Gees' 'Staying Alive' starts to play.

MACCALLAN
Crank it up.

The volume increases and Robertson starts singing along. Maccallan stares at him for a moment, impressed with his voice.

MACCALLAN
We need some disco lights.

Someone begins flicking the lights on and off. When the lights are out it's possible to see the street outside. A mass of zombies is approaching. Maccallan joins in with Robertson and both men climb onto the large reception desk. They start hamming up a dance routine. The CD player gets louder and more people start singing or cheering.

Close-up on Robertson. He is singing a long high note and has his eyes closed. At the end of the note he opens his eyes. As he does this the lights flick off.

Shot changes to Robertson's POV. The faces of three zombies are pressed up against the glass. Behind them dozens more are shuffling forward. Only Robertson is aware of them.

ROBERTSON
(Shouting)
Shut it off, stop it.

The lights are back on now and the plate glass is

only showing the reflection of the party. Nobody realises the dangers or understands what Robertson is shouting. He jumps off the reception desk and runs toward the window. At the right-hand side of the window we see a pile of weapons. Robertson's axe is on the top, along with Maccallan's machete. Before he gets to them, a crack appears in the glass. Close-up on Maccallan as he realises the danger.

MACCALLAN
Okay, everyone, we got gate-crashers.

The partiers turn to look in the direction of Robertson. Cut to Robertson as he grabs his axe and Maccallan's machete. As he straightens, the glass gives way and the first zombies break through. The one at the front is trampled by those behind and it is cut open on the broken edge of glass. In one fluid movement Robertson, not appearing to even look, swings the axe through a sweeping arc and takes the top from the skull of a zombie. Carrying on the motion he uses the machete to take down the next zombie.

Maccallan has now reached Robertson's side.

MACCALLAN
Here!

ROBERTSON
What kept you?

Robertson tosses the machete to Maccallan. Maccallan uses it to despatch a zombie that has appeared on Robertson's blindside.

MACCALLAN
I hate to leave a good party.

Movie Madness Forum > General Discussion > Movies > Year of the Crow

FanguRobertson
POSTS: 45
Does anyone know how true to life Maccallan's death scene is? I know a lot of people say Crow's Kingdom is more fiction than fact, but I've read Robertson's book and I can't find any mention of what became of Maccallan.

****
tHATmOVIEgUY
POSTS: 787
The film is fairly accurate in some respects. The route the Crows take across London and the set dressing are supposed to be very accurate for example. The signs and posters, shown in many of the earlier scenes, are direct copies of the ones issued by the UK government and the NHS.
The events directly involving the characters are largely made up. The description of Miller in the book bears no relation to the character in the film. His suicide isn't alluded to at all. The book's references to Maccallan are fairly ambiguous. The tone of it would suggest Maccallan and Robertson weren't comrades in arms, and not really friends.
There is a fleeting reference to Maccallan's fate in the book. On page 56 (at least in my edition) Robertson describes when Maccallan makes contact with the Crows, and says that it might have been better if he'd stayed in hiding because he would have survived. To answer your question: I don't think Maccallan's death in the movie is based on reality.

****
A2ZEE
POSTS: 70
No offence to tHATmOVIEgUY, but you've not answered the

question you've just given your opinion.
I read the book and agree that Robertson indicates Maccallan is dead, what's interesting is the implication that he (Robertson) feels guilty about this.
I know Malik interviewed Robertson at length to prepare for the film, and that the script writer also spoke with him. I suspect Robertson may have revealed something to them that he wasn't happy about putting in the book.

****

tHATmOVIEgUY
POSTS: 788
No offence to you A2ZEE, BUT you're calling me out on giving my opinion? Then you come out with some wild idea about Robertson confessing to something he was too ashamed to put into a book, but was happy to tell a film crew about?

****

A2ZEE
POSTS: 71
I was offering my opinion, as were you. I did not state it as fact or claim I had answered the question.

****

Big_Foot
POSTS: 36
This is only an opinion. If Robertson had accidentally killed Maccallan, he might well be racked with guilt. Friends or not, they would have been through a lot together. It could be that he couldn't bring himself to write about it, but felt he could talk about it to someone who was going to take over the story, EG Malik.

****

THATmOVIEgUY
POSTS: 789
I think everyone is forgetting who Robertson is. He is

the last of the Crows, the ultimate survivor. If he had killed Maccallan, he wouldn't confess it to someone who'd go and make a film about it. Why would he put himself at that kind of risk? Do you really think a man like Robertson would want to go to prison?

****

A2ZEE
POSTS: 72
THATmOVIEgUY, what are you talking about? Why would he go to prison for something that happened during the Lockdown?

****

THATmOVIEgUY
POSTS: 790
And that is why my opinions are worth more than yours. Get your facts straight. There has never been an amnesty for events that took place in the Lockdown. If the events in the film are true and if the writers were told they were true by Robertson, then he'd be admitting to manslaughter. Which he could still face a prison sentence for.

****

A2ZEE
POSTS: 73
BULL SHIT. That would mean anyone who killed a Grippy during the Outbreak would be liable for arrest.

****

tHATmOVIEgUY
POSTS: 791
Technically they could be.

February 14th, 2021

The crows had returned to the carrion, the background rattle of their presence quieter than usual. Miller had filleted the Gonzo, reducing it to a collection of wet parts. He'd worked methodically at dividing the cuts, evenly, around the yard. Spoilt for choice, the crows were relaxed, and their feeding wasn't troubled by territorial squabbles.

"Have you seen this?" Sol asked.

Robertson answered with a grunt. It was a rhetorical question. The three of them were standing on the loading dock at the rear of Miller's van.

Miller was sitting cross-legged, his knives spread in front of him once again. A man Robertson had never spoken to, but who'd been with them since the first day of the Lockdown, was cleaning them. As he finished with each blade he put it reverently back in it place. Before picking up the next one he would pause, gathering himself. Two women were washing Miller's hands. They had an arm each and worked with the same self-aware precision as the knife cleaner. Miller's attention was on the crows.

From the corner of his eye, Robertson saw Maccallan touch Sol on the shoulder and point to the far end of the loading yard. Two people, a man of about twenty and a woman who might have been his mother, were pacing along the wall that formed one side of the site. They were leaning forward and moving slowly around the feeding birds. Crows strutted away from them, not bothering to flap into the air. Sol muttered something that Robertson didn't catch. As they watched, the young man knelt and carefully picked a feather from the ground. When he straightened up, there was a pause as they both admired the find.

"We need to get moving," Sol said.

"We need to strip this place first," Robertson said. "Then find someplace to hide the cadge."

Sol shook his head. "Look at them, they're building a god."

"It doesn't matter. As long as they follow him. All hail the chief."

Sol gave him a furious look.

"And what happens when the chief decides he prefers the company of acolytes to the council of advisors?"

"All he wants is a ready supply of Gonzos to hack up. I can keep him happy."

"It's the crowd you need to work, not Miller," Maccallan said. He was squinting at the man cleaning the knives.

"Who fucking asked you?" Robertson stepped round Sol, who was positioned between him and Maccallan. "You're here on my say-so, nothing more."

Maccallan took a half step to the side. Not directly putting himself behind Sol, the intent of the movement was still clear. Sol turned his head a fraction, watching him. It was only fleeting but Robertson saw the flash of contempt on his face.

The old man put a hand on Robertson's shoulder and held eye contact with him.

"Let's calm down. There's truth in what he says. If our little band of scavengers reinvents itself as a cult, they might decide on who's in and who's out."

Robertson waited for Sol to look away. When he didn't, Robertson pointedly turned his gaze to the hand on his shoulder. Sol took it away, but at the same time shifted more to his right, shielding Maccallan to a greater degree.

"I'll take care of Miller, and his fucking cult." He craned his neck to look round Sol. "You take care of your fucking side of things. Got that?"

He waited until Maccallan nodded before making his way over to Miller.

Chapter 19. Unsettling in Pink

Holing-up (Laying-up)

The practice of laying up provisions and barricading oneself into a bolthole or siege-house. Although common during the Outbreak, terms such as bolters, holers and uppers are increasingly used as derogatory descriptions of the people who survived (or attempted to survive) in this manner.

Snuff-Box

A bolthole fitted with a booby trap intended to kill or maim intruders.

Shit-Safe

A bolthole where the occupant/s had succumbed to HV-Tg. The term was a reference to the smell from such locations. By the time the practice of laying-up had become widespread, HV-Tg had mutated from a fatal disease into a condition that caused severe psychosis. Victims of HV-Tg-induced psychosis would often lack the cognitive ability to free themselves from their boltholes. Almost invariably they would smear the confines of their environment with their own faeces. It is believed this was a disease-driven action, similar to the change in behaviour seen in domestic cats with pre-HV-Tg. Infected cats would forget their house training and ceased hiding or burying their stool.

The A to Z of Gondii Names

From recording of police interview with Colin Robertson (8th April 2028)

Winslow - We searched your flat. Lovely place, did you decorate it yourself?
Robertson - Yeah, I've got Homes and Gardens booked in for a photo shoot, so if we could wrap this up, that would be great.
Winslow - Good, you've got a sense of humour. I hear it helps when you're sitting in a cell, pissing in a bucket and wondering who's getting the next turn on you in the shower.
Robertson - I'll tell you what's funny, Lincoln: you trying to put the frighteners on. Now, if she was telling me scary stories, I'd be inclined to listen.
Cross - Why don't you give us some straight answers? As you're so keen to get out of here.
Robertson - Well, if I was in here with two real coppers, instead of you pair of clowns, no doubt someone would have asked me a fucking question.
Winslow - Alright, here's a question. Are you aware there's a trapdoor cut into your bedroom floor leading to the flat below?
Robertson - No idea what you're talking about.
Cross - Then how do you explain that the flat below yours has been shut up tighter than a drum from the inside? The only access is from your bedroom.
Robertson - You're the coppers, you explain it. Or better yet, prove I knew something about it.
Winslow - I think you're overestimating how much weight your hero status is going to carry with a jury.
Robertson - Now that is funny, seriously, that is funny. So far you've held me six days without charging me, and the nearest you've got to an accusation, not a case, an accusation, is illegal entry to unoccupied property. You're going to try to take that to court? Jury, what fucking jury?
Cross - It's not an unoccupied property. There's a listed owner, care to guess who?
Robertson - Not really.
Cross - You don't want to know who owns the trapdoor in your bedroom floor?
Robertson - If we can get all this bullshit over and done with … tell me.
Winslow - Rodger Maccallan.

April 7th, 2028

After his initial burst of tapping Winslow had been unusually quiet as he looked around the room.

"What is going on here?" he finally said.

The bedroom directly below Robertson's had belonged to a young girl. Even by the light of the low-energy bulb, the wallpaper was clearly princess pink. The shade around the dingy bulb was a mass of fabric butterflies and unicorns. The paper had started to peel away from the plaster and the unicorns and butterflies, dancing around the light, were thick with grime.

Winslow appeared to be fixated on the collection of computers.

"Doesn't look like a bolthole," I said.

He still didn't look away from the blank screens, but he nodded his agreement.

The room was creeping me out; it was too close to my daughter's room. The one I practically ran out of the last time I'd seen it. Late getting into the cab and worrying about missing my flight. Too many years ago and counting. Cabs, schedules, flights out of the country. Everyday things back then that had felt important. I wondered if Maria's room had begun the gradual creep from girl's room to young woman's private space. Disney posters giving up ground to boy bands or pretty actors. Back home, was Malik Connally brooding against an expanse of pink wallpaper? Maybe not. Malik would have been my choice; perhaps Maria was more a Ryan Morgan gal. Would I have been, before tracking across the ruins of Paris?

Winslow was tracing the wires from the back of the computers. Down the wall, along the baseboard. The collection of power cords, thick as my arm, vanished through a hole in the plasterboard wall. I imagined Robertson slicing it away with his axe. The door opened onto an annexed room that was little more than a cupboard. One of those near useless additions that appear in converted buildings where somebody has turned a house into a two-story rental investment. There was no clue as to the room's previous use. The walls were hidden behind a selection of mattresses bound in place with a chaotic network of clothes lines.

The room housed a pair of generators and a score of five-gallon jerry-cans stacked in one corner. The sickly oil smell was worse here, full enough to reveal itself as diesel fuel.

More boards had been pulled up here and another hole cut, this one below floor level, through to the burnt-out house next door. The exhausts of the generators were routed through the gap via aluminium ducting tube. The gaps where the ducting pierced the rough-cut hole had been plugged with rags. When they were running in their soundproofed hideaway, the generators would dump their fumes beneath tons of soot-blackened rubble.

Winslow had knelt beside one of the generators. He began rapping a knuckle against it. I assumed he'd reverted to type, until he shuffled around to perform the same act on the second generator.

"Tanks are empty, and they're both cold." Before he stood again, he did another knuckle rap against one of the machine's control panels. "They're ready to go though."

I didn't need the explanation. Working a generator was a common skill among survivors. The two machines had been left running and only stopped when their tanks ran dry. I took hold of one of the jerry cans and had a struggle to lift it. It was full, so were the next two I tried.

"Why bother though?" Winslow said. "This building's on the grid. He can plug all his hardware into the mains." I'd asked myself the same question. "Shall we?"

He had hold of one of the jerry cans.

"Let's do it."

Winslow emptied the diesel into one of the empty fuel tanks and yanked on the starter cord. The cold engine took three attempts to catch. We closed the door behind us when we stepped back into the pink room. The mattresses did a fair job of hiding the noise.

Half the computers on the bed base responded to the power supply with glowing LEDs. I switched the two closest to me on and their screens flickered to life, demanding passwords. I tapped in 'password', lower-case, upper-case, five in place of S, zero in place of O. Of course, the screens just blinked back my failure. That shit only works in the movies.

"You know anything about hacking computers?" I asked Winslow.

"Nothing. Let's get out of here."

There was a tension in his voice that made me look round. He blinked three of four times in quick succession. I expected him to turn away quickly or to make some defensive remark, but he just grimaced as though he was in pain.

"Sorry," he told me, "This room's too much."

He was halfway up the ladder before I had a chance to reply. I closed off the generator before I followed him. When I went back to the room with the fuel store and the mattresses, there was a square of buff-coloured paper lying just inside the threshold. It hadn't been there when we'd first opened the door and I had a moment of something close to panic wondering who had put it there. It wasn't much of a mystery; the generator was bolted to the floor. The vibration it was putting out as it pumped electricity ran tremors through the boards. Even as I watched, the square of paper shuddered through ninety degrees and began dancing away, back towards shelter.

It was a ration coupon, officially stamped and entitling the bearer to twenty litres of diesel oil. It wasn't something many people would let slip through their fingers.

Winslow was sitting on the edge of Robertson's bed. He hadn't been crying but he was a shade lighter than he had been. It was pointless to ask if he was okay, but I did anyway. He nodded a lie and added:

"Sorry."

"Little girl's room?"

He nodded again.

"All that pink," he said

"How old was she?"

"Seven." I thought that was all he had to say on the subject, but then he stood and stared into the hole in the floor. It glowed softly pink; I'd forgotten to switch the light off. "She came down with something. We were scared it was Toxo. Jenny took her to the hospital."

"Was it Toxo?"

He stopped looking at the hole and made to leave.

"Don't know. The hospital was burned down the night they went there."

"I'm sorry."

"Robertson's right, everyone's got a sob story."

"I don't know if Robertson has."

"Not yet, but I'm working on it."

April 7th, 2028

At the station they told us they'd let Richard go. Thrown him back out into the big wide world he was doing his best to retreat from. The charge sheets detailing his arrest for breaking and entering with assault were quietly misfiled, lost or simply thrown in the trash.

The pretence of conditions had been given their due lip service. Richard was told he was required to attend his rehab session and if he didn't, he'd be back in a cell. He was smart enough to know nobody was going to waste manpower on wet nursing another hopeless junkie. He was also smart enough to know we could afford to play the waiting game. It was just a matter of time before he was pulled in for something, unless he cheated the odds and OD'd first.

The hostel he was living in was a grade two: single males, able-bodied, no history of violence. The building had been an office complex and in common with most commercial buildings close to the Thames, most of the windows on the ground floor were plyboard, stencilled with the official HMG logo. The carpets had been stripped out, though the smell of their rotting dampness was still in place. It was playing second fiddle to the collective musk of close-quarters living.

The beds were a mismatched collection of salvage and rickety Department of Supply foldaways. A uniform wall of lockers completed the furnishing.

The hostel's two caretakers were both women in their fifties. They had a solid squared-off look to them that made me think of prison warders. They watched the activity in the living space in a way that did nothing to dispel the notion.

It was late in the evening and fully dark when I paid a visit. A dozen low-energy bulbs were strung across the ceiling, casting light like a stain. Four or five men were already bedded down for the night, another ten were milling aimlessly. Half a dozen of the beds, including Richard's, were unoccupied.

When I asked if they expected Richard to appear anytime soon, one of the caretakers looked pointedly at a clock on the far wall. The hostels were the logical progression of unemployment or addiction. It was an hour before the mobile systems shut down; it represented the start of the working day for those with a habit to feed.

"He won't show until gone midnight. Come back at breakfast. That's when we're full."

"This place have a landline?"

Caretakers one and two narrowed their eyes and exchanged a look.

"We've got a landline," caretaker one said. She was trying for nonchalance but squared her shoulders slightly as she spoke.

Landlines had gained the status once only afforded to mobiles that were all singing and dancing. If you weren't rich or important enough to own one there was kudos to be had in having one entrusted to you.

"When he shows, give me a call." I gave caretaker two a card with my mobile number on it.

Chapter 20. Market Forces

From Soldiers of Misfortune, by P. Sullivan, Oakfield Press (2026)

By the middle of 2021 HV-Tg would reach its peak. The destruction of much of Europe's infrastructure and the massive restrictions on intercontinental travel had largely stopped the spread to the USA, Australia, Japan and much of the subcontinent.

It was little comfort to those in Europe and the UK to know the rest of the world would, for the most part, be spared the suffering they were enduring.

As late as November of 2021 the army still pursued the policy of merging depleted regiments. As with so many of the disastrous steps taken during the HV-Tg pandemic the chain of responsibility has been lost or denied.

Deployment of troops in the early stages of the pandemic – as peacekeepers to shore up the crumbling and overwhelmed emergency services – resulted in the infection of hundreds of men. In the tightly-packed barracks and troops transport, HV-Tg transmission progressed at faster rates than within the civilian population.

Survivors of the infected and decimated regiments were almost certainly incubating the Toxo parasite. Their transfer to the nearest available regiment introduced the disease to a new set of hosts. Most of the MoD records from that time are locked away from public view until the thirty-year ruling allows right of access. It is doubtful that by the end of 2021 anybody was maintaining records of any worth. By then far more pressing matters were facing a massively depleted staff.

Figures that do exist paint a distressing picture. Extrapolating from what is known to fill in the many blanks – or give an alternative to the obviously fantastical – doesn't make the picture any brighter.

By the kindest estimates the British army was at less than thirty percent capacity by the start of 2022. This figure was to fall further still, even after the radical reordering of military practice to stop the intra-force spread of HV-Tg.

After destroying much of the southern half of the country, Toxo edged north. The demoralised and overstretched services found themselves fighting their own countrymen, with a lack of resources and in conditions no one had prepared them for.

Figures for the rates of desertion are unavailable. However, Karl Sanderson's infamous article in *The Times* (later syndicated across most of the US and African news outlets), suggests unprecedented numbers of men and women abandoned their posts. The UK Government's refusal to grant an amnesty for the period covering the officially-recognised national crisis has done little to clarify the picture.

At the time of writing, public feeling towards the military continues to be mixed. Attempts to cover up the shooting of civilians at the start of the Lockdown have resulted in a prolific rumour mill. The resultant stories have turned a tragedy into an atrocity. The wealth of urban myths concerning the actions of uniformed men and women is startling in its brutality and profligacy.

The stories of Captain Clark-Billings and his rogue battalion are a case in point.

Americans always ask about guns. We had a few, maybe three or four. We wouldn't have had much use for them if we'd had more. The fighting we had to do was close quarters, face to face. Start shooting off guns in that set-up and all you're going to do is kill your own people. If the Outbreak had reached the USA, they'd have lost more people to friendly fire than Gonzo, believe me. The biggest killer in those days wasn't the disease or the psychos, it was stupidity.

May 2nd, 2021

The sounds of gunfire started shortly after dawn. At first, two or three isolated shots, then a more concentrated and rhythmic pattern. Short bursts from automatic weapons. The distant firefight lasted until the sun was fully up. The rhythm barely deviated; the level of control suggested discipline and training.

"Army?" someone asked.

The whole group were awake. Most of them were gathering at the windows on the fourth floor. There was a strange buzz in the air, swinging between excitement and fear. The only ones not looking over to the skyline across the river were Miller and a half dozen of his more devoted followers. They were busy with their morning rituals, content as long as their idol was. Miller seemed oblivious, aware only of the sound of his blades against the steel.

"Is it the army?" Same voice, belonging to the woman Johnno constantly trailed after.

Robertson knew the face but hadn't bothered to learn a name to put with it. She had a collection of black feathers stitched along the shoulders of her jacket. He was about to tell her to shut up when Maccallan answered her.

"It must be. Who else would turn up with a pair of helicopters?"

The two Chinooks had appeared when it was still dark. The air was still and damp; the hollow thumping sound of the machines had rolled over the river and bounced against the glass frontage of the office building. Robertson had already been awake and had seen them drawing in from the north long before he heard them. After the months of seeing nothing in the sky other than crows, the light-studded shapes were hypnotic. He'd watched their progress without thought until they settled across the river, over the illuminated section of the city. Then he'd woken Sol.

As soon as they'd found the building, Sol had set up camp in an oversized office that had been designed to display status. Robertson had commented that it had been better furnished than his flat. The old man had barked out a laugh.

"They say crime doesn't pay."

He'd sounded angry. Rather than walk round a glass-topped table, he'd overturned it. When the thick carpeting cushioned its landing and the glass hadn't shattered, Sol had sworn at it.

Robertson had noticed Sol's mood changing as they got closer to the river. The crumbling affluence they passed through seemed to amuse or enrage him in turns.

He'd laid out his bedding on a sofa upholstered to match the leather-topped desk. The comfort it offered was the only thing about the office that hadn't annoyed him; even then he'd managed a bitter remark about sleeping where the boss-man would have been screwing the secretary.

Sol had cursed him when he shook him awake, waving the torch beam away from his face.

Robertson cut across the tirade, "There's two choppers hovering across the river."

Sol had fallen silent and thought for moment.

"They above the bank?"

"Can't tell from this distance, but they're hovering over the area where the power's on."

Sol's face screwed up, in thought or pain; Robertson couldn't tell. After what felt like a long time he relaxed and turned away. Talking to the sofa cushions rather than Robertson, he said:

"So, you want I should do what? Fly over and scare them off?" He pulled himself deeper into his sleeping bag. "Go back to sleep. You want company to worry with? Wake up Maccallan."

Robertson had a moment of white-hot anger. He swallowed it down but knew he'd come close to slamming the heavy torch into the back of Sol's head.

For all his professed indifference, Sol hadn't been long in joining Robertson on the fourth floor. One of the Chinooks had remained on point, wavering slightly over a fixed spot. The other was describing a tight circle around the area. Spotlights cast beams from the machine's belly, even though daylight was beginning to appear along the horizon.

"Has Maccallan seen this?"

Sol spoke quietly. The steady pulse of the engines had woken others and they were pressed against the glass. Some of them were chattering nervously, waking others. Robertson shook his head.

"You're right, there's nothing we can do."

"I think we should tell him," Sol said.

"Then you go and fucking tell him."

It was then the guns had started. Within a minute the whole group, including Maccallan, was awake.

"Why are they here?" Robertson resented being the one to ask the question. The implication was that it was Maccallan and Sol who'd have the answers. The three of them had moved to the roof of the office block. Johnno was stationed at the base of the access stairs, maintaining their privacy.

"I'd guess they're collecting the bullion," Sol said.

Robertson looked directly at Maccallan, "You thinking that?"

"Yeah, I can't see what else they'd be doing."

"It doesn't really matter what they're doing. The question is, what do we do?" Sol said.

"I think that might be out of our hands," Maccallan said, then fell silent.

It was a trait Robertson remembered from the days of working under the man: introducing a subject but not volunteering any information on it, compelling people to ask. He had another sudden surge of anger, the way he had when Sol had initially dismissed his concern about the Chinooks.

Maccallan had subtly changed his position. They were near the edge of the roof, still watching the helicopters, but Maccallan had shifted. Moving no more than half a step, he'd managed to set himself apart just enough to be slightly to the front. Robertson let the anger cool and turned to see if he could judge Sol's reaction. Not unusually, all he could tell was that the gears were in motion.

The top of the building hadn't been meant for public access and the parapet enclosing the flat roof was barely waist height. Robertson stepped behind Maccallan, grabbed the back of his collar and bent him onto the low wall. One hand on his collar, the other on his belt, he tipped him past the balance point. Maccallan panicked, then realised he wasn't falling and froze, arms held out ridged, as if ready for flight.

Robertson leaned in as close as their odd position allowed.

"Nothing, absolutely fucking nothing, is in your hands. You get that?" When Maccallan didn't answer he inched him forward, "I said, do – you – get – that?" with each word another inch.

"I get it, I get it. I'm sorry, alright, I'm sorry."

Somewhere behind them, Sol cleared his throat. Maccallan's legs failed him when Robertson spun him back onto the roof. He took three faltering steps before allowing himself to sink onto his knees. It was Sol who broke the silence.

"Out of our hands, how?"

Maccallan swallowed twice before finding his voice.

"If they are running the power across there so they can pull out the bullion, they'll probably shut it all down again afterwards." He shrugged and looked helpless, then caught Robertson's eye, and looked frightened. "If they cut the power there's nothing I can do."

"Why would they power up a chunk of the national grid just to move the gold?" Robertson asked.

Maccallan's voice failed him and he had to swallow again, "It could be the vaults have time locks that need powering up. I don't know for sure."

"The gold reserves are kept underground," Sol said. "Up to five tons of the stuff. They'll need the lifts to work."

"There'd be backup power," Robertson said. "Emergency generators."

He was watching Maccallan closely.

Maccallan nodded and finally got to his feet. He was calming down again. As he considered the situation across the river, his breathing slowed, returning to normal.

"You're right, you're right they would. We could be worrying about nothing. If they are just here for the gold, they'll take off again once they've got it. We–" aware that Robertson hadn't taken his eyes off him, he clipped the sentence off and reordered it as a question, "–do you think we should just wait and see what they do?"

Happy with the submission, Robertson turned to Sol.

"Wait?"

The old man had his attention back on the other side of the Thames. One of the Chinooks was still hovering; the other had vanished from sight. The gunfire had lessened. The regular patter of automatic fire had become spasmodic. Single rifle shots could be heard again.

"No," Sol said, "we keep moving. Getting this far was the easy part. This close to the bridges we'll be knee deep in switched. Then we need to find a way to cross the water. What do we gain waiting?"

Chapter 21. Colours

Doing a Benny (Going Benny)

Slang within the British forces to describe the act of succumbing to HV-Tg psychosis. The term is believed to have originated decades before the HV-Tg pandemic among members of the RAF stationed in the Falkland Islands. Originally 'Benny' was a disparaging term for the Falkland islanders, being an unsympathetic reference to a character in a TV soap opera of the time. It seems likely that the term travelled back to the UK and continued to be used as a sign of disrespect. It is unlikely that many of the men and women using the term were aware of its origin.

Cat's Eye (Kitty's Eye, Red Eye)

A reference to the eye lesions victims (human and feline) display in the early stages of Toxoplasmosis gondii.

The A to Z of Gondii Names

Letter received by Laura Freeman, Head of Project Development, Lithograph Studios, in response to enquiry made to Julian Clark-Billings, Service#:78695312, Military Corrective Training Centre, Colchester (2028)

Dear Miss Freeman,

My apologies for the delay in responding to your letter. As a convicted member of Her Majesty's forces I am permitted only a limited amount of correspondence and so I have to give some consideration as to how best to use my allocated allowance. I must also apologise for the quality of this writing paper. Rationing of such items is still in force for miscreants like me.

I am happy to recount my part in the events that took place towards the end of the so-called Lockdown. However, to protect the reputations and, in some cases, liberty of others, I will refrain from identifying additional participants. I do not know the whereabouts or status of many of the men I fought alongside, and I fear naming them might compromise their security. I beg your indulgence in this.

I wish to state clearly that I take full responsibility for all actions carried out by the men of ███ company, the battalion during the period from 15/01/2021 to 20/06/2021. I was a captain in ███ regiment for three years prior to its absorption into ███. All my men maintained their loyalty to me, their superior officer, and as such should not be held to account for my decisions.

███ had been mobilised to ███ on ███. Until that point, we had been on deployment in ███ as part of the Iraq ground coalition. On our arrival in Peterborough it became clear that our battalion was one of the few untouched by the HV-Tg pandemic. Having been stationed in ███ we had no contact with the disease other than via news reports or communications from home. I believe I wasn't alone in feeling completely unprepared for what awaited us when we landed back in England.

We came back on a mix of commercial and military jets flying out from ███ airport. I remember the mood on the flight was very strange. Very few planes were flying by then and the airport had been like a ghost town. We'd had army transports to mobilise us from our base in ███. The withdrawal had happened incredibly quickly and there were concerns that Islamist fighters would try to pick off the vehicles at the rear of the convoy.

In the event, nothing of that sort happened and when we first reached ███ airport the mood was high. After all, we were going home. The mood faltered when the men realised we'd been taken to a civil airfield. I could feel the worry begin to settle in as the trucks passed the airport buildings. There were so few people there.

The car parks were deserted. The only activity I saw was in a sectioned-off area where a barbwire fence had been erected to contain people. I assume now they were refugees. There were five or six tents in there and I saw what appeared to be [redacted] police wearing flame [redacted].

The drivers had been instructed to take us straight to the planes. The tension heightened when we saw how crowded the runways were. There were scores of big passenger jets just sitting there and of course it was quiet, none of the noise you would expect at an international airport.

Our orders were to board our planes with all expedition. I can't give enough credit to the sergeants at this point. They knew how uneasy the men were by then. They used the standing order as an excuse to turn boarding the planes into a drill exercise. One of them announced that each platoon would be timed according to how long it took them to get from the trucks to their allocated seats. The platoon with the worst time would be on jankers for a fortnight once we'd landed. The sergeants set about screaming orders and double timing the men through the embarkation.

From arrival on the runway to closing the cabin doors, the men's feet did not touch the ground. No one had time to worry or think about how wrong everything felt. Once we were in the air it was different. The strangeness of the situation began to creep back. There was a lot less chatter and noise than I'd expected; the excitement of getting home was turning to unease. Obviously, something had gone badly wrong.

Once we were in the air the men were shown a short film about spotting the signs of HV-Tg infection. One of the main symptoms was bloodshot watery eyes. The air in that plane was thick with bleach and nearly everyone was rubbing their eyes and blinking because of the smell. Naturally, some wit made the connection and shouted out, "Effing hell, I've already got it". It got the desired laugh but the humour was forced. One of the sergeants asked my permission to let the men smoke. I agreed and about half the men lit up. There was a grumble or two from the non-smokers but I agreed with the sergeant; the smell of cigarette smoke was preferable to bleach.

Even with a cabin full of nicotine the mood became progressively bleaker. When we entered European airspace it was fully dark. It was a mixed blessing. On one hand it stopped us seeing the extent of the devastation on the ground. On the other hand, passing over at night made it clear how many major areas of population were in darkness, and how many fires were burning. By the time we were over the Channel, the plane was practically silent.

We touched down at the old [redacted] airbase. It was shortly before dawn and there was grey drizzling rain. Despite the mood, there were a few cracks about the weather. We were still in our desert fatigues and it did seem funny, in a desperate sort of way, to be landing a plane full of sand-coloured soldiers in the rain.

The sergeants did the same trick again getting the men off the plane, turning the exercise into a fast-paced drill. On this occasion nobody timed them. Later, a lot of the men told me that they knew they were being distracted and were happy to go along with it.

I've had time to think about things lately. Life in here, waiting for sentencing, is almost the opposite of what my army career was. I can't help but ask myself if that wasn't the appeal of the military, for me. There used to be a rather unpleasant phrase about enlisted men; people would describe them as being led from behind. I think it meant the regular fighting men were pushed into battle ahead of the officers, men like myself. Thinking about it now, I believe I was pushed just as much as any of the regulars. Maybe that's why I did what I did. Leading the mutiny was possibly the only time in my life that I fully took command.

I'd been told while we were still in ██████████ that on arrival we'd be put under quarantine for a period of eight weeks. That didn't happen. The men disembarked and lined up at the edge of the runway. We were waiting in the rain for ten minutes before someone came to collect us. It was another of those jarring points of discordance. Another captain pulled up in a civilian Land Rover that had been militarised by painting the word 'Army' along the side.

He drew to a halt about twenty feet away, opened the door and, without leaving the vehicle, bellowed, "Are you clear?". We didn't know what he was talking about. I took a step towards the vehicle and he slammed the door shut and made a shooing gesture at me. It looked ridiculous.

Of course, he was talking about the infection. Did we have HV-Tg? Shouting from his car, he told us to head to the ████████ barracks and pointed towards ████████ before driving away.

There was a certain amount of muttering in the ranks as we marched the men over to the site. You develop an ear for the grumblings and banter of the men under your command. It pays you to listen to it. What I was hearing that day was worry. In a group of civilians, I may have been inclined to call it fear, but these were men who'd seen active service in ████████ and faced lethal force, as part of their job, on a daily basis. But still.

I had expected a medical facility of some kind. Medical orderlies and brisk, no nonsense army nurses. What we arrived at was a standard barracks. The only things out of the ordinary were the streaks of discolouration on every surface and the smell of bleach. The sergeants began shouting orders and getting things put away.

While the men settled in, I went to make contact with the base commander. Given my orders regarding the quarantine I'd been expecting to be confined to barracks or at least an isolated area of the base. What happened instead was that I was intercepted by a sergeant in regular issue camo clothes. He looked over my desert uniform and quickly made the connection. He saluted and signalled that I should halt before we were within metres of each other and then asked if my men had any symptoms. I told him I didn't know because we had not had a medical assessment. By that point I was getting angry. I'd picked up on the mood of the men, and the strangeness of the whole situation was making my hair stand on end. I may have appeared aggressive because the sergeant put a hand on the stock of his gun.

It was an awkward moment, to say the least. I found out later that the base was running at less than twenty-five percent capacity. At the same time, the number of HV-Tg victims going into the psychotic stage was incredibly high. The term used on the base was 'going benny', I've no idea why. Anyone unknown showing any signs of aggression was very likely to be shot. With hindsight, I was lucky to survive the encounter.

I'll deviate from my decision not to name individuals at this point. The sergeant who nearly drew his weapon on me was . He was without doubt one of the most capable men I have ever encountered. His death in my opinion can be directly attributed to the mismanagement of airbase.

Eventually I calmed down and explained that I was expecting to be isolated for several weeks. Sergeant told me there was no time or manpower for that and repeated the list of symptoms to watch out for.

I was handed a set of standing orders: muster a group of twenty men to be picked up in four hours. The platoon's first deployment was to be riot control/guard duties at a local hospital.

I put myself in the first group of men as an observer. I'll never forget the briefing we received. We were told that in the event of encountering aggression or threat, regardless of the source, we were to meet it with extreme prejudice. No warning shots were to be given. What I found truly chilling was the advice to aim for the head. We were dealing with British civilians and being ordered to shoot to kill.

The base was twenty miles from . The platoon was driven out in two trucks. We left at 07:00hrs before it was fully light. It was the first time I'd been to that part of the country and I wasn't familiar with its usual pattern of activity. As we drove towards the town proper, I'd formed the impression that we were in a rural part of the country. I was shocked at size of the town we entered. The lack of traffic and noise was misleading.

We were met by a checkpoint on the main road. I was in the cab of the truck with the driver, not one of my men. As we drew closer to the town, he'd pulled a face mask on, not one of the army issue respirators but a small blue and white affair. Several of the men had them and I later learned they were getting them from hardware or DIY stores. Often, I'd see men wearing them or going about their business with scarves pulled up over their mouths. It was more an article of faith than practicality.

The checkpoint was manned by two squaddies. Their insignia identified them as members of two different regiments, the ████ and the ████. One of them was holding a Heckler and Glock and the other was behind a L111A1 heavy machine gun. Until we reached the checkpoint there had been a background mutter of noise from the back of the truck. As the driver slowed, I was aware that it had gone quiet. On the side of the road leading to the improvised gate were three hulks of disabled cars. They were all clearly civilian vehicles. One of them was burned out. It must have been sitting there some time because it was beginning to rust. All three cars were peppered with bullet strikes.

We'd been on tour so of course we'd seen burned-out vehicles before, as well as wreckage left behind from IEDs, but they were different. Those vehicles had been in context, the furniture of a war zone if you like. They'd also been in a foreign country. This was home, the place we came back to on leave to get away from the death and destruction.

We were waved through the checkpoint. I remember the driver lifting a hand in greeting to the man at the L111A1. The gesture made me feel ill. It may have been the banality of it. We were driving into a town on the British mainland and seeing bullet-riddled wreckage, and the driver was saying, 'how do' to a man with a machine gun.

The first two days we were active were largely uneventful. Our main duties were disposing of corpses and providing an armed presence at any point where trouble was likely to spark: anywhere official, or anywhere with supplies of medication or food. It wasn't until the third day that anyone was engaged. Two of the men had been sent to keep order at a health centre. They were to provide back-up for a nurse who was questioning people about their symptoms before they were allowed in.

A car pulled up with a man and woman inside. They half carried a teenage boy from the back seat. We were already familiar with the signs to look for and it was clear to the nurse, and both my men, that the boy was infected with HV-Tg. The long and the short of the story is the boy went benny on them. My men, to their credit I believe, hesitated before opening fire. The nurse was attacked and in the process of pulling the boy away from her one of my men was bitten. At that point, his partner did open fire. Of course, it was too late.

We hadn't experienced HV-Tg first-hand until that point. We'd been lectured on it since getting home, seen all the information films, and the posters were everywhere. But it's very different being told about something to actually seeing it.

The boy's parents became hysterical, which was only to be expected. The nurse, who thankfully wasn't injured, ran inside the health centre and locked the door behind her. My men ordered the parents away at gunpoint and radioed the incident in to base control. I happened to be there to hear the report coming in and jumped a ride with the crew sent out to the scene.

My man with the bite didn't want to leave his post. It was a macho thing and of course we didn't know what lay ahead. The 'medics', I use that term loosely, who were part of the response team were old hands. I hate to think how many of their comrades they'd watched die by that point. In the end I issued a direct order to my man to go with the orderlies. The remaining squaddie stayed on duty.

I accompanied the bitten man back to base. We travelled in the rear of a long wheelbase Land Rover, along with the body bag containing the dead teenager. Blood leaked all over the floor and the soles of our boots were resting in it.

The civilian hospital in ████████ had been attacked. I don't know the details about that, but there were a lot of lives lost. The army had its own infirmary on the edges of the airfield. It was a long, low, brick affair: typical military spec, ugly as sin and barely fit for purpose. It had hit maximum capacity weeks before we got there, and tents had been set up round the main building.

The smell hit us before we were out of the car. The only way I can describe it is roast pork. Except bigger, if that makes sense. It wasn't pork of course; it was the incinerator. Four men from my regiment had been assigned there. When two of them came to the car to remove the body bag, they were drunk. It wasn't uncommon. Men expected to undertake body disposal for long periods are often given a ration of spirits. It was battlefield psychology: keep them too drunk to truly understand what is happening.

The men assigned to disposal worked in teams of four. Two would be sent out in a truck or van to collect the dead. Two would dismember the corpses to fit them in the incinerator.

When we got to the actual infirmary, my man was told to report to one of the tents. It was where the increasing number of patients were taken. The reality of the situation was that new cases were brought to the surrounding tents and either died or showed signs of aggression. Then they would be bundled into the main building. A number were shot dead. All the medical orderlies were military personnel, and all were armed.

My man was led to one of the tents. As the flap was pulled back the stench poured out. It must have been all around us already, but the pork smell had blotted it out. I think it's possible that I had fixed on the smell of the bodies being burned and blanked out anything else until it became too intense to ignore.

It was unbelievable. The vilest thing I had ever encountered. In retrospect, I must praise the doctors and nurses who attempted to work there.

My man took a step back from the tent and told me he'd sooner take his chances without treatment. An orderly, a big man with the bearing of an MP, told him he had no choice. All infected personnel had to be registered and report for treatment.

Now, I'm inclined to think that orderly was in fact one of the Porton Down specialist research ████████████ company.

I was horrified at the thought of a man under my command being led into such a place, and when the two of them began to argue I pulled rank. I squared up to the 'orderly' and told him I wasn't going to let any of my men enter that pigsty of a hospital. I told him he should be ashamed of himself for allowing such a slack operation. And so on, and so forth.

In short, I exhibited the same attitude that I now blame for the mismanagement and poor handling of the whole affair.

The 'orderly' saluted and we drove away. I understand fully that my actions that day caused the deaths of at least twenty-four of my men, and I can only guess at the subsequent death toll after that event. If I could only meet that orderly again, I'd ask him why he didn't shoot me dead on the spot. I have my own theories on that. Soon after the new government initiatives and redeployment took place, there were rumours that the Porton Down facility directed the disease be allowed to spread in selected, observed areas.

We got back into the Land Rover, with all the blood congealing in the back, and I told the driver to take us to the barracks. Again, the order was blinked at, but no more than that. Looking back, it seems odd that men who'd been serving in a high-intensity area, under the most arduous conditions, gave way so easily.

Perhaps I'm becoming paranoid. I wouldn't be the only one around here. Prison does that to you. I suppose it's part of the punishment. It's not just about stripping you of your freedom, it's a way of rebuilding the person you are into something they deem acceptable.

We got back to the barracks. I took him in, and we dressed his hand with a field dressing. We poured about a litre of saline over it and every drop of antiseptic we could find.

It did no good. Two days later he had all the symptoms we'd been told to be on the lookout for. His eyes were puffed and red and you could feel the heat coming from him. I honestly didn't know a human being could produce so much sweat. When he started vomiting, he was taken back to the infirmary.

I wasn't there when that happened. They carried him over in the back of a flatbed truck. On the way he began shouting and waving his arms. The two men who rode with him tried to calm him down; it did no good. At one point he was trying to jump out of the vehicle, and they had to forcibly restrain him. In the process they were smeared with sweat and vomit.

At the medical centre a doctor told them to hold him down while he was injected with something, a tranquiliser I'd assume.

Over the next two weeks twenty-four of the men in the barracks went down with the disease. Five of them died in front of us; the others either took themselves to the infirmary or were forcibly taken. One took his own life.

I was told by a captain from ██████ battalion that my men had learned quickly and came off lightly because of it. At least three other barracks had men hiding their symptoms for as long as they could, or had friends covering for them. In two of those barracks a man had gone benny and run amok. At first the damage looked minimal but the injured invariably came down with HV-Tg.

Somebody on the base said something I found quite chilling. They described the events in the barracks and the spread of the disease as "a learning curve". As I say, I might be getting paranoid.

I think I'm correct in saying the ████ battalion was the last to be brought home from an overseas deployment. We had been stationed in ██████ from ████████ to ████████ personnel being on permanent rotation. At no point was there a time when a company from the ████ battalion wasn't on active service. In that time we lost ██ men. In the five months we were stationed at ██████ we lost three-quarters of our people. Of those I can only verify that ███ men are actually dead. The rest were taken to the infirmary for 'treatment' or went missing while suffering from HV-Tg induced psychosis.

By the winter of 2021 the feeling was that we were no longer maintaining order. It felt as though we were under siege. The men had no faith in the chain of command and I felt the same.

There was a lot of grumbling in the ranks. They say it's a soldier's right to complain. I agree with that. We ask a lot of our forces personnel.

While it's a soldier's right to complain, it's an officer's duty to listen. It's also common sense. No officer with an ounce of sense thinks he can run into battle alone. You listen to the men and try to hear the truth behind the grumbling.

The truth was we'd been abandoned. The high command, wherever it was based at that time, had forgotten us. We didn't really mutiny; we just took the logical next step and became an autonomous unit. The final order, or should that be the final straw, was the order to ████████████████████████████. To kill a man, or a woman, who had turned into a monster as the disease drove them on, was sometimes necessary.

Kill or die. Every solider knows that creed and knows they may have to live by it. To be ordered to kill your comrades as they lay helpless and in need of treatment, even for the most hardened men, was too much.

We gathered our remaining men and took what supplies we thought we could reasonably use. And weapons. It was pretty clear what was happening, and we met little resistance. What we did meet were men from other regiments who wanted to join us. Men from the ████████, the ████████ and the remains of the ████████ threw their lot in with us.

I have heard people making excuses for us: a few lone voices that may have understood some of what went on. Most of them talk of an understandable mutiny, but I really don't see it that way. We didn't desert or change our allegiances. We merely took the job of soldiering out of the hands of incompetents.

Stories that circulated about us are largely untrue. We didn't become brigands and thugs. The myths that have arisen about the insignias we adopted are wholly false. I'll admit we did paint the skull and cross bones on our vehicles but that wasn't a nod to pirate traditions as has been claimed. We were no longer members of Her Majesty's forces. As we were no longer under the colours of our old regiments, operating under them would have been disrespectful. The skull and cross bones held no meaning; it was merely a symbol on the side of a truck, something to gather under if you will.

I maintain we stayed loyal. The men maintained their discipline. They never stopped being soldiers. They kept their ranks, they saluted and obeyed orders. My men remained true; it was the world that went wrong.

I'm not bitter about being held to account for what happened. I'm proud to have lived and fought among those men. I'm proud and humbled that they put their faith in me and followed me. They never let me down and I won't let them down now. The situation in ████████ became untenable and mutiny was the only possible response. What does make me angry is the unjust way the stories about London have been told.

History will judge us, and in all likelihood it will do so more than once. Were we heroes? No, we weren't, and we have never claimed to be. Nor were we villains. What we did, many others did. Some others did far worse and are being hailed as heroes and kings.

Sincerely,
Julian Clark-Billings
Service#:78695312,
Military Corrective Training Centre,
Colchester

Chapter 22. In the Shadow of the Plant

April 7th, 2028

The phone rang twenty times before David picked up. I wanted to think he was caught up with some domestic task, stopping a pot from boiling over or cleaning cake mix off his fingers. Something that gave him a legitimate reason not to snatch the handset up before the first ring had ended. I even waited for him to offer an excuse, when he finally answered. There was no excuse of course, he didn't even say 'hello' in that hurried, questioning way people do when they're worried that they're too late.

And neither of us acknowledged that I was calling a few minutes later each night, edging the calls closer to the ten p.m. communications downtime.

Not that we communicated exactly. I asked how his day had been and he recounted alien events taking place in a world I'd visited once. Complaints about store owners who wouldn't take cash anymore, and insisted people used hand sanitiser before approaching the checkout. Delays on cryptocurrency transactions. Bitcoin to dollar exchange rip-offs.

I hedged when it came to talking about my day, hid behind words like 'confidential' and 'ongoing'. I'm not sure why. It allowed David the illusion that investigating the King of the Crows was heroic and charismatic. But for whose benefit?

We both admitted that we'd run out of conversation with ten minutes to go before the phone blackout. We'd already pretended indignant outrage at the seemingly arbitrary restriction on our time together. We did that at least once a week, both making loud and pointless noises about the British Government, the mobile networks, the gods.

David dug deep and came up with nothing.

"Shall I put Maria on?"

I said, "Yes," and closed my eyes.

I opened them again quickly when the blackness was filled with a mental picture of Maria, frantically mouthing, 'No, no, no,' and waving her hands at the proffered phone.

I watched the clock grind through four minutes. School, classes, friends. Names and events I should have been a part of but wasn't. I mourned the little girl I'd left five years before and mourned the interest I should have felt about the stranger I was talking to now.

The disconnect took me further from home with each word. Made them feel less a part of my life with each minute closer to the cut-off.

We hadn't had the conversation about official documentation to get me home in weeks. It always came back to the same thing, the same rant from David about the cost of lawyers and thus onto the rant, again, about stores that wouldn't take cash.

We hung up and pretended we'd have spoken longer if the restrictions permitted, ignoring the three minutes of 'precious' time still left to us.

I tried to read and couldn't. Then tried to get drunk and couldn't do that either. Both activities required an enthusiasm I didn't possess and getting drunk required access to something that didn't taste like cooking oil. For want of anything better to do I paced the floor, counting my steps.

I wasn't good with my own company anymore. Which was counterintuitive if I took the trouble to think about it. Something I avoided if I could. I'd worked my way across Paris, watching it burn and getting hardened by the heat. Lost Juan at the mouth of the A86 tunnel and followed Dog Boy into one of the worst decisions of my life. Made it through to the other end and carried on, with the dead weight of the injured.

I should have been a cross between Batgirl and Wonder Woman. The most self-assured, independent creature on the face of the planet.

But.

But, but, but.

I'd never taken on board the lessons learnt and hadn't totted up the victories. I came back to the losses, always. Juan, leaving us at the mouth of the A86. Dog Boy, staring at his leg and actually laughing. The irony of being spared Toxo, only to fall to gangrene, triggering some European vein of humour that was beyond me.

I'd reached a count of 509 steps when someone knocked on my door. I stopped mid-step and nearly lost my balance. I waited, I don't know for what, then the knock came again. I went to the door via the bookcase and peeped through the spy hole. The lens was badly ground, and Winslow was a distorted caricature, his mouth dragging the rest of his face behind it. He knocked again and I recognised the rhythm.

One, two. One, two. One, two.

I began unlocking the door and realised I was still holding Dog Boy's pistol.

I called, "Just a minute," and returned the gun to its hiding place.

My rank in the Washington Police might have allowed me a firearms license but I'd never registered the gun and didn't want to risk having it confiscated if the permit or pass – whatever the British required – was refused.

"Richard York's turned up," Winslow said as soon as I'd opened the door.

"And good evening to you."

He waved my sarcasm away, "He's been murdered, over in Southwark. I'm heading there now. Do you want to come?"

Winslow had got hold of a car; an ex-squad unit that had been stripped of its rooflights and decals. It ran like shit and was insanely loud, the exhaust having fallen victim to the network of potholes that had once been a road system. Southwark was only a few miles away, but it took half an hour to get there. The program to clear the roads had been grinding steadily to a halt. The main thoroughfares had been restored in fairly short order by bulldozing abandoned cars to one side. The task of removing the wreckage was proving more problematic and we drove down a corridor of rusted hulks. Side roads were way down the list of priorities. Getting to Cole Street involved half a dozen detours.

Winslow nursed the car over the broken roads, cursing each time the wheels sunk into the cracked tarmac. What the tracks of the bulldozers had started, unchecked weather erosion and nature looked set to finish. The weeds growing in the cracks were almost level with the doors of the car.

At the entrance to a road made up of storefronts, about half of them burned out, Winslow said, "This is as close as we're getting."

The engine shut down with a noise like a death rattle. In the silence my ears rang. At the far end of the street, work had begun on demolition. Figures were milling around in the yellow flare of arc lights. It took my shell-shocked ears a while to register the bass tone of a generator.

A bulldozer and another tracked machine, with a pneumatic drill on a hydraulic arm, were the main focus of the arc lights. At the end of their day's work, both machines had been left on the mountain of rubble they'd produced. The thing with the drill on its arm looked precarious to me, but the figures I'd seen when I'd got out of the car seemed unconcerned. They were a pair of uniforms and a woman wearing a hard hat and dayglo vest. She watched Winslow and I approach without interest until we got to the edge of the rubble pile, then she became animated and started making self-important shooing motions. Regardless of the arc lights washing over the scene, she was holding a torch and she pointedly shone it in each of our faces.

"Go on, out of it, this is private property." Her voice was flat and pitched somewhere over talking level but below shouting. "Private property," she repeated carefully.

"Police," Winslow told her, and flipped open his ID with a fluid motion that required practice.

"You can't come in here." She shone the torch at him again. "This is pry-vet prop-per-tee."

One of the two uniforms, who had been balancing on the rubble alongside the tracked machine, appeared at the woman's side.

"It's okay, Mary," he said, and had to squint when she directed her torch at his face, "they're with us." He gently put a finger on her wrist and guided the glare from his eyes. With a hand on her shoulder, he turned her carefully round. "Why don't you go and check the genny's alright, okay?"

Mary nodded – slightly too slowly for anybody who understood what was going on – and cast a scowl at Winslow. The uniform softly vouched for us again and she ambled away, over the broken bricks and concrete.

When he was sure she couldn't see, the uniform put a finger to his temple and traced a small circle.

"Mary used to live around here. When the demo team turned up, she was sleeping rough in an old shopfront. The workmen sort of adopted her. She thinks she works here."

The uniform delivered the explanation without a trace of humour. It made me wonder what was waiting for us at the scene.

"Was it Mary who found the body?" Winslow asked as the uniform turned and led us towards the drilling machine.

The bricks clinked over each other as we trod on them. The sound was vaguely metallic, at odds with the sight of so much dust. The uniform stumbled and swore before he answered Winslow.

"There's an official watchman, not much brighter than Mary, to be straight about it. They gave him some radio gear, for emergencies. We logged the call at nine twenty. I was in the area and got here about five minutes later. Mary was the only one here, apart from the victim. The guard had done a bunk."

"Done a bunk?" I said.

"By the account Mary gave, he got sick and had to go." The uniform made a drinking motion and rolled his eyes. "We've got an address for him, a hostel." He rolled his eyes again. "The body's behind the big plant."

The 'plant' was the machine with the drill attached to it. The point of the drill had been left buried in the wall of the next building due to be destroyed. It was the outstretched arm that made the machine look unbalanced and ready to topple. I had to assume the operator had known what he was doing, because Richard's body had been dumped in the shadow cast by the angle of the machine's tilt.

It had been on the tip of my tongue to ask if there was any doubt it was murder. First sight of the corpse put such ideas to bed.

Richard lay on his back and, even in the restricted light, the massive wound on his chest was visible. Lacking anything to tap on, Winslow click-clicked his fingers a couple of times before asking if it was possible to reposition the arc lights. While the uniform went to see to it, Winslow pulled out his mobile and put the torch on. He made me jump by laughing.

"What's funny?"

He played the tiny light around the body.

"Look at us, joint Anglo-American policing task force. And crazy Mary's got a better torch."

I might have seen the funny side too, had the punchline not coincided with light from his phone landing on Richard's face.

His mouth had been forced open, and tufts of grass had been pushed into it.

Chapter 23. Inner Circles

MI.X (Mix, The Mix)

Reference to a clandestine branch of British Military Intelligence connected to the Porton Down research facility. There is no official record or recognition of such a branch of Military Intelligence, and little has been offered in support of its existence. This hasn't stopped numerous rumours and accusations concerning MI.X being one of the most discussed subjects on the internet. Within Europe, MI.X is the twelfth most common subject of internet search (statistic provided by Chinese search engine, Baidu). It has been suggested that this statistic is misleadingly low, as it does not include searches made on the dark web.

Porters (Dark Porters, Night Porters, Shadow Porter)

Members of a supposed branch of British Military Intelligence. (See MI.X.)

The A to Z of Gondii Names

Has anyone heard from Tor_t lately? Been very quiet for a while now.
Member:Triple3

****

The last posting I saw from Tor_t was on the Facts_U_Can_Keep message board. That was over a month ago.
Member:L_eyes

****

Tor_t's website has gone cold since he posted that piece about MI.X poisoning the cannabis supplies.
Member:Trooth_Fairy

****

He was getting close to something.
Member:Triple3

****

Yeah, that stuff about the poison weed makes a lot of sense. A good friend of mine picked up some weed in Salisbury about three weeks before he went down with Gondii Tee. That dude smoked every day of his life and nothing. Then three weeks after smoking Salisbury Pure he gets sick.
I reckon Tor_t got TOO close to something.
Member:KittyLitter

****

We shouldn't panic. We don't know what's happened to Tor_t, yet. Remember, this site is about facts. It's a little premature to start talking about him in the past tense
Member:L_eyes

****

WTF, L_eyes? Read your own posts. The last thing Tor_t

wrote about was MI.X putting toxic cannabis on the streets. Then it all goes quiet.
U think that's a coincidence?
Member:KittyLitter

****
I just read Tort_t's article, it wasn't about toxic cannabis being put on the street. He was reciting a rumour that part of the Porton Down remit was to produce a herbicide that worked exclusively on hemp. That was back in the 1980s, when the government was trying to gain a monopoly on the recreational drug trade and wanted to put all the private growers out of business.
Member:Ma$k

****
Tort_t's posted stuff since that article anyway. I just re-checked. My bad
Member:L_eyes

****
Stuff has BEEN posted on Tor_t's site. That doesn't mean it was posted by him, dude. And how do we know that the article Ma$k read is the one Tor_t wrote?
All I KNOW is my bro bought an eighth of Salisbury Pure and was dead one month later.
Member:KittyLitter

****
R.I.P Tor_t.
Miss you brother.
Member:Triple3

****
Respects to Tor_t
Fuck MI.X and fuck the Porters.
Member:Hate_the_Lie

February 19th, 2021

The man, Robertson thought his name was Mel, had crow feathers worked into the hood of his sweatshirt. With the hood pulled up, the feathers framed his face. There were others in the room behind him sporting similar adornments. Before moving aside to let him in, Mel, if that was his name, paused. It was brief, no more than a moment. Robertson didn't realise it had happened until he was past the feathered man and inside the old boardroom. Once he had registered it, he filed it away in a mental drawer labelled: problems.

Miller was seated at the oversize table, deep in the embrace of an expensive leather chair. Nine or ten of his apostles, Sol's word for them, were hovering about. Three of them were dividing food between a collection of mismatched bowls and plates. The remainder were watching Miller. Some were intent on him, almost awestruck; others appeared more casual but were careful to keep him in sight. Most of them were honing blades.

The scene had almost become a set piece. If the group was holed up anywhere with a meeting room or a canteen, Miller would be led to a seat at the table and people would station themselves around him. It had happened half a dozen times before Sol had pointed out the apostles never guided Miller to the head of a table. He was always situated centre place. The way Christ was for the Last Supper.

Robertson was getting fed up with the old man's clever-clever observations, and Miller's bizarre behaviour. Corralling their 'leader' was becoming increasingly difficult. And Robertson was physically tired. The lookout, posted at the door of the building's grandiose reception, had dozed off in the small hours. He'd woken up when a pair of Gonzos had been on top of him. Robertson had been first to arrive at the screams. Miller had been close behind him, but even with the unexpected speed he possessed, both the Gonzos were dead before he'd drawn a blade.

The lookout was one of the apostles. He was bent double, his arms pulled tightly against his stomach. It had been a clear night; the blood dripping from the man's wound was cast black in the moonlight. Robertson had braced himself for the denials or the hysterics. Most people went for one or other, almost no one was stoic. No one counted the days they'd survived as a bonus; endurance was another addition to the tally of bitterness.

Five more members of the group had made their way outside to investigate the noise. They all had hooded shirts or jackets. None moved with any sense of urgency. Four of them stopped at a respectful distance from Miller and stood in observance. He'd started work on the Gonzos Robertson had killed and seemed barely aware of anything else.

The fifth figure was Johnno. He glanced at Miller and then made his way across to Robertson and the injured lookout.

"What happened?"

It wasn't clear who he was asking. When Robertson didn't reply, the man, still doubled over, offered his hands in explanation. The right one was supported in the left, forming a cup that was overflowing with blood. The moonlight hadn't been enough to make out the details, but it was clear that the damage was bad.

"Bite?" Robertson asked.

The man nodded and pulled the injured hand back to his body.

"I'll be okay," he said.

Robertson had felt rather than seen Johnno shifting his weight from foot to foot. He expected him to be watching the injured man, but Johnno was looking at him. He continued shifting his balance. Robertson felt a thread of unease.

"What do you think, Johnno? He going to be okay, you reckon?"

The way Johnno moved, and the hesitation in his response, suggested he'd been aware of Robertson adjusting the grip on his axe.

"We could get him some painkillers, Boss. See how it looks in the morning?"

Still bent over his bleeding hand, the lookout had begun moving towards the knot of people around Miller. As he neared them, one had broken away and gone to Johnno's side. It was the woman with the feathers woven into the shoulders of her coat, another member of the group Robertson couldn't put a name to. She and Johnno didn't touch, but it had been clear there was some connection between them.

"He's almost finished, Peter."

She'd addressed the statement to the lookout, who'd nodded his head in reply. The movements of his head were short and jerking.

The woman had stood in Johnno's shadow, practically in silhouette, but her posture made Robertson think she was watching the injured man with an air of approval.

He tapped Johnno's shoulder and took him to one side, walked him away from Miller and the hooded people.

"Painkillers?" he said. Johnno began the shifting from foot to foot again.

Robertson waited for him to say something. When no reply came, he leaned close into Johnno's space. "You need to take a piss, or something?"

He was relieved when Johnno backed away slightly, widening the gap.

"Boss, Boss, I know, I know, Pete's already dead, I know that. It's just …" he started shifting his balance again but stopped when Robertson made a sharp hissing sound "… it's just some of the guys they … they think Miller can sort of … keep them safe."

"Keep them fucking safe? From Toxo?"

"They've seen him going at it with the Gonzos, then the stuff he does afterwards. They think he's immune."

"And you buy into that shite?"

"No, course I don't, it's just …"

Robertson jerked his axe in the direction of the woman with the feathered shoulders, "It's just you're burying your brains in her snatch every night and going along with this crap."

"Look, Boss, maybe it's not a bad thing. People need something to believe in."

The wet sounds that had been drifting over from Miller, had stopped. Robertson had kept his attention on Johnno, but from the corner of his eye, he saw Miller stand and step away from the collection of parts he'd spread over the pavement. He was breathing heavily. The woman took Peter forward. They both moved slowly; it lent their motions a sheen of grace.

"Has this happened before?"

"They've got a couple of guys at the moment."

Johnno sounded the words out carefully; his intonation almost turned the answer into a question.

"They?"

"The ones who sort of hang out with Miller a lot."

"Couple of guys?"

There was a pause before Johnno answered, "Four."

"Does that include …?" Robertson jerked his head in the direction of Peter.

"Five."

"You isolated them?"

"Oh hey, Boss, it's not me, it's them."

"How many of them are we talking about?"

Miller and his selection of followers were making their way back into the building. The woman appeared to be leading them.

"About twenty, I'd say. That includes the … the couple that are injured."

Robertson watched the group walk into the darkness of the office building's reception.

"You take over the watch," ed told Johnno.

"Alright. What do you want me to do about that business, Boss?"

He nodded at the spot on the pavement where Miller had left the arrangement of bone and flesh.

"You do fucking nothing. Just stay awake and keep your eyes open."

Back inside the office building, Robertson took a few steps up the stairs and stopped, listening out for the sound of Miller's party. He could hear people on the floor above whispering enquiries about the noise. Someone, he didn't recognise the voice but assumed it was one of the men with the hoods, gave an over-loud assurance that all was well.

"No problem, all sorted; just some Miller Mince for the crows to clean up in the morning."

Someone laughed. Robertson waited for the sounds to move away before climbing the rest of the flight and finding the side room he'd set his bedding in.

He hadn't told Sol about the situation with the bitten and almost certainly infected man. He'd debated whether he would or not, but when he'd found Sol the next morning, he was already in conversation with Maccallan. Robertson wasn't in the mood to listen out for the subtext of his old manager's patter.

Miller and his crew, Robertson tried not to think of them as apostles, were on the third floor. He'd been spending less time with Miller lately. Conversely, Maccallan had been trying to gain the man's favour and was constantly engineering ways to put himself in his presence. It wasn't a position Robertson envied. He could see Miller breaking apart and was expecting something to finally snap. He'd regard it as a bonus point if Maccallan was in the way when Miller blew up.

Watching Miller, he could see why Sol had named his people The Apostles. The Last Supper comment had been on target too, though the messianic analogy ended at the collection of butcher's knives.

Johnno was there already, not quite in Miller's orbit. He was talking to the woman from the previous night. She had her back against the frame of a doorway and was laughing softly at something Johnno was telling her. He was leaning over her, supporting his weight by bracing one arm against the door jamb. Not especially short she had to angle her posture in order to fit under his outstretched arm. The lack of subtlety was lost on Johnno.

Robertson looked around the room taking note of the people wearing crow feathers in one way or another. He recognised most of them but couldn't put names to faces. A few were complete strangers to him, but four – five if he counted Johnno – were men who'd been part of the group almost from the start. One of them was eating at the long table. The other three, like Johnno, were busy being led by their dicks. There was no sign of the injured man.

The man eating at Miller's table, Patrick, had noticed Robertson and nodded a greeting to him. He'd pulled out the seat next to him as Robertson had approached. Robertson ignored the offer.

"One of this bunch got himself bit last night. You seen him?"

"Pete? Yeah, he's with the others." The pause before he'd answered was a blink-and-you'd-miss-it moment. Robertson didn't miss it.

"Show me."

Patrick stood, not without reluctance. As he made his way through the room several heads turned to follow his progress. Robertson was pleased to see that the old hands, the men he regarded as his people, had picked up on the tension and were watching what was happening. He waved a hand above his head, half pointing at Patrick, half beckoning.

Patrick led him to a door at the far end of the room. There was a heavy-set man to the side of it; sitting cross-legged, inevitably honing a knife. As they approached, he got to his feet and moved half a step to his right, not quite blocking the door. The frayed hood of his sweatshirt was pulled as far forward as it would go, almost obscuring his eyes. He hadn't sheathed the knife.

Patrick had slowed as he neared the man. Robertson hadn't. He looked as if he might barrel over the doorman and burst through into the next room without breaking pace. He stopped with less than a palm's width between their faces. At the edge of his vision he saw the knife hand twitch, but no more than that.

"You better get the fuck out my way, sonny."

A hand, Johnno's, reached from behind Robertson and patted the doorman on the shoulder.

"It's alright, Josh, we're just here to see how the lads are doing. Okay?"

He patted Josh on the shoulder again, this time directing him gently away from the door. Robertson was aware that behind him the room had quietened. There was only the teeth-edge hiss of a single blade running along a steel. When he was sure Josh wasn't planning on using his blade he turned round; Miller, indifferent or unaware of what was happening, was fine-tuning the edge on one of his filleting knives.

Josh was sitting cross-legged beside the door again, his knees poking through rips in his jeans. Robertson pushed the door open with his foot. Before walking through he placed the head of his axe in Josh's lap, letting the weight settle against the man's crotch.

"You stand in my way again holding a knife, and I'll cut your bollocks off. You understand me?" Back braced against the wall, Josh nodded. "I asked you a fucking question, sonny. Do … you … understand … me?"

More nodding, faster.

"Don't mind him, Boss. He just ain't speaking."

As Johnno spoke, he moved past Robertson, shuffling sideways and threading himself between him and Josh. Without intending to move, Robertson found himself inside the room.

The room was a smaller version of the one they'd just left. It had been equipped with a scaled-down table that someone had pushed against a wall, clearing space on the floor.

There were over a dozen bedding rolls laid out. Five of them were occupied. Robertson recognised Peter from the night before. He was curled on his side, with his eyes between open and closed. His injured hand was lost inside a mass of gauze. Thick as the bandaging was, it was still struck through with blood. Next to him was a woman on sodden bedding. Writhing in pain, she was attended by a man holding a damp cloth.

The three other patients were sleeping or unconscious. The one nearest Robertson was naked apart from a pair of shorts. Without needing to get closer he could see the swollen glands at the man's neck and armpits. There was a trio of scratches above his left eye, running down his forehead. One of them had bisected his eyebrow. Robertson took a step back.

"Those scratches, they from a Gonzo?" The man sponging the woman down glanced across at Robertson and nodded. "Then what the fuck is he in here for? He's probably riddled with fucking Toxo, just look at him."

The medic shook his head, put a hand on his own chest and tightly clenched it into a fist. Robertson waited for an explanation, but the man still didn't speak.

"He's not talking either, Boss," Johnno said.

"I can fucking see that."

Johnno put his hands up as if admitting defeat.

"No, I mean they don't speak. It's like a vow."

Robertson turned so he could make eye contact. He kept his movements slow, not trusting his temper to stay in check.

"A fucking vow?" Johnno nodded; the silent response might have been an attempt at humour. "You better start fucking talking."

Johnno made the surrendering gesture with his hands again.

"Alight, Boss, alright. It's Miller, see?" He dropped his voice to a whisper. "He ain't spoke for five days now. Some of these soft bastards have taken a vow not to speak until he does."

"So, what's all this crap in aid of?" Robertson jerked a thumb at the five casualties on their improvised sick beds.

"They think Miller can cure them. It's like I said: belief. It's a kind of faith thing, you know?"

"No, I don't fucking know. How long's this been going on for?"

"Dukey there got scratched at the start of the week. He tried to cover it up, but someone saw he was cut. They took him to Miller. We thought he'd tell him to fook off out of it, but he didn't. He didn't say anything, just sat there, not a word. And he ain't spoke since."

"So, what was that? A sign?" Johnno didn't answer. "And you were too busy getting your dick wet to tell me about this?"

"We didn't think it'd matter." It was Patrick. He was leaning through the doorway, keeping his voice low, the same as Johnno. He flicked a look over his shoulder before continuing. "Dukey probably won't last another day. We figured it would ... well, resolve itself."

"Well it fucking didn't, did it? You got five of the bastards now."

"What do you want us to do, Boss?" Johnno asked.

Robertson walked out the door and slammed it shut behind them.

"Do what you should have been doing all along: isolate that room and put a guard on the door. One of our lot." He noticed for the first time that Johnno had a long black feather threaded into a hem on his jacket. He pulled it free and dropped it. "And cut that shit out."

BROTHERS! SISTERS! DO NOT FEAR!
THE CHILDREN OF THE CROWS ARE HERE!

Medium: Oil based black paint on concrete, applied by brush.
Location: First-floor frontage of commercial tower block. One of the largest pieces attributed to Miller's group. It is the first time the identifier 'Children of the Crows' is used.
Date: Between January 2021 and March 2021 (estimate based on locations of other dated examples)

From The Writing on the Wall

As we got closer to the Thames, encounters with the infected became more frequent. We were moving towards a more densely populated area. More people, more infection, more switched. On the first day of the Lockdown loads of people had rushed to the bridges.

I have no idea how many people made it away from the Thames on the first day. If the size of our group was an indication, I'd say not many. A lot of those left behind would have been infected. Add to that the injured, plus the ones who'd already switched, and the numbers are frightening. We'd find or be attacked by Gonzos two or three times a day.

By that stage food was getting harder to find, so were medical supplies, bleach, disinfectant. The best policy, or so we believed, was to stay mobile. Closed communities withered.

We encountered plenty of streets that were barricaded with burnt-out cars or piles of furniture. Sometimes, we'd find a road that had been blocked and there'd be a warning sign that the street was diseased. That could have meant anything from a maze full of switchers to a cholera outbreak.

The signs were heartbreaking but at the same time wonderful. They meant a group of survivors was probably about to die out. They also meant that even at that stage somebody was humane enough to post a warning.

We'd never investigate the streets that had been shut down. It didn't seem likely that we'd find anything good.

As the number of infected we met increased the encounters with other survivors dropped off. Worse, was the number of people we began to lose. We had learnt the lessons about cross-infection, but it became harder to keep up standards as water and supplies became scarce. No matter how careful you were some things would get through.

It was hard knowing things you'd have shrugged off before the Outbreak could now kill you. A bad case of flu or diarrhoea, things that had been inconvenient, had become lethal. The worst thing, and this is another subject people don't talk about, was not being able to help. People had to not get sick. It was feeling like the end of days.

At the time we didn't know things were starting to turn around. South of the river there was no power and, because we stayed on the move, we seldom had access to generators. Even if we had it's not likely we'd have spent time charging up mobile phones and checking the internet. We believed all that had gone. And, even if we had got onto the UGOV site none of us would have trusted it. The government had let us down, the army had fired on us, medical science had failed us. Why would we listen to officials anymore?

Chapter 24. Burying the Past

UGOV (UHEALTH, UNHS)

Official website of the British Government from 01/01/2021. The united government (UGOV) site ran alongside the government's pre-Outbreak website (www.gov.uk) before replacing it entirely on 01/06/2021. Initially, it was a separate entity from the standard official websites, dedicated solely to standardised information and advice concerning the HV-Tg pandemic. It's companion sites UHEALTH and UNHS carried identical content but were presented as separate sources of information.

UMUG (ULIE, UDIE, URKIDDING)

Slang terms reflecting the public's lack of trust in the UGOV website.

The A to Z of Gondii Names

April 10th, 2028

One of my first memories of school is of a boy called Noah. One morning, during recess, he announced that his dad had taught him to drive and would let him use the family car on weekends. Another boy duly claimed he too could drive, then another and another. When Mom collected me that afternoon, I was chatting excitedly about all my six-year-old classmates and their wondrous automotive abilities. It hadn't occurred to me they were lying.

I wasn't stupid. If I'd given it a moment's thought, I'd have spotted the lies. The problem was I didn't really want to spot them. I wanted truth to be a constant, so I'd be able to accept things at face value. I held on to that hope for as long as I could, until I saw I was crossing the line between trusting and gullible.

I thought about that a lot in later years and decided it was why I'd become an accountant. Math provided my reliability fix. Columns of numbers don't lie, not unless they're corrupted by human error or deceit.

Some part of me still wanted to believe people, but it didn't stop me checking and rechecking the numbers they presented to me. But I always held on to a grain of hope that they'd add up. I wanted to be proven a cynic, so I could stop being disappointed with the people around me.

The more I worked with Winslow, the more I doubted he'd ever gone home excited and full of second-hand lies. He wanted suspicions confirmed. Maybe it made him feel superior to the people he got to arrest.

"Robertson," he said. The assertion was accompanied by with the tap-tap of his finger tip on the coroner's report.

Richard had died from a shotgun wound to the chest, delivered from close range. Death would have been instant. His heart had effectively ceased to exist. The amount of shot found in the body indicated two shells had been used. The even distribution of the pellets suggested they had been fired simultaneously, probably meaning a single shooter using a twin trigger double-barrelled weapon. All of which we might have guessed from just looking at the corpse.

More importantly, at least to us, was the examination of the rubble the body had been found on which revealed no significant amounts of blood or tissue.

Meaning Richard had been killed at another location. He had also had all the fingers of his right hand broken. The coroner hadn't speculated on whether this had occurred before or after death. Since neither myself nor Winslow could think of a scenario that required breaking a dead man's fingers, we worked on the assumption that it had happened while Richard was still breathing.

Tap, tap. Tap, tap. Tap, tap.

"Robertson," Winslow said again. "This connects to Robertson."

"How?" I didn't argue the point.

"I don't know, but it does. I can feel it."

Robertson was brought up from the cells with a mug in one hand and a PC in the palm of the other. Both men were chuckling at some private joke. It rankled me, as it did every time I saw it, but I could almost feel the heat radiating from Winslow's anger.

The uniform caught sight of us waiting to receive the prisoner and quickly put on his professional face. Robertson flicked a sideways look at him that he didn't see. If he had his hero worship might well have ended there and then. Of course, he didn't see it. I wondered if myself and Winslow were the intended audience for the contemptuous glance but shook the thought away as a paranoid delusion.

Winslow dismissed the uniform with a nod. I caught the man's eye and although I was probably no more impressed with his professional face than Winslow was, I told him thanks. I resented being made into the peacemaker.

Robertson took the mug into the interview room ahead of us and made himself comfortable at the table. Winslow and I sat opposite him. Winslow hit the record button but before he could state the date and those present, Robertson said:

"Aren't you bored with this shit yet? How many times have we been through this? You drop a name now and then or ask a stupid question. I wait for the punchline and then … there isn't one. You really should think about letting me go or at least telling me why I'm here."

"For the benefit of …"

"…the tape: April tenth, present are DC Winslow, DS Cross and Colin Robertson."

Winslow sighed heavily and started over. Robertson sipped his drink. It was coffee, real coffee. I could smell it now we were at the same table. Until he was formally charged Robertson was allowed the use of his ration coupons. Assuming someone was willing to take them to the canteen on his behalf. Otherwise he'd have had to suffer the foul ersatz garbage issued to most inmates of the cells. I remembered the passage in Robertson's book, about having his nose broken and losing his sense of smell. The real coffee aroma was wasted on him.

Robertson had seen my attention was on his mug. He took another sip and made an over-loud noise of appreciation. Then softly blew across the surface of the coffee, sending more of the smell my way.

"Don't you just love that smell?" he asked, smiling.

"I got more of a taste for tea since I've been living here," I said.

I was lying and he knew it.

"Ring a bell?" Winslow threw the coroner's report in front of Robertson.

He'd opened the report folder so an A4 photo of Richard York looked up hollowly. The image had been produced by a black and white printer. The picture's low quality made him look vacant rather than dead.

Robertson looked at it with a blank expression, squinting.

"Looks like Rich York. I worked with him before the Outbreak."

He pushed the folder back towards Winslow. It spun through a half circle.

"Mr York was arrested a few days ago. Breaking and entering, assault." Winslow had spoken without looking up from the folder as he sifted through the pages. He finally met Robertson's eye to say, "Looks like he was feeding a drugs habit."

Robertson rolled his eyes. He had been sitting forward with his forearms resting on the tabletop. Now he sat back in his chair and folded his arm across his chest.

"Am I a drug dealer now? Is that your latest idea?"

"When did you last see Mr York?"

"I haven't seen him since before the Lockdown."

"That would be more than six years ago. Are you sure about that?"

"Yeah, I am."

Winslow's head snapped up and he tried to nail Robertson with his intense stare. It didn't work; he'd either timed it badly or Robertson had anticipated the move. Either way the penetrating glare landed on Robertson's ear as he turned his head to yawn.

"Richard told it different," I said, when he'd finished yawning. "He was telling his arresting officer you and he were big buddies."

"'I'm in with The King of the Crows', were his exact words." Winslow said this with a sheet from the folder held in front of him.

I doubted he'd found the right page in the short time since I'd spoken, certainly not in a coroner's report.

Robertson laughed at us.

"Well, I am the King of the fucking Crows, and I hadn't seen him since I got the sack."

"Any idea why he might lie about it?" I said.

He laughed again. "I get letters from people, people I've never heard of, or can't remember. They all start the same, 'You may not remember me but …'. But they went to school with me, or they were one of the people the Crows 'saved'" – he put the word in finger quotes – "or their brother was one of the Crows. And then they all end the same: 'If you could just give me a little help with …'. I don't even read them anymore. They go straight in the bin."

"So, you're not going to be shedding any tears then?" Winslow said.

"About what?"

Winslow didn't bother answering. He pushed the folder across the table again, this time opened at a different photo. Robertson leaned forward, blank faced again and looking bored. He regarded the new picture without apparent interest and leaned into the chair again.

"Nothing to say?"

"You fellas must have one hell of an arrest technique."

The photo had been another shot of Richard. This time head, shoulders and torso, taken on the coroner's stainless-steel table. It was another sheet from a black and white printer, but the gaping chest wound left no doubt the subject was dead.

"You don't seem particularly upset," Winslow said.

"Why would I be? I worked with Rich over six years ago. I lost touch with him before everything went to shit and hadn't seen him since. We weren't friends, we just worked in the same place."

He didn't bother pushing the folder back this time. Winslow had to reach across to retrieve it.

"So, this means nothing to you?" he asked. He didn't bother with the pretence of studying the report this time. He just did his annoying tap-tap routine on the folder's cover.

Robertson leaned forward again the way he had when he'd first sat down, forearms on the table and his fingers entwined, holding his hands in place.

"I'm sorry he's dead. There, that's what you're supposed to say isn't it? Sorry, tragic waste, very sad. All that. But I hardly knew the guy. The time I spent with him was when we sat next to each other in an office and watched the clock together. We didn't bond, we weren't brothers. Since then I've fought in the streets with men and women who risked their lives for me, because they knew I was doing the same. We kept each other alive and we saw others die and get killed and go mad. Their deaths mean something. That guy? He's just a face in a photograph. Sorry."

He sat back again and folded his arms. There was silence for a moment, then Winslow brought his hands together four times, clap, clap, clap … clap.

"Very good. Never mind Malik Connally, you should have been in the film. Did you write that yourself? Beautiful piece of scripting, beautiful."

He wiped an imaginary tear from his eye. Robertson regarded him with obvious contempt.

"What do you fucking expect me to say, Lincoln? Give me a clue, eh? I'll give you the right answer and maybe we can get all this bollocks over and fucking done with."

"Okay, Mr Robertson, I'll give you a clue. Richard York got himself arrested and mouthed off about his connection with you. On account of us having a mutual friend, so to speak, we sat Mr York down, right where you're sitting now, and had a little chat. He told us, among other things …" – Winslow paused to see if there was a reaction – "… that your mate Maccallan couldn't wait to get shot of your services. Told us you were on his shit-list for quite some time. He also told us Maccallan was scared of you."

"So what? I used to work with someone I didn't like. A lot of people work with dickheads." He kept eye contact with Winslow but pointed at me. "Ask your colleague."

Winslow didn't rise to the bait and if he took offence, he hid it well.

"You see, Robertson, that's sort of the point here, isn't it? I can ask my colleague because, whatever she thinks of me, I'm still alive to ask. Whereas someone who didn't like you, and by all accounts you didn't like back, is dead. And the only one who saw that happen is you."

Robertson laughed.

"You know something, Lincoln? You are one of a fucking kind. I'm going to miss you when I'm out of here. Have you seen what's left out there? The last I heard the best estimate, the best estimate, puts the death toll in London at over five fucking million. That's just one fucking city. Go outside and throw a stone. Whoever you hit will have seen people die, know a dozen more that vanished into thin air." He laughed again. Humourless, the sound was one of contempt. "Is that why I'm here? Someone I didn't particularly like is one of five million corpses? Fucking hell, if that's all it takes, you'll need to build bigger holding cells."

"What happened to Maccallan's body?"

Extract from the screenplay of Year of the Crow. Lithograph Studios, California (2026)

EXT. PARKLAND – DAY

It is raining. POV is from inside a grave Robertson is excavating. Despite the rain he is wearing only jeans and a t-shirt. He is breathing hard and is caked with dirt. After watching him throw three shovelfuls of dirt from the hole, the camera spirals up to show the viewer the extent of his work. The grave is at least six feet deep and soil is piled high around its edges. The aerial view allows us to see the parkland is overgrown and choked with weeds.

Scene change. From a distance the camera tracks a line of figures moving across the screen. The figures at the head of the line are carrying a wrapped body on their shoulders. The only sound is the cawing of crows. A great number of them are circling above the procession. In a series of jump cuts, we close in on the figures at the front of the line, Chan and Miller. Both men are stony-faced. The procession reaches the grave. Robertson now stands beside it. He is the only one there and it is clear he alone has dug the grave. As the men carrying Maccallan's body begin to manoeuvre it to the ground, Robertson steps forward to take some of the weight.

MILLER

We can take it from here.

Robertson opens his mouth to speak but closes it again without making a sound. He shakes his head and insists on helping them lower Maccallan to the grass.

As they lie the body down, the cawing of the crows

changes, becoming urgent. From a tangle of overgrowth, visible over Robertson's shoulder, a zombie appears. Robertson looks over his shoulder and sees it a fraction after the viewer.

ROBERTSON
No! Not now, not here.

He stands and takes hold of the shovel again, then strides toward the approaching zombie. Miller moves to go with him, but Chan puts his arm out, blocking his way.

CHAN
He needs this.

Robertson is running hard as he reaches the zombie.

ROBERTSON
(shouting)
Not now you bastards.

He swings the shovel at the head of the zombie. The first blow slices its scalp away. The second blow cracks its skull open and it falls. Robertson continues beating the zombie. He is shouting at it and punctuating the words with blows from the shovel.

ROBERTSON
(shouting)
Not. Now. Not. Now. You. Bastard.

Cut back to the other mourners who are watching the scene blank-faced. Out of shot Robertson stops shouting, and the only sound is of the shovel striking home.

Fade to black.

Filming the funeral was pretty full on. The scene in the final cut is only a few minutes long but it's the part of the film everybody remembers. The atmosphere on set the day we filmed it was real intense, really … well, real, I guess.

There was one scene and after doing it I was in tears. Benny, that's Benjamin Cole, the director, wanted to show Robertson climbing back into the grave he'd dug, pulling the body of Maccallan in after him. He, Benny, wanted the symbolism of Robertson being willing to go into the grave ahead of Maccallan. Acting out the way he'd have preferred it to be, going in place of Maccallan, giving his life for him. It was a hard scene to film, technically and emotionally. They had a cameraman down below ground level with me. We used a weighted dummy, so it would look right as I pulled it into the grave. That thing weighed about two hundred pounds, and I was dragging it down from above me. Because I was standing in mud it was hard to get my footing, and they were spraying rain all the time we filmed. It took nine or ten takes to get it right. Either I'd drop the dummy, or I'd fall over, or the camera would get splattered with mud. Nine, ten takes. When Benny finally called cut and said he was happy, I burst into tears.

It was harrowing, I was exhausted and black and blue from struggling with the dummy and I was in character; I was putting my best friend's body in his grave, again and again.

And of course, after all that, it didn't make the final cut.

Is it true that the burial scene was filmed in the actual Hide Park, England?
Username:MovEElov

****

I don't know where U heard that, but it's not true. The whole film was made in the USA. Even the long shots of London were CGI. The set they built for the funeral scene is a replica of Hyde Park, where Maccallan is buried.
Username:4kneeK8

****

Is there any kind of monument to Maccallan?
Username:MovEElov

****

There isn't an official one, but there is a spot where people leave flowers and messages. There are companies that arrange shipping to England and arrange for someone to take tributes to the site.
Username:4kneeK8

****

My friend sent a tribute to be laid on Maccallan's grave. She used a company called Grateful to the Heroes. They've got a range of statues and plaques. You pick the one you want and the message you want on it. They arrange to have it put in place. They even take a photo of it, so you've got something to show people.
Username:Blambie

From recording of police interview with Colin Robertson
(10th April 2028)

Robertson - Maccallan's body? We left it for the fucking crows. Same as all the others.

Chapter 25. Wake up and Smell the Coffee

April 10th, 2028

Winslow wrinkled his nose at Robertson's comment about Maccallan's body. We'd known the answer already. Robertson wasn't a man given to sentiment. He'd snorted a laugh at Winslow's expression of distaste.

"Yeah, I know, not the way you did things up in the badlands of Lincoln."

Winslow was very still and quiet. No tap, tapping, no finger clicking. I wondered if there'd been a burial for his wife and daughter, other than smoke-blackened rubble.

"You know, Robertson, if someone offered me the choice of being you or being Maccallan right now, I'd be Maccallan. I'd sooner be picked over by the crows than be whatever it is you've become. I've met Gonzos that were more human than you."

Robertson didn't answer, except to square his posture slightly and give Winslow the hard-eye treatment. Winslow gave it right back to him and refused to look away. The policing instinct I was trying to develop kicked in and I checked the time. It was a full minute before anyone gave. It surprised me that it was Robertson. He broke the silence with a gunshot crack of laughter.

"I fucking knew you'd go for a staring contest, you macho prick. Did you try staring out the Gonzo you met? You wannabe hard-men are all the fucking same." He laughed again. "If you'd fucking lived it, the way I have, you'd know to keep looking around you …" and at that point he quickly cut a glance at something behind Winslow's shoulder.

Winslow didn't actually jump but his head snapped round to look behind him, as did mine. We both registered the empty space behind us as Robertson laughed again.

"Interview suspended at nine twenty-six a.m.," Winslow said and turned the recorder off.

I had a solitary ration coupon left for coffee. I'd been holding onto it for the last week, unwilling to give it up, juggling cravings against the fear of having nothing in reserve. Craving had become need, so I suggested we headed down to the canteen. Winslow nodded; his expression carefully blank. I almost told him not to let Robertson get to him but decided to keep quiet. We left Robertson in the interview room, with the door locked.

The building the Met had taken over was better equipped for food preparation than policing. Whatever the workers and executives of the establishment's previous life had done, they'd done it on a full stomach. The serving counter was easily twenty feet end to end and the surfaces were wrought with thick plates of some mottled brown stone that shone with the lustre of money. Surrounded by opulence, the Met's catering department served food fit for pigs.

In one corner, tucked away with typical British discretion, was the limited selection of items worth having. Food produced using fresh eggs or real meat, and of course real coffee. The few people who went there to hand over their personal coupons invariably looked faintly embarrassed. Those lining up for the regulation slop were allowed the pride of penitents at an altar.

By chance, as I was buying my guilt-laced caffeine fix, I spotted the uniform that had brought Robertson up from the cells. He was sitting alone with his own mug and the remains of a sandwich laid out on the table in front of him. I didn't give it any thought until I saw him take a sip from the mug with obvious pleasure.

No one else was waiting to be served but the woman who took my last coupon hustled impatiently as she poured the coffee. The coupons were issued in the form of a blocky book with detachable pages. You handed over your coupons and received your goods. All very simple. The books were printed on grey recycled pulp-stock. Cheap and nasty. The printing itself was another matter; that was delicate and hugely elaborate. Insanely ornate fonts offered such delicacies as 400g of dried egg or a single cup (150ml) of coffee that might not taste like shit. The only plain script to be found was the line of digits running down the left-hand edge.

The numbers were unique and said who the coupon belonged to and how long it was valid for. The sequences of figures were encoded and unreadable to the bulk of people using them. And they were almost never checked. The real security was the fancy lettering.

"How many coupons have you taken today?" I asked.

The woman found a cloth to wipe the counters with, sharp, busy movements achieving nothing. She was around twenty but harboured an ambition to be taken for sixty.

"I don't know, not many." She hustled some more, and I waited it out. "I'm busy," she snapped when she saw I wasn't going away.

"I'd like to see the coupons you've taken today."

She wiped again at a surface she'd already smeared with disinfectant.

"I'm busy."

I stopped the pointed motions of her cloth by putting my hand over hers. When I leaned over the counter, I could smell coffee on her breath.

"Now, listen to me. I don't want to see you unemployed, but I know full well one of the prisoners is sending up coupons to buy himself a coffee." I kept my voice low so no one else needed to hear.

"That's allowed."

She tried to sound outraged but was pitching her voice lower than mine, keeping the subject below the radar.

"I know that's allowed. What isn't allowed is accepting tips from detainees, because that can be construed as bribery. That goes for all police employees, not only serving officers. Show me the coupons you've taken today."

The coupons were kept in a tin box with no lock on it. They were worthless once they'd been exchanged. Scored through with red ink they were ready to be tallied up by the Ministry of Supply. She hadn't been lying about not taking many. It didn't take me long to find three with matching code numbers. I told her they were being held as evidence.

Before we went back into the interview room we went to the cells and asked to see the property Robertson had with him when he'd been brought in.

The plastic box contained what I'd expected: an ID card with a low-resolution photo that might have been anyone, a leather belt, a cell phone with a flat battery, a multitool that folded in on itself, matches, a bottle of hand sanitiser. His wallet had three banknotes folded into it that wouldn't have bought a dozen eggs. His driver's license was pre-Outbreak. The photo was better though it still took a little imagination to connect the bland-faced non-entity in the picture to the cocksure alley cat in the interview room. According to the dates the photo was eight years old. They hadn't been kind years. The last item was a key ring with three keys and a metal-bodied USB stick, with IRONKEY printed along its surface. And of course, the ration book.

"We'll be taking the keys and the ration books," I said, picking them from the plastic box.

"They'll need signing for," the special said.

He pulled an envelope from the box and pulled a sheet of paper from the envelope. Both were soft with overuse. The sheet of paper was A4, titled 'Personal Property Record'. There was the usual mass of official printing that nobody ever reads and spaces for prisoner ID, staff ID, dates. The texture of the recycled paper made most of the printing illegible. Impatience had done the same for most of the handwritten notations.

I signed for the keys and ration book and the special signed as well, adding the time, date and reason: evidence/investigation. He also noted how many pages were left in the ration book. The previous notations showed that four different PCs had taken pages from the ration book. The envelope contained chits signed by Robertson giving his okay. Either he drank coffee by the gallon, or he was a big tipper.

From recording of police interview with Colin Robertson (10th April 2028)

Winslow - Do you recognise this? For the benefit of the tape, I am showing Mr Robertson a standard issue Grade II Civilian ration book.
Robertson - Like you said, it's a ration book.
Winslow - For the benefit of the tape, would you read aloud the name on the front of the ration book I have just handed you.
Robertson - Colin T. Robertson.
Winslow - You're willing to confirm that this is your ration book.
Robertson - Obviously it's mine.
Winslow - Where did you come by it?
Robertson - From a Ministry of Supply office, same as everyone else.
Winslow - They'd remember you collecting it would they?
Robertson - I doubt it, they're busy places.
Winslow - Convenient.
Cross - Notice anything about your ration book?
Robertson - Can't say I do.
Winslow - For the benefit of the tape, Mr Robertson, would you read aloud the date of issue for the ration book I am giving you. It's inside the front cover, top right.
Robertson - It says, seventeenth of April, this year.
Cross - Can you explain how you came to be in possession of a ration book that isn't due to be issued until next week?
Robertson - Obviously there was a foul-up at the printers somewhere. Oh, my Lord, is this it, charge time? You keep me in a cell all week and all you can come up with is black marketeering? You pair of clowns.
Winslow - Mr Robertson I am placing you under arrest.

Chapter 26. Myths

C-man (Seaman, Seefer)

Certified Firearm Chaperone (CFC). Armed member of hospital staff. These were deployed throughout NHS hospitals in response to the increasing occurrence of HV-Tg-induced psychosis. Inadequately trained and supplied with ad hoc weapons, CFCs were responsible for at least twenty-seven shootings of NHS staff members. Effective from March 2021, the practice of arming hospital staff was discontinued in July 2023.

The A to Z of Gondii Names

Q: What's the difference between a Gonzo and a CFC?

A: One's uncontrollable, dangerous and should be put to sleep. The other's a victim of HV-Tg.

Joke told by A & E staff

Calais was practically deserted. Somewhere there's probably an account of what happened there, but someone else will have to find it. And read it.

I was tired by the time we reached the port. Not normal tiredness that comes from sleep deprivation and hunger. This was something different, sinking through flesh and bone and into the meat of my soul.

I'd forgotten whatever twisted logic we'd had for heading to the coast. I'd forget at times that I was trying to get home. I had a single photograph that I carried in an overpriced designer cardholder: David and Maria. Taken somewhere with a flower bed that I had to concentrate to recognise as mine. I'd had a program of checking the photo once a day, so I'd remember their faces. By the time I got to Calais I'd memorised the faces in the photo but forgotten why.

Life had become a series of random events, repeated at irregular intervals. Scavenge, hide, run, sleep, run, hide, check a map, scavenge. The parts merged into something less than its whole. People came, went, lived, died. All meaningless really.

I've wondered if going through it in a second language saved me from insanity. Then I wonder if I'm sane. I'd thought I was fluent in French, boasted, if only to myself, that I spoke it like a native. That level of linguistic command doesn't start at the tongue. You have to think in the language. It's common for bilingual people to think in their second language until they hit the numbers. Nearly everyone slips back into their mother tongue to tot up figures. Not me; it could happen in either English or French. I could divide five into quinze, multiply the answer by three and come up with neuf. I'd have said French was hardwired into my system, was as much a part of me as the colour of my eyes and the length of my limbs, but once I left Calais, I never spoke it again.

I only speak English these days, at least when I'm awake. My nightmares are exclusively French.

We headed to the remnants of the ferry port. The wind, heading inland, had been laden with soot. Dog Boy's face was smeared with streaks of blackened sweat; when he coughed he brought up wads of glossy black mucus. Once we sighted the scuppered hulks in the harbour, he stopped walking. No drama, no speeches. He just stopped, used the walking stick we'd found as a brace and lowered himself to the sidewalk. He tried to rest his weight on just his right buttock but couldn't. He gritted his teeth as his left thigh settled on the paving slabs. The ragged fatigues, which should have been baggy, were taut against the bloated flesh of his leg. The smell cut through the acrid mist of burnt air.

"I'm done." He coughed up another wad of black snot. "You know what hurts most? Knowing Juan was right." He tried to laugh but couldn't do it. "Do you think he's still alive?"

I tried to make up an answer but couldn't. Dog Boy was probably beyond caring anyway. We'd left Juan, or he'd left us, at the mouth of the A86 road tunnel. Quickest way from the city and on to the coast.

We'd probably gone less than a quarter of a mile before knowing we'd made a mistake. Why did we go on? On those occasions when I'd think about it, I put Dog Boy's determination to keep going down to male pride. Risking death rather than turning back and admitting to Juan that the tunnel was a bad idea. I remember being scared to turn round and make my way back alone. Juan had walked away before I'd even gone into the tunnel's entrance. I had no reason to believe he'd be there if I should emerge again. That fear, now, looks ridiculous.

I've heard accounts since of the 'Tunnel of Tears'; there are even rumours about another Hollywood movie deal. Whoever gets their name tacked onto a film deal, it won't be me. There were no heroics involved in what Dog Boy and I did. Hiding and cowering, we did plenty of listening to others who weren't lucky enough to find a hiding place. We weren't destined to be heroes. Our luck stayed with us that far at least.

We made it through without a scratch; I don't know how long it took. The tunnel is, was, ten kilometres start to finish, nearly all of it in darkness. Too tired to keep track and too hyped to sleep, we might have spent less than a day or more than a week in there.

When we came out into the light, surprised at the muggy heat, the last obstacle was the twisted remains of yet another pile-up. Survivors had long since left their cars or been pulled from them. The dead rotted where they lay.

Dog Boy, with an enthusiasm that looked out of place on his painfully young old man's face, pointed above head height. A dozen birds, I've no idea what kind, were performing an elaborate dance in the air. The beauty of the display belied the fact they were feeding on the flies. Dog Boy started to say something and then yelped and jumped with a twisting motion. There was a moment's panic followed by misplaced relief. Dog Boy had only walked into a piece of wreckage, torn into an edge by the forgotten impact. We dismissed the cut and took another moment to admire the swooping birds before moving on. The infection set in a few days later.

"I'm sorry," Dog Boy told me.

He'd given up. Whatever reserves he'd been drawing on to get this far were deserting him.

"I thought, I thought …" but he didn't know what he'd thought.

That we'd hop on a ferry and sail off? I accepted the apology he didn't owe me and sat next to him, resting my back against the wall. We sat without saying anything for a while. Then I said, "I wonder where everyone went."

He jumped. He'd been drifting into sleep. I could see it took a while for his eyes to focus on the world around him, longer still for him to make sense of what he was seeing.

"Looks like it was bombed," he said, and swallowed back a coughing fit.

I unscrewed the cap on one of our last bottles of water and offered it to him. He shook his head and told me to save it. When I tried to put it to his lips, he turned his head away, repeated the line about saving it.

"You need to drink, and we need to find shelter so you can rest."

"Save it, you need the water. I'm done."

I put the bottle against his lips and tipped it, so he had no choice but to drink.

"Come on." I got to my feet again and grabbed his arm. Even through the heavy police issue jacket, he felt hot against my skin. "Come on, on your feet."

He didn't move. In a film, a movie like *Year of the Crow* , it would have been the part where the plucky hero hauls their fallen comrade upright and throws them over their shoulder. Reality, as ever, failed to be so photogenic.

Dog Boy wouldn't be moved. He wasn't a great deal heavier than me by then – he'd lost bulk to the hunger of our journey while I'd gained muscle from the relentless activity, but lifting his dead weight was beyond me.

I gave in and slumped next to him again. He took the water when I begged him to.

"You'll make it without me," he said.

He fumbled with the catches on the straps of his rucksack, loosened them to their fullest extent and managed to shrug one of them off his shoulder. He gave up on the second and let his weight settle back into the pack. Then he began emptying the pockets and pouches of his uniform. The pile of treasures it yielded was barely worth the effort it cost him. The final act was unhitching his gun belt and letting its ends flop loosely on either side of him. Lifting his hips to pull it from behind him was too much.

He should have died then. Noble last words, grand gesture, ultimate sacrifice and then a quiet dignified passing. It wasn't like that. I doubt it ever is. He drifted back into sleep and I waited.

I'd seen others die, too many to count by then. I'd despatched the infected who'd attacked us, or the well who'd crossed us at the wrong time. But it was always fast. We left the dead at a run in the normal course of events. You didn't wait for last words.

Shadows began to lengthen. The stillness began to feel ominous more than peaceful. Dog Boy's breathing was slowing; more than once I thought it had stopped only for him to catch a breath and suck in a mouthful of air. When I tried to pull the gun belt from under him, he jolted with a cry and looked around him. Amazingly, he smiled, then mumbled something I couldn't make out and drifted away again.

The sky had darkened to a purple smudge when he started babbling nonsense and trying to stand. He managed to roll over onto his side and tangle himself in the webbing of his backpack. Groaning and crying for help he attempted to stand and fell heavily. Then he tried again. When he began to thrash and shout at the backpack, I grabbed the end of the gun belt and yanked it. It came with almost no resistance and I fell backward. The pistol clattered from its holster and was lost in the shadows. Dog Boy was still trying to stand and calling out to something I couldn't see. He fell heavily again and let out a cry.

I remember the feeling of disconnect as I looked for the pistol. The part of me that only remembers when I think in French might be related to that feeling, the separating of myself from what was I doing. As Dog Boy wept and cursed and tried to stand, I put my hand on the cold weight of the firearm. Someone, who was me, racked the slide, pointed the gun and waited for Dog Boy's scrabbling to face him away from me.

He was floundering, limbs doing little more than slapping the ground. But I'd seen the ones who'd switched and knew the disease overrode what their bodies told them. I'd seen them walk on rotted stumps, stride through shotgun blasts, screaming in pain and barely breaking their stride. When Dog Boy's thrashing placed him so his back was to me, I stepped as close as I dared and levelled the gun at his head.

It's another one of those Hollywood fallacies: the mercy killing.

When it's scripted, there's a shot, maybe a flash and then cut to black and silence. The first bullet didn't kill him. My aim, even at such close quarters, was off. Dog Boy rolled. Miraculously the motion freed him from the webbing of the backpack and allowed him to flop onto his back. The light had faded sufficiently that I was spared seeing the exit wound in his face. It was the only mercy gifted to the operation. The second shot missed entirely. The third finished the job.

Someone, who was me, cleared the chamber and put the gun back in its holster.

Nursing Times Editorial, Jan 2021

With cases of Human Variant-Toxoplasmosis gondii (HV-Tg) on the rise, recognising the early signs of induced psychosis is of increasing importance to nursing and auxiliary staff. This is especially true for staff working in accident and emergency units and paramedics working in the field. However, the signs of a patient entering an irreversible psychotic state are something all healthcare workers should be aware of. In the current climate of uncertainty, many HV-Tg sufferers conceal signs of illness and deny symptoms. Also, with the vectors of the disease not fully understood, it is possible for infected patients or potential carriers to be admitted to hitherto clean wards.

There is a lack of reliable information regarding the causes of the chronic psychotic episodes associated with HV-Tg. The limited evidence available suggests the time from infection to psychotic state has a wide variant. Unconfirmed observations have recounted time frames as short as twelve hours and as long as eight days. It is unclear what factors account for these variations. Less varied is the time frame for first signs to full episode. All accounts place the time frame, from initial agitation to full psychosis, at between two and seven minutes.

The most important thing to note for ward-based staff is the similarity between the early signs of switching (as it has become known) and those of terminal agitation. Unlike patients undergoing terminal agitation, sufferers of HV-Tg will find no relief from pharmaceutical intervention. It is vital therefore that any patient showing signs of terminal agitation be treated immediately with high-dose pharmaceutical intervention. If this is not effective it should be assumed that HV-Tg-induced psychosis is occurring. Until HV-Tg-induced psychosis has been ruled out, the presence of a CFC is essential.

Chapter 27. Chains of Command

April 11th, 2028

The super didn't like me. I didn't take it personally; he would have felt the same about any member of a foreign police force that happened to be foisted on him. He didn't like Winslow either.

"So, this is it?" He held up the charge sheet. "You've had a national hero in custody for a week and we're going to charge him with black marketeering." Winslow opened his mouth to speak but the super's look made him shut it again. "Black marketeering, to the tune of a single ration book. A civilian ration book."

There was a pause that dragged on until it was clear one of us was expected to answer.

"Yes," I said.

I was the ranking officer. If there was a shit-storm to weather, then I was the one to weather it. Which sounds noble. The truth was I knew Superintendent Taylor hated dealing with me and I had no desire to make him comfortable. Given the choice, he'd have ignored me altogether. But choices in this brave new world were rationed out almost as strictly as real coffee and petrol.

I tried to picture Taylor pre-Outbreak. It was something I found myself doing a lot; it was becoming a habit that annoyed me more each day. It was another of those things that put everything around me at a remove, and that provided an element of comfort that was as false as any child's fairy tale. It didn't make any difference if Taylor had been a kind and generous soul with a ready laugh and a love of life before the Outbreak. The version of Taylor I had to deal with was a cheerless and bitter man with responsibilities wider than his shoulders. Like so many of the people I met in London, he'd cheated death only to be cheated by life.

He wasn't a leader. No matter how big the room he'd commandeered was.

"Yes?" He repeated my answer back to me. Everything he'd said so far had obviously been rehearsed. Whatever reply he'd been prepared for, 'yes' wasn't it.

The office was another example of the building's grandiose design. It was the ideal setting for reminding subordinates of their place. Taylor was so taken with the idea of being on the other side of that equation that he was blinded to the irony. The double aspect windows where a parade of chief executives had looked out over miles of hyper-expensive real estate – imagining it was all a reflection of their achievements – now looked out over ruins.

The great reclaiming process, a natural follow-on from the fabled, and largely mythical, Takeback, had yet to start. The huge machines like the one overshadowing Richard York's body weren't building anything. They were still in the process of pulling down the husk left by the violence and neglect. The people moving through the streets of the capital were on a par with Robertson's crows, doing nothing more than stripping a corpse. The other irony lost to Taylor was the shallow splendour of the office. Even in its heyday, it would only have bolstered egos equally lacking in depth. The whole of the building we were occupying was in the shadow of taller buildings. Glass-sided monoliths that put me in mind of vertical aquariums. In comparison we were in a goldfish bowl.

"Yes?" Taylor said again.

I didn't know his personal history, but his bearing made me think he'd missed out on the worst of the hand-to-hand slaughter. Robertson was right: everyone had a sob story. Losses to mourn or question marks over gaps in their family. People who'd fought and killed didn't have a monopoly on suffering or trauma. But as a rule, they didn't try to scare people with a hard stare or a harsh word. They knew threats could be either ignored or acted against. Speculating about survival is very different from the day-to-day grind of fighting for it.

Winslow was another case in point.

"Sir, I think …"

And we were back on script.

"Oh, you think do you? Well I'm glad to hear it. But I'm going to tell you what I think. I think you have wasted your time. And the time of your suspect. And, most importantly, my bloody time."

He stood at that point and brought the flat of his hand down on the overbearing-by-design desk he was behind.

Winslow and I both missed our cues and failed to jump.

"DC Winslow was acting under my instructions," I said, largely to the side of Taylor's head. He was busy giving his best stare to Winslow. Now he turned the stare on me.

"In future, I suggest you try to remember the chain of command."

I moved forward a step. I was already on my feet; the chairs in the room were all stationed on Taylor's side of the desk and were clearly invite-only. I leaned into his space, deliberately getting too close.

"This operation is a joint force undertaking, Superintendent Taylor. You might do well to remember that."

Taylor drew himself up to his full height and I had to force myself not to roll my eyes. Instead I cut a sideways look at Winslow. It was less confrontational and quicker, which was all I cared about really.

Taylor's backdown was so sudden it was comical. Pre-Outbreak I would have laughed, but the post-Outbreak version of me didn't have a sense of humour, so it was just pitiful. Except pity had died alongside humour. Both of them mouldered in unmarked graves along with the spent cartridges from a French police pistol.

"What was that all about?" Winslow said once we were out of Taylor's office.

Before we were clear of the doorway Taylor had bellowed for his secretary. The man stationed at the modest desk outside the immodest office was a civilian, tagged with an ID declaring him an auxiliary. He answered the bellow with the resigned expression of a man protecting a job. He had a similar presence to Robertson, watchful and detached. Preloaded was the way I thought of people like him. Not exactly stressed but waiting to be. I suspected he was just a few bad days away from falling into a pit of memories that wouldn't give a soft landing. I suspected too that I looked that way.

"Taylor being a jerk." I told Winslow.

"That wasn't what I was talking about."

I was going to tell him I didn't know what he meant, but maybe some cord of preload snapped under the strain and I motioned him to follow me.

It was getting cold outside as the evening drew in. The thing I missed most about home was the weather. Tricks of my memory no doubt, but in my mind the weather, stateside, was more decisive. It was raining or it was sunny; if it was snowing, white flakes landed and settled, and you could hear them crunch under your boots. England's skies seemed to be a constant variation on the theme of off-white smeared with grey.

Winslow pulled a rectangular tin from his coat pocket once we were on the sidewalk. It opened to reveal a dozen of the thinnest cigarettes I'd ever seen. When he saw me scrutinising them he asked if I smoked. That peculiar British habit of paying lip service to generosity. I was tempted to say yes out of meanness. I only rose above the instinct to see myself in a better light. He covered his relief well.

"Only good thing to come out of this," he said, slipping the mean tube of paper between him lips. "I'm smoking less."

It was the closest he came to making a joke at his own expense.

"If I ever get back home, I'll send you a carton of Marlboros."

He put a light to the end of the tube and sucked on it as delicately as a maiden aunt sipping sherry. The self-rationing still used almost an eighth of the roll-up.

"That the goal? Back to the US of A?"

"There's nothing for me here," I said. Winslow nodded and teased a little more smoke into his lungs. Held his breath to trap whatever hit the tiny measure of nicotine was producing. "I guess it's different for you. This is your home turf – you've got history here."

"Not really. This isn't history is it?" He waved a hand at the street we stood in. "It's ruins and graves. Where we grew up just doesn't exist anymore. This is something else."

I could imagine how this scene would have played out in the film. I would say something poignant and noble about building a new future. Cue someone, Chan or Robertson, breaking the tension with a witty aside. Then there'd be a zombie to deal with before anyone had time to question the triteness of the whole spectacle.

Winslow finished the cigarette off with one good draw, and a look of satisfaction briefly passed across his face. I looked away. It was an unguarded moment and I didn't want to intrude.

"So why did Taylor back down so quickly?"

"This stays between us, you understand?"

"Scout's honour."

He did a funny salute putting two fingers to his forehead.

"This joint ops situation between the Washington State Police and the Met, the official line is that I have superiority at the investigation level, but Taylor has overall authority."

"I take it there's an unofficial line, then."

"The official unofficial line is that Taylor is on an equal footing with his counterpart in the Washington PD."

"The official unofficial line?"

"Yeah, it's a sop to smooth all the ruffled feathers. The bottom line is Washington is calling the shots. The only reason Robertson was brought in is because I said so."

Winslow sighed and muttered a curse. I couldn't say I blamed him. The flimsy thread of aid coming from the US to the UK was a source of embarrassment to people and government alike. As was the knowledge that the only thing the UK had to offer was obedience. The low-level resentment was underpinned by the knowledge that the special relationship was as fragile as a Fabergé egg and nowhere near as valuable.

"So, why are the Yanks so keen to see Robertson in the frame? Don't get me wrong, I want to see him go down, but really … what does it matter? Maccallan's just one more body."

He looked around the street. The building opposite was a shell. Gutted by fire it was held up by a series of timbers, doubtless pulled from other ruined properties, wedged into the brickwork at angles. Most of the timbers were smoke-blackened. It wasn't a restoration; they held the collapse in check until it could be dealt with in an orderly way. Winslow was right: it wasn't history.

"Beats me," I lied.

February 20th, 2021

Johnno approached Robertson carefully, stopping at the foot of the stairs and calling up to him.

"Alright, Boss?"

Robertson looked and beckoned the man forward, without speaking. He was sharpening his axe by grinding it against the concrete step he was sitting on. It was something he'd taken to doing in private. It distanced him from the people sharpening blades as an act of worship, eager to show their piety to the world.

Johnno made his way up the steps. It was getting late and the light from the open door at Robertson's back was fading. Even so, the big Scouser turned his torch off. Batteries were still relatively easy to find but people, at least some of them, were beginning to obsess about consumable items.

The increasing shortages of fresh foods and medicines were becoming a worry. Though not among Miller's band of acolytes. Warm in the embrace of their 'faith', they didn't worry.

Robertson made no move to stand and Johnno stopped a few steps down from him, so their heads were on a level. He said a name that Robertson didn't recognise. Said it in a way that implied he should, then added he was dead.

"You were right about the Toxo. Bastard switched."

"We talking about the kid with the scratches?" Robertson ran his fingertips down his own forehead. Mimicking the placement of the wound he'd seen in the 'sickbay' Miller's followers had set up.

"Yeh, Dukey." Johnno said, an edge of impatience in his tone. "He switched over first light this morning, he …"

"First light? Is it dealt with?"

"Yeah, but …"

"But, fucking what? Did you deal with it?"

Behind him, on the rooftop, he could hear Sol and Maccallan talking. He couldn't make out what was being said but it was beginning to grate on him anyway. Getting the details of their conversations after the event was close to becoming the norm. Now Johnno was giving him hand-me-down information.

Johnno took a step back. Then maybe realising it put him at a disadvantage, he climbed the last few steps and stood on the landing.

"I didn't get a chance to deal with it. Miller took him out. I got told all this after the event, alright, Boss?" When Robertson didn't reply he said again, "Alright?"

Robertson stood up and put himself close to Johnno, close enough that the man tried to back away. He couldn't, his back was against the wall of the stairwell. From somewhere below, on the flights of stairs, sound drifted up. There were others down on the unlit confines of the steps.

"You bring a few friends along?" Robertson asked, his head tilted to one side as he listened.

"No. Boss, whoever's down there, they ain't there for me."

Robertson carried on listening to the sounds. After a while they became more defined. Two voices. One sounded female and a shrill giggle confirmed it. Shortly after, whatever words were being exchanged were replaced with urgent breathing.

He took the heavy-duty torch he carried from its belt loop and shone it down into the dark. A few floors below he could make out the pale outline of naked legs.

"Fuck off," he shouted.

The legs scrabbled from view and someone, male, shouted back, "What do you think we're trying to do?" There was another giggle and a door slammed.

"What happened?" he said to Johnno.

"Dukey went for the other patients."

"You had them isolated by then, yeah?"

"Yeah …"

"Go on."

Johnno was shifting his weight; his signature move when he was nervous.

"Miller took Dukey out. When it kicked off in the sickbay, he was in there like a shot. He practically took Dukey's head off. Then … you know, did his thing."

"All of them?" Robertson already knew the answer.

Johnno shook his head. "When he'd finished, he just sat down watching the four wounded guys. Someone asked him if they should take care of the others. He finally spoke. He said, 'Leave them, they'll change'."

"And where the fuck where you while all this was going on?"

"I was asleep. Patrick saw it going down. He only came and got me when the dust had settled."

"So, where's Miller now?"

"He's still down in the sickbay, waiting for 'em to switch."

More shifting his weight. Robertson realised he'd been inching forward, getting closer and closer to Johnno. He backed off and took a deep breath, forcing himself to calm down.

"Aw, fuck it. What's it matter? They'll go Gonzo, he'll hack them up. Problem solved." Johnno didn't reply. "Oh, for fuck's sake, what else?"

"The soft bastard's doing the vow of silence bit." Johnno hesitated, watching Robertson, trying to gauge the coming reaction. "Well, now he's talking again they dropped the vow of silence, but they're just repeating what he said, 'They'll change, they'll change,' over and over. It does your head in, Boss, I'm telling you."

Robertson muttered an oath, "They still follow Miller, though?"

"Yeah, but that's not all. A couple of them are sat in the room with him. They're with the wounded ones, waiting for them to switch over. It's like they want to go too."

"And the body? This Dukey that got minced?" Johnno didn't answer, which told the story. "The body's still in there, yeah?" More silence, other than the creak of boot leather as Johnno shifted his weight back and forth. "Fuck's sake."

"I wanted to take it out, Boss. I tried to tell them, but they won't have it. It's down to Miller. If he says he wants it moved, it'll move. Otherwise ..."

"Is Miller clean?"

"Yeah, Ally went in to him and washed him, soap, bleach, the works. The works, Boss."

"Ally? She that bird you been knocking off? The one with all the fucking feathers?"

"Aye, Boss, that's her."

Johnno had paused before the reply. Robertson took another deep breath and let it go. He wanted to speak slowly and enunciate the words clearly, so Johnno would understand the risks and take on board how serious the situation was becoming. But when he spoke the words came in a rush.

"Right, so we've got a torn-up and infected corpse, in the building, rotting as we speak. There's four more wounded down there waiting to switch. We got two more dozy bastards waiting for their bloody turn and your girlfriend's in there playing doctors and fucking nurses with Miller."

Johnno opened his mouth to answer and Robertson closed in on him again. So close that Johnno, pressed against the wall, had to turn his face away.

When he tried to speak, Robertson's voice was little more than a hiss. He had to make an effort to unlock his jaw.

"Shut it, sonny, understand? Just fucking shut it."

Johnno nodded his head as best he could. Robertson counted four breaths before he trusted himself again. He took a step back, and then another. Johnno allowed himself to ease forward, away from the wall. He was breathing hard.

"This has been going on since first light. It's fucking dark now, and you've only just thought to mention it?"

"I was trying to get it all sorted. Anyway, that's why I'm here now. I'm looking for Sol and Mccall …"

The air came out of Johnno in a rasping groan and he folded forward around Robertson's fist. While he was off balance Robertson grabbed the back of his neck and used the man's own momentum to bring him down. Johnno landed on his chest, his head hanging over the top step of the stairway.

Robertson heard himself hissing again. This time he didn't bother trying to calm down.

"You do not report to Sol or fucking Maccallan, you cunt." He was on all fours, snarling into Johnno's ear, putting most of his weight against the back of the man's head. "You report to me. Me. Have you fucking got that?"

"Yeah, I get it."

Johnno choked the affirmation out in a panic. Robertson took a moment, decided it was enough and let him up. The big man used the metal bannister to lever himself upright. He stood with his hands on his knees, gasping.

"You alright?" Robertson asked.

"I'll live. Jesus Christ." He straightened and stood to his full height; one hand spread over his stomach. "I get it, alright? I get it, you're the boss. I just thought …"

"If you want to think about something, think about sorting out those fucking lunatics downstairs."

Johnno nodded without meeting Robertson's eye and fumbled through his pockets for his torch. As he made to descend back into the building, Robertson put a hand on his shoulder. The big man didn't flinch, but Robertson felt muscles tense. When he turned round, his expression was neutral. Robertson had intended to offer a word of explanation or apology but something about the blank face wiped the idea away.

"You make sure Miller's safe, make sure there's always a few of our guys with him."

"Yes, Boss."

"And tell our guys, if I see any of them playing dress-up with feathers, I'll break their fucking legs."

Chapter 28. Crow-Headed Jesus

Extract from the screenplay of Year of the Crow. Lithograph Studios, California (2026)

EXT. TRAFALGAR SQUARE – DAY.

Seen from above, the remains of Miller's band of survivors are gathered around the broken pieces of Nelson's Column. The camera pans to a second-floor window. Miller is standing at it surveying the scene below. Robertson is beside him. He is resting on his haunches. Both men look exhausted. Their clothes hang in tatters and, although they are smiling, their expressions are hard to read.

ROBERTSON

(Voice-over)

I think in those last few hours, Miller was sort of lost.

During Robertson's voice-over, the camera swirls away from the window, moving quickly and making the scene blur. The movement ends suddenly. Close-up on the face of a young male. He is looking vacantly into a point slightly to the side of the lens, just short of looking directly into the viewer's eyes and not quite breaking the fourth wall. There is a sharp crack of unidentifiable sound and the scene changes to a brightly-coloured montage of still shots. They show the young man with a woman and child. The montage is fast, snapshots of a happy family. The first few images are on screen long enough to register. The man and a woman at a party, the same couple on a beach, then getting married. The images change more rapidly as they become less happy: a hospital interior, a darkened child's bedroom. The pictures blur into each other, finally settling back on the blank face waiting in Trafalgar Square. The camera pans slowly across more faces. They all look tired and blank, some of them are talking to their neighbours but the viewer can hear no sound other than Robertson's voice.

ROBERTSON

(Voice-over)

It was as if everything we'd been doing for the past months had been leading to this point. Reaching that end gave us the time to look back and face the madness of it all.

The camera comes to rest on another face, a woman in her sixties. Like the young man she is staring blankly and almost meeting the viewer's eyes. The same crack of sound introduces another rapid montage. This one is faster and shorter, images of people we don't know interspersed with images of the violence she had just lived through. Again, it ends by coming up to date and showing us the old woman staring and waiting. The camera pans across fewer faces before coming to rest on another individual. There is no sound this time, just the rapid montage bringing us back to the moment and the blank stare. This sequence is repeated again and again as Robertson narrates.

ROBERTSON

(Voice-over)

In the end we waited, waited for the salvation we had fought for. Wondering what we'd do with it. Except, I don't think Miller did wonder. I think, in his mind, he was the bringer, the giver not the taker. It made no sense for him to contemplate life after the Takeback. The point of it was knowing he'd brought others to it.

The montages and Robertson's voice-over both stop as if a switch has been thrown. The screen is black and silent for a few seconds. The screen remains black as Robertson's voice returns.

ROBERTSON
(Voice-over)
I think he was at peace with that. I hope he was. Because it was short, a short-lived fucking peace.

The screen bursts into life along with the roar of an engine. The images on the screen are of something rapidly moving and swirling. The camera pulls back until the confusion of shapes and lights reveals itself to be the wheel of a truck. The camera follows it at close quarters, so it fills the screen. The sound of an engine gets louder as more engines join it. The camera pulls away until we can see a complete truck. It is an army transporter and is very clean. The back is open and two soldiers are standing in there, obviously excited. The camera stops panning and the truck moves out of shot; another and another and another follow it. The noise increases as we jump cut to a blank screen. The camera drops away to reveal more of the 'blank' until it resolves into the silhouette of a Chinook helicopter seen from below.

INT. OFFICE - DAY.
Miller and Robertson. The room they are in was once an official office of some sort. The walls are covered with posters about the Outbreak and maps of the city, all of them with large areas marked out in red. The two of them are still standing at the window gazing out, but their faces are now animated and stricken.

ROBERTSON
Fucking hell.

MILLER
They're going to draw them right down on us.

Both men turn from the window and run. The door they leave by has at some point been smashed down and there is the wreckage of a desk to one side of it. As they exit, the camera settles briefly on a detail of the desktop. An old-style blotter, with an official-looking rubber stamp on it, has been gouged through with four long scratches that could have been made by a human hand. The blotter is stained with blood.

EXT. TRAFALGER SQUARE – DAY.

About half of the people waiting around the broken sections of Nelson's Column have realised the danger and become animated, picking up weapons and looking for somewhere to run to or make a stand from. Others appear unaware of the situation but pick up on the excitement. They are cheering and waving at the helicopter which is now hovering and throwing up dust. Still others haven't moved and are staring blankly into the chaos.

POV changes: same scene shot from above.

In a series of three jump cuts the camera moves higher until it is at the height of the helicopter. The image of the crowd below becomes black and white and we freeze. A white grid is superimposed over the image. Various symbols and number adorn the picture letting the viewer know this is an official military photograph. An old-fashioned shutter noise accompanies a change of picture. Six or seven different stills show the crowd gathered in the square. In the first one there is a black mass visible in the top right-hand corner. With each shutter sound the mass gets closer to the crowd.

The military grid vanishes and the picture becomes colour again. Three jump cuts take us back to ground level and into the thick of the mass. It is a group of zombies attracted to the noise.

EXT. WRECKAGE OF ORNATE DOORS AND THE REMAINS OF A BREACHED BARRICADE – DAY.

The remains of the door burst outwards and Miller

bolts out of the building. Robertson is close behind. He is carrying his axe.

MILLER
(Shouting to be heard over the noise)
Get them moving, get them to the trucks. I'll hold them.

ROBERTSON
But …

MILLER
Please.

Robertson glances to his left. The camera follows his gaze and we see the zombies are about to enter the square.

MILLER
Please. Get them out of here.

Robertson nods, suddenly takes Miller into a one-armed embrace and then hands him the axe. He turns and grabs one of the staring people, dragging them along with him away from the zombies. At the other end of the square the trucks arrive. The sense of urgency has finally reached the military who begin physically hauling people into the vehicles. Robertson throws the man he is hauling toward the soldiers and kicks him in the ass to get him moving. He grabs someone else who is limping and supporting themselves with an improvised crutch.

Jump cut to street containing the zombies. The horde is spilling out in the square. The wreckage of a car lying on its side is knocked over onto its roof. Camera cuts to petrol leaking onto the road.

Jump cut to the back of one of the army trucks at the edge of the square. A soldier with a grenade launcher is loading a canister onto the end of the weapon. The camera briefly settles on the metal case from which he has taken the canister. The word 'incendiary' is stencilled onto it. The solider discharges the incendiary grenade toward the mouth of the street where the zombies are coming from.

Cut to extreme close-up of someone's back as they walk away from the camera. As the figure moves away we see it is Miller. He is walking calmly toward the oncoming zombies. His pistol is in one hand, Miller's axe in the other. As he moves toward the horde, he lifts both arms stiffly away from his body. As his arms reach shoulder height the incendiary grenade lands and ignites the petrol from the wreaked car. In the flash of flame we see Miller's cruciform shape in silhouette.

Fade to black.

Chapter 29. Fourth Floor: Acolytes, Blades and Chanting

Coffin Coin (Crypt Coin)

A term used to denote distaste for the actions of one hoping to benefit financially from the victims of the Outbreak, eg. he's chasing some Coffin Coin. These types of phrases were originally used in regard to American lawyers who attempted to bring a tort action against the UK Government on behalf of the families of victims of the Lockdown Massacre.

The A to Z of Gondii Names

February 28th, 2021

Without looking at Robertson, Maccallan asked, "Are the scouts back yet?"

He and Sol were at the edge of the rooftop. Neither of them had turned to acknowledge him. Robertson ignored Maccallan's question and sat on the low parapet with his back to the view of the river. With the night drawing down, the glow of lights across the river was beginning to show. There was even enough ambient light to throw a few highlights on the ebb and flow of the Thames. Thankfully the folded ruins of London Bridge weren't visible against the silhouettes of the buildings along the opposite bank. Knowing they were there was enough.

Maccallan finally looked over to him.

"I said …"

"I heard what you fucking said," Robertson told him. "We got a problem." He spoke to Sol.

"You mean we have another problem," Sol said.

He still hadn't looked at Robertson. Maccallan manufactured a laugh. In the cover of the growing darkness Robertson settled his hands on the shaft of the axe. It would be easy enough. Slam the flat side of the weapon against his temple, push him forward a couple of feet while he tried to gain his balance. He'd be a mess on the pavement before he'd had time to scream. He dismissed the thought. For the time being Maccallan had a purpose.

Robertson turned to the right, cutting the two men from his line of vision. He watched the sun setting. It was a spectacular display; it had been most nights for a long time now. It was one of the things he liked about the new way the world was ordered. Colourful sunsets and problems you could generally solve with an axe.

It wasn't all bad.

He pushed himself up from where he'd sat and made to walk away. Whatever the situation was with Miller and the strange splinter group forming around him, he'd deal with it. Sooner rather than later. Maccallan had a job to do. Until that job was done, he could wait.

He didn't bother with the torch, even when he was back inside the stairwell where it was now completely dark. He'd pulled the door closed behind him and waited. The landing at the top of the stairway wasn't much bigger than a good-sized desktop but he didn't plan on hiding for long. He'd heard Sol following him as he'd walked away. The old man's step was steady, but it didn't have Maccallan's cock-of-the-walk assurance to it. A difference he attributed to age rather than humility.

Despite the size of the landing at the top of the stairway, the door onto the rooftop opened inwards. Robertson stood behind it. The light from Sol's torch preceded him, the circle of light it cast shaking in sympathy with the old man's hand. It performed a zig-zagging scan of the stairwell as Sol tried to find him.

"Looking for me?"

Robertson had stood directly behind the old man to speak. Startled, Sol dropped the torch and it bounced down the steps making a swirling cartwheel of light. It came to rest on the landing below. Surprisingly it still worked. Sol had almost performed the same descent and Robertson doubted he'd have fared so well.

"Is it a heart attack you're trying to give me?" Sol asked.

Robertson could just about make out the pantomime he was performing; hand clutching chest, shuddering deep breaths. He'd caught Sol's feeble-old-codger act before. Usually in the moments before he announced checkmate.

"You wanted something?"

Sol stayed with shuddering breaths but the hand he was clutching to his chest transferred its grip to the stair rail.

"You said we had a problem?"

"Did I?"

He stepped round Sol and made his way down the steps. Sol muttered something that wasn't in English but was clearly a curse. Robertson could hear he was struggling to negotiate the stairs in the near darkness. He didn't slow his own pace.

At the lower landing he waited for Sol to catch up. He waited again while the old man stiffly bent to retrieve the torch.

"So, what is this problem?"

Robertson switched his own torch on and trained it onto the run of steps leading down into the building. From somewhere in the depths of the building voices carried up to them. Other than that, they were alone.

"Miller's getting worse. He's down on the fourth floor with a room full of infected, waiting for them to change so he can hack them up."

"I thought you could control Miller."

"We need to get moving. That pack of freaks he's got down there with him are setting up house. If we don't leave here soon this whole building's going to turn into a plague pit."

"We need word from the scouts."

Robertson laughed despite himself. Maccallan had started applying military-style labels to things. The 'scouts' were a married couple in their mid-forties who happened to be kayaking enthusiasts. When the idea of sending someone across the river to see what was happening was mooted Johnno had sought them out. They'd volunteered their encyclopaedic knowledge of the city's boating supply shops.

The scavenging process for a boat had been surprisingly fast. That they should make the crossing under the cover of night had been a logical progression. Or so everyone had thought.

They'd been gone for over a week. Robertson was beginning to doubt they'd return. The helicopters hadn't been seen again but the sound of gunfire would occasionally carry over to them.

"Yeah, well while Maccallan's up on the roof pretending to be Napoleon I've got Crow-Headed Jesus down in the boardroom sharpening his knives and waiting for his people to switch so he's got something to fucking play with."

Sol nodded and began climbing down the stairs. He'd set up quarters on one of the higher floors despite the inconvenience. The old man contentedly slept between ranks of filing cabinets holding records of transactions that had once been important. On occasion Robertson would find him sifting through files as if they were photograph albums of old friends. Robertson had stuck with the second floor, high enough to gain breathing space from wandering infected but low enough that leaving in a hurry was still an option.

Maccallan had taken up residence on the top floor.

Sol's descent to his quarters was laboured, and Robertson wondered how much of it was genuine. He didn't actually know the man's age. All he could say about him for sure was he didn't trust him.

Robertson looked in on the fourth floor on his way down to his own billet. He stood in the doorway of what had been a vast open plan office and was now the main sleeping area. He didn't go in.

Miller's people were settling down for the night. The man himself, presumably watching over the infected members of his flock, wasn't in residence. Without his lead to follow the scene wasn't greatly different from the normality on the second floor: puddles of feeble light cast from torches or candles, vague movements in the near darkness as people carefully arranged their limited bedding.

The two details that did jar were the grouping and the noise. On the second floor people tended to stick to the four or five members of their scavenger group, at least in terms of physical distance.

Here the groups were bigger and the chatter was different. Though still muted from habit, it was rhythmic. He had to strain to hear it, but the carefully versed sound resolved itself into a hushed chant.

"… leave them be. They will change, leave them be. They will change …"

In the dull glow from a huddle of tea-lights Robertson could see half a dozen people being led in the chorus. The choir master's face was lost in the shadows of his hood.

And of course, underscoring the chant, the metallic throbbing of blades against steel.

His first thought was to go and see Miller. He held an affection for the man, or at least the memory of the man he'd been, and he was aware that Miller represented a key part of their investment. But he was hesitant about stepping into the communal space. During the day his position felt more secure; at night, the fourth floor and people on it put doubts in his mind. He was still debating whether to go in and find Miller when Johnno called to him.

Johnno had come up to the floor via the main staircase. Though not massive – the building had been designed to be travelled by lift – it was intended as a front of house thoroughfare; corporate art on every landing and brushed stainless steel hand rails. Robertson favoured the unadorned concrete of the service stairs.

"Hey, Boss."

He jogged along the corridor, lowered the torch that he'd shone onto Robertson's face. Robertson was quietly relieved to see him, until he noticed he was breathing hard.

"What's wrong?"

"Alyson's back."

Alyson was one of the 'scouts'.

"Just Alyson? No …" He left the question to hang when he realised he didn't remember her husband's name.

"Alyson reckons those bastards shot him."

"Fuck it. Was she followed?"

Johnno didn't answer straightaway, and Robertson guessed that he hadn't thought to ask. Which probably meant no one else had.

Finally, Johnno confirmed that he didn't know. "I saw she was back, and when I heard her say they'd shot Neil I ran to find … you, Boss."

"Take me to her then, come on."

He'd taken a few paces towards the stairs before Johnno, who hadn't moved, called out again.

"She's on the second floor, Boss, in the old kitchen. A couple of the guys are with her."

When Robertson looked back, he could see Johnno was intending to head into the open-plan office. He wondered who he'd been planning to report to first, Miller or Sol.

Robertson didn't bother arguing the point and left him to vanish into the chanting mass of Miller's acolytes.

Chapter 30. An Ordered Monument to Life in the Midst of Chaotic Death

Gondii Town (Stomp Down, Stomp Town)

Uninhabited areas deserted due to the effects, or after-effects, of the HV-Tg pandemic. Although the various terms have been likened to the phrase 'ghost town' they are often applied to very small geographic areas – such as a single street or, commonly in built-up areas, a tower block – that have been rendered unfit for human habitation. The phrase Stomp Down, or Stomp Town, is occasionally used as a verb to describe the poor condition of an area, eg: That housing estate has been stomped down, or the whole place was stomp towned. Stomp Down and Stomp Town have their origins in the American term, Gondii Stomp. Its use is prevalent among extremist right-wing and Christian groups and carries the implication that the HV-Tg pandemic was a form of divine judgement.

The A to Z of Gondii Names

April 12th, 2028

The block where Maccallan had lived and built his bolthole had survived the Outbreak, the Lockdown and the Takeback with barely a scratch. Had he stayed put when he'd seen Miller's rag-tag collection of survivors, he'd have probably been able to unlock his door six months later and begin picking up the threads of his life again. That much of Robertson's account was true.

The lack of damage to the building wasn't particularly significant. For domestic buildings the violence that had rolled across the city was a hit and miss affair. It wasn't unusual to see an unscathed row of houses and a line of burnt-out ruins divided by fifteen feet of blacktop. Shops and storefronts had suffered a more even spread of desolation.

It helped that the tenants of Creston Towers had been professionals. Young and single, many of them would have fled the city in a money-cushioned escape bid. Or at least headed back to a family home. The less privileged, and those bound to spouses and offspring had a harder job breaking for the border.

Many tower blocks had been turned into fortresses when their residents decided to pull up the drawbridge. It had been a practice common in Europe and Britain, and usually ended badly. The sealed communities tended to break down from the inside out. Either the 'community' splintered into civil war as supplies dwindled or cases of undiscovered Toxo came to light when the infected switched. As the ad hoc forces of the emergency government began the clear-up, stories began to emerge of high-rises that had become charnel houses.

There were rumours too about what had happened inside the nation's prisons. The Official Secrets Act meant they'd be no more than rumours for at least thirty years.

We had wasted days trying to obtain a search warrant for Maccallan's old flat. I had suspected Superintendent Taylor of putting up some objection, but the truth was less sinister. Old-fashioned red tape, combined with the makeshift communications systems, had meant the request had spent days bouncing, slowly, from desk to desk and then department to department. Finally, the reply came via the American Embassy in Absence. The British police authority's jurisdiction didn't extend to Creston Towers. When Lithograph Film Studios Ltd had bought Maccallan's flat, they'd bought the whole block it came in and its sovereignty. Maccallan's bolthole was now on American soil. A fact that sped things up. Washington granted permission for the search within six hours of my request. Superintendent Taylor had handed me the printout of the paperwork himself. His only comment was to ask how much more time I intended wasting.

The only external sign that we were technically crossing into the US was the quality of the security measures. Where most unoccupied buildings were encased with splintered sheets of plyboard, the first two floors of Creston Towers were sealed tight with made-to-measure steel sheeting. Printed signage, no spray paint stencils here, warned wannabe intruders that the structure was protected by Sycamore Security Services. To deter the illiterate, any surface that might have lent itself to climbing was wrapped with razor wire.

As Winslow pulled aside the heavy security door, something scurried away from the intruding daylight. He muttered 'rats' under his breath, as though he didn't want to disturb them. I don't know why but dark spaces make people lower the volume. That was something I remembered from picking my way through the A86 tunnel. Already in hushed sympathy with the dark, Winslow and I both jumped at a sudden burst of noise high above. When we realised it was a pigeon we'd frightened from its roost, we both laughed though neither of us found it funny.

There was more light than I'd expected. The building, built on the plan of something bigger, had an atrium capped with a latticework of glass panels. The roof allowed enough light through for us to find our footing.

"Must have been a nice place once," Winslow said.

Once upon a time. Whatever gap the pigeons had found had also been letting rain in, and the air was rich with the smell of mouldering fabrics. The entrance floor was stone or tile of some sort. Liberally seeded with bird shit and stagnant pools of water, it was slick underfoot.

Someone, I assumed Maccallan, had barricaded the staircase to the residents' flats at some point. The barricade now lay in the mess of droppings and mould.

The stairway was an enclosed space and had been spared the worst excesses of the pigeons. The footing was better, but we lost the benefit of the glass roof and climbed by torchlight. Maccallan's flat was on the sixth floor and there was another barricade. Put together using scavenged items from neighbours' flats, it was familiar from the tedious collection of images catalogued in *Scenes from a Crow's Nest.* Except in the photo the panels had been swung aside and left there, evidence of Maccallan's uncompromising flight towards heroism. Now we had to sift through a collection of keys to unlock the new owner's investment.

The barricade led onto a short landing with four doors leading from it and a window at one end. The walls had been painted an inoffensive shade of grey and the carpeting was a hard-wearing brown; probably described as chocolate to hide its industrial roots. Three of the four doors were open. The last, Maccallan's, was shut tight and secured with yet more locks. As an afterthought another Sycamore Securities sign had been fixed to it.

Tap, tap. Tap, tap. Tap, tap.

Winslow's finger against the grey wall. His mannerisms never ceased to annoy me but giving him the response he wanted brought them to a quicker end.

"What?"

"I'd assumed Maccallan had this building to himself. Lone survivor sitting in his bolthole, right?"

"And?"

"Well if that's the case, why is this hallway empty? Surely you'd use it for storage; try to make the flat more bearable."

"Maybe he didn't think it through."

I was struggling with the locks securing Maccallan's flat. Winslow made a grunt and tapped out a rapid sign-off against the wall: taptap, taptap.

His silence as I opened the door was comeback enough. Clearly, Maccallan had thought it through. Every inch of the flat had been utilised. I'd thought I'd known what to expect from seeing the photograph back at the station but Gordon Price's pictorial essay, even with the quasi-academic gloss, didn't do the scene justice.

The hallway was tiny even by the standards of housing this close to the centre – the miniature scale of living spaces found in London still surprised me. What space there was had been filled. Cans, row after row of them, lined one wall. The attention given to their placement made the food store resemble an art installation. I remembered some of the pages of Price's book and the cataloguing of Maccallan's bookcase. There had been several on art, and, looking at the carefully arranged labels all facing one direction and all the right way up, I wondered if Maccallan had been trying to make some abstract statement. Had he given this work some self-consciously cryptic title, the sort of thing people who buy corporate art just lap up – An Ordered Monument to Life in the Midst of Chaotic Death?

I shook the thought away, irritated. I hadn't gone there to deal with whatever ghosts Maccallan had left behind. The only thing of interest for me was the paperwork spread over his bedroom floor. As I fussed with my coat to extract a torch, Winslow tried the light switch. We hadn't expected the building to have power and weren't disappointed. He flicked the switch half a dozen times to turn the non-result into a rhythm.

The living room was in close to perfect darkness. The floor-to-ceiling picture window had been blacked out with a double thickness of cloth. I was vaguely disappointed when I pulled a section of the material away and sunlight flooded the room. It looked stupidly small, much smaller than it appeared in the book; Price must have taken most of his photos with his back pressed against a wall. The contents rendered it smaller still, although here the hoarding lacked the abstract quality of the entrance hall. The living room had obviously been where Maccallan relaxed and maybe tried to pretend the world outside hadn't gone to hell. There was a lot of IT gear in the room. I wasn't a devotee of computing equipment, but I'd worked with it long enough to know Maccallan had favoured top of the range electronics. The furniture consisted of a two-seat couch and the famous glass-topped coffee table. It had been left as it appeared in the iconic photograph. The book, open on a picture of a luxury car, the piles of coins and, of course, the bowl and cup. The only change had been the cleaning away of the mould. The bowl and cup gleamed under the film of dust that had gathered.

"What do you think they're going to do with this place?" Winslow asked.

He was looking around the preserved room with a mildly puzzled expression.

"Tourist attraction. If that asshole Drumph ever lifts all the travel bans, this place will be knee-deep in my fellow Americans." I imitated President Drumph's squawking accent.

I'd expected some acknowledgement from Winslow, but he was lost in thought. I opened the window a few inches to let the air circulate.

The bedroom was beyond small and into claustrophobic. If the living room was about relaxation, this room was a workspace. There was more IT gear, including the shattered laptop that still lay on the floor where Price had photographed it. There was more food here, water too, and fuel. A pair of small generators had been tucked beside the bed. The bed, like almost every other surface in the room, was acting as a tabletop. The room was a shrine to paper. When I pulled the blackout layers from the bedroom window the dimness of the room retreated and the pages revealed their contents.

Figures, row upon row of blessed, truth-giving figures. The knots of tension that I'd carried in my shoulders had been there so long I barely noticed them anymore. In the presence of so much certainty they dissipated so fast; I felt a moment of light-headedness.

There was a walkway formed between the layers of accounts. I made my way to it and stood staring at the pile of information, deciding where best to start.

Chapter 31. Crossing Over

Bastard Jay (Bee-Jay)

Derisive term for members of the British Armed Forces, especially the Army. The term Bee-Jay is derived from the term blow job (BJ) and is a reference to the destruction of the bridges that crossed the Thames during the first day of the London Lockdown operation. The 'blowing' of the bridges and the subsequent gunning down of civilians is regarded as a war crime by many legal groups in America.

The A to Z of Gondii Names

Julian Clark-Billings, Service #:78695312, Military Corrective Training Centre, Colchester (2028)

I am aware that I have no right to ask for people's understanding or forgiveness. Events that I failed to control led to a great deal of suffering. I accept that to many people I am beyond the pale. However, I ask one thing: please, for the sake of my surviving men and for the memory of those who've died, make it clear that we had no part in the atrocities that took place on London's bridges. I and the men under my command were not in the country during March 2021. The stories that have been circulated, connecting us to shootings on the first day of the Lockdown are heinous. What occurred when we encountered the Crows I can't deny. Nor do I deny that I was responsible for actions I now regret. The Lockdown massacre was not one of them.

Robertson is surprisingly calm when I ask about the fate of the Crows. In fact, his control borders on sanguine. However, there is still a hitch in his voice. It would barely be noticeable in a less softly-spoken person, but it's there. Or rather they are there: tiny pauses that creep in from time to time, almost as if he's checking everything is in place before he continues his account.

"We'd lost a lot a people by the time we crossed the Thames. We'd been living hand to mouth for almost two years by then. The winter had been bad. We were very weak."

There is a moment when I think Robertson's composure is going to break. Then it's gone. He smiles sadly and continues.

"We weren't making great decisions at that point. We saw a helicopter hovering over North London, over the lights, and we just made a big push to get over to them. We thought they'd come to help. I'm not apportioning blame here, please don't think that, but Maccallan and Miller were the moving force in that decision. He was so fired up about getting over the river before it was too late. We lost three people before we got across."

Extract from the screenplay of Year of the Crow. Lithograph Studios, California (2026)

EXT. BANKS OF THE RIVER THAMES – TWILIGHT

Close-up shot of Miller. His face is contorted with effort. It looks as if he is fighting for his life.

MILLER

(Through gritted teeth)

Come on, come on.

Camera tracks back showing the figure of Miller in full. He is wearing mud-caked combat pants and is stripped to the waist. He is hauling on a rope with both hands. His body is at a forty-five-degree angle as he leans his weight into the task. The rope is looped across his back and wound across his chest. Blood trickles down him where the rope has dug into his skin. Jump cut further back. We see he is standing on a pile of shattered concrete and stone.

ROBERTSON

(SHOUTING)

Okay, done.

At this moment we jump cut into a long shot. Robertson's words echo over the expanse of water we are now looking across. From this POV we can see the two ropes span the width of the river forming a makeshift bridge. Still from this POV we see Robertson take hold of the upper rope and use it to hold himself upright as he shuffles his feet along the lower rope.

February 28th, 2021

Alyson had been crying. She'd stopped by the time Robertson found her but the grime on her face was striped where she'd rubbed her eyes.

The kitchen area on the second floor served no practical purpose but had become a semi-communal area through a quirk of habit. People would gather, still sticking to their own sub-communities of scavenging groups, to eat together. Paranoia usually kept the rotation of use short and clean. Now a dozen people were pressed into the room. Unnerved by Alyson's sudden return and her distress, Robertson wondered how much of her story had been heard, or how much she might have blurted out.

Alyson was at the far end of the room, sitting on the long table with her back to the wall and her arms wrapped around her knees. For the moment she wasn't speaking. A stooped man, who Robertson recognised as one of Alyson's scavenging group, was comforting her. Another man and a woman, both just faces to him, were exchanging worried looks and mouthing questions at each other. Everyone else in the room appeared to be waiting for something to happen. The number of torches lighting the room added to the impression of a stage play and a restless audience.

Robertson drew focus from the main act by tapping the head of his axe against a glass partition wall. The heads swung round en masse at the sharp sound. A lot of the torch beams followed them, and Robertson had to squint against the light.

"Give her some room."

He jerked his thumb over his shoulder. When no one moved he felt the pit of his stomach drop. It reminded him of sitting in the car on tense family holidays, his father always oversleeping and making them late. "Late for what?" he'd always demand as Robertson's stepmother hurried them through the door. "You think they're going to close the beach if we don't arrive before noon?" The argument would sit in the car with them all the way, then follow them down to the sand. And there had been nothing he could do about it.

He gripped the shaft of the axe, hanging onto the feeling of control.

"Come on." He said the words softly, but people started to filter out. The relief made his knees go weak.

The man with the stoop remained. The couple who'd been miming questions over Alyson's head were the last to leave. As they passed Robertson, the woman carefully mouthed something that might have been, she's not right. He ignored her and went to Alyson, who still hadn't spoken. The stooped man looked up as Robertson approached. Robertson's presence made him nervous and he gently put a hand on Alyson's shoulder, almost anchoring himself to her. Clearly, he didn't want to leave.

The jeans Alyson wore were soaked to mid-thigh and plastered with mud up to the knees, both of which had ripped open. She was shivering. Now he was closer, Robertson could see her hands were grazed and bleeding.

"Alyson, Alyson," the stooped man said, stooping further so their faces almost touched, "where's Neil, what's happened to Neil?"

Alyson shook her head and looked down, avoiding the question. Robertson felt his stomach lurch again. Whatever the dynamic was here, it was something that ran deep, and it wasn't a situation he could fix with an axe.

He put a hand on the man's shoulder, mirroring the gesture he'd made with Alyson. Despite his efforts to be gentle the man started and looked scared.

"We need to get her warm and into some dry clothes. And we'll have to clean her hands up. We can't risk her getting an infection." The man looked ready to argue the point, but the moment passed, and he nodded. After that he just looked old. "Could you find some clothes, and get some water on the boil?"

The man nodded again and said, "We don't know where Neil is."

"We'll find him, but …" he finished the sentence by looking pointedly at Alyson's scuffed knuckles.

He noticed that as the man left, Alyson's eyes, though still downcast, followed him to the door. Once he was out of sight the eyes snapped onto Robertson.

"Neil's dead. I can't tell Barry that, it'll kill him too."

Her breath caught and Robertson thought she was about to start crying again, but instead she pressed one of her bloodied knuckles to her mouth and made two hard grunting sounds. It seemed to be a way of keeping the stress in check.

"I can't tell him," she repeated.

"I'll break it to him. Just, first, tell me what happened."

She made the grunting sounds again and cast a look to the door.

"It'll kill him," she said again, to herself this time. She didn't look at Robertson. As she told him the story, she kept watch for Barry's return. "We got across okay, but there's Gonzos by the dozen on the other side. It must be the noise and the lights." Robertson thought she'd lost the thread of her thoughts. He was about to prompt her to continue but she picked up again, biting her knuckle and making the grunting noise.

"We spent two days just dodging packs of the things and hiding out. We couldn't find a damn thing to eat. There's nothing left over there, everything's gone. Gonzos, flies and bodies, that's all there is. We had to go all round the houses to get to them, but we just kept following the noise. They're set up in the Bank of England. They've barricaded the streets and they're just cleaning up the Gonzos with a machine gun when they get too close."

Robertson tried to remember the streets around the main bank. He had a vague picture in his mind of narrow roadways hemmed in by tall walls.

"Are they really army?"

"I think so, they're well-equipped and they're organised. We spent two nights in an office block that overlooked them a bit."

"Any idea what they're doing?"

"Digging, they've got a JCB in there."

She finally looked away from the door and regarded him with an expression he couldn't understand. It made him uncomfortable. He realised she was waiting for him to ask what the information had cost.

"What happened to Neil?"

More knuckle biting and grunts before she continued.

"They shot him. Cold blood, just …" – she made her hand into the shape of a gun – "… boom."

"Why?"

"The Gonzos let up for a bit; I think there was some big noise down the road and they drifted off to … to whatever. It was a chance to make contact. Neil ran off, down the stairs. There was a sentry on this barricade they'd made up. When he saw Neil heading towards him he just …" She finished the sentence by making the gun shape again.

Robertson tried to process the information. Neil wasn't the first person they'd lost to 'normal' human violence. Since the stocks of food available to scavengers had begun to run low, acts of violence were as likely to be sparked by desperation as HV-Tg infection. But an army unit picking off individual civilians felt outlandish.

"Did the gunman mistake him for a Gonzo?"

Alyson looked away again, went back to keeping a vigil for Barry's return.

"No." She was speaking quietly, more so than before. "Neil put himself in the open, had his arms in the air, announced himself. That bastard saw him coming and took aim, he took his time. I can't tell Barry," she said again. "It's going to kill him."

Julian Clark-Billings, Service #:78695312, Military Corrective Training Centre, Colchester (2028)

I thought you would want to know about the bullion. That's to be expected, I suppose, but I'll have to disappoint you, I'm afraid. As I have stated repeatedly, neither I nor my men removed the gold bullion. I won't deny that we did go to Threadneedle Street with designs on the vault. The evidence of the attempt is still there to be seen, I understand. However, our attempted bank robbery was an unmitigated failure.

February 28th, 2021

"Digging equipment?" Sol repeated.

His voice was neutral and with the only light in the room coming from the candle stubs he'd lit, his face couldn't be read. Robertson assumed the old man was thinking aloud and didn't reply.

Maccallan was pacing back and forth between the ranks of desks. He'd been on his way down to the second floor – and Alyson – as Robertson had been making his way back up the building. He'd chosen the main staircase for the ascent, knowing Maccallan favoured its grandeur. When their paths crossed, he told him he'd already spoken to the woman and got her story. Maccallan had announced he'd go and check for himself and Robertson had grabbed his arm, pulling him back.

"It's sorted," he told him. "Now, fucking leave it."

The beam of another torch played over them as someone came down from the floors above. It settled on Robertson's face, then moved onto Maccallan's. Maccallan shook Robertson's hand off and squinted into the light.

Johnno's voice, "You right, Boss?"

"Yeah," Maccallan and Robertson both answered.

There was a beat of total silence. Robertson could feel the blood pounding in his head. Johnno held the light motionless. He'd stopped where he was, one staircase above theirs.

"I want to talk to Alyson myself. I want to find out what happened over there," Maccallan said.

"She told me what happened. I don't want her telling everyone else, in case it starts a fucking panic. The less she says the better."

"How do you know she's not shouting it out right now?" Sol's voice caught Robertson by surprise.

He swung his own torch to the direction the question came from. The old man was on the stairs above, alongside Johnno. He started walking down and closing the gap between them and the big Liverpudlian followed behind.

"She was cut up pretty bad. I told her she'd have to go into quarantine. Her father-in-law's the only one who'll be in contact with her. He's in pieces."

Sol nodded an approval.

"So, where's quarantine?"

"Down on third, there's an executive suite down there. No one's visiting."

Sol nodded again.

"Good, come on." He turned and started to climb. Robertson waited for Maccallan to follow before he fell in. He'd expect Sol to take them back up to the higher floor he'd laid claim to, but he turned into the corridor at the end of the first flight of steps. The room he led them to seemed to be a random choice, but Robertson noted it had a view of the river and the blur of lights on the other side.

"Save the batteries." Sol waved impatiently at their torches and produced candles from one of his pockets. He found a chair and sat in it with a dramatic sigh. "Okay, tell me the story."

He'd listened without comment until the JCB was mentioned. Then he'd sworn.

"So, we were right," Maccallan said. "They are trying to get the gold out."

"That's not the point," Sol said.

Maccallan halted his pacing and spun on his heel.

"Then what is the bloody point?"

"The point is they're trying to get into the bullion vault in the Bank of England, using a mechanical digger. If they were here on official business, they'd have the keys, the codes and the combinations. These fellas aren't army, not anymore. They've crossed the Rubicon."

Chapter 32. Profit and Loss

LEAKED BANK OF ENGLAND SECURITY TAPE

Video taken on the Bank of England's in-vault security camera. Shows British Army personnel removing gold bars. This proves that the UK's bullion reserves were removed and hidden by the British government!

Views:35,042 Likes:7,098 Dislikes:75

(78) Comments on Video: Leaked Bank of England security tape

****

Cactus
All I see is men in camo gear taking gold out of a safe.

****

ZooLooz
Those are British Army uniforms, if that is the bank of England vault it proves the theft of the gold was officially backed.

****

JinnySnack
Fake!

****

SAXbeats
London was over-run with the toxo infection when the gold was lost. Why would there be cameras running in the vault? I call bullshit.

****

Johnny5
The power was restored to parts of London during the Outbreak. The Bank of England was situated in one of the parts that was powered up. The security cameras were probably activated by motion sensors.

****

ProudBrit
THIS VID PROVES THAT THE GOVERNMENT IS HIDING THE COUNTRIES WEALTH AND KEEPING ITS OWN PEOPLE IN POVERTY. WAKE UP!

****

JinnySnack
Oh please, all this video proves is someone, somewhere has a cellar, three camo jackets and a video camera. There isn't a time code on the film even. This is amateur hour stuff.

April 12th, 2028

Winslow realised I didn't need help and, if I had, he wasn't the one to give it. I heard him wandering around the living room for a few minutes, tapping out rhythms or clicking his fingers. Then he called out he was going to look around and I heard the front door closing behind him.

I waited for a few minutes after he'd left the flat. I didn't realise I was waiting at first, less still what I was waiting for. As the quiet sank in and I allowed myself to trust it I saw that I'd been waiting to be alone. Alone with the ledgers and printouts and columns of figures. Figures don't lie. The people who set them on the page are a different matter. For possibly the first time since seeing Dog Boy shoot a man's pet in Paris, I felt that I was home.

Home comforts were lacking. The room smelled bad: old air, frustration and fuel. The generators and their store of gasoline had left the air heavy with that leaded smell of dead oil.

There was also the smell of money. Not in a romantic way, not a way to politely denote ostentation, but as a physical fact. The air carried the slight musk that money picks up as it passes from hand to hand to hand. Maccallan's pretentious flat was stuffed with banknotes.

More accurately, once upon a time it had been stuffed with banknotes. Now it was stuffed with carefully printed and numbered waste paper. The window for exchanging old, pre-Outbreak currency for new had been brief. Less than three months at the start of 2021.

It was doubtful if more than a handful of the country's survivors had the time or the means to get to an official government bank had they wanted to. For most people it would have been a waste of time. Hyperinflation had rendered pounds sterling practically valueless. Even Maccallan's hoard would have translated into little more than a pair of shoes.

I'd seen the backpack loaded with cash in the photos of course. What Gordon Price's tediously obsessive camera work hadn't captured was the story under the bed. Maybe his remit hadn't extended to capturing anything beyond what future movie audiences would need to see on a set; maybe he was held back by a sense of respect for a dead hero's privacy.

Having left such high moral concepts on the other side of the channel, I lifted the bedding and poked my torch under the bed.

The larger of the two suitcases, an anonymous nylon item, contained a small collection of clothes and toiletries, a wallet with cards and a fat layer of euros folded into it, and a key with a USB stick dangling from it.

I counted the fold of notes; it came up just light of three thousand. Not an insignificant sum pre-Outbreak, but nothing that would set off any alarm at a baggage check. Maccallan had planned, or least made provision, to leave the country at a run. It wasn't that uncommon. Riots at airport and ferry terminals had been all the rage in 2021. What was unusual was the orderly packing. This wasn't a rushed throw-in-everything-that'll-fit and run.

The other case I found under the bed was slightly smaller, but more expensive. It was neatly packed with stacks of notes; sterling and euros. I didn't count but I estimated something in the range of a hundred thousand in sterling and the same again in euros. Worthless now, but at one time a considerable nest egg.

I pushed the cases back under the bed and stood for a few minutes staring at the paperwork that had overtaken the room, looking for some form of order beyond the obsessively neat arrangement.

February 28th, 2021

Robertson had dipped back down to the second floor to collect his sleeping bag, then climbed up to the tenth. Sol's billet, among the filing cabinets and records, was on eleven.

The tenth floor stood apart from the other areas of the building that he'd explored. The quiet smugness of the corporate styling had been suspended here. The imposing marble cladding and the safe corporate art had been blunted with warmer colours and softer surfaces.

Robertson suspected it had been home to an advertising agency or design house of some description. It had an air of wackiness that was too controlled to be unintentional. It might have been a nice place to work at one time; most of the desks held a clutter of personal touches.

True to the cut and paste layout of the other floors, the staff breakroom/kitchenette was pushed out of sight into a corner space with a double aspect view of the bigger building next door. It held the usual Formica table and chairs and a beaten down sofa. He dragged the sofa from the room and across to the stairs and set it along the mouth of the stairwell.

If Johnno intended going over his head, literally, to either Sol or Maccallan, he'd have to physically climb over him. He unrolled the sleeping bag and lay under it rather than climb in. The axe stayed by his side.

March 1st, 2021

It was light when the sound of Johnno's boots on the steps woke him. He could recognise the big man's tread; he tended to catch his toe on the risers of stairs. The steel caps of his Doc Martens made a hushed clang.

When he appeared round the corner from the lower floor, Robertson was waiting for him.

"Right, Boss?" He stopped with one foot on the bottom step when he caught sight of Robertson. "I been looking for you."

Robertson was sitting on the edge of the sofa. The head of the axe between his feet and his fingers laced together on the end of the handle. He rested his chin on his knuckles and parodied an expression of surprise.

"Looking for me? Really?"

"Yeah." Johnno started to climb again, slowly, as if expecting Robertson to tell him to stop. "I brought you a brew. It'll probably be cold by now. I've been all over the second floor. No bastard knew where you were."

When Robertson stopped the wide-eyed act, and glanced at the lidded mug he was holding, Johnno picked up the pace. He still stopped a few steps down to offer the mug.

"Cheers."

Robertson put the axe aside and took the drink.

As an afterthought he patted the space on the sofa.

"You right, Boss?" Johnno said again as he sat next to him.

"Yeah, I'm fine." He had to fiddle with the cap on the mug to open it. The coffee inside was tepid. "So, what you want?"

Johnno stretched an arm out and made a jabbing motion with his hand, pointing vaguely at the descending steps and, Robertson assumed, the floors below.

"There's a few less sick in the sickbay."

"Meaning?"

"Pete, the one that got injured that night, the one you saw? He went the full Gonzo first thing. Then two of the others flared up soon afterwards. It's like Pete going for it and switching channels set the buggers off."

"Dealt with?"

"Aye. Miller. When I left him he was arranging the parts."

"Fucking hell."

"Aye, fucking hell's exactly what it looked like."

"Is that all the injured gone then?" Johnno didn't answer and the sofa creaked as he shifted his weight.

"It still leaves one. One of the guys that switched wasn't wounded, but he'd been sleeping in the sickbay. Trying to prove how devout he was, or something."

Robertson sipped the lukewarm coffee and tried to work out the sequence of events.

"This idiot that switched, did he have symptoms already? I mean before he started sleeping in the Toxo wing."

"No. He was fine. As fine as anyone is at the moment. It was Josh. You saw him, he tried to stop you going into the sickbay. You threatened to cut him."

Robertson remembered the heavy-set man who'd sat cross-legged at the door of the sickbay. The hood of his sweatshirt pulled forward like a monk's cowl; fitting, given his vow of silence. He hadn't shown any signs of illness.

"When did he get sick?"

"I saw him yesterday," Johnno said. "He was fine."

"No symptoms to full Gonzo in less than a day?"

"I guess so."

"Are there still people in there, people being devout?" Johnno nodded. "Miller?"

"He's in there too. Ally went in and cleaned him up, carbolic soap, bleach, the works. No worries on that account."

Robertson got up and rolled the sleeping bag into a tight tube.

"Come on, I want to see what's going on down there."

Johnno's movements were slow as he got to his feet.

"Should I go and tell Sol?"

Robertson put the sleeping bag beside the sofa and picked up his axe.

"No, I want you with me."

There'd been a change in the open plan space that housed Miller's followers. It wasn't immediately apparent to Robertson what, but as he and Johnno made their way across the floor it struck him. The bedding and clusters of belongings that marked personal spaces had been rearranged. They formed a loose collection of curving rows. The focal point was the sickbay, where Miller waited. Standing, sitting, a few still lying; everyone on the fourth floor had the doorway to their idol in sight. Robertson could feel eyes on him as he passed.

Close to the sickbay a line of six hooded figures sat, heads bowed, each sharpening a blade. Their movements were synchronised to the beat of their chant, the blades hissed along stones or steels at the end of each line.

Leave them be – scching – They will change – scching

Leave them be – scching – They will change – scching

Ally, her collection of crow's plumage grown to cover most of her shoulders, was standing at the door. She alone was facing away from the sickbay. She made no overt sign that she intended to stop him, but Robertson felt something shift in the crowd as he came up against her. He was conscious of Johnno standing behind him. It took an effort not to turn around.

"Miller in there?"

Ally nodded and smiled.

"It won't be long now," she said.

Something ran through the crowd; a ripple of … approval? … excitement? Robertson was about to ask what wouldn't be long when the question answered itself. There was a crash from inside the sickbay and a series of stuttering yelps. He pushed Ally to one side and kicked the door open, nearly overbalancing when it offered almost no resistance.

Miller was at the far end of the room, on his feet and with a butcher's knife in each hand. The floor around him was strewn with uneven shapes. Flies buzzed. Nearer the door, in tangles of dirty bedding, two of the faithful sat. A man and a woman, both wide-eyed and each wearing an expression of awe. A second woman, the one brought to the bay with bites on her face, was emitting the yelping noises. She was naked and her bowels had emptied. She trailed shit behind her as she limped towards the figure of Miller.

Another figure stood to one side, a painfully thin man who looked about thirty but was probably younger. He was shaking wildly and might have been having a seizure, but for the fact he was standing upright. As he shook, his clothes were moulting feathers.

There was another crash from the far end of the room. Miller had kicked a chair sending it flying into a wall. He did it again, drawing the yelping woman towards the sound. She took a few more limping steps, then bent double as the yelping sounds became a flood of vomit. As if the gesture had been a sign he was waiting for, Miller, and his knives, were suddenly on her.

As the switched woman fell, the shaking man made a dry retching sound. Ignoring Robertson and the seated couple, he lunged across the room.

He made straight for Miller, shouting, "Me, me, me, me."

Robertson smacked him square in the face with the flat side of the axe. He let out a shout of pain and fell backward landing hard on his back.

"Oh, shit." He spat out a wad of blood, then swore again. When he made to get up, Robertson stamped him down.

"What the fuck are you playing at?"

He rested the weight of the axe on the man's throat.

"It is my time."

The man tried to roll, but Robert stamped his boot into the man's stomach, pinning him underfoot.

"What's that meant to fucking mean?"

"It is my time, my time to join the blessed." Amazingly the man smiled, blood dripping from his mouth. He was looking past Robertson. "Now is my time."

Robertson jerked around to see what the man was smiling at. Miller stood behind him. His chest and arms were soaked red. He still held his knives.

The man under Robertson's boot began shaking again and added a chorus of retching to the performance. Robertson backed away, sidestepping and turning to face Miller, who scarcely registered him.

He looked dispassionately at the shaking man and with slow, deliberate movements put both butcher's knives on the floor. Then he took a step closer and appeared to wait for the man to do something. At the edge of his vision, Robertson saw the couple in the tangled bedding, gently rocking back and forth; their whispered chant was just audible over the shaking man's theatrics.

They will change let them be, they will change let them be.

Miller lashed out, kicking the shaking man in the crotch. The force of it made Robertson's stomach clench in sympathy and he heard himself gasp. The shaking and retching ended with a shrill howl. The man pulled himself into a ball, knees clamped to his chest.

Robertson had waited for a coup de grâce that didn't come. Instead, Miller bent, grabbed the man's collar and hauled him into a sitting position. Then dragged him to the door.

Scrabbling painfully, the injured man made it to his feet just as Miller propelled him out of the sickbay. He staggered a few steps before losing his footing again.

With the graceless exit, the chanting had stopped. The silence felt total, almost palpable.

"Fake," Miller spat the word out and closed the door.

The silence held its ground a little longer before a single voice repeated: *fake.* Then another and another. It became a new chant.

Fake ... fake ... fake ... fake.

Miller collected the knives he'd placed on the floor and returned to the body of the infected woman. Rather than watch him work, Robertson turned to the couple still sitting in the matted collection of bedding. They were quiet now, but he could see their lips moving in time to the new chant.

Stretched out alongside them, also in a tangle of stained bedding, a man flickered on the edge of consciousness. His skin hung on him and it seemed likely that he'd once been heavy; now he was slim, almost skinny. It would have been hard to gauge his age but for the smoothness of his cheeks. The only sign of facial hair was a tuft of wispy growth on his chin. He was slick with sweat and the skin at the angle of his jaw was swollen and red. A filthy bandage had begun to unwind from around his forearm; the exposed wound was feeding flies.

It was impossible to know what he was infected with. Given the conditions in the sickbay it might have been anything. The risk was that Toxo was tricking his body into staying alive.

Outside the room, there was the sound of glass shattering, and the chant of *fake* stopped dead as though a switch had been thrown.

Robertson lifted his axe and let it fall.

Chapter 33. Working in the City

Block Party

Example of black humour used among the members of official clean-up teams. A Block Party referred to a closed community that had been wiped out by internal violence. Most often these events seem to have been the result of HV-Tg-induced psychosis. On some occasions it appears to have been the result of community breakdown due either to stress or competition for limited supplies.

The A to Z of Gondii Names

April 12th, 2028

Lithograph Studios had put in a formal request that the flat and contents be left undisrupted as far as possible. It was a plea for courtesy dressed in legalese rather than a document that held any weight. Museum piece or not, the search warrant had turned Maccallan's flat into part of an ongoing investigation. So, I stole a can of some generic brand cola from Maccallan's supply store.

It was only slightly flat and would have fetched a reasonable price on the black market. I figured Lithograph Studios could sue me if they wanted. It was worth it.

Perhaps it's my accountant's brain, but it was the little details of life post-Outbreak that got to me. The big-ticket items: not seeing my family, Dog Boy laying in a pool of blood; those I could package up and put in a mental file marked deal with later. The little details, however, slipped out and picked at me: living through the Outbreak, then not being able to find a bottle of decent shampoo, or a bottle of coke. Things like that crept up on me and reminded me how shit life had become.

I took the cola, pilfered from the kitchen cupboard, and sat at the famous coffee table. The sofa was nowhere near as comfortable as it looked, and it had a definite fragrance to it. Maccallan's months of enclosed living had sweated their mark into it. I'd sat on worse.

The paperwork in the bedroom had taken thoroughness into the hinterlands of obsession. The room had become a shrine to finance, laid down by a high priest. Each transaction was detailed with the devotion of the zealot. Black and white truth, column after column of it. Precise, honest and correct.

And, in accordance with my experience of religion, it didn't make an ounce of sense when you exposed it to the light.

I finished the coke and stole another, finished that one too, before I gave up waiting for Winslow to return. His location was easy enough to trace in the stillness of the empty building. I could hear his foot tapping on the floor of the flat above.

The corridor above was identical to Maccallan's. Four doors and a window at one end. Three of the four doors had been forced open. The entries hadn't been made with any finesse. The flat Winslow was in, the one that sat directly above Maccallan's, was alone in having an intact door.

Like the corridor, the structure of the flat was a direct copy of the one below. The limited size of the rooms meant even the layout of the furniture was similar.

Winslow was sitting in the middle of a sofa facing another coffee table. My footfall sounded harshly when I walked into the room. Where Maccallan had favoured thick carpet, the owner of this unit had gone in for hardwood flooring.

"Nice place, eh?" Winslow said by way of acknowledging me. He kept up the tap, tap, tap of his foot.

"Yeah, I guess."

The answer was rewarded by a thin smile.

"I am particularly impressed with the modern art."

Without turning to look, he pointed over his shoulder. Towards the bedroom.

The flat had been finished with minimal clutter and a great deal of white eggshell paint. Around the doorway to the bedroom the calming lack of colour had been defiled by a spray of darkness. It kinked through a right angle at the juncture where the wall met the ceiling. The general shape was roughly ovoid, but it broke down into irregular tendrils along the bottom edges where runs had formed. On the other side of the doorway, two or three feet into the bedroom, the floor held a shapeless black witness mark.

"Blood?" I asked, in case Winslow had any other theory.

"Don't see what else really."

"Someone caught a Gonzo." The tapping on the floor started up again. I gritted my teeth. "You have another idea?"

"That was my first thought, but …" He stopped the toe tap and did his 'I'm thinking' act instead, rubbing his fingertips into his temples. "This is the seventh floor. I've not seen many Romeos that had the coordination to manage seven flights of stairs."

"It takes people different ways."

I was thinking of the attack on the quarantined street in Paris, and the fast moving Gonzos in the earlier days of the Outbreak.

"Maybe, but how many did you ever see with that sort of coordination or cognition … even with your vast experience."

I conceded the point, but mostly so he could have his victory. Male pride has always held a higher value than a woman's argument. Some things the Outbreak hadn't changed.

"Then maybe a resident switched. They're lying in bed waiting for the Toxo to kill them, only they switch instead. Whoever else was in the house …" I waved at the pattern of blood sprayed over the wall.

Winslow made a pinched face of disappointment. Then he ran his fingertips along the arm of the sofa he was sitting on and made a show of inspecting them for soiling. The white leather upholstery was clean.

When people started dying there had still been enough of an infrastructure left to keep records and file reports. There had probably been enough 'civilisation' left about the place for people to argue about who should fund the research, while they filled out expenses claims. Deaths attributed to HV-Tg had been well documented. Reports after the disease mutated, or evolved, or was altered in secret underground labs – take your pick, the internet is rich with theories – were thinner on the ground. With resources stretched to breaking point and beyond, speed and safety become the priorities. Detailed clinical reports of the point of 'switch over' weren't so common. The few there were, and of course the raft of anecdotal stories, nearly all agreed on one point. Come the end, be it the loss of life or the loss of mind, the body emptied. Gut, bowels and bladder. Whatever the body held it lost.

I took a step nearer to the blood-stained doorway. There was more evidence of blood loss; drops and smears that I avoided treading on even through they'd been dry shadows for years. The bed was an oversized monster that filled most of the space. At the far side of the room it abutted the floor-to-ceiling window. It had been made up with a heavy cotton sheet. It bore a few creases from use and there was a small patch of black mould where it was touching the window glass. That aside, it was clean. No stained rings from body fluids. Also, no blood.

"You see the bed?" Winslow asked. "See the problem?"

"Too clean for a sick bed."

"And …"

I tried not to sigh heavily, and failed.

"Look, Winslow, I understand, I get it, okay? You're a real cop reading a crime scene, and I'm a jumped-up accountant with no idea what any of this means. I accept that, but I'm sorry, I'm all out of medals to give. So why don't you just tell me what I'm meant to be seeing here, so we can get on?"

There was pause and I thought we were about to fill it with a shouting match. Then Winslow pushed himself up from the sofa and came to where I was standing. He didn't get into my personal space but the look of contempt was as good as a slap in the face.

"Okay, Detective Sergeant Cross, I'll tell you what you're not seeing. I just thought you might want to think it through, so you could get some idea of the job you're meant to be doing."

He turned away from me before I had a chance to come back at him. That was good; I didn't have anything to come back with.

"This," he made an impatient gesture that encompassed the bloodied doorway and floor, "is where someone was murdered in cold blood."

"And what about it? Go anywhere in this city and throw a goddamn stone, you'll hit a spot where someone got killed. You're in London now, not Lincoln."

Winslow gave me another contemptuous look.

"You don't have a bloody clue, you know that? Not a bloody clue."

"And you think you do?"

Winslow didn't bother with any more scathing looks. He turned his back on me and crossed the room to the sliding glass wall. He tried the action of the window and found it slid with some effort. There was no balcony, just a waist-height sheet of safety glass. If he'd intended to let fresh air in then it had been a vain attempt. The smell of the city seeped in.

London had a particular odour to it. Maybe it always had. I'd never visited the city before the Outbreak, so I couldn't say. It wasn't anything I could put a name to, it was just something not right, sick and … slow. I'd never smelt it when I was in France. There the stench was immediate: smoke, blood, shit. London smelt of something just out of sight, creeping up behind you.

Maybe that was what Winslow smelled too; perhaps that was what he wanted me to pick up. He stared out of the window for a few seconds, then spat before turning round to face me again.

"I get told I'm going to be part of the Historic Crime Department. I'm going to be investigating crimes committed during the Lockdown." He jerked his thumb over his shoulder, at the view of the city. "The city's dying on its feet. I lost count of the reported robberies the first day I got here. I can't remember a single week when we didn't get a rape come in. But what do I get told to do? Pull in Colin Robertson, because someone in Washington thinks he killed Maccallan."

He stopped talking and I wondered what I was meant to say. I settled for telling him I was in the same boat.

Winslow nodded.

"Why?"

"What do you mean why? Rule of law, justice. Take your pick."

"I mean why you? There's plenty of US citizens got caught on the wrong side of the pond. Why are you handed a gold star and told you're the sheriff?"

"Financial experience. If there was a financial gain to be made it gives motive …"

Winslow waved my words away with his hand. I had to fight the urge to run across the room and shoulder him out of the window.

"Spare me the bullshit. Do you honestly believe anyone in the US gives a toss about Robertson killing Maccallan? If they did care, I'd be standing here with a detective, not a bloody accountant."

"There are other considerations." Winslow stared at me with a blank expression. The only indication of how he felt was the depth of his breathing. Slow and controlled. "The bullion in the vaults …"

I didn't get to finish. Winslow shook his head in disgust and crossed the room again, leaving the window wide open behind him.

"I'll tell you what, you stick to your story and crunching your numbers. If we get to put that dickhead Robertson away, I'll live with not knowing why you pretend to care."

The outburst seemed to have run its course. He pointed at the dried blood sprayed round the door frame.

"Whoever died here, they weren't a Gonzo, or a plague victim and they died running away from someone they probably knew and trusted. And I'd say it's a fair bet whoever killed them also killed the tenant in the flat next door and whoever was in the flat upstairs. I'd say if Robertson did kill Maccallan he did it here. I don't think anyone left this flat alive."

From Kings of Crows: Life on the Wrong Side of the Lockdown

I can't imagine there's anyone caught up in the Lockdown who doesn't have regrets. We were desperate, scared. We had to hold on to the hope that we'd get through it and get back to normal. Some days that wasn't easy; it wasn't easy to think straight.

Looking back, it's easy to see the signs that Toxo had run its course. We saw air traffic more. Not huge amounts but we saw planes from time to time. It's easy, now, in hindsight to think we were stupid not to realise that things were being pulled under control again. But a lot of our people had died; it had been over a year. That sounds like a short time. It's funny to think that the pandemic has been over for more time than it was active. But that was a long, long year. Especially when you consider how quickly everything had fallen apart.

My biggest regret is crossing the Thames. All of us that had been through so much crossed the river thinking we were heading to the promised land. And we were mown down by those scum. At the time we thought they were official army. I didn't find out they were deserters until later. Not that it matters.

I should have pressed harder to stay on the south side. But I followed Miller. I think that's one of the reasons he killed himself. He blamed himself for the deaths of the people those deserters murdered.

From recording of police interview with Colin Robertson (10th April 2028)

Winslow - You talk about Miller like he didn't care about any of the people in the group. So, why did he hang himself?
Robertson - Is that your latest idea? I murdered Miller?
Winslow - This is off the record. I'm just wondering why he killed himself.
Robertson - No Toxo. Killing was all he did, no more Gonzos equals nothing left to kill, equals nothing to live for.

March 1st, 2021

He'd washed as best he could. His last bottle of bleach was almost finished, and he'd used a weaker solution than he'd have liked. He'd used most of it on the front of his combat trousers. Now they clung to his legs as he climbed the stairs to Sol's floor.

The axe he'd held off cleaning. He knew he'd have to do it but couldn't face the idea of maintaining the weapon so soon after killing the infected man on the fourth floor. He'd had to do the same to others. It was something he made an effort not to get used to; despite the effort it was getting easier. Along with corralling Miller, dispatching the infected before they turned – while they were still human, in effect – had fallen largely to him. Maccallan was one of the few others willing to undertake the task. For Robertson, it was another reason to dislike the man. It made him wonder how the other members of the group regarded him.

Sol was boiling water when he found him, using the open drawer of a steel filing cabinet as a grate. Smoke was gathering along the ceiling before being drawn through a ragged hole smashed in the window. Robertson had done that with his axe. It had been strangely disappointing. He'd anticipated a destructive burst of energy. Instead the toughened safety glass had put up an almost passive resistance, refusing to shatter in a satisfying way.

"You want tea?" Sol asked.

"If you're offering."

Through other, intact, windows Robertson could see grey banks of cloud moving along the jagged horizon. If the weather was going to turn bad it would be harder to cross the river. He pushed the thought to one side.

"We need to get moving," he said.

Sol added another file to the blaze before looking up.

"We need to wait for the solider boys to move on."

"Miller's getting worse. This cult he's got buzzing around him is frying whatever fucking brain he's got left. We need to get moving again, get people active."

Sol nodded to himself. He wasn't looking at Robertson now; his attention was on feeding the fire with sheets of filing paper.

After a while he said, "Does Miller still listen to you?"

Robertson moved nearer the filing cabinet, putting up with the smoke to take advantage of the warmth.

"If I'm telling him something he wants to hear. I don't know how much longer that's going to hold for."

"But his … people, they still follow him?"

"Yeah, but it's almost like he's playing a part. It's hard to describe."

"We make our gods in our own image; you need to remember that."

"Yeah, very fucking deep. We need to get out of this building. The floor Miller and co are building their church in is a fucking cesspit. It we stay here much longer we'll be riddled with fucking cholera."

"Have you spoken with Maccallan?"

"Fuck Maccallan."

"We need Maccallan."

"Not for this. Once we're over in the city proper, yeah. But this is where you need me."

Sol shrugged and took hold of the kettle. The tremor in his hands was pronounced.

"How do you propose getting everyone across the Thames?"

"We can still cross on Millennium Bridge. They fucked it up when they blew the charges. Alyson said there's a couple of places that need swimming but only about twenty yards. I reckon we can get most people across."

Sol pulled a zip-lock bag from a pocket and struggled to open it. Robertson watched him for almost a minute before taking the bag and extracting one of the teabags.

"And if it collapses halfway over?"

Robertson dropped the bag into a mug that Sol had waiting on the top of the filing cabinet.

"Alyson said it's pretty solid. It's how she got back across, that's why her hands were so cut up." He could feel Sol's expression before he saw it. "I didn't say it was easy. But we'll be doing it in daylight, we'll be ready. Alyson had just seen her husband shot dead, then she'd had to make her way back through all the Gonzos."

"We won't get everyone across," Sol said.

"We don't need everyone. If we get Miller and his band of arseholes across that'll be enough to deal with the Gonzos. Then we find out if Maccallan's big talk translates into something other than empty yap."

"And if it doesn't?"

"Then I'll do what I should have fucking done when I first saw the twat –

break his legs and leave him to crawl back home."

Sol produced another mug from a drawer. The office block was a seemingly endless source of obsolete paperwork and mugs. As he poured water, his tremor seemed less pronounced.

"Maccallan will come good," he told Robertson.

Chapter 34. Room at the Top

Butcher's Block

A residential high-rise/tower block where a large group of residents/survivors gathered in hope of escaping HV-Tg infection or the violence that followed in the wake of the pandemic. These endeavours had a low success rate and attempts to sustain a closed community within a single structure usually led to a concentrated loss of life. Most of the buildings/communities were abandoned as they began to fail but, in some cases, huge numbers of bodies have been discovered on one site.

The A to Z of Gondii Names

April 12th, 2028

Winslow puppy-walked me through the crime scenes. At first, he'd been angry and condescending. Leaving gaps in the explanation for me to fill, knowing I couldn't. As we'd worked through the building, he lost patience with his own performance and just delivered his findings.

Another detective, a real detective, might have been able to pick holes in his case, but that person wasn't me.

Whoever had died in the apartment had sprayed blood high enough to hit the ceiling. It had been directed at the doorway. The pool of blood on the other side of the wall suggested they made it through before falling over and bleeding out what little blood was left to them. The living room, the hallway and the front door were all intact, no splintered frames, no overturned furniture. Someone had walked in without fuss, got to the front room and, or so Winslow surmised, pulled out a heavy bladed weapon and hit their victim as they panicked and ran.

"You thinking of the famous axe?"

Winslow shrugged.

"As you keep pointing out, this city was a war zone. Axes were ten a penny." He shrugged again. "But, yeah."

The kitchen was bare, completely stripped of edibles. The bathroom had been similarly stripped – soap, toilet rolls, shampoos all gone. Winslow pointed out a box of sanitary pads and a near empty bottle of feminine hygiene wash.

"Male assailant," he said pointlessly.

It was on the tip of my tongue to tell him I could guess that, but I bit the response back. Until that point, I'd gathered nothing from the crime scene other than blood loss. I hadn't earned the right to be talked to like a fellow police officer.

The doors on the floor's other three apartments had been forced. On two of them the wood of the frames had been levered away until the locks had nothing to hold onto. The third was just as badly damaged but the door had the addition of a sole pattern, from what looked like a trainer. It was repeated half a dozen times round the lock.

"Pick a dawr," Winslow said, trying to do an American accent. He stood in the hall, sweeping across the options like a fifties gameshow host.

I picked the one with the footprints stamped into it. He nodded, but otherwise didn't indicate that I'd made a good choice. The pattern of blood loss here was different. The tastefully pale colours were in evidence here too, but without the big picture windows the lighting didn't do the effect justice. The splatters of blood appeared black on grey in the dimness. There didn't appear to be the clear-cut areas of loss there had been in the first apartment. Both sides of the narrow hall were marked with abstract shapes. The only one that really told me a human had been involved was a smudged handprint about halfway down the hall, two or three feet from floor level.

I made my hand in the shape of the print and orientated myself so the direction of my finger and thumb matched. My thumb pointed down towards the chocolate brown carpet and my splayed fingers faced the front door.

"Whoever was bleeding fell backward while they were facing the door. Slapped their hand against the wall to try to save themselves?"

Winslow nodded, "That's what it looks like to me."

I shone my torch onto the carpet. Its dark colour had done a good job of soaking up and hiding the blood but in the beam of light it was possible to see the weave was matted and congealed. Even allowing for what had soaked away it seemed a modest amount after the blackened puddle in the bedroom next door.

"Could they have survived?"

"I don't think so. If I'm reading this right, this fella …" – he gestured at the patch of stained carpet – "… took on whoever smashed through the door. He gets injured, and gets knocked on his arse, or trips. Once he's down…" – he tapped himself in the centre of his forehead, denoting a killing blow – "Gonzo style."

Hollywood had chosen to ignore the facts about HV-Tg, the better to produce a good zombie film. The victims of the pandemic, driven into psychosis by the brain lesions it caused didn't need a head wound to kill them. It was simply the surest way. Gaping stomach wounds, punctured lungs, even hacked off limbs could be ignored as the disease drove its host to spread the word.

But dead was dead.

Marksmen tended to go for the chest and try to blow the heart out. Blunt trauma or swinging blades were better directed at the skull.

Brain death was quickly followed by organ shutdown. The heart stopped beating. Unlike the high-pressure bleed-out from a severed carotid artery, most of the blood would have stayed in the body.

The rest of the apartment told the same story as its neighbour. Stripped of everything useful, but with no signs of disease or hurry. All the kitchen cupboards were bare, but their doors had all been closed. In the bedroom the bed had been stripped.

I asked Winslow if he'd been into the other apartments on the floor.

"Yeah. They've been stripped bare but there are no signs of violence."

His tone of voice implied there was a 'but'. Rather than tell me what it was he pointed at the ceiling.

The floor above held only two apartments. Bigger than the ones below they were the closest the block could claim to having a penthouse. They didn't run to rooftop gardens but they both had oversized balconies dressed with potted shrubs.

The doors of both apartments were open. In an echo of the floor underneath, one of the doors had been smashed open while the other was just open. That was where the similarity stopped. The landing on the top floor had been used as a junkyard. At one end a pile of drinks bottles had accumulated. Most of them were broken. It looked as if they'd been hurled the length of the corridor once they'd been drained. Emptied food cans and boxes had been tossed out. There were other items too, a pair of laptop computers lay on the floor along with a huge flat screen TV. They'd all been smashed. At the top of the stairwell there was a three-piece suite and a bed frame. They'd been stacked to form a barricade but the builder had lacked the skill of whoever had fortified the lower floors. Someone had shouldered their way past.

The apartment with the broken door didn't interest Winslow much. He showed it to me but didn't bother pointing out things I might be missing. It looked like a lot of emptied property I'd seen on my way across Paris. It had been looted. Not in the way the apartment below had been stripped; this was a sloppy job. Someone had gone in and grabbed whatever they saw. The kitchen was coated with knives and forks where the drawers had been pulled out and upended. Two of the cupboard doors had been torn off in a fit of rage. Probably because they'd been empty. Because I'd seen it before I recognised it for what it was, an abandoned home that had been ransacked.

The apartment with the intact door was a mess too but in a different way. There were more food wrappers here and more bottles. Emptied too, but left where they'd fallen. Soiled plates and cutlery had been left around the sofa. You could see the holes in the plaster where the flat-screen TV had been ripped out before being completely destroyed in the corridor. Clothes, most of them dirty, had been left on the floor.

Like its neighbour the apartment boasted a pair of bedrooms. In one the bed was covered with a shambles of dirty sheets and duvets. In the other, the king size mattress was completely bare and stained rust brown. More blood.

"Kitchen's stripped," Winslow said. "I doubt there was much to take though, looking at this."

He kicked a wine bottle. It rolled less than a foot before coming to a halt against a box that had contained luxury biscuits.

Whoever had occupied the apartment had cracked up. Not everyone who went mad had Toxo. I didn't have Winslow's detective training, but I could make a fair guess at what had gone down on the top floor. Someone made a bolthole for themselves and then cooked their brain in their own company. Boredom, desperation, frustration, building up over the days. The TV stops, the internet breaks down, the lights go out. Nothing to do but drink and worry.

"Do you think this guy was our killer downstairs?"

"No. Whoever did the killing down there was clinical about what they did. I'm more inclined to think this apartment was just the last stop on the tour."

He pointed at the doorway of the bedroom with the blood-stained mattress. This apartment had been carpeted throughout in deep cream. It was hard to find an inch of it that wasn't stained or littered with waste. The detritus had served to leave a record of something heavy being dragged from the bedroom, across to the sliding glass window and out onto the patio/balcony.

The make-believe roof-top garden hadn't fared well on its own. Something that resembled a scaled-down palm tree was rotting quietly in a corner. Next to it was a mound of fabrics, tangled and black with mould. When I looked closely it was possible to make out the remains of a human torso.

A crow was perched on the chest-high railing that secured the balcony's edges. It watched the pair of us as we stood gazing at the mutilated corpse. Maybe it was trying to figure out why we weren't tucking in. In the tangle of rotting bedding, things were moving. Winslow waved his arm at the crow and made a hissing noise through his teeth. The bird stretched its wings, then decided we weren't worth the effort of flight and merely shuffled a few feet along the railing.

Aside from the corpse and the remains of the potted landscape, the balcony had held a metal café table and chairs. There were half a dozen empty wine bottles on the table and a wooden knife block. The block was a swollen ruin now, but it looked expensive. The sort of thing men dress their kitchens with and seldom, if ever, use. One of the knives had been left out, resting on the table. A huge butchering blade, it was far larger than anything required in a domestic kitchen.

Neither of us were speaking and I could tell the crow wanted us to hurry up and go.

"Okay," I told Winslow, "unless this fella wants his tax returns done, you're the expert here, so what's happening?"

"Disposing of the bodies. Our man drags his kills up here, probably wrapped in the bedding stripped off the mattresses. Hacks them into manageable sized pieces that he can just sling over the side." He pointed at the railing and the watchful crow. "Keeps the rot out of the building."

"And disposes of the evidence."

"I don't think that was a consideration. Purely practical. He's made no attempt to cover up what's been done. Why would he? From what I'm forever being told, about what it was like in London, a lot of people must have thought it was the end of civilisation. No more laws, no rules."

"So now what? What's the next police move?"

Winslow laughed, but not at anything funny.

"That body's been out here for years. Even if we had the facilities to run something resembling a forensics department, we don't have the staff to work it. We get to file a report. Fill out some forms in triplicate about suspecting foul play. Then someone else files it."

He pulled one of the café chairs out and checked it for debris before sitting on it. I could feel the frustration coming from him.

"Did you want to be a detective?" I asked. "I mean before the Outbreak, was that your game plan?"

"My game plan." He tried, again, to do an American accent and I bridled at it. He saw he'd pissed me off and held his hands up. "I'm sorry, I'm sorry. Yeah, I wanted to be a detective ever since I was a kid. He lifted one of the bottles from the table and threw it at the crow. It hit the retaining wall a few feet to the bird's left. With a rattle of caws, it flapped away. "Now here I am, living the dream. Look, I'm sorry if I've given you a hard time. The truth is you're more of a copper at the moment than I am. You've got Washington behind you, the old …" He rubbed his fingertips together in the universal sign language of money. "What you flag up will probably be acted on. Me? Forget it."

Cue the awkward silence.

"I don't think Washington's going to give a shit about what I've found out."

He stood and avoided eye contact by pretending to brush dust from his knees.

"Come on then, let's go through it."

Chapter 35. Travel Plans

Primary Stage (Type One)

Quasi-scientific phrase relating to the different expressions of HV-Tg. The mutated form of the Toxoplasma gondii parasite was highly unstable and displayed several variations, some of which differed from region to region. In the early months of the Outbreak victims of HV-Tg-induced psychosis were, in cognitive terms, indistinguishable from clinically-diagnosed psychopaths. In parts of Northern Europe there were incidents of the infected orchestrating mass attacks and even staging sieges. This phenomenon was short-lived and has been incorrectly categorised as a primary-stage infection.

The A to Z of Gondii Names

March 3rd, 2021

The support cables running along the right side of the bridge had broken into uneven lengths. The centre span of the structure twisted as it drooped into the water. Crossing it was going to be more climb than walk.

"We might be better off trying to find an intact boat," Maccallan said.

"I did a head count," Robertson told him. "We currently number fifty-two. Twelve of them are too young or too sick to cross. I'd say another six will opt to stay with them. Which leaves around thirty-five."

"If we find a boat, everyone can get across," Maccallan said. He was looking sideways at Robertson.

"We won't find a boat that'll carry fifty-two punters. We won't find any fucking thing in running order, and even if we did, what are the chances of finding any fuel that'll still do anything?"

Maccallan didn't want to let the idea go. "So we round up a load of little boats."

"Little boats? What do you think this is, fucking Dunkirk?"

"I'm saying …"

Robertson spat in the direction of the twisted bridge.

"All you're fucking saying is, 'Look at me, look at me.' If we find ten boats, plus oars we're still looking at five trips. And how much fucking rowing have you done lately? Same as everyone else, bugger all. Alyson can find another kayak and paddle over if she wants, but it's no safer than climbing that thing."

"That's what you say. Try telling everyone else that. See what they think of it."

Robertson spat again, ignored Maccallan.

"How many of those freaks has Miller got up on the fourth?"

Johnno pulled a face, "Twenty. Twenty or thereabouts."

"Twenty-three," Robertson corrected him. "Two of them currently keeping Miller entertained in the sickbay."

Johnno nodded rapidly.

"Miller's clean though, boss. Ally sees to that, she's solid. Straight as a die, you can rely on her."

Robertson looked at the man without speaking.

When the big Scouser started shifting his weight from foot to foot, he said, "I'm relying on you, Johnno. You understand?"

"Yeah, Boss. I get you."

"You're planning what exactly?" Sol said. It was the first time he'd spoken since the four of them had gone to look at the bridge.

"Same plan as always, 'cos it works. Miller leads, others follow."

"I think you're overestimating his pull. Have you seen the state everyone's in?"

Robertson nodded. He knew it better than any of them. Maccallan was spending his days in glorious isolation in the luxury offices at the top. Sol was keeping clear of the great unwashed on the second floor. Even Johnno was restricting himself, as far as Robertson would allow him to, to the fourth floor. Robertson couldn't work out if the man was tied up with the cult or just infatuated with Ally. Either possibility worried him at some level.

The cult of Miller, as Sol called it, was getting more insular. Sol's cryptic remark, that people made gods in their own image, had got stuck in his head like an unloved song. He was beginning to see what the old bastard had been getting at. The cult was going to outgrow its idol if things were left to stand. Some action, some drive, was overdue.

"I'm not talking about the whole group. I'm thinking about the freak show on four, with the feathers and the chanting. If Miller says it time to cross the river, they go."

He was aware of Johnno shifting his weight from side to side again. He waited for him to speak.

"Ally's got a lot of sway with the Crows." He laughed, but it was forced. "That's what they call themselves, the Crows. Because of the way the crows …"

Robertson waved a hand to shush him.

"I get it. You're saying she's going to stop them following Miller?"

He'd moved in close to the man without realising he was doing so. They were inches apart.

"They don't really follow Miller, Boss. It's like they follow the crows. They act a bit like Miller's the king of the crows. It's all a bit weird."

Maccallan snorted a laugh. He was standing a few feet to Johnno's rear. Robertson caught the dismissive glance he cast at the Scouser's back.

"Well that's great isn't it?" Maccallan said. "The one thing your pet psycho's any good for and now you're even losing that."

Robertson's head began to pound, and he felt his knuckles crack as his hand tightened on the handle of his axe. He pictured putting the blade through

Maccallan's face. The moment of madness passed, though the anger was still there.

With an effort of will he let go of the axe and, with both his hands free, grabbed the front of Johnno's camo jacket. Caught by surprise the bigger man stumbled back, only keeping on his feet because of Robertson's grip on him.

"Get this fucking straight, pal, and make bloody sure that daft tart of yours knows it too. I am the King of the Fucking Crows, me."

He let go his hold on the dirt-glazed jacket and Johnno, again caught by surprise, had to take three or four hurrying backwards steps. When he was fully upright, he looked ready to fight, but Robertson had used the time to pick his axe up again. The big Scouser, breathing deeply, took another backward step, slower this time, distancing himself.

"What do you see?" Robertson asked, making a huge effort to keep his voice steady.

He pointed across the river. Low over the opposite bank, a huge flock of birds circled.

"Crows," Sol said when it was clear no one else was going to answer.

"We move out of that fucking cesspit tomorrow morning. Everyone. You," he pointed at Johnno, "tell your high fucking priestess, or whatever she is, we're off to feed the birds. I'll tell Crow-Headed Jesus there's more Gonzo over there for him to butcher."

April 12th, 2028

"This type of thing bores me to tears," Winslow said.

He was standing in the doorway of Maccallan's bedroom, doing his best to look disdainfully at the piles of numbers. I'd seen the pose too often to be fooled by it. People, men especially, don't like to admit ignorance; better to affect indifference. Or in Winslow's case, disdain.

"If you want to know less about the investigation just say so," I told him. "Teaching you math isn't on my bucket list, okay?"

Winslow made a production number out of agreeing to listen. In truth there wasn't a lot to tell him. I gave him the overview. The massive collection of paper was a blow by blow account of financial fraud that had gone on for years. Detailed with obsessive care.

If pressed I'd have said it was a boy thing. One of those male habits like putting CDs in alphabetical order and keeping coins in a saucer by the side of the bed. Pointless activities that achieve nothing but give an appearance of order. Or more importantly to the male ego, control.

The sheets of paper on the bed told a single self-contained story. Maccallan had been skimming money from the letting agency he managed since day one. Modest amounts to begin with but getting progressively bigger until, by the end of the second year, they plateaued. The sums weren't huge, but they represented a steady income. Clients were targeted by their ability to take a loss without feeling it. I'd seen enough similar transactions and misdirection to know better than think the victims were being shown mercy.

The morality of the piece was lost at the first theft. Victims weren't being chosen on the basis that they could afford it; they were picked on the basis that they wouldn't notice they were being robbed. It was a common set-up. What set Maccallan's efforts apart was that he'd kept to the plan. The majority of people I'd watched sweating into their expensive suits had gotten greedy. Once that happened, they took a little more, then a little more, then someone noticed.

Maccallan hadn't made that mistake; in fact, reading through his records he hadn't made any mistakes. He'd set up some cash cows, took a modest amount of their yields and settled in for the long game. He'd even had the good sense to sit on the money rather than burn through it like a two-ended candle.

Then Europe had fallen apart and taken the world economy with it.

The biggest skims were taken at the end of 2020, just before I was trapped in Paris and the US banking system bolted the doors and stopped trading. The last document Maccallan had added to the list was a bank transfer that had been cancelled before the skim took place. A slightly bigger amount than usual.

The bland line of text stating the transaction was N and V had been highlighted in dayglo green, then a border had been drawn round it in contrasting yellow. The final marker had been a circling of red biro that had worn through the paper. I could picture Maccallan sitting with pen and paper, putting a circle round this last detail again and again.

"Why would he do this?" Winslow said. "It must set some record for the world's most detailed confession."

"Look, Winslow, I'm not trying to say you had an easy time in Lincoln, but it was different in places like this, here, and Paris. It wasn't just a national emergency, it was game over, there was no law and order. At least, that's how it felt. We thought it was Judgement Day, and everything was over, no more government, police, radio, electricity. We were heading back to the caves."

"No accountability?"

"Exactly."

Winslow looked uncomprehendingly at the pages of figures.

"Still, why?"

"Mourning and regrets. What was it Robertson came out with, everyone's got a sob story? This is Maccallan's." I picked up the sheet with the highlighted cancellation on it. "This is the day after the American banks stopped trading with non-domestic economies. I'm guessing Maccallan's long-term plan was to hide money away until he had enough to settle back and spend the rest of his days being rich."

The trouble with having 'rich' as goal is it's never enough. Maccallan had shown admirable restraint in the executions of his scam, but I would have bet a ticket back home that he hung on too long. Wanting just a little more. Then time had run out. In fairness, the speed of the Outbreak and the collapse of the world economy had taken everyone by surprise.

I showed Winslow the suitcase tucked under the bed, packed for a getaway. He shifted through the contents and thumbed the wad of euros. With a grin that was unpleasantly childlike he took a knife from his jacket pocket and used it to cut the lining from the lid of the case. Behind the fabric were three packages of clingfilm, held in place with strips of duct tape. Through the layers of clingfilm we could still see the packets were made up of high denomination notes.

"This was definitely break-for-border packing." He rocked back on his heels and eyed the contents of the case. "Why didn't he grab this when he left the flat?"

"What was the point? The money was no good by then."

"I know that, but there's soap and shaving kit here, changes of clothes. If you've got a case already packed, why leave it?"

"He left in a hurry. His breakfast was still on the table when they opened this place up. Maybe he just upped and ran."

After he'd tapped out a few beats he shook his head and pointed at the wardrobe.

It had been the subject for one of Gordon Price's iconic photographs: the door hanging open revealing gallons of bottled water and, on the floor just in front of it, the laptop computer with its broken screen. It would have been a banal detail in most settings, but amongst the obsessive order of the apartment it jabbed you in the eye.

"That cupboard is more or less full. The only gap is on that top shelf. That laptop wouldn't have filled it on its own."

Accountant or not, it was easy to see the point he was making. When Maccallan had left the apartment, for whatever reason, he grabbed one thing and ran with it. Snatched it from the top shelf, knocked the laptop down and left it where it landed.

He closed the lid on the case and started a tap-tap-tap. After he'd worked through a few paradiddles he pushed the case back under the bed.

"There was no passport in the case," he said.

I looked away from him in case my face gave anything away.

"Maybe he carried it with him all the time. If he thought he might need to run on short notice."

Winslow nodded to himself and seemed satisfied with the idea.

"So, what's all this?" He waved at the other set of accounts that carpeted the floor.

"I think that's a list of Robertson's crooked dealings."

From recording of police interview with Colin Robertson (14th April 2028)

Winslow - For the benefit of the tape I am showing Mr Robertson a sheet of A4 paper. Does this mean anything to you?
Robertson - It's a copy of a letter from Redman and Green's Properties Agency.
Winslow - A copy?
Robertson - The lettering is all in black. Redman and Green's headed paper had Redman printed in green and Green printed in red.
Winslow - Subtle.
Robertson - Head office thought so.
Winslow - For the benefit of the tape, would you read the content of the letter.
Robertson - "Dear Mr Brinkly, please find enclosed details of your account with Redman and Green's Properties Agency. Also enclosed is a contract for you to sign and return. We are pleased to welcome you to our list of clients and hope you will be satisfied with our service. If you have any questions, please do not hesitate to contact us."
Winslow - Would you tell us who signed the letter you've just read?
Robertson - There's no signature. This is a printout.
Cross - It hasn't been signed but a name still appears at the bottom. Would you read that out?
Robertson - C. Robertson.
Cross - Do you remember writing that letter?
Robertson - I worked at Redman and Green for bloody years. One day was much the same as the next: answer the phone, talk to some wanker wanting to let a flat out, write some letters, then go home.
Winslow - So, you deny writing it?
Robertson - I wrote a lot of letters, I don't remember them all. My name's on that one, so it's probably one of mine.
Cross - You're not curious as to why we're asking?
Robertson - No. I'm just bored with your double act. I've never liked clowns.
Cross - We searched Maccallan's flat. He'd documented, very carefully, several years of embezzlement. He'd misappropriated hundreds of thousands of pounds. He'd put some away in Swiss bank accounts, some into offshore holdings of American banks. And another chunk was lying around his flat in cash. If the Outbreak hadn't come along, he was on the path to being very rich.
Robertson - Then the world economy goes belly-up and all his sterling's worthless and all the US banks pulled up the drawbridge, so his dollars are lost.
Cross - Exactly.

Robertson - Just as well he's dead then. The disappointment would have killed him.
Winslow - For the benefit of the tape, I am showing Mr Robertson a page – of the book Scenes from a Crow's Nest by Gordon Price. Page ninety-three shows a photograph identified as four point zero seven. Do you recognise this, Mr Robertson?
Robertson - No.
Winslow - You don't know where this photograph was taken?
Robertson - I can read the caption. You want me to read it?
Winslow - Please.
Robertson - The caption reads: Bedroom floor. View on entering bedroom.
Cross - You don't recognise the interior of Mr Maccallan's flat?
Robertson - Look, me and Maccallan weren't friends. We worked together, and frankly we didn't like each other. We didn't socialise, we didn't invite each other around for tea and cake. And if we had, I very much doubt I'd have been looking around his bedroom.
Cross - Do the papers on the floor and the bed mean anything to you?
Robertson - No. Nothing at all.
Cross - The ones on the bed detail Maccallan's activities. They're very careful and precise. I've been sniffing out financial fraudsters for years, and I'll tell you, if the world hadn't gone all to shit, he'd have got away with it.
Robertson - Bully for him, shame he's dead.
Winslow - At least being dead, he won't be arrested for embezzlement.
Cross - The stuff on the floor is rank amateur level. Mickey Mouse tricks anyone with a calculator would spot.
Robertson - This is fascinating, really.
Cross - So, I find it very hard to imagine Maccallan, who obviously knew his way around a set of crook books, would do anything so clumsy. And the only name we have to connect these crocked transactions to is yours.
Winslow - Nothing to say?
Robertson - Oh, sorry I must have dozed off. All the excitement's wearing me out. What was the question?
Cross - Why is your name printed all over Maccallan's accounts of a fraud, perpetrated against Redman and Green and thirty-seven of their clients?
Robertson - The only thing you've got connecting me to any fraud is one sheet of paper, taken from a printout, with my name on it. Not even my signature.
Winslow - For a man who never visited Maccallan's flat and wasn't that close to him you seem to know a remarkable amount about what we did or didn't find there.
Robertson - If you pair of clowns had anything to pin on me, you'd have

charged me by now. And you, Lincoln, you'd have pulled in a wad of paperwork a foot thick and rubbed my nose in it.

Winslow - So, you've never been in Maccallan's flat?

Robertson - Catch on quick, don't you? I can see why they made you a detective.

Winslow - So, you don't know anything about the three murders that took place there?

Robertson - No.

Winslow - Did you know about the murders?

Robertson - No.

Winslow - You don't seem particularly surprised. Three murders in a building you have a connection to.

Robertson - First off, I have no connection to Maccallan's property. And secondly, I saw dozens, probably hundreds, of people die. Sorry if I don't have tears to shed for three more.

Winslow - The problem is, we only have your account of how Maccallan joined up with you and Miller. And what you've told us is a man leaves a very secure and well-stocked bolthole to traipse across London with, by your telling, a maniac and an old colleague who despised him. But what we're looking at is a very skilled financial fraudster who can implicate you with a piss poor rip-off job and who vanishes from his bolthole leaving three murders behind.

Robertson - Well you'd need to talk to him about that.

Winslow - But we can't, because he's dead.

Robertson - Him and the three others in his tower block. You trying to pin those on me as well?

Cross - What did Maccallan bring with him? When he joined your group, I mean. What did he turn up with?

Robertson - Nothing. He was empty-handed.

Chapter 36. Blessing in Black

In his book, Robertson talks about finding dead crows not long before they cross the Thames River in London. They don't make any reference to that in the film. Anyone know why?
User name: SinDee

****

I think they left it out of the film because of the occult/satanic overtones. That wouldn't have gone down well with some of the companies funding the film.
User name: tHATmOVIEgUY

****

But they were OK with making a zombie film?
User name: SinDee

****

The zombie thing was a result of the disease. The stuff about dead crows turning up was something else, something spooky.
User name: tHATmOVIEgUY

****

Not everyone believes the thing with the crows even happened. Robertson himself said they were strung-out by the time they got 2 the river. They may have left it out of the film to keep it real.
User name: A2Zee

****

There was nothing occult about the number of dead crows they found. In the lead up to the lockdown in 2021 the UK's cat population was massively reduced because of primary stage toxo (and the bounty on stray cats). For most birds in western cities, not just crows, the main predators are the domestic cat and road traffic. During the Lockdown there was a massive reduction in both.

Plus, the amount of dead lying in the streets meant the crows and other carrion feeders had a very good year. The number of Gonzos/Infected had already been reduced. In part due to the efforts of groups such as Robertson’s. The natural die back of corvids wasn’t increasing, it was just catching up.
Username: DOCTOR_CROW

March 5th, 2021

Ally led the group of Crows. They moved, in total silence, three or four paces behind her. She kept a similar distance from Miller. The solemnity of their measured paces was out of kilter with their idol.

Miller was excited, he was never still, breaking stride suddenly to peer into a doorway or through a shattered window. Robertson had to stop himself laughing; the man reminded him of a dog that had been kept inside too long. The only time he was calm was on finding a dead crow. He came to a halt without warning and dropped into a crouch. Robertson, already on edge, scanned the surrounding buildings, wondering if Miller had spotted some danger.

Karan, her measured pace undisturbed, walked up to Miller until she was almost on top of him. She made a sweeping motion with both arms. The group of followers swarmed past her and settled into a loose circle.

For a long time nothing happened. Then, mindlessly, one of the followers began to mutter, let them be, they will change. The low hum of gibberish was picked up and passed around. Soon everyone present was chanting.

Robertson had been keeping Miller in sight but maintaining a distance. It was mostly through habit. The 'cult' were ignoring the lessons of the last year and clustering together like sheep. The chanting occasionally lost a voice to a fit of coughing. Now with his view obscured by the Crows he stopped and adjusted the grip on his axe and waited.

The few members of the Crow people that didn't have hoods – tugged far forward so they resembled cowls – had laced strips of cloth with feathers and were wearing them as headbands. It had been Sol, as always, that had pointed out the resemblance to a crown of thorns.

Johnno and Patrick were close to the crowd but keeping a space around them. The sun was low, and Robertson had to squint to scrutinise them. They were in ragged jackets and jeans, unevenly grey from frequent splashes of bleach. No feathers, no hoods.

Johnno had climbed onto the roof of an abandoned car and was looking down into the knot of chanting people. Robertson gave a shrill whistle to get his attention. He pointed at the crowd and pantomimed looking baffled. Johnno shook his head and made a calming gesture with his hand, patting the air.

"That's meant to mean something?" Sol said.

He'd seen the big Scouser's mime of reassurance. Robertson grunted in reply.

The chanting stopped without a warning. The silence was so sudden Robertson started. When Sol patted him on the shoulder and told him to calm down, he jumped again.

The circle of people around Miller parted and Karan walked out with her hand held in front of her. She was holding the dead crow. Following some signal that he didn't see, three or four people – all of them with hoods – made their way to her. It took Robertson a moment to see what they were doing: plucking feathers from the dead bird. He saw Karan talking softly to the people, now clutching feathers. They broke away from her when she nodded.

One of them went over to a pair of the people from the second floor, the people Robertson had begun to think of as the regulars. With much gravitas he handed one of them a single feather and murmured something. The woman he'd given the feather to nodded and took the offering. Unnerved, she clearly had no idea what to do with it. The man drifted off and climbed onto the bonnet of the car Johnno was standing on. Johnno took the offered feather and bowed his head with every appearance of sincere gratitude. When he saw Robertson was watching him, he shrugged helplessly.

While hooded men distributed the feathers around the regulars, Ally made a beeline for Robertson and Sol. She kept her gaze level with Robertson's. He couldn't tell if she was being defiant or if she was oblivious of his hostility. She stopped a few feet short of them. Turning to Sol she selected one of the feathers with overacted care.

"Miller would like you to have this, with his blessing."

The delivery of the words was slow and in a slightly breathless way, as if addressing a toddler. Sol took the feather and told her, 'Thank you', mimicking her tone of sugar-sweet awe. She gave no sign that she'd noticed the sarcasm.

When she presented a long tail feather to Robertson, she smiled benignly.

"No thanks. Is Miller okay?"

The figures clustered around Miller were either staring at him fixedly or honing their knives. The knife sharpeners did it in harmony, synchronising the scrape of blade edge along steel. Miller wasn't joining in; he was still on his knees, staring at the patch of road in front of him.

Ally tried to give him the feather again. The benign smile was tightening against her teeth.

"I don't want a fucking feather, understand?" He batted her hand aside. "Is Miller alright?"

Ally took her time answering. Finally, "Miller thinks the crow is a bad omen. It's the seventh one we've seen since we left. The crows were thriving. Now we find them dead in the street." There was another pause, but Robertson waited. She hadn't broken eye contact or made to move on. "Miller would like you to have this feather. I would like you to have this feather."

He was about to tell her to fuck off, but Sol cleared his throat, pointedly. Without saying anything Robertson took the feather and made his way towards Miller. Not meaning to, he broke stride when he reached the loose circle surrounding their idol. One or two of the knife sharpeners lost the beat as he moved inside the circle that contained Miller.

Miller had gained weight. He guessed the Crows must have been donating a portion of their own rations to him. Where everyone else was shedding pounds, Miller had gained the beginning of a paunch.

He didn't look up as Robertson approached. The excitement of earlier was over.

"Hey, you okay?" He'd softened his tone slightly and the sound of his own voice surprised him. "What's the matter?" he asked, over-compensating and sounding harsh.

Behind him somewhere there was another catch in the harmony as the sharpeners lost the beat again. Robertson was glad to see Johnno moving towards him.

Miller still hadn't answered. Robertson squatted in front of him and had to crook his neck to see the man's face. His eyes were glazed.

"Hey, hey Miller." He tried to keep his voice neutral.

"Hello, Col." His voice was flat, and he sounded tired.

Somewhere behind him four, maybe five, voices murmured, "Hello, Col."

"We should be moving on, you know," Robertson said. "Getting over the river, heading to the big city and the bright lights."

His voice had softened again. He didn't bother correcting.

"Keep finding crows, Col. Why is that?" Miller shook his head, though the movement was one of confusion, not denial. "Why are the crows dying? They like us."

The same voices, "Why are the crows dying? They like us."

"Maybe they're trying to tell us something."

Robertson looked up. The suggestion had come from one of the hooded men giving out the feathers. He'd arrived at Miller's shoulder silently. Robertson could see Maccallan wasn't far away. From the way he was watching the exchange it was clear he'd instigated it in some fashion.

Miller looked uncertain. He didn't look like someone to lead the masses.

"Tell us what?" Robertson said.

He'd stood and hissed the question into the man's face. The man took a step back and Robertson had to make a conscious effort not to go after him and square up.

"Telling us it's time to move away. Telling us … telling us…"

"Forgotten the script?" Robertson spoke quietly.

The confusion looked genuine. Robertson guessed the man was being played, rather than complicit. The confusion vanished in a flash of fear when Robertson put the flat side of the axe against the man's shoulder and ushered him aside. All the while he had his attention on Maccallan.

Maccallan had one of the dead crow's feathers pushed into the lapel of his shooting jacket.

"You think the crows have got something to fucking say?" He shouted at him. He'd meant the question to sound like ridicule. It hadn't come out that way, he was too angry.

Maccallan didn't make his move until everyone's attention was on him. He ignored Robertson and stepped round him. Putting a hand on Miller's back, he bent to speak into the man's ear. Miller barely acknowledged him, but the posture gave the impression of intimacy. When Maccallan spoke, he kept his voice loud enough to be heard.

"Perhaps the crows want us to move on. This place isn't fit for them anymore. They're on the other side of the river now. The crows have crossed over."

He intoned the last phrase, raising his voice slightly. When he'd finished, it seemed too quiet, too still. A woman's voice, Robertson was sure it was Ally, picked up the idea.

"The crows have crossed over." She didn't shout but the expectant stillness was eager for something to fill it, and the cry was picked up and became a new chant.

Miller was excited again, by the idea of crossing the river or just the sudden rush of noise – Robertson couldn't tell. Suddenly on his feet, he pulled two of his biggest knives free of their webbing and began running. Thankfully in the right direction.

Now the chanting was ragged, cries and yells overlapping and mingling. The followers abandoned the measured pacing and silence and ran to catch their idol.

The exception was Ally. She held herself with studied detachment and strode in their wake, making no attempt to keep up. Johnno kept pace with her. He was still holding the 'blessed' feather he'd been given.

Maccallan watched them go. Before he made to follow, he gave Robertson a wide smile.

"And that, Collie, is how it's done."

Chapter 37. Flotsam

KINGS OF CROWS, BACK BY POPULAR DEMAND!
2021 LONDON BRIDGE TAKEBACK TOUR!

Medium: Top line, black spray paint. Bottom line, red spray paint.
Location: Remains of concrete concourse leading to south side of Millennium Bridge.
Date: Although this piece had no date other than the year, eye witness accounts put the time of Miller crossing the Thames somewhere between late February and early March.
Note: It is likely that this piece was intended as a tribute to Miller's group and was applied sometime after the events it celebrates. Aside from the obvious error in referring to London Bridge, it is also the only example of graffiti alluding to the Takeback, or to use the identifier Kings of Crows.

From The Writing on the Wall

From Kings of Crows: Life on the Wrong Side of the Lockdown

The group split at the Thames. Not everyone wanted to risk climbing across the wreckage of the bridge. I'd guess about a quarter of the group stayed in the south of the city.

We lost three people in the crossing.

From Locked Out: Stories of Survival During the London Lockdown, edited by Breda Chilton. Coltrane Press (2026)

Lorraine Corbet

Both Lorraine Corbet and her late husband, Frank, were native Londoners and had spent their lives in the capital. Despite their emotional bond to the city, by spring of 2021 they agreed the situation in London had become untenable. With the safety of their eleven-year-old son, Peter, at the forefront of their minds, they made plans to leave. The intention was to travel from the capital to the relative security of Cumbria, where Frank's sister lived.

On 6th March, one day before the Lockdown was instigated, Frank was taken ill. He succumbed to HV-Tg-induced psychosis less than a week later. Lorraine and Peter were lucky to escape alive (Note: Since the restoration of the British Government in 2023, Peter has changed his name to Frank, in memory of his father).

Although we weren't part of the Crows, we were with Miller's group for a time, about four months. No more than that. We had been living day to day on a deserted housing estate about two miles from where we'd lived before the disease came.

Frank Jr and me were lucky, if that's the right word, we were both resistant to the cat flu. Neither of us had so much as a sniffle. Frank, big Frank, come home from work early on the Monday and he'd switched over by the weekend. We, Frank Jr. and me, just ran out of the house. We never went back. I think we were in shock. We didn't make any plans, didn't think about moving on or what we'd do in the long term.

We stayed close to home for a few weeks. We could normally find an empty house to hide in. There had been a lot of deaths on our street in the early days; people got scared and left. I don't know if any of our neighbours made it safely over the river. We went from house to house, we'd break a window and live there until the food ran out. After that we just drifted to the next one. That's how we wound up on the housing estate.

It was what they used to call a low-rise estate. What that really meant was a lot of cheap houses crammed into an area the size of a handkerchief. The developers would build as many maisonettes as they could, to squeeze as much profit out of the land as possible. There were never enough services to go with them. They might leave a plot aside for a corner shop and maybe a health centre.

I reckon that's why it was deserted; there wasn't much to loot, so people moved on. There was quite a lot of fire damage too. That happened a lot just after the Lockdown. People panicked; if they got word that someone had the disease, they'd petrol bomb their house.

Miller's group saved us from a pack of Switchers. I don't know how long we'd been drifting around the estate by then, months, I think. There weren't many places left that we hadn't stripped, and we'd wandered towards a more built-up area with a lot of Switchers in it. We'd seen others of course, and Frank obviously, but they'd normally be drifting about on their own. When we saw them, we'd run before they got a sniff of us.

This time we were in a road that was blocked by a burned-out building that had collapsed, so we were pinned. We thought that was it. There were ten of them. I counted afterwards. At the time I thought it was more.

At that point we didn't know about fighting them properly. We were throwing bits of rubble at them and that wasn't doing anything. Frank Jr. hit one of them right in the eye with a chunk of brick and it didn't even flinch. We were both screaming for help. That sounds stupid but we were terrified.

Then these people appeared at the end of the road, only three of them. You could tell they were normal. They all had weapons of some sort. I always remember one of them, a woman called Barbara, had a shovel. She'd filed it on one side, so it was like a blade. They killed the Switchers so quickly it made my head spin. Then they took us with them.

At the time we didn't really know it was Miller's people. It wasn't until much later when the power came back on and the army and police started up again, that we started hearing the stories. We realised then that we'd been part of Miller's group.

I'd heard a lot of people talk about being with Miller's lot. I don't believe most of them. It wasn't the way they tell it. They talk like it was a gang or a family, they nearly all go on about the bond. It wasn't like that, not for most of us. We kept in very small groups, to avoid infections spreading. We didn't tend to mix much.

I only saw Miller once or twice. At the time I didn't know who he was, or that it mattered. He was insane. I know a lot of people will hate me for saying that, but it's the truth. The first time I saw him he was killing a Switcher. We all did at some point; it wasn't that hard to be honest. Most of them were in a bad way and if you had something to swing at them, an axe or a sharpened shovel, you could finish one off quite easily. It was the packs that were the real problem. It was just something we did, like looting supplies or cutting your hair off so you'd not get lice. Miller wasn't like that. He went into frenzies with them, hacking at them even after they were dead. He scared me more than they did.

The second time I saw him was when we left the group. This was just before we were meant to cross the Thames. There was a sort of group within the group, a set of people who stayed close to Miller and treated him like he was a movie star, or a royal.

We'd been squatting in an old office block. There was a group of us on one floor and Miller, and his special people, were on another floor, higher up. We'd been there a while, I don't know how long exactly, but longer than usual. We moved around a lot normally. One day the word came around that we were going over into North London, and we all moved out.

Something happened to Miller. I didn't see what but the whole group stopped walking. We used to move in small groups of four or five, again to stop infections spreading. No one knew what was going on. Then one of the Miller people came towards us. He had a sweatshirt with a hood that had feathers stitched around the face hole. I thought he was stoned because he was grinning like an idiot. He handed me a long black feather and said, "Miller wants you to have this", or "This is a gift from Miller", something or other like that anyway. I took it because I was scared not to. Then he wandered over to Frank Jr. and gave one to him.

When the group started moving again our pack – me, Frank Jr., Barbara and three or four others – slipped away. That night I cried with fear, being so cut off again. But that shows you how much Miller scared me.

Extract from the screenplay of Year of the Crow. Lithograph Studios, California (2026)

EXT. RIVER THAMES – DAY.

We hear an amplified heartbeat. Miller, bare-chested, is wading into the river. POV changes so we see where Miller is heading. A woman wearing a ragged pea coat and army boots is clinging to one of the piles of rubble we saw Robertson attaching the ropes to earlier. She has frozen to the jagged structure and has her face pressed into the shattered concrete. Close-up on the woman's profile. She is breathing fast and wide-eyed with terror. There is blood on her face from where she has pressed herself into the debris. The camera moves in closer on her face until all we can see is her profile. Behind her we see only the expanse of water she is trying to cross. The image of the rock and the river in the background blur into abstraction.

We hear a voice as though far away and only just audible over the sound of the woman's heartbeat. The voice gradually becomes clearer until we can make out the words. The first word that we hear is 'trust'.

MILLER

Trust me. I know you're scared, I know you can't swim, but trust me. You're going to be fine. It's all going to be fine. You need to trust me. I'm coming.

POV changes to show Miller. He is still wading out into the water. We see fast-moving flotsam bumping into him. Out of shot we hear Robertson.

ROBERTSON

For Christ's sake be careful, that's a rip tide coming in.

POV changes to show the scared woman. She appears to be glued onto the pile of debris. The camera pulls back, and we see the surface of the river is awash with fast-moving flotsam. Miller comes into shot swimming toward the woman; he is being buffeted by pieces of the floating junk.

POV switches to the other side of the woman. A badly scuffed and scratched row boat is riding the flow of the river and bangs into the remains of the pylon. It jams into the jagged edges and stays there. The camera remains with the boat long enough for us to see that it is not empty.

Return to close-up of woman's face. As before the background is out of focus. As the sound of the heartbeat decreases in volume the woman blinks. A darker blur appears in shot and as we watch looms larger. The woman blinks again as she begins to calm down. The focus changes so the background image sharpens. The dark blur is revealed to be a badly rotten zombie. Camera cuts away as the woman becomes aware of its presence. The woman screams as the camera cuts back to Miller, still some distance from the pylon, and unable to help. The camera stays on Miller and the sound of the heartbeat increases in speed and volume, then suddenly stops, leaving us in total silence.

MILLER
(Whispering)
I'm sorry. I'm sorry.

March 5th, 2021

Miller and the first half dozen Crows swarmed across the shattered concourse of the bridge. Robertson watched Miller abandon the backpack he carried, throw himself into the twenty yards of open water and strike out for the wreckage of the first pylon. The six following him, three men and three women, hesitated. They were carrying heavier packs than Miller and had more they wanted to keep. They also carried weapons that couldn't be slipped into webbing. They desperately tried to secure machetes and pickaxe handles into belts or rucksacks, while trying to match Miller's pace. He threw himself from hand-hold to toe-hold without a second's pause.

At the centre of the river, Miller threw himself back into the freezing water and struck out again. The first to follow was one of the women. Still wearing her pack she hit the water and had time to yell twice before sinking without trace. The five others froze. Four of them were staring at the point where the woman had vanished, the fifth was keeping track of Miller. Miller, who hadn't looked behind him, was scrambling onto the twisted slope where the next section of wreckage rose from the river.

One of the men lowered himself into the water, still with his pack on. He managed to get halfway across before he began to flounder and had to fight free of the straps. He barely made it across to solid ground. He laughed stupidly and punched his fists in the air.

The others finally learned the lesson and abandoned their backpacks and weapons. Once on the other half of the damaged bridge they rushed to catch up with Miller. One of the men, the one who'd obsessively traced Miller, missed a handhold and fell backwards down the steep angle of the old walkway. Robertson thought he heard a dull crack as his head connected with the concrete base.

"Shite," said Johnno as he watched the man, unconscious or dead, float away.

"Fucking morons," Robertson said. "Get Ally to talk to the others. Get them organised, before they all get themselves killed."

Chapter 38. No Charge

Civvy Rash

Short for Civilian Rations, the term is also used to describe a pale unhealthy complexion or general lack of vitality caused by poor nutrition. This is a reference to the poor-quality food provided under rationing in post-Outbreak Britain. Rationing was introduced in October 2021 in order to ensure equal distribution of supplies. Allocation was controlled by the use of coupons, supplied bi-monthly in the form of a ration book. The quality and quantity of the goods provided was dependent on the grade of book issued. The three-tier system of rationing attracted much criticism. The most common type was the Grade II Civilian (G2C) book, issued to citizens employed in non-civil roles and with no dependants. Grade I Civilian books (G1C) were issued to citizens with dependants. Grade III books (G3) were issued to the unemployed. Non-civilian ration books (HMGB), issued to members of the police force, the civil service and military, were based on a detailed thirty-four-part tier system. Unlike civilian books these were protected with chip and pin security. They could also be legally exchanged for digital currency.

Werx (Paper Werx, Paper Work)

Term for a fake ration book, normally a G2C. Attempts to forge the highly elaborate civilian-grade books were seldom successful. The penalty for being in possession of a forged ration book was a three-month term on a custodial labour crew. As the value of the books was so low, forgers rarely attempted to use their own handiwork in person. Commonly the fake books were exchanged for black-market or stolen goods. This trade was almost exclusively practised with victims of drug or alcohol addiction.

The A to Z of Gondii Names

April 14th, 2028

The standard issue ration book from Robertson's personal property, and the coupon for diesel I'd found in the genny room under his flat, were genuine. I had that on the grudging authority of the specialist Ration and Currency Fraud Division.

The uniformed sergeant whose opinion I'd asked had glanced at them and sighed heavily. He was one the Met's hefty number of desk-bound officers. Most of them were veterans of the force. Like Winslow, they'd been coppers going into the Outbreak and been coppers when they came out of it. Like Winslow, nearly all of them had been moved into London from other regions. I never met one that wasn't bitter about something. Or one that didn't come with a chip on their shoulder.

A lot were disabled. The lack of medical supplies and doctors had made minor problems into major events.

This one had lost a leg. He looked at me as if I'd pulled it off personally.

"Yeah, they're real," he said and spun on the swivel chair, so I was looking at his back.

He picked up a sheet of paper with about a dozen words printed on it and pretended to read it. I waited the performance out and he started to fidget. Paper rationing meant there wasn't a great deal of paperwork on his desk to look busy with. When he started tidying the contents of a drawer, I grabbed the back of his chair and spun it round.

"How can you tell?" I asked him before he had a chance to complain.

He saw my I'm-pulling-rank expression and raised me an I'm-talking-to-an-imbecile voice.

"The current batch of grade two coupon books have this security stamp imprinted onto the paper."

He picked up the ration book and waved it in the air, too fast for me to see it. I had to hold my hand out like a child asking for sweets so he'd give it to me. There was what appeared to be an official rubber-stamped crest in the top right corner. He'd fallen silent again and I had to ask him to explain the significance. He took his time opening another drawer and lifted out a wooden box, the type used to store chess pieces. A collection of rubber stamps rattled around in it. He shook it at me, his expression saying, 'Get it now?'. I didn't.

He smiled in that way men do when they explain clever things to women. Probably popping an erection while he did it.

"The black-market boys spend hours making these little fellas." He held up one of the rubber stamps for my inspection. The stamp had been made with a degree of skill I'd never have, but the way he was talking implied a wasted effort. He waited for me to ask for the explanation.

"Just cut to the chase, okay? Then you can get back to tidying your desk and I can get on with some police work."

The noise level in the room dropped a couple of points. I could feel eyes on my back and heard something muttered behind me. It was too low to make out the words. It didn't matter, the sentiment was loud enough.

"This isn't stamped." He pointed at the crest on the ration book. "It's printed onto each page before all the other print work is added. If anyone takes the trouble to look" – he tilted the ration book in the light, looking at something I couldn't see – "they'll see the 'stamp' is printed over. None of the black-market boys have the sense to look. So, they make up their little stamps, print out their fakes and stamp, stamp, stamp."

I took the book from him again and tilted it the way he had. I still couldn't see what I was meant to be looking for.

"Stamping the crest on leaves dents in the paper," he explained. "And if you've got an eye for it, you can see the shine of the ink on top of the marking."

"Is it the same for the diesel coupons?"

"They don't bother with the stamp business on fuel coupons. The paper they're printed on has a metallic thread woven into it. It's practically impossible to reproduce if you're working out of an old lock-up somewhere."

He gave me a smile that most rattlesnakes would have been proud of.

"So where did these come from?"

"In my opinion, they're genuine. That means, they are not fake. Which makes it … your problem, Detective Sergeant."

He spun round in his chair and I was looking at his back again. The buck had just been passed. I heard someone snigger as I left the room.

Winslow smiled when I gave him the news.

Like my one-legged friend in the counterfeiting squad he had his back to me. I wasn't flattered. The performance was for the masses, not just me. He was staring fixedly at the section of wall that he'd tacked the details of Robertson's case onto. It was a thin collection of notes and scraps. It would have fitted onto a side of A4. Maybe he thought putting it on a wall made it more impressive.

"What's good about it?" I stood between his chair and the wall, making him acknowledge me.

I dropped the ration book and coupon into his lap. His eyes flicked towards them briefly, but he didn't stop rubbing circles into his temples.

"Robertson being in possession of a genuine ration book that shouldn't have been issued for another week gives us a legitimate reason to charge him."

I got the feeling he was waiting for me to ask him to explain. Even if I had needed it spelled out to me, I wouldn't have given him the satisfaction of obliging.

If it was genuine, the ration book with the wrong date on it was big potatoes. As a fake it represented someone buying forgeries; as an official document it showed someone had access to official supply lines.

"And what does that achieve?" I asked.

Winslow got out of the chair and deposited the ration book and coupon in a drawer, holding them between finger and thumb as if they were soiled.

"If we have a real criminal case to bring, we can keep him here and sweat him some more, see if he gives anything away."

"He isn't sweating. He's down there, sending your uniforms out for coffee and eating three meals a day which the Met's paying for."

"So, you suggest what exactly?"

He stayed on his feet resting his thighs against the edge of the leather-top desk. It was a picture straight out of a middle manager's repertoire of commanding poses. I had planned to give a breakdown of what I proposed. Instead I said:

"We let him go."

Winslow blinked, maybe waiting for the punchline. When it didn't come, he shook his head, equal parts disbelief and contempt.

"I am not about to …"

I cut across him using my superior officer tone.

"You are not about to do anything. I am letting him go."

From recording of police interview with Colin Robertson (14th April 2028)

Robertson - Do I get an apology?
Winslow - It's in that letter.
Robertson - I'm not talking about an official, rubber-stamp apology. I mean an apology from you two fucking clowns. I've been wasting my life away in your poxy cell for the last week and now you say, off you go. That's it, is it? No sorry Mr Robertson, our mistake?
Cross - You're free to go. If you feel you've been poorly treated, you can lodge a formal complaint.
Robertson - Fuck you.

April 14th, 2028

Robertson left the building with a cock of the walk strut.

"I hope you're right about this," Winslow said. It wasn't the first time.

"Relax. If it's a mistake it's my bad. I get a reprimand from Washington and you and your fellow Brits get to roll your eyes. The super will probably buy everyone tea and cakes."

We were on the sidewalk outside 'the station'. The words POLICE STATION had been stencilled directly onto the stonework above the entrance. Official blue spray paint, to denote it as a law enforcement agency. Ministry of Defence got to play with green paint and the civil service got red. It was the sort of petty bureaucratic detail that would keep me awake some nights. I wondered how many sallow-faced men had sat around a table somewhere deciding which department got which colour. And how long they'd spent doing it. I didn't doubt the table was all male, cushioned from events outside their door by a buffer of gender and rank.

Robertson had squared his shoulders as he emerged into the daylight. He'd made no requests for phone calls or even asked that anyone be informed where he was. There was no one to meet him, certainly no entourage. The King of the Crows still walked down the steps like he owned the place. There was something fitting about it, the borrowed glory of the marble steps, the crumbling sidewalk and a self-proclaimed monarch with no one to acknowledge his reign.

We watched him walk out of sight, turning left off the main thoroughfare. The last thing I saw him do was exchange a casual salute with a uniformed PC. I heard Winslow laugh softly. When I looked at him to explain the joke, I found he was already looking at me.

"What's funny?"

"The way your eyes just narrowed. Do we have a word with that bobby then?"

"Not yet. Do you know him?" Winslow nodded. "We'll know where to find him then."

On the opposite side of the street a figure pulled itself from a doorway and slid across the road. I noted the quick glance cast in our direction before the figure disappeared down the same turning as Robertson.

Winslow clicked his fingers in his irritating double-time rhythm.

"I hope you're right about this."

I didn't bother reassuring him again. I was hoping the same.

I'd offered Winslow a lift to the police housing unit he was living in, but he declined, saying it would be faster to walk. Which was probably true, though I suspected the real reason was more to do with pride than anything else. The police accommodation, at least for those below the rank of inspector wasn't known for its splendour. In comparison, my damp-smelling Victorian flat was five-star.

I'd let myself in and waited in the hallway for a few seconds, wishing there was something to hear. In Paris, quarantined and cut off from home, I'd longed for silence. The city had collapsed within earshot, not with a bang, but with a drawn-out groan of panic and violence. Now the silence had finally arrived it wasn't peace, it was just despair. And some days not even that; it was just empty.

The only sound I could hear, no matter how hard I strained, was my own breathing. A road clearing team had thoughtfully bulldozed the shattered remains of a dozen cars across the only route that I knew, so I'd had to park half a mile from 'home'. The walk to my door along the weed-choked sidewalk was exhausting. The day had faded into darkness and the air, always leaden with dust, had an aftertaste of damp soot. There was always a fire somewhere, people keeping warm or just burning rubbish.

The clean air had been the only good thing I could find to remember about Calais. The bombing had reduced the town and port to rubble and bone, but the wind blowing in from the sea scoured the air with salt.

I didn't know it then, had no way of knowing, but by the time I got to the coast the Outbreak, the plague, the end of days, the Gondii Stomp – call it what you will – was effectively over. HV-Tg had wrung itself out. If you care to read them, there are papers by the hundreds explaining Toxo's decline. When Hollywood told the story, the world rejoiced. Reality was less buoyant. Toxo stopped killing people but people kept on dying. And keep dying still.

Though by the time I got to Calais, there was no one left there to die. Those that had weathered the plague, the riots, the stampeding attempts at exodus had then either fled or perished in the bombing. No government has ever laid claim to the destruction of Calais or Marseille, or any other of the port towns that had ceased to exist.

I'd whittled down my list of essentials to the contents of a small backpack.

The only things I held were a plastic jerry can of petrol and Dog Boy's pistol. That was how I thought of it: Dog Boy's pistol.

After I'd left Dog Boy, left his body, the only humans I encountered were the occasional Gonzo. They were rarely a threat. Whatever was left of their cognition, it didn't extend to operating can openers or picking over the looted shells of shopping centres. As gathering food became a more sophisticated operation, the infected were succumbing to starvation. Unconcerned with such matters, the disease kept firing neurons and the Gonzos kept on twitching, trying to spread the creed. I stepped round their fallen bodies and saved bullets to scare away packs of feral dogs. The petrol was for starting fires.

Calais should have filled me with despair, but I don't think I had room for any more. My idea of taking a boat to Britain and finding an intact American Embassy had never really been more than a trick of the light, something to keep me moving forward, even if forward was just an illusion.

The first night I set up camp in a triangle-shaped room formed by the collapse of a cast concrete frontage. Somewhere in the back of my mind was a memory of an instructional video of what to do in an earthquake, or it might have been a nuclear attack. Whatever disaster it was meant to equip them for, the video urged its viewers to stay away from the centre of rooms, because that was where the ceiling and roof would land. So, I headed to the sides and put my faith in the geometrical wonders of the triangle.

I poured a cap of petrol onto a collection of flammable junk and sat in the glow of the fire. In the dark silence the crackle of flames sounded loud and powerful. It scared away, or least drowned out, the scrabble of vermin in the rubble, and the smoke kept the flies at bay. I slept, not really waiting for the morning or even waiting to wake up. I was just waiting to stop sleeping. Trust me, there is a difference.

The sound of seagulls woke me. They at least had thrived. About thirty of the things circled and swooped in the morning sky. Three or four others that looked too big to fly stood on the roof of a burnt-out car. Regarding me with their suspicious sideways glare, possibly wondering if I was dead. I thought about trying to shoot one and inviting it to breakfast. But it was no more than a passing thought. If killing Dog Boy proved anything, it was that I couldn't shoot straight. Unable to shoo away the memory of Dog Boy's last moments I threw a chunk of masonry at the gulls and scattered them instead.

Then I started walking towards the sea, not expecting to find anything likely to float.

I finally felt up to going into the depths of my flat and making my nightly duty call to David and Maria. Maria was out and David had friends over. We had to shout down the phone line to be heard over the sounds of the game.

Chapter 39. Taking Charge

From Kings of Crows: Life on the Wrong Side of the Lockdown

I couldn't really say what we'd expected when we crossed into North London. The lights we'd seen on the horizon had got us thinking something was happening. At the time anything that changed the status quo felt like a good thing.

I've seen people's reactions when they hear stories from places where the infection was rife. They either look fascinated or horrified. What doesn't occur to them was how draining the whole thing could be. Not only physically, mentally as well. The life we lived during the Lockdown was largely pointless. We worked, scavenged, fought with no goals other than staying alive.

Imagine being on a roundabout, motion that takes you nowhere, but no one knows how to stop the ride. It feels like you're on it forever. That was how it felt. I believe that was harder on people than the moments of terror. At least at those times the adrenalin would kick in and blot out everything except what you were dealing with.

So, a lot of people thought crossing the Thames was going to change things. Which it did.

Julian Clark-Billings, Service #:78695312, Military Corrective Training Centre, Colchester (2028)

Discipline had not broken down. I cannot state that enough. My men – the men now either sitting in stockades or running and scared for their lives – followed orders or acted on their initiative, in a manner appropriate to the time and the conditions under which they were operating.

What had broken down was the chain of command, communications and the mental and emotional reliance of the men. Every one of them had lost family and friends. They'd been pushed from deployment overseas, often leaving wives and children behind. The way they are being vilified now is a national disgrace. It's no better than the way the enlisted men of the First World War were treated. Court-martialled for cowardice when they were suffering with PTSD.

We made the decision to leave ████████ not because we intended to rob the Bank of England but because we genuinely did not believe the high command were capable of making informed decisions any longer.

The losses of military personnel, of infrastructure and intel were unbelievable. Had the situation been a conventional war, I believe the only route would have been the negotiation of our nation's surrender. That wasn't possible of course. What should have been done? I do not claim to know. I will say, however, that the decision to deploy ████████ to ████████ ██████ was totally unconscionable. We were given word we were to be deployed on ████████. Just two days before, three of our company had been diagnosed with HV-Tg and marked for summary execution. The medical staff by that time had fled or were sick themselves. ████████████ was in overall command of ████████. He made the decision that the last official action of my men, before deploying to ████████ would be to carry out the executions. He called it a 'disposal'.

I cannot imagine what he was thinking. To issue such an order was madness. My men had been forced to fire on British soldiers before, but that had been in self-defence. Before most of the medical staff had died or left there had been a large contingent of HV-Tg victims on the base. Already, we had had two incidents of Romeos breaking free.

The term psychosis is wholly inadequate to describe the effect that switching-off has on a man. It is truly terrifying. The actions of the men affected were beyond deranged; they became animals. At that point they were no longer recognisable as human beings, never mind soldiers and comrades. When it became clear that the disease had changed, and infection would invariably lead to psychosis, it became practice to euthanise all those infected. The doctors had drugs and training for that. We only had bullets.

Imagine being told you are required to shoot a man in cold blood. Not only that, but the man would be one of your friends. Someone you might owe your life to. On diagnosis of HV-Tg, the man in question would be restrained. My men were expected to shoot their comrades while they were bound to hospital beds.

From transcript of preliminary meeting between Corporal Ameer Khan and Roland Cartwright, acting for the defence in The British Armed Forces vs Clark-Billings (2023)

- I saw Captain Billings go into the office of the base commander. When he came out again, he was shaking and white as a sheet. He told me our orders were to dispose of Privates Skerrett, Smith and Kelly.
- What did you understand by the term 'dispose'?
- We were to execute them.
- Did Captain Billings explain why?
- He didn't need to. Skerrit, Smith and Kelly had been infected. A Romeo, that's what we called people who'd switched, had attacked a patrol three days before. She, the Romeo, bit or scratched all three of them. It was understood that they would have to die.
- How did you feel about that?
- It was horrible, but I thought it was necessary. Anyway, we, the battalion talked about the disease a lot. Everyone said they wanted to be shot if they got the disease. No one wanted to turn into a Romeo.
- Had orders to shoot infected men been issued before?
- On two other occasions.
- Were the orders carried out on those occasions?
- They were.
- Who by?
- Once by me and once by Private Skerrit.
- What was Captain Billings' reaction on those occasions?
- It upset him, it upset everyone. This time it was men from our own company.
- What did you say when he told you about the order to dispose of the three men?
- I told him I'd do it if he didn't feel able.
- And his response?
- He didn't say anything. He shook his head and drew his sidearm. Then he walked to the medical block.
- Did you go with him?
- Yes, I did.
- Did he request this?
- No. I was acting on my own initiative.
- What happened when you got to the medical wing?
- Skerrit, Smith and Kelly were on separate beds. They'd been restrained. Their ankles and wrists were handcuffed to their bedframes.
- How did the men appear to you?
- Smith and Kelly were very feverish and were asleep. Asleep or unconscious.

Private Skerrit was awake, he didn't look sick. He was managing to sit up in the bed. When he saw Captain Billings and myself he began to plead with us not to shoot him.

- What did Captain Billings do then?
- He said he was sorry and walked to Private Skerrit's bed. When he was about four feet away, he lifted his sidearm and aimed it at Private Skerrit.
- But he didn't fire?
- No, he stood with his weapon raised but didn't discharge it. Then he said it wasn't right. Something like that: this isn't right, or this can't be right. I don't remember his exact words.
- What did you do?
- I didn't do anything at that point.
- You stated before that you had offered to carry out the order to dispose of the men.
- Yes.
- Did you not reiterate that offer?
- No. Until then I hadn't seen the three men. When I saw them, well, when I saw Private Skerrit, I began to wonder if he had been correctly diagnosed.
- Okay. Carry on, what did Captain Billings do then?
- He reholstered his sidearm and told me that we couldn't do this and that we should go.
- What did you understand him to mean by 'we'?
- At the time I thought he was referring to me and him.
- What was your response?
- I told him that I would rather stay and take care of the three men.
- By take care, you meant?
- I meant execute.
- Even though you had doubts about the diagnosis?
- It was a direct order.
- And Billings' reaction?
- He nodded. Then he repeated that we should go. That was when he turned and left.
- But you didn't carry out the orders to shoot the men?
- No. When Private Skerrit saw Captain Billings leave, he turned to me and begged me not to kill him. He said he wasn't sick and to give him a few more days to prove it.
- Did you shoot any of the men, in fact?
- Not at that point. The medical bay was almost empty by then and they were already in restraints. The medics were either dead or had slipped away. I didn't think they posed a risk of spreading infection. I kept Skerrit as comfortable as

I could and waited.

- How long did you wait?

- Four days in all.

- What was the outcome?

- Private Skerrit became sick but only in a minor way. He made a full recovery. Private Smith switched and I was required to execute him. Private Kelly didn't switch and survived, although his recovery was only partial. I learned later he suffered a degree of brain damage.

- When did you learn that the rest of your company, along with Captain Billings, had deserted?

- I wasn't told formally until almost a week later, but I saw a pair of transporters drive past the hospital window shortly after Captain Billings left me with the sick men.

March 5th, 2021

From the South Bank Robertson watched Miller's followers make their way across to their idol. With Ally's guidance they had started an orderly transition. Robertson had intended to let them all get across ahead of anyone else. He wanted to keep them together, rather than have them interacting with the regulars. He hadn't wanted a repeat of the business with the blessed feathers. Now most of the Crows were on the other side he wasn't sure it had been a good plan. Even with the expanse of water between them, he could see the bedraggled group were doing nothing more than watching Miller.

Johnno and Maccallan were standing back from the activity around the bridge. Listening to Maccallan, Johnno was nodding rapidly and obviously not understanding what he was being told. Maccallan had taken to spouting-off about IT equipment and practice; the closer they'd got to the lit-up parts of the city, the more self-assured he'd become. Beyond the figures of Johnno and Maccallan, one of the regular squads of four lookouts/fighters had drifted together. Robertson couldn't hear their conversation, or see their expressions, but they were clearly wary of the river crossing. He found he didn't blame them. Two people had died already and now Miller's group of freaks were waiting on the other side looking weird. Weird and dangerous.

Sol's voice made him jump, "You need to get over there."

The old man wasn't looking at him. He was peering to the far side of the river and the concourse where the Crows appeared to have stalled.

"If the soldiers at the bank are as hostile as Alyson claims, we need them" – Sol jabbed his finger at the stationary Crows – "to be organised."

Robertson didn't respond and continued scrutinising the situation around him. Ally was talking, maybe preaching, to the remainder of the Crows. They hung on her words, heads nodding in unison. If he'd strained, he might have made out what she was saying but he purposely didn't listen. She'd been told to keep them on a leash, let them cross in groups of four or five only. So far, that was what she'd done.

Patrick was stationed at her side; Robertson hadn't wanted her to be left with Johnno.

"If we …" Sol began.

Robertson cut him off, "Shut up fucking bleating. I know what needs doing. You worry about getting across without getting yourself drowned."

He walked away before the old man had a chance to reply.

Maccallan and Johnno were on the footpath which ran along the river. It had once been a busy tourist and commuter route. Now it felt eerily empty, despite the bulk of the group being there. Maccallan was sitting on a bench and wrapping a Tupperware box with layers of plastic bags. He didn't look up from what he was doing. As Robertson drew near, Johnno said:

"Alright, Boss?"

He had the idea that the Scouser's greeting was intended to alert Maccallan to his presence. He shook his head to knock the thought aside.

"I'm going to go over soon. I want you to keep an eye on the freak show. You good to keep it together over here?"

It was Maccallan that replied, "Yeah, we're good."

Robertson stared at Johnno, "I asked you a fucking question. Can you keep it together?"

"Yeah. It's alright, Boss. It's under control."

Without turning to look his way, Robertson jerked a thumb over his shoulder in the direction of Sol.

"Make sure you get that old bastard across in one piece."

"I'll sort it, Boss. Don't worry yourself about him."

There was a sudden ripping noise which was familiar but which Robertson couldn't place. It caught him by surprise, and he spun on his heel, half in a crouch. The sound had been Maccallan pulling a long strip from a roll of duct tape. Robertson's overreaction had, in turn, startled him and he froze with one hand in the air, holding the end of the tape. He extended the moment for comic effect before using the tape to anchor the plastic bags to the box he'd wrapped. He exaggerated the actions, making the movements overly slow and careful, as if he was discarding a weapon while someone held a gun on him.

"Jumpy, aren't we?"

"Just do your fucking job."

A dozen Gonzos had gathered on the northern side of the shattered bridge. Robertson could see more shuffling out of the side streets behind them. The concourse, where the bridge blended into the road was largely intact. At the narrow point of the entrance, rusting tangles of barbed wire and a redoubt of rotting sandbags marked where the army had once closed the way.

The majority of the Gonzos had become entangled in the barbwire. One of them, bleeding from a score of lacerations where the barbs had caught, groaned every time he pressed forward. The pain wasn't stopping him inching through.

Miller was picking off the Gonzos that had got past the wire. He was approaching them almost casually, waiting for them to lunge or swing at him, before driving one of his butcher's knives into their throat or sidestepping them and hacking at their knees. The followers weren't moving. Gathered in a knot they watched. A congregation keeping a silent vigil.

Robertson shivered in the cold. He'd stripped off his outer layers and wrung them out as best he could. The chill wind from the river stole his body heat. The people gathered, watching Miller, had made no attempt to get dry. The ground where they stood was turning into a pool as they dripped water.

As Robertson shook more water from his jeans, one of the Gonzos, either by chance or design, dropped and rolled under the barbwire. It staggered back onto its feet and made towards the group of watchful Crows.

"Hey."

No one turned. When he called louder someone began a chant of, "Leave them be, they will change."

Robertson cursed and pulled his wet clothing back on. Still shivering, he walked over to the Gonzo. He killed it, with practised efficiency: two clean swipes, one in the knee to fell it and the second into the crown of the head.

Minimum splatter, letting the weight of the axe do the work.

Miller was busy with another Gonzo. Going at it with the butcher's knives, alternating left and right. It had once been a man, big and well-muscled, but the switch had been a long time ago and it was in bad shape. Naked apart from boxer-shorts, its skin was mottled with infections and neglect. Robertson waited until Miller had taken a step back, then he came up behind it. Again, two strikes: knee then head.

As the big Gonzo fell, two or three people gasped, and the rhythm of the chant faltered. Miller himself appeared not to care. The number of Gonzos pressing at the barricade were an embarrassment of riches and he began work on another. Several of the Crows, Robertson saw, were no longer watching Miller. They were now watching him.

He could see the press of infected, straining at the wire, was increasing. Dealt with systematically, their contained arrival wouldn't have been a problem. The group of followers – still chanting and watching Miller as he plied his trade – should have despatched them as they tangled themselves in the wire. Half their number could have completed job. Now, wary of having the Crows at his back, he was caught between their attention and the number of Gonzos building at the old barricade.

As he dithered, another group began hauling themselves from river. Another point that needed his attention. He locked eyes with one of the people watching him. A woman, barely out of her teens.

"Miller needs help with the Gonzos," he shouted at her.

The young woman's gaze drifted from him to the figure of Miller. He was delicately cutting the features from a tall Gonzo whose arms he'd hacked down to stumps. He showed no concern for the other bodies adding their weight to the press. When Robertson looked back to the woman, she smiled and joined in the chant again. This time shouting it loudly, but only the first line.

"Leave them be … Leave them be … Leave them be …"

Behind him something gave way. He risked taking his eye off the crowd and saw the wire had pulled free under the weight of bodies. Seven or eight, maybe more Gonzos had fallen into a heap. Their limbs flailed as they struggled to get to their feet.

Robertson could see that Miller, happy as he was, was about to be overwhelmed. Unsure if he was worth the risk, Robertson hefted his axe and ran towards the break in the wire. The chanting stopped and he felt, more than heard, the crowd behind him break ranks. He swung at the flailing mass of Gonzos, randomly picking a face to target. The axe connected and hit home. As steps moved in at his back, he pulled the blade free, used the momentum to carry him around so he faced the people closing down on him.

The Crow people weren't running. Their steps were even and deliberate. He brought the axe up and felt his lips drawing back into a grimace, or a snarl. Somewhere, in the back of his mind, a voice he recognised as his own, issued a number.

Five.

Five, he'd take out five of these fuckers before they brought him down.

He did a rapid scan of the approaching crowd. Found the woman who'd rejigged the chant.

And she'd be number fucking one.

"The crows," someone shouted, and for a second everything seemed to freeze. "The crows need feeding."

The last words were drawn out like a sport commentator's excited call of a goal: feeeeddddiinnnngah.

Patrick, bare-chested and fresh from the river, ran past him. He was wielding the pickaxe handle he favoured. Ally and two more of the Crow people followed close on his heels.

The locked focus of the group broke. Heads began to move in different directions, some looking a Patrick and the Crows who'd crossed with him, others at Miller, others overhead where the black outlines of real crows circled against the cloud.

Only the young woman still stared at Robertson.

He jerked his head in the direction of the barricade and turned to carry on dispatching the Gonzos.

It took longer than he'd have liked to find shelter. The numbers of Gonzos at the end of the shattered bridge hadn't been a one-off. Robertson couldn't remember seeing so many infected since the first days of the Lockdown. They encountered two or three on every street or building they moved through. In itself, that wasn't a problem. Most of them looked to have switched weeks or months earlier. The imperative of the disease was the only thing keeping most of them going. Several times they found near dead people, too weak to stand, lying in the streets. It was Sol who'd pointed out, through chattering teeth, that they were often stationed in front of buildings that had lights on.

What slowed them was Miller. He stopped to fillet each Gonzo they encountered. In the end, purely to speed up their progress, Robertson took up a knife and joined in the butchery. They left streets full of crows in their wake.

The light was beginning to fade when they found a commercial street with a largely intact three-storey department store. The bottom floor had been gutted as thoroughly as one of Miller's Gonzos. Robertson had beckoned Johnno to follow him in. Broken glass crackled as they walked through. The wide stairwell leading to the upper floor had been blocked at some point with the remains of a counter and a confusion of clothes racks. A tumble of tubing at one side showed where someone had exited.

The two of them crept up the stairs. The floors up there were largely untouched. In a far corner of the top floor a bed had been formed from a pile of clothing. A scattering of tins and plastic water bottles surrounded it. Slumped behind a cash till were the remains of a body and half a dozen empty blister packs. A scrawled note on the counter read, *Got sick. Fuck you.*

"Suicide," Johnno said, and screwed the note into a ball. He threw it at the corpse and hit it in the chest. "Fook you too, soft lad. You think he'd have turned the lights off."

Robertson ignored the comment and looked through the clothing, discarding his jacket in favour of a parka-style coat.

"Get everyone up here. Tell them to get some dry gear before we all freeze to fucking death."

"What about this soft bastard?" Johnno poked the corpse with the end of his baseball bat. It toppled sideways and landed wetly on the floor.

"Find a window. I'm going to try sort out some security."

The head count was down to twenty-eight. Twelve of the regulars had elected to quit the group and stay in the office block rather than risk the north side.

More had slipped away after watching how the crossing had progressed.

They'd lost another Crow before finding shelter. He'd made a run at a trio of Gonzos. Robertson had the feeling it had been a suicide dash. He wondered if that was why Johnno was angry at the long-dead body upstairs. The Crow had screamed when the Gonzos bit him, but as he drifted back he looked serene. He held his hands out from his sides with the palms forward. The right had been bitten at the base of the thumb and blood welled from the wound, trailing onto the road behind him. The left hand was less picturesque, the two remaining fingers broken and twisted.

He'd begun a slow dreamy chant of, "Let them be, they will change." Before anyone else picked up the refrain, Robertson sunk his axe into the man's skull. He didn't want the sickbay scenario starting again.

Sol was coming up the steps as Robertson was going down. He was shaking badly and had a second coat pulled round his shoulders adding to the weight of water. Maccallan was at his side.

"There's clothes up there, get him into something dry," Robertson told him.

"Is it clear up there?"

"No, it's full of Gonzos. Of course, its fucking clear. Where's Patrick?"

Maccallan didn't answer him.

Patrick was talking with a woman in Crow regalia. In crossing the river she'd moulted; the few feathers she'd retained were matted and broken. The effect was almost funny, made more so because she was obviously trying to be flirtatious.

Robertson broke the spell by whistling loudly through his teeth. Patrick looked up, startled.

"We need to get sorted. Get upstairs, get some dry gear on, then you, him, him and her get back down here for first watch."

The two men he'd pointed at looked at Patrick, waiting for him to confirm the order. The woman, the one who'd led the rejigged chant, just nodded, her eyes not leaving his.

Chapter 40. Dream Team

Getting across the Channel to the UK wasn't that hard in the end. I drifted around Calais for a few days, breaking into various houses and flats. I'd given up checking supermarkets and corner shops for food long before. They'd all been stripped bare, turned into fortresses or burned to ash in the battles for their contents. I encountered the odd Gonzo, so wasted and disease-eaten it could barely drag itself towards me. They posed no kind of threat but sometimes I killed them. To this day I'm not sure why. It may have been mercy on my part, or just an outlet for the background anger and fear I'd lived with for more than a year. It was probably habit.

The silence unnerved me. I'd become immune to the soundtrack of misery in the city: weeping, screaming, panicked footfalls, random shots and of course crows. I'm sure there were other birds growing fat on the lack of cats and the wealth of picking, but the crows and the ravens were the ones the new world was for. You couldn't miss their dark shapes spread across the sky or fail to hear the rattling cries. Calais didn't have the same soundtrack.

The most common sound was the wind, whistling through gutted buildings and shattered glass. If it was blowing in from the sea, it smelt of salt. From the land, the smell was ash and decay.

I spent three nights in a house that had been hidden along with five others behind a high wall. It was ornate in a way that I've only seen in Europe, as if the owners were embarrassed to have property worth protecting. It may have been nothing more than good taste, but to my money-trained American's mind it looked like an admission of guilt.

Hopefully the owner's angst was eased by the bombardment that had turned most of the discreet security measures into rubble. I approached the abandoned homes cautiously, looking out for barricades or furtive movements at windows. There was nothing. I listened until the silence ate away too many nerve endings and I had to call out.

Bellows in French and then English elicited bilingual silence. I picked the first house I found that still had all its walls intact and eased myself through the front window. Whoever had lived there had left in an orderly manner. Most of the disruption I found had been caused by the blast damage. The main bedroom showed signs that someone had left in a hurry. Drawers were hanging open and a suitcase, a huge Samsonite, was laying on the still-made bed with its lid folded back. It was holding more clothes than you could run with and was only half-filled. The case that had been left half packed had only women's clothes in it.

There was a framed photo on the wall of a bride and groom. Sometimes I wonder what happened in that room before I found it. Did they bicker over the packing the way I did with David when we went away together? You can't take all those clothes, what do you need that for? Or was it a widow, deciding she'd be better off with a smaller case?

Like so much that happened that year, seen and unseen, it probably didn't matter.

I checked the house, found a reasonable stack of tinned food and a bottle of white wine. Along with all the windows the house had lost a large part of its roof. All the rooms upstairs, including the main bedroom, were sodden, the walls black with mould. Uneasy about sleeping on the ground floor with its broken picture windows, I spent the night in the bathroom. The bathtub and tiling had stood up better to the ingress of the past winter. The mattresses were all ruined, so I filled the oversized tub with sofa cushions and lay there, with the door bolted and Dog Boy's pistol next to me.

I didn't sleep much; with so little to hear my ears invented sounds to amuse themselves with. At some point in the small hours I dozed off and snapped awake convinced I'd been woken by Gonzos scratching at the door. In the hard confines of the tiled room the pistol shot I fired off was insanely loud. Strangely, I slept after that, my ears ringing and deaf to the silence.

By the fourth night I'd adjusted to the new soundscape and tuned into the noises that had doubtless been there all along: gulls, rats shifting under the floors of the homes I scavenged from, thunderstorms rolling along the coast. The sound of a place the people had left.

When I heard the regular chunting rhythm of a diesel engine, I was almost disappointed.

I had almost forgotten my idea of getting to the UK. Concepts like embassies and American consulates had become so abstracted in my mind that the point of crossing the Channel was lost to me.

The boat was a private yacht. To me it looked huge, possibly because it was the biggest moving structure I had seen in almost a year. The crew consisted of a man and woman who could have been anywhere between thirty and sixty. Their eyes were big, and their skin hung on them. The woman was called

Mariam; the man – who I assumed was a husband or partner – never gave his name. Or if he did, I lost it in the blur of Scandinavian vowels. We met each other over the barrels of a shotgun.

The yacht, Bella-Kay, was taking on water. Not in a major way but fast enough to scare Mariam and her gun-toting husband ashore. They'd picked the Port of Calais because it was the least likely to be occupied. Being tongue-tied nearly cost me my life.

I can't really say what I'd been doing, moving randomly from house to house, or maybe moving systematically. I'd like to believe my logical accountant's mind was following some sort of plan, even if the rest of me had checked out of the thinking process completely.

I listened to the noise of the engine echoing around the empty port for a long time. It didn't feel important to me. It was too nonsensical; a marching band or a Disneyland parade wouldn't have been any less out of place. When I did make my way to meet the newcomers to my dream, I drifted rather than rushed.

The yacht had come to rest against a section of jetty that had somehow survived the bombing. At the time I didn't question how it had navigated the graveyard of scuppered wrecks. I later found out it was blind luck.

Mariam's partner had climbed out of the jetty and was about to start scouting for materials to repair the leak. He'd had a five-minute delay trying to calm Mariam down enough that he could leave her with the boat. By the time he encountered me, stumbling mutely towards him, his nerves were shot. Drawing down on me with the Remington had been a panic reaction. One I'd have had in the same situation. Luckily, I'd registered the reality of the gun more completely than I'd registered the yacht, and I put my hands up.

The yacht, as far as I could tell from the finger-jabbing at maps and broken mix of French and English had been hugging the coast most of the way down from Norway. Mariam mimed shivering and traced a route on the map from the Netherlands down towards Calais. I made a guess that they'd escaped the colder weather by heading south. The details of how they'd been surviving were lost in translation. Mariam hardly spoke English and her partner hardly spoke at all. Because I didn't know his name, I called him Captain. It translated and amused them both.

I showed them where to stock up on food. Mariam stayed on the boat. We had three days of stocking up and repairs. Captain, always with the Remington slung over his shoulder, scoured the remnants of the town for arcane supplies for patching hulls. I collected tins, carrying them in my backpack, until Captain found a wheelbarrow.

Mariam stayed in the boat. Each day Captain would spend longer and longer talking her down from her morning bout of hysteria. She'd retreat below deck in tears and the last sound we'd hear was the bolt being thrown on the hatch.

I didn't look back when we left. There was nothing to see that I'd want to remember. Mariam tried to persuade me to stay with them. I couldn't follow the argument that followed but the division of opinions was clear. Mariam wanted company and Captain didn't want another mouth to feed.

It made no difference to me. I had no desire to starve to death at sea. I pointed at the map, pinning the town of Folkstone. Mariam pleaded. I probed the same point and tried to smile. There was another bout of jabbering that I couldn't understand.

Mariam cried.

Captain shook his head.

Then he set the tip of his finger to the left of mine, on a place named Brighton.

The location agreed, Captain set course. The engine took a long time to start, the starter motor grinding out slower and slower complaints as the battery drained. It caught just as I was giving up hope. Captain said the longest string of English I'd ever hear him mutter.

"Shit fuel. Old."

The engine beat unevenly but got us clear of the jetty. Once on open water, Captain hoisted the sail.

Chapter 41. Lines of Enquiry

THE CHILDREN OF THE CROW ARE HERE!
THE NEW ORDER IS NOW!
Jack-Wing and Raven
Forever with the blessed

Medium: Red spray paint.
Location: Side of commercial building in St James, SW1.
Date: Unknown

From The Writing on the Wall

April 15th, 2028

I'd asked Winslow if he trusted the people tasked with tailing Robertson. The affirming nod he'd given me was too self-assured to be anything but false. I'd recommended he try to find officers who'd been in London for the Lockdown. I was working on the angle that they wouldn't be star-struck by their celebrity assignment. He'd told me he knew his men. I left it in the hands of a god I didn't believe in and tried not to roll my eyes.

We headed down to the canteen mid-afternoon.

The uniform Robertson had been sending out for refreshments was called Ben Haddan. He was still drinking real coffee. Winslow and I sat down either side of him after he'd settled in with his paper and mug of fresh-ground.

"That smells good," Winslow told him and pulled the drink towards him. He took another sniff. "That's the real thing."

"Yeah."

Ben pulled his mug back towards him and gave Winslow a sour look. When he made to drink, Winslow put a hand on his forearm. The move caught him by surprise and some of the coffee slopped onto his paper. He tutted loudly. But no more than that.

"I bet you don't get many of those to a ration book," Winslow said.

"A friend gave me a coupon."

"I wish I had friends that good," I put in.

It took some time for Ben to realise it was his turn to speak. Winslow and I stayed quiet and waited for him to work it out. He put two and two together but evidently math wasn't his strong suit.

"I've got another couple, if you fancy a coffee."

His intonation turned the statement into a timid question as he realised his mistake; fancy a coffee?

Winslow, who still had his hand on the man's forearm, gently guided his hand and the coffee down to the tabletop. In the process more of the expensive liquid swam over the lips of the mug. Winslow held his other hand out and twitched his fingers in a 'give' gesture.

The uniform reached inside his tunic. The pocket he needed was on the same side as his free hand and the movement was angular and ungainly. He avoided Winslow's eye and didn't attempt to free his other arm.

After much fumbling, he withdrew a pair of coupons and put one on Winslow's open palm and the other in front of me. He also offered up a shaky smile. Winslow smiled back and produced an envelope from his pocket. It was an official one. The Met's crest was printed on the top right corner along with the words: INTERNAL POST NOT FOR CIVIL USE. Like most stationery it had been used before.

Winslow made a performance of crossing out the last item on the envelope – the front was divided into a grid of sixteen rectangles – and, in the next space, writing 'evidence'. As an encore he leaned over and squinted to read the PC number on Ben's uniform. He added the digits to the contents of the box.

"Any more?" Winslow said when he'd finished.

He put his hand out again. Ben's mouth worked like a fish two or three times before he realised he had nothing to say. He produced a fold of coupons about half an inch thick and handed them over, without comment.

Once he'd folded the envelope over on itself, Winslow began tapping it on the tabletop. His favourite rhythm.

Tap, tap. Tap, tap. Tap, tap.

"Don't let your coffee go cold," I said.

Ben looked between me and Winslow, hoping I presumed for a reassurance that drinking the coffee was okay. Neither of us offered him anything. In the end he shrugged and picked up the mug. He drained it in one go, probably not even tasting it.

Tap, tap. Tap, tap. Tap, tap.

"Do you know where these are going?" Winslow asked him. Ben shook his head. "Upstairs, to the fake and forgery boys."

"They're genuine."

Winslow drew a sharp breath through his teeth. A habit that seemed particular to the British.

"Let's hope not, for your sake."

"What's that meant to mean?" Tap, tap. Tap, tap. Tap, tap. "What?"

"This many coupons, all real?"

The canteen wasn't busy. It was the lull just after lunch and before the scramble of preparing the evening menu of disappointments. Without the cram of bodies or the ovens and hotplates working, the canteen was bordering on cold. But, in the harsh glare of the strip lighting, Ben's face had a sheen to it.

Winslow was enjoying himself and started another round of tapping.

"Here's the thing, Constable," I explained. "Low ranking operative, like yourself, with a wad of black-market forgeries … who cares? Misdemeanour.

Something that's barely worth entering on your record. Your duty sergeant or someone chews on your ear, for form's sake. And it's all forgotten."

Ben was nodding his head quite slowly, wanting to back up my assertions, but bright enough to know no one was levelling with him.

Winslow picked up the ball again. "But, if they're not fakes it's a very different story." He held the envelope up, pinching one corner between finger and thumb, and jiggling it, gauging the weight. "Big wads of coupons, all genuine, don't just appear. The boys in fakes and forgeries won't be interested, but the Department for Professional Standards might be."

Tap, tap. Tap, tap. Tap, tap.

We watched Ben sweat some more.

"I'm not on the take. A friend gave them to me."

Winslow jiggled the envelope again and feigned surprise at the weight.

"You're a policeman. If you've got a friend in a position to give away this many coupons, you've got a duty to ask him how he's coming by them."

"Who's this friend?" I asked. No answer. "Was it Robertson?"

He glanced around the near-empty canteen before nodding.

"Yeah."

"Why would he give you coupons?"

"When they're in the cells, they're allowed to use any ration coupon they have on them, yeah?"

"If a helpful policeman is willing to be their fetch and carry man," Winslow agreed.

"Well, sometimes, if someone's willing to go to the canteen for them they'll … tell them to get one for themselves."

"And you do this, even though the regulations expressly forbid it?" I said.

Ben licked his lips and glanced around the near-empty canteen again, making sure no one could hear him throwing them under a bus.

"Look, we all do it. Everyone does it." He leaned forward and gave the confession in a hurried whisper. "Everyone."

"Just the prisoner's way of saying thank you?" Winslow suggested.

Ben grabbed the idea and nodded eagerly.

Winslow jiggled the envelope again.

"Looks like Mr Robertson had a lot to thank you for."

The nodding turned into shaking with a speed that must have hurt. The motion petered away to nothing in the silence.

"What are you going to do?" he finally asked.

Tap, tap. Tap, tap. Tap, tap.

"Well, if it was down to me," Winslow smiled. "I'd throw the book at you and then have that uniform you're wearing fumigated. Because I was a policeman before the world turned to shit, and there is nothing, nothing I hate more than a bent copper." Ben opened his mouth to say something, but Winslow jabbed an index finger at him like he was holding a knife. "Shut it. If you want to keep your job, just shut it." He slumped back in the chair and lifted the envelope again, so it was level with Ben's face. Then tossed it across the table so it landed in front of me. "But, it isn't down to me."

Having made his disgust for the pair of us known he stood up and walked away.

I let him get out of the room before I picked up the envelope.

"You deal with me, or you deal with him. It's up to you."

"I'm dealing with you then, ain't I."

I took Ben to an interview room. I told him it was so we could talk in private. Keeping it forefront in his mind that this was where official proceedings would put him added a subtle layer of pressure. He would have known that was my play. But that didn't stop it working. I also kept my hands in front of me on the table while we talked. That way he could see me fiddling with the envelope and the word 'evidence' written on it. I don't know how it stacked up as police work, but it was the sort of tactic I'd used on a dozen audit results.

"We all do it," was the first thing he said once we'd sat at the table. "I mean, everyone takes the odd cup of tea or coupon."

I drummed my fingers on the envelope and let him wind down. The envelope contained a lot more than the odd cup of tea. We both knew it.

"What favours did you trade for these?"

"He wanted proper coffee. I offered to get it for him."

"For a coupon?"

He shook his head, "No, I just told him I'd get him one if he had the coupons. He said he did, but they were with his personal property. I went and signed them out, it's in the …" he stopped abruptly.

"Property book?"

I got a shrug, then a nervous nod in answer. My accountant's brain settled into a smooth tick-over.

"Let me get this clear. Robertson is picked up on the fourth of April. According to the report, at eight p.m. on his way home from an officially licensed bar. When asked if he wanted to go to his place of residence before going to the station he replied, 'no'." I spun the envelope round and round. I could see the step change to official language hadn't been lost on him.

"I don't know anything about that."

"Are you on the take from a lot of the detainees?"

"I'm not on the … I just … No."

"So, these came from running errands for Robertson?"

"Yeah, that's right."

"All of them?"

"Yeah."

I stopped spinning the envelope and sat up straight in my best sincere professional stance.

"Here's the thing, I believe you, and so will Winslow. And that's the problem. Because if these are all Robertson's, it begs the question, why was he walking home at night with a stack of coupons this big in his wallet. Any ideas?"

He realised the hole he was in wasn't about to get anything other than deeper and didn't say anything.

"If I go and find DC Winslow and tell him this is okay, just a collection of technically illegal, but very minor, infractions of regulations, what do you think he's going to do?"

Still nothing to say, Ben suddenly found the ceiling very interesting. He winced as he pictured a disciplinary tribunal and a future without his uniform. He knew full well what Winslow would do.

Eventually he said, "He'll check the personal property book."

"Not quite," I told him. "We've already checked the detainee's property book. Every item, including coupons, that Robertson checked into his personal property box when he was brought in. Every coupon you signed for when you were getting his morning coffee."

And of course, the figures didn't add up. Which meant the stack of coupons Ben was holding, courtesy of Robertson, had been obtained from outside the station.

"If DC Winslow gets his teeth into this, you'll be lucky if you don't do jail time."

"What do you want?"

"The truth. You tell me exactly what you did for Robertson, exactly what he gave you and exactly how the two of you worked it." He winced again and nodded. "And do not lie to me, understand?"

March 5th, 2028

They barricaded the stairs from the lower floor and ate the little food they'd managed to bring with them. Despite the hunger and the cold most people were in high spirits. Being in a building with working lights was a luxury.

Someone had found a radio CD player and coaxed it into life. Robertson didn't recognise the song, it was middle-of-the-road pop music, but for a few minutes everyone had fallen silent. When the track ended, three or four people applauded. Robertson thought he heard someone weeping. Someone else, in a different part of the room, murmured, *It's going to be alright.* It sounded like a prayer of thanks. The next track on the CD began and broke the spell.

"Ready?" Patrick asked him.

The other two men and the woman who'd led the chanting on the bridge were behind him. They were wearing mismatched clothes they'd pulled from racks, but they'd all hung onto their jackets or coats, fluttering with the tattered remains of crow feathers.

"Yeah." Robertson looked over the small group. They were tired and obviously not keen on leaving the party. "I just want to have a quick scout around, check nothing major's headed our way. Then we head back in and get some sleep. Couple of hours tops." He made a point of getting eye contact with each of them. "We all good with that?"

Nods, a few yeahs.

They climbed through a gap in the barricade and stood on the stairs letting their eyes adjust to the gloom. Then the gap closed behind them and blocked the light again.

Robertson split the group when they were on the street. Patrick and the two men went left, he and the woman right. The group had paused for a fraction before stepping onto the pavement. It had been a collective act. After the months of darkness, entering a street bathed in sodium light seemed surreal.

Patrick gave Robertson a quizzical look when he'd sent him off with the two men. When he was sure the woman couldn't see, Robertson had given Patrick a smile.

"I'll be about an hour."

He winked.

Patrick glanced at the woman, who was holding herself a slight distance from them. He grinned and, leaning close to Robertson, said, "What you going to do for the other fifty-eight minutes?"

Robertson told him he'd think of something and slapped him on the shoulder. When the two groups parted Patrick glanced back and told him to call if he needed help. Before they left his sight, one of the other men laughed.

They walked in silence, staying clear of the darker patches. Two streets west of the shop they'd commandeered, they encountered a lone Gonzo shuffling down the middle of the road. Like the group they'd encountered on the bridge and the others since, the switch over had been a long time ago. Robertson had lifted his axe and made towards it. Before he got there the woman had overtaken him. She was holding a kitchen knife, one of the shorter-bladed weapons some of the Crows seemed to favour. He'd heard them referred to as jaggers.

She swung back-handed at the Gonzo, driving the knife into its face. The momentum of the blow carried it over on to its back. She let it fall then pulled the knife free and used both hands to punch it into the top of its skull.

"You got a name?" Robertson asked.

She'd started the filleting routine Miller followed.

Robertson let her get on with it while he kept watch for any more Gonzos.

"You got a name?" he repeated.

She looked up briefly from the carcass.

"Raven."

Her head dipped back to what she was doing.

"Raven? Jesus, do you arseholes think this is a fucking game?"

"No, this isn't a game. This is the new world."

She dropped an organ on the road, regarded it critically and changed its position.

"What was with all that crap in the sickbay? People waiting to switch?"

"You wouldn't understand."

"So, explain."

She didn't respond at first and he thought she was ignoring him. After making another adjustment to the display of offal, she turned and sat back on her haunches. Head tilting first to one side then the other, she regarded him.

"There's a new order coming. The old world is gone." She waved her hands at the ruined streets around them. "This" – she indicated the disembowelled Gonzo – "is part of the new form."

"And how does you guys offering yourselves up to get butchered change that?"

Raven carefully cleaned the knife, wiping the blade against the side of her heavy boots.

"We are not trying to change it." She spoke very clearly and carefully, the way she might have addressed a young child. "We are changing. Changing in order to fit into the new paradigm. We are the children of the crows."

"Very poetic."

"The old gods talked about the wheat and the chaff. Well now we have the crows and the butchered. These are going before us, to feed the crows."

"So where does Miller fit in with all this?"

"Miller leads the way, Miller has the tongue and the ear of the Bone Crow and speaks to their eyes."

"And you think this is it? No more law and order, no more government? Just crows and Gonzos?"

"New world. Children and chosen. Everything before …" she snapped her fingers, "… gone."

"And the lights coming back on?"

"They are the lights of the old world. The dying flame of a guttering candle."

Raven was beginning to raise her voice. Excitement or anger, it was impossible to say.

"So, what was all that shit on the bridge? Leaving Miller to fend off a pack of Gonzos while you all have a sing-song?"

She didn't speak, but in reply put her arms out to her sides and let her head hang loosely. It took Robertson a moment to realise she was enacting Christ on the cross. Or at least a Christ on the cross.

Robertson saw another Gonzo approaching. He lifted the axe and hesitated briefly. Raven, her head still bowed in the parody of crucifixion, didn't spot it. He swung his axe in a high arc and brought it down squarely for a clean kill.

She died without knowing she'd been hit.

The Gonzo was homing in on him. It was in worse shape than the first one. Missing an arm and dragging a near useless leg, it moved in a series of lurching semicircles. He let it get closer, intending another clean finish, then realised it was speaking. The words were barely audible. Cracked sounds shot through with gaps as the thing's voice box failed it.

"Jam to … bread … row … jam today …" On repeat.

He circled the thing half a dozen times, trying to untangle the message, as it lunged at him. When it was finally clear he stepped back.

"Jam today, bread tomorrow," he said. "What does that mean?"

The Gonzo made another weak swipe at him and over-balanced on its damaged leg. Robertson put his foot in the centre of its back to keep it down. He let the collection of words run through another cycle before asking what it meant again.

"Jam to … bread …"

He lifted his foot and stamped down. He felt ribs break. The words became gasps and wet gurgles. He stamped again.

"What does that fucking mean?" He carried on stamping, felt more bone giving way. "What … does … that … fucking … mean?"

He was still shouting the question after the Gonzo was dead and his boots were covered in gore. When he stopped, he had no idea how much time had passed, and he realised he had tears running down his face.

Chapter 42. In from the Cold

Excerpt from speech given by Presidential Candidate Mason J Drumph

I intend to pass the legislation needed to stop the entry, into our great country, of so-called 'medical asylum seekers'. The practice of immigrants entering the US, carrying viruses and diseases such as French Cat Influenza, Cat Scratch Fever and Toxic [SIC] Gondii will be outlawed. Anyone wishing to gain lawful entry to our great land will need to prove they have had no exposure, zero exposure to the plagues currently raging in Europe.

I will keep a permanent armed presence along land borders with Mexico and current border crossing points will be closed. Entry, into US air space, from another sixteen nations will be prohibited entirely. These policies are the only way to keep our people safe.

Transit through American seaports and airports should be for US citizens only. A vote for me is a vote to make America safe again.

Together we can make America safe again. Together we can save American soil for American sons.

We didn't make land. Captain gave me a lifejacket and raised a hand in farewell as I lowered myself over the side. My boots filling with water, I told him thanks and let go. The lifejacket kept my head in the air and pulled me into a slant. Face-up, floating at an odd angle, I struck out for shore.

Captain's wife hadn't been on deck to see me off. She'd hugged me once that morning and stayed below, crying. I'd tried to ask Captain if she'd be alright, but the language barrier had been too high to jump. He'd shrugged helplessly and beckoned me towards the bright orange lifejacket he was holding up.

The tide was with me. I assumed Captain had timed matters that way, but I might have been wrong.

Leaving the yacht had meant leaving my supplies. I took the kitchen knife I'd carried since Paris and a few packets of vacuum-packed, processed meat. Captain had watched the selection of meats I took. I had the feeling he might have been weighing the humanity of his actions against the loss of supplies. I let him catch sight of Dog Boy's pistol and the scales tipped in favour of humanitarian aid.

The water sucked the warmth from my body. I kicked harder with the mixed agenda of getting to land quicker and keeping my core temperature up. Beyond that, I didn't allow myself to think. The idea of making for the island nation had been a touchstone for so long I didn't want to risk questioning it.

There was a strange transition from sea to land. When my feet touched down, the weight of my wet clothes and the buoyancy of the lifejacket conspired to keep me bobbing along at an angle. I flapped around for a while before managing to haul myself upright in the shallows. Wriggling out of the lifejacket was beyond me; it was stuck fast, and my fingers were too numb to work the fastening. In the wind, wearing sodden clothing, I could feel the last shreds of heat leaving my body.

The beach was a blanket of pebbles that slid from underneath me as I tried to walk. The water ended about two hundred yards from a blank wall of concrete, where the high tide had left a black-green witness line. A stairway, cast in the same black-slimed concrete, led to a point some twelve feet above. Shivering and weighed down by my clothing, I climbed the steps on all fours.

At the top of the sea wall I turned and looked out to sea, hoping, for some reason, that I might catch a glimpse of the Bella-Kay. Rain was drifting in from the east, reducing visibility, and all I could see was water.

In the other direction the sea wall tapered away into a ragged trailer park with a collection of static trailers that looked impossibly small. About a third of them were burned out.

Other than gulls, I seemed to be the only living thing.

I slid down the grassed incline and finally got a break from the wind. I listened for shuffling steps or streams of gibberish. When I didn't hear anything, I forced myself up and made my way to the nearest intact trailer.

The storm arrived shortly after I'd managed to force the lock. The trailer acted like a sounding board and the noise of the rain made my ears ring. At last, free of the wind and the rain, I fumbled with the lifejacket and my clothes, and finally shed the wet layer. Then I pulled down all the drapes I could find and wrapped myself in them.

When I woke up it was dark, and the rain had stopped. The drapes had gone from damp and cold to stiff and humid. I sat in the dark and listened. The silence began to spook me. It was easy to imagine I'd trekked through France only to land in a dead country. From there it wasn't far to imagine the air was toxic with infections and I was just waiting to fall ill and die.

It's funny the things the mind clings onto. Some neuron in a corner of my brain reminded me I had vacuum-wrapped meat stuffs. It was enough to drive away thoughts of death and insanity.

After I'd carefully chewed through all my supplies, I thought about trying the cooker top in the microscopic kitchen. I turned on one of the rings and there was a faint hiss and the sharp chemical tang of gas. I lit the ring and left it burning to give the illusion of warmth. Something about the smell or the quality of the flickering light, reminded me of being a kid again. I sat in the trailer listening to the hiss of the gas flame and gazing into space.

The next day I systematically searched thirty-one trailers. After the tenth, I had breaking and entering down to a fine art. I found a tire iron early on and sped up the process immeasurably. The haul I got didn't reflect my expertise.

The few trailers with food in them had been visited by vermin long before I got there, and the only clothes were invariably beachwear or children's coats. I left with seven boxes of matches, three tin openers and a selection of blankets. I used the kitchen knife to slit a couple of the blankets and turned them into serviceable ponchos. Then I set off inland.

The trailer park gave way to patches of unkempt scrubland and the occasional empty house. The only signs of life I saw, apart from gulls, were a few feral cats and a near skeletal cow that regarded me with complete indifference. I walked what I estimated to be three miles before coming to a sign crudely painted onto a square of plyboard:

REPORT TO CHECKPOINT FOR REGISTRATION

Underneath that, an arrow pointed along the right-hand spur of the road.

There was no clear border to the town. Its outer limits were a sprawling collection of shops and arcades that could have been built anytime in the last hundred years. Styles and formats mixed in an unplanned mess. There was very little damage here: broken windows, signs that doors had been kicked opened, but not much of the rubble and ash I'd seen most of Paris reduced to. Like the walk down I saw few signs of life, other than stray animals.

Signs of humanity came hand in hand with barbwire and officialdom. As I walked further inland, the sprawl of buildings congealed into a knot. I followed signs that promised a town centre and found a traffic circle with an army truck parked diagonally across it. Coils of barbwire tangled around criss-crosses of timber and the fire-gutted shell of an automobile.

Getting closer I saw the truck had a pair of mountain bikes propped against its rear wheel. Closer still, I could see the truck was sitting on flat tires.

I was about twenty feet from the circle when a man in army fatigues appeared.

"Okay, that's far enough. Halt."

The fatigues flapped in the wind and, even with the distance I'd been kept at, I could see his face had the sharp shrunken look that came with rapid weight loss. The same look I was wearing.

He had a blunt-looking rifle held high on his chest with the barrel pointing down. The stance was neutral but the practiced efficiency of it was intimidating. He was clearly a professional solider. I stopped walking and put my hands up.

The solider looked at me and tilted his head to one side.

"You on your own?"

"Yeah, it's just me."

He lifted his eyes at my accent.

"You American?"

"Yeah."

"You sick?"

"No, I'm not infected."

"Where have you come from?"

"I don't know. I caught a ride on a boat from Calais. I got here last night."

"How many of you on this boat?"

"It's just me. They didn't land, I had to swim ashore. I slept in a trailer park, a couple of miles that way."

He glanced in the direction I'd pointed and looked at me as if I was speaking in tongues. Then he laughed.

"Oh, the caravan site." For some reason the exchange pleased him. He took his hand away from the gun and found a length of webbing to hold instead. "Welcome to England. We better get you sorted out."

Things had a strange stop-start rhythm after that. Not knowing the British called trailer parks 'caravan sites' seemed to be proof enough that I wasn't dangerous.

A second soldier appeared carrying an armful of branches. He made a fire and, maybe to prove I had washed up on the British mainland, he made tea.

Via a walkie-talkie, contact was made with an HQ somewhere in the town. There was a flurry of communications and an order to bring me in. The solider who'd made the fire asked me if I could ride a bicycle. I said yes, which spared me a two-mile march.

Civilisation, or at least its kissing-cousin bureaucracy, had returned. I was met at a second perfunctory checkpoint by a man in a fancier uniform and a woman in a ragged fur coat.

The man introduced himself by rank, which I instantly forgot, and introduced the woman by profession. She was a doctor and could have been any age between thirty and ninety. I'm sure she had a story to tell, but I had no more interest in hearing it than she had in telling it.

I was led to a building that looked like it had been a school. A collection of beds in a dozen different styles had been slotted into the old classrooms. Most of the rooms I was led past had at least one patient in them. I wondered at the time why so much of the equipment was cobbled together from bits and pieces. I didn't find out until much later about the spate of hospital burnings.

I was given a rapid medical. After being held prisoner in a Paris boarding house and seeing the sick executed, I was surprised at the speed of the process.

"It looks like the disease has run its course," the doctor told me. "We haven't seen any new cases in three months. There have been reports of people recovering."

She shrugged as though that was a fairy tale she might choose to believe.

It took me a while to digest what she'd said.

"So, it's over?"

She laughed, too loudly for the near-empty room we were in.

"It's just starting."

I didn't ask what she meant, and she didn't elaborate.

I was told I was going to be in quarantine for two weeks and to expect a debriefing. She put on a deep voice when she said debriefing. Obviously mocking someone.

Quarantine was the first hiatus. I was confined to the drafty room the examination had taken place in. I saw very few people. Fresh bedding was left at the door after the first seven days and two meals a day were handed to me at the door. Other than the three-daily bathroom trips I was allowed, that was as exciting as it got. After two days the uniform with the forgettable rank turned up with a notebook and a clipboard. He informed me I was about to be debriefed and I gathered the doctor had been mocking him.

He was the first in a long line of people that I was to meet – all of them men – promoted far beyond their capability, and too vain to know it. He said 'debrief' with a degree of self-importance that told me everything I needed to know about him. He was probably responsible to a large degree for my dislike of Winslow.

I answered pointless questions about the situation on the continent and followed the motion of his ballpoint. He was getting about an eighth of what I said down on the record. When he started asking about military placements and civilian armament levels, he was clearly playing at being a general. I lost patience.

"Is there an American consulate operating in this country?" I asked.

He told me he would be asking the questions. I told him, as an American citizen, I'd be ignoring them. He tried for a cold stare and an air of authority. I wondered if it would have worked before Paris.

The next hiatus lasted three days while I waited for someone with real command experience to appear. In one of those rare moments when the universe cooperates, Colonel Pinkman was a woman. Mid-fifties with the grey hair to prove it, she came to me while I was eating the second meal of the day and asked if I had proof of US citizenship.

She looked over the threadbare passport I had given her and nodded.

"Eliss tells me you claim to have been in Paris."

"I don't claim anything. I was in Paris."

I told her the story, shortened and minus Dog Boy's shooting.

She nodded occasionally and gave the impression of keeping better records than her male colleague.

"That ties up with what we'd heard about France. Bloody mess. Can you tell me something about the boat you came in on?"

I fabricated a new name for the Bella-Kay and glossed over most of the details with a mist of language barrier.

"We've located an acting US Consulate in Tunbridge. I'll arrange for you go over there as soon as we can. But there's very little that happens quickly now. I'll try to organise a phone link."

Four days later, I was crammed into the passenger seat of a truck hauling fish across country.

The acting consulate was in a building that resembled a wedding cake. In common with every building I've since encountered in the UK, it was freezing cold.

The staff consisted of three people and I never quite worked out what their diplomatic mission was. I dealt with another man who'd been shunted up the chain of command by chance alone. To his credit, Herb Shackly at least knew it. To everyone else's detriment, he'd adapted to his new role by turning bitterness into an art form. He sat hunched over his desk and opened my passport with a deep sigh.

"Miranda Cross. Citizen of the US of A and once proud resident of New York State."

His desk was a modern style thing in a pale wood that had been lacquered until it looked like plastic. The surface was covered in a thin layer of papers, forms, folders and junk. The whole collection represented about an hour's worth of work, or a week's worth of excuses. Like Officer Debrief, he made a big deal of taking notes and making records.

"What do you think I can do for you?" he said.

I was back in the clothes I swam ashore in, but I'd managed to replace the blanket ponchos with a bright yellow coat that smelled of kerosene and would have fit me twice over. I could see Herb eyeing it enviously. Without taking my hands out of the pockets I told him,

"I want to get back to the States, I've got a …"

I didn't get to tell him about David and Maria waiting at home. He was laughing.

"Sure, sure no problem. You want a window seat? There's twenty flights a day and Drumph'll roll out the red carpet for you."

The name Drumph rang a bell, or rather tolled one. I remembered a scaremongering clown, tacked onto the end of political newscasts for comic relief. Shackly told me that while the world was going to hell, America had made the clown president. He'd rolled in on a tidal-wave majority, votes bought and paid for with paranoia and pig-ignorance.

When Herb got agitated, he emphasised his words with hand gestures. He used both hands at once and wouldn't lift his elbows from his desktop. The effect was similar to an amateur puppet show.

"The problem is, this goddamned crisis hit North Europe and the UK hardest. Now it's got everyone peeing in their panties, all because the goddamn limeys got no second amendment. If they'd stamped the damn things out once and for all, we'd be home right now."

He finished the speech with both hands open, fingers spread wide.

I wanted to ask him how many gondii psychotics he'd met and how many riots or running street fights he'd been in. And how many times he'd fired a gun. But I didn't. I knew the answer anyway and I was too tired to shake him from his John Wayne fantasy. I let him wind down in his own time.

"So, is that it, are we British now?"

Herb looked like he was about to launch into another fantasy-based explanation. What he said was just as disappointing.

"I'll give you the forms to fill in to have your case considered. But I'll warn you, the last communique I had from Washington was recommending a five-year quarantine on unemployed US citizens overseas. Unless they can prove residency in a safe area for the duration of the Outbreak."

"Unemployed?"

"There's currently seventeen percent unemployment in the US. They're deporting illegals as fast as they can to ease the situation, but still. If you've got employment waiting for you it speeds things up."

"I worked ..."

He gave me one of his double-hand gestures to cut me off.

"Just fill out the paperwork. It'll all come out in the process."

He made a three-course meal out of finding the forms to hand over. Then he pointed me to a table in the corner. Unlike the high-tech modern thing he was nesting behind, this was a rickety table that had been customised by fixing screens of plyboard to it, turning it into a booth.

When I sat at the table/booth, I saw it had been further customised by bolting a length of cable to it. On the end of the cable was a ballpoint pen and, on the wall, directly in front of me was written:

THINK! PAPER IS HARD TO GET.
FILL OUT YOUR FORM CAREFULLY.
AVOID WASTE.

There was a red-brown smudge underneath that looked like blood but on closer viewing was an attempt to add an official stamp to the official graffiti.

The form ran to ten pages and at first glance was obsessively geared to proving citizenship and health. In reality, it was asking what funds I had access to.

Strangely, it made me feel like I was on my way home.

Chapter 43. Guilty Parties

From Behaviour Patterns in Corvids, by Dr Nina Amin. Oxford (2027)

The commonly-held belief that flocks of crows would follow in the wake of violence during the HV-Tg pandemic is a fallacy. It stems in part from the romantic notions of the film industry and flawed observations made by people living under stressful conditions.

Crows, being territorial, would not be inclined to move as a group. It is likely that what people witnessed were similarities in feeding patterns across different groups of corvids.

In cities, where most accounts of 'crow following' arose, crow populations were already relatively relaxed in the presence of humans. It's likely that local crows, in various locations, had quickly made the connection between the presence of humans (infected or otherwise) and the sudden increase in carrion.

The tailing away of this rich food source would account for increased aggression, within urban flocks, during territorial squabbles.

Once we were over the Thames the number of infected we encountered increased dramatically. They were drawn to the powered-up section of the city too. We'd find groups of them milling around shops where the lights still worked.

We passed one where a sound system had survived intact. It must have been on a timer. With the power back on, it had kicked in again and the tape or the CD, whatever, started playing. There, in the middle of a street half smashed to rubble, was a shoe shop blasting out drum and bass music.

It was full of Gonzos, wandering around the racks and shelves. Some of them were holding trainers and there were shoes scattered everywhere. I think they'd been picking things up and not remembering what they were for, then they'd drop them, or they'd knock into something and lose their grip.

This sounds morbid, but it looked like a party. If you half-closed your eyes, they were just people.

In hindsight, and I may be deluding myself, I think that moment was a turning point. That was when we started getting our humanity back. In a way that was unsettling. It made us face what we had become.

And if we forgot, the crows followed in our wake to remind us. They seemed unsettled as well. The flocks were louder and more aggressive.

Maybe they knew more than they let on. We saw signs of change but didn't fit them to a bigger picture. Everything was personal at that stage. We didn't know the Toxo gondii mutations had largely burnt themselves out.

April 15th, 2028

Robertson's tame uniform sat in the back of Winslow's car and jabbered his story out without pause. Winslow sat in the driver's seat with his arm spread along the backrest. He didn't interrupt or smile, and totally unnerved PC Ben Haddan. Which was the intention.

Ben had been star-struck by Robertson's presence in the station. He'd been more than happy to sign out a coupon so his celebrity ward could have a decent coffee in the morning. Taking the offer of one for yourself was understandable. I'd have done it myself, so would Winslow, though I doubt he would have admitted it. The next step was questionable at best. And at worst a sackable offence.

"After a couple of days he asked me how many were left. He was getting really low by then and I told him so. Then he asked if I could fetch him some more. He said he'd had a fresh book issued the day before he was picked up. Only it was at his place. He said if I could go and get it … he'd … appreciate it."

When he'd told me the story in the interview room he'd faltered at the same point. It was the tipping point where being thanked for a favour began to look like profiteering. Winslow picked up on the hesitation too. He showed it by nodding slowly.

"I knew I wouldn't be allowed to sign his house keys out so next time …" another tipping point. Instead of signing property out the next time he made a coffee run, he palmed Robertson's keys.

"So I went to his flat and picked up the ration book. It was in a drawer in the kitchen. When I told him I had the book he told me to take half for myself." When Winslow didn't comment, he added, "He said you'd be keeping him as long as you could, so he wouldn't be needing them for a while."

He stopped talking and I began to suspect he was as dim as Robertson had taken him to be. We had pulled a damn sight more than half a ration book out of him. He'd already told me the next part, and thinking he'd be spared telling it to Winslow was a further exercise in stupidity.

Winslow still didn't speak; he drummed his fingers instead. Ben, slow as he was, got the message.

"He asked me if I wanted some more. This was a day or so later. I wasn't that fussed at the time, I'd been careful with them, you know."

"Being frugal, clever," Winslow deadpanned so completely that, for a moment, Ben genuinely thought he'd done something right.

"Yeah, well you …" He swallowed dryly, "But I said yes, because, because …" He trailed off leaving Winslow and me to mentally finish, because you're greedy and stupid.

Tap, tap. Tap, tap. Tap, tap.

"He told me if I'd do him a favour there'd be 'a drink' in it for me." He jigged his fingers up and down making quotation marks in the air. "He gave me a letter, to deliver to a friend of his."

"What was in this letter?"

"Don't know. It was in an envelope. He said it was just to let a friend of his know he'd be out of circulation for a while."

"He had the envelope and some notepaper with him, did he?" Winslow asked. Ben began to answer but Winslow waved the excuses away. "Who was this friend?"

"I don't know. Some old man. When I gave him the envelope, he opened it and read the letter. Then he gave me the coupons."

"Where was this?"

"A flat over this drinking den. I can't remember the exact address, but I can find it again."

"Describe the old man."

"I don't know. He was just an old man."

"This was on the sixth." I said this to Winslow, but Ben picked up on my tone of voice and swallowed again.

Tap, tap. Tap, tap. Tap, tap.

"What time did Robertson ask you to contact this old man?"

"Lunchtime, when I went down to the cells before I went to the canteen to get the prisoner's meal. I wanted to know if Robertson …"

"Wanted anything extra, yeah. What time did you deliver the letter?"

"That evening, right after my shift finished. About eight?"

"We had a young fella pulled in on the fifth. He claimed to know Robertson from before the Outbreak. We mentioned this to Robertson. The day after you delivered your letter our young fella was turned loose. He was murdered the same night."

We all sat in the car and listened to the silence. The only sound for a long time was the relentless drumming of Winslow's fingers.

"What's that got to do with me taking someone a letter?"

"You mean, facilitating an illegal communication between a man in custody and an unknown individual for payment in illegally-procured government-issued coupons," Winslow said.

The colour drained from Ben and his breathing became shallow and fast.

"Here's what we're going to do," I said. "Detective Constable Winslow and I are going to pretend we didn't hear you telling us about taking bribes and obstructing the course of justice. You are going to pretend to be a real policeman and direct us to the drinking den and the flat where you met the old man. And you're going to do it right now. Is that clear?"

It was.

March 5th, 2021

Robertson was limping when he got back to the clothes shop. The music from the first floor was muffled, reduced to a series of soft pulses. Three Gonzos had gathered at the broken shopfront. Two of them were too far gone to manage the step up required to get through the window. He took them down with little effort.

The third one was in better shape. It was another chanter. Sing-songing the same five words over and over, *Swan and button blue song.*

Robertson lifted the axe and hesitated a fraction, caught, despite himself, trying to make sense of the gibberish. It gave the thing time to take a swipe at him. The new set of instincts he'd built over the months killed it.

On the other side of the barricade the party mood had slowed. Not exactly sombre, the people sitting around listening to the music were thoughtful. It put him in mind of parties he'd been to in his youth. Everyone looked like the booze had run out and now there was nothing to do but wait for the hangover. He felt bad for adding another layer of woe.

"You alright, Boss?"

Johnno had opened the gap in the barricade. In the brightly-lit room, Robertson's blood-soaked jeans and freshly-used axe became the centre of attention.

"I'm okay. Are the others back?"

Johnno shook his head. Behind him there was a sharp click and the music cut off. The whole room was staring at them.

"What happened, Boss?"

"We split into two groups. Patrick and the two fellas went east, I went west with Raven. We walked right into a pack of bloody Gonzos. She didn't make it."

Johnno swore under his breath, "Big pack?"

"No, but …" He motioned with his head to the big Scouser that they should leave the room. When they were on the stairs, away from the watchers, "It shouldn't have been a problem, but she just walked straight into them, dropped her weapons and …"

Johnno swore again and then fell silent. In the room above them someone put the music back on. More bland pop. A teenager singing about heartbreak and trying to sound worldly.

"Listen, how much sway have you got with this Ally?"

"I don't know about sway, but we get on alright."

"Have a chat with her. If all these Crows of hers are intent on getting themselves killed, we need to know. Alright? If we got a suicide cult tagging on to us, we might as well give up now and leave the army boys to it."

Before he got an answer, they heard boots approaching the shop. Robertson recognised the step of Patrick and the two other Crows, but he made a pretence of jumping at the noise.

"It's alright, Boss. It's just Pat and the other boys." He patted Robertson's shoulder. "I'll see they're okay. Go get yourself cleaned up."

Patrick's team had returned with a report of clear streets, and a collection of fan heaters. They took the news of Raven's death without question or surprise. The only recognition the news received was a sympathetic glance from Patrick. Robertson blanked it, unsure of how he would have reacted to the situation Pat was imagining.

With the addition of heat, the 'party' picked up again.

March 6th, 2021

They dropped back into the pattern they'd adopted on the south side of the river. Small, largely self-contained groups, acting together, each in sight of a least one other.

Robertson was walking beside Sol. In front of them was a Crow, behind them Patrick. He'd arranged the teams so the one with Johnno and Maccallan was always in sight. It meant the Crows were largely unobserved, but he already knew he couldn't rely on them.

"Any idea what this means?"

He passed Sol a strip of paper; it was a piece torn from a roll of till receipts. Sol held it up for inspection. It was the string of words the Gonzos from the previous night had been muttering. Sol sounded the words quietly and nodded to himself.

"You recognise it?" Robertson heard the note of surprise in his own voice. Surprise and excitement.

"I don't recognise it, but I know what it means."

With his shaky fingers he carefully folded the strip of paper into a small pad. Robertson had stopped walking, all his attention fixed on the old man.

"So, what does it mean?"

"It means," Sol lifted the tiny pad of paper until it was level with his face and stared at it in silence for a moment. Then flicked it away and laughed. "It means you've been listening to a lot of gibberish. I told you, they're mad, stop wasting your time. Or you'll end up mad yourself."

Sol, despite his drenching in the Thames and the cold trek to shelter, was in high spirits. Unlike Robertson, he regarded the crossing as a success. One more hurdle that had been cleared.

His optimism grated on Robertson.

Chapter 44. Praying God Doesn't Exist

Crypt (Digi Crypt, Digital Crypt)

Slang term popular in most English-speaking countries. It replaces the official term 'purse' in reference to individual cryptocurrency accounts. The term first appeared in an online article written under the byline 'Anony Mouse'. The article condemned the increasing use of government-endorsed cryptocurrency throughout the US. Anony Mouse claimed the adoption of the 'inland bit-coin' was an attempt by the US to increase border controls by allowing external trade without human interaction. Maintaining the move was symptomatic of a culture of dehumanisation, the article closed with the line, 'the bit-coin purse should be renamed the bit-coin crypt'.

Though adopted internationally, within the US its use is taken as a barometer of an individual's political leanings. The right-leaning / conservatives tend to use the conventional term purse. The term crypt has become associated with the political left and those holding a negative view of America's isolationist policy.

The A to Z of Gondii Names

Shout out to avoid Lou Lou's Home Town Supplies, in Mississippi. Inbred tosspot in some pass-fuck-nowhere 'convenience' store, refused to accept an N-kode transaction because I mentioned I had a crypt full of coin. They only take coin from purses 'cos we is Ameeriicaan here, y'all'. Told me he'd call the police if I didn't get out of his shithole of a store. Dickwad.
Username: EnWhyGurl
Posts: 898

April 15th, 2028

The drinking den PC Haddan directed us to was a private house that neighboured a burnt and boarded shell. We knocked on the door and a woman with a face of sour milk answered.

"You here to drink?" she said.

Winslow flipped out his warrant card. The way he did it made me wonder if he stood in front of a mirror practicing the move. If that was the case, the woman's reaction must have been gratifying. Already pale, she drained of colour to the point where she was almost transparent.

"Yeah, we fancy a drink. What you got?" Winslow said.

She tried to backpedal manically until I quietly shushed her. Without her prattle, we could make out the murmur of voices from the 'empty' building next door.

"We're here to speak to the man upstairs," Winslow told her.

The front door had opened onto a hallway with another door at the end of it, and a grease-clotted kitchen beyond that. To the right there was a staircase. Nonplussed, the woman took a backward step and began to mutter about the upstairs being nothing to do with her.

We ignored her and Winslow told Ben to lead the way. I watched the old woman's face as we started up the stairs, curious to see if she'd recognise him as a regular. She carried on backing away as we climbed.

The upper floor had been converted into a separate unit. The standard of the work suggested it had been done pre-Outbreak. Even in the dim shadows of the landing the walls showed every scratch, dent and cut-corner to full effect. It clearly had a long history of being a piss-poor property.

Ben was waiting for one of us to do something. Winslow prodded him and mimed knocking on the door. He knocked. Then knocked again. On the other side of the door we could hear someone moving around.

"Who's there?"

The voice was an odd combination of caution and outrage. A quality I associated with New York; for a split second I was homesick.

Winslow prodded Ben again, "It's me, Ben. Robertson's …" He stopped, not sure how to describe the relationship in front of two people who might yet become his arresting officers. He gave up and finished on, "… from the police station."

There was another sound from the other side of the door. I guessed whoever was inside could see out. It took a moment to spot the spyhole in the landscape of the door. I waved at it.

"Who are the other two?"

"They're from the station."

"Show me some ID."

We fussed about with warrant cards for a minute or two more before we heard bolts being drawn.

"Come in, come in. Don't let all the heat out."

Winslow, gallant or possibly cautious, motioned me to go first. Before I did, I turned to Ben.

"Go home. Take every single coupon you got from this deal and get rid of it. Throw them in the street, flush them down the john, burn them, whatever. But lose them, because if I even think I've seen you using one, I'll see to it you lose that badge. You understand?"

He nodded rapidly but didn't move. I told him again to go home and he almost ran down the stairs. Winslow watched him go with a look of disgust; he had enough left over to spare some for me.

I followed the old man inside.

The flat he led us into was obsessively tidy and appeared austere when it wasn't. The living room was furnished with a large leather couch and an office chair of the type fat-cat executives used to sit in. At least in TV shows. The chair was set in front of a table that was, in turn, tight against the room's only window. There was a flock of desk lamps there. One consisted of a magnifying lens surrounded by a circle of LED bulbs. There was a selection of boxes and small items spread over the table. It was impossible to see exactly what any of them were. Despite the collection of high-output lights, the room's only illumination came from an oil lamp standing on the mantelpiece of a small fireplace. There was a gas fire in the grate showing the barest flicker of flame.

The old man took a seat on the couch, near to the mean excuse of a fire, and hauled a blanket around his shoulders.

Downstairs we could hear an exodus. The old biddy on the ground floor must have tipped off the den that the police were nearby. It wasn't an uncommon set-up. The dens would crop up from time to time. Normally an abandoned site with a supply of home-brewed hooch or beer. The more upmarket ones tended to leach power from an officially owned residence. That way they could run an internet connection and make exchanges in Digi Coin.

There was probably a closet under the stairs leading to a hole in the wall.

Technically it was all illegal, but so long as no one went blind drinking the bathtub swill, no one really cared.

Winslow sat in the executive chair, as I'd known he would. And, I suspect, as the old man guessed he would.

"And who are you?" Winslow asked him.

The old man pulled the blanket more tightly to his shoulders and managed a shiver.

"Solomon Abrahams. I'd say I'm pleased to meet you, but I'm not sure if I am."

His hands trembled but the movement seemed unconnected with the temperature in the flat, which wasn't especially cold.

"I'm DC Winslow, and this is DS Cross."

Winslow pointed at me with one hand and used the other to do his trick of flipping his ID wallet open. Solomon leaned forward and took the card. He held it a few inches from his face and squinted at it.

He handed it back and said, "If this is about what goes on downstairs, it's nothing to do with me. I mind my own business. Abby, God rest his soul, he told me, in this life a man has enough to do minding his own business without minding everyone else's."

"We're not interested in a bunch of jokers paying good coin to drink anti-freeze." Winslow inflated slightly before adding, "We're CID, we deal with the big stuff. Murders."

"Oi, so now I'm a murderer? I'm an old man, I can barely lift a knife and fork, and now I'm being arrested for murder."

His voice cracked on the word murder and he tried to shrink further into the blanket.

The only other seat in the room was on the couch. I hadn't wanted to sit next to Solomon, so I'd stayed on my feet. I didn't bother offering him my ID again. I was pretty sure he'd seen it well enough through his spyhole.

"No one's accusing you of murder. You know Colin Robertson, King of the Crows?"

He didn't answer immediately, and I suspected he was running through a list of possible replies. And weighing up the wisdom of an outright lie.

"I know Robertson. We were both caught inside the Lockdown. They blow the bridges to bits and leave us to die. Robertson, Maccallan, Miller, all the big shots I know. Did they make a film about me? Pah. What does anyone care what happens to an old ...?"

Winslow clicked his fingers and pointed at Solomon, "You're Chan."

I'd already got there with that one, and the temptation to make some snide remark about 'real coppers' was pretty strong. But I had bigger things on my mind.

"Mr Abrahams," I said, "You can drop the act. It's not fooling anyone."

My eyes had adjusted to the gloom enough that I could see the light switch. I flicked it on and noted that the bulb, a low energy one that should have taken a while to warm up, emitted light at once. It was still warm from its last use.

"I don't need to act. You're looking for a murderer? I look like a murderer to you?"

In the glare of good light, the helpless old geezer act was even less convincing. There was a hardened shine to the fella's eye that no one in their right mind could have mistaken for a twinkle. And the blanket he'd pulled tightly around his frame wasn't outlining a hunched set of shoulders.

But he was right, I wasn't looking at him with a murder charge in mind.

"You knew Maccallan too?" Winslow said.

"Maccallan, yeah I knew Maccallan. God rest his soul."

"You think his soul's likely to be at rest Mr Abrahams?"

"What are you asking me? You come here to discuss religious beliefs? I'll tell you something – anyone who's seen the things I've seen prays every night that there is no God. Because any god that lets his people go through that is insane or evil. Pah. Maccallan, God or no, is dead and nothing will change that. Dead with a million others."

"Did you see who killed him?"

"I've seen more people kill and be killed than I can count. I see that all the time, in my sleep, in the mirror. I see ghosts walking the streets and think they're still alive."

"Did Robertson kill Maccallan?"

"Maccallan died. Miller died. Patrick, Ally, Raven, men, women, children died and died and died. Millions. Don't you understand that? Millions upon millions." He had shed the blanket now and, in his anger – the only thing I'd seen that looked genuine – he shed the old man act too. I put his age in the low eighties. Old by the standards of the day, but he wore it well. He stood and turned the oil lamp off, then looked to myself and Winslow. The look he gave us was past contempt and into a whole new field. "And you two are looking for a murderer."

"The governments, UK and US" – Winslow nodded at me – "never granted any kind of amnesty for crimes committed during the crisis, not even those committed inside the Lockdown region."

Solomon laughed.

"Then you better be ready to arrest the whole of this city. No one survived without looting, stealing, fighting. Killing? You think anyone had a choice?

Gonzos. You think you can reason with them, frighten them away, pay them off?"

"We're not talking about the infected. We're talking about Maccallan and possibly the parade of corpses littering the tower block he was bolted in. So, maybe you should think about what you saw."

Whatever shreds of the harmless-old-man shtick Solomon had been clinging to he brushed away.

"Alright little man, have it all your way. But what do you think I'll be telling you? I was one of fifty or sixty people that stayed together to survive. The rest are God-alone-knows where or dead. Maccallan's flat I've never even seen. He tagged onto the group and got himself dead when those pigs in the bank opened fire."

"You're saying Maccallan died in the incident with Captain Billings and his men?" I asked.

Solomon gave me a strange look. Not quite contempt, it was maybe disappointment.

"Incident?"

"When the group of survivors, known as the Crows, was fired on by the group of army deserters known as the Billings Boys, yes," said Winslow. "That incident."

"Probably, that's where most of us died."

"You stayed in contact with Robertson?"

Solomon's smile had not a trace of humour in it.

"Is that a crime too now? Why are you here, talking to me about murder? Why aren't you out looking for those bastards that shot us?"

Winslow repeated the question.

"Yes. I have been in contact with Colin Robertson."

"What was in the letter he sent to you?"

"He was just letting me know he was alright. I'm an old man, he helps me out with a few bits and pieces. He knew I'd be worried about him."

"So instead of just asking us to inform you of his detention, he involves you in bribing a police officer?"

"Bribe? Someone brought a message to me, I gave them a tip."

"What did the letter say about Richard York?"

"It didn't mention anyone, I don't know any Richard York."

"When did you first meet Robertson?" I asked

Solomon gave the first straight answer since he'd started speaking. Possibly the first in his life.

"March third, twenty twenty-two. Ring a bell?" Though I'd asked the question, he addressed the remark to Winslow. "That was the day the men who stayed in the army blew up the bridges, shot civilians and locked the survivors in." Still looking at Winslow he said something that I recognised as Yiddish. I couldn't translate it, but the feeling behind it was pretty clear.

"So, you were with Robertson for the duration of the Lockdown?"

"Yes, him and Miller. Others too. Dead now, murdered by your reckoning."

"Recognise this?"

I took the passport I'd found in the case at Maccallan's flat and held it out at arm's length.

Chapter 45. S.W.A.L.K

Exhibit 19.D: Letter from Private Thomas Welsh to Vivienne Reeve (nee Welsh). Obtained by Ms Reeve's solicitor on 14/01/2023. Submitted as evidence against Thomas Welsh in The British Armed Forces vs Welsh

Dear Vi,

I heard Jimmy, from my last posting in Peterborough, had been in contact with you. He was in here last month visiting his brother who is on the same wing as me. I couldn't talk to him because there are crazy strict rules about visiting. It was pure chance he spotted me as he was being led to the visitors' area and asked his brother to pass a message to me. I'm so glad to hear you made it through. I'm sorry about the baby, but in some ways, maybe, it was for the best. I can only imagine what it would have been like going through labour during the Outbreak.

I don't know if the army has been in touch with you about my situation. If they have, or if you have heard the stories going around, it may explain why you haven't been in touch.

I'm writing this to you, almost hoping you haven't tried to contact me because you thought I was dead. If that is not the case and you have been avoiding contact in light of what is being said, please read this letter before closing me out of your life.

I will not deny what happened. I and the remains of my company, along with Captain Billings, did desert. Along the way we picked up other deserters and together stole a pair of choppers. In the process of stealing them, three innocent members of the crew were killed. All I can say on that count was that I was not directly involved. It is also true that we attempted to steal the bullion reserves from the Bank of England. Also true, and I'm ashamed to admit this, we did kill a gang of survivors. But please hear my side of the story. I'm not trying to justify our actions, or my own, but I want you to know that we were not monsters. The things we did were not carried out in cold blood (which is what people are saying). We were scared, scared for our lives. The mutiny was the idea of two sergeants. Billings, who you could see cracking up under the pressure, was just carried along. I have heard over the grapevine that he is trying to take the fall for what happened. I'm sure he's acting out of guilt. He had no real say in what was going on. By the time we'd got to London and started trying to smash into the bank, he was a nervous wreck. Having broken the chain of command we were really at a loss for what to do. A dozen of the men broke away entirely and said they were heading for their homes. I have no idea if they managed it, or what they found when they got there. I expect most of them are dead by now.

The idea of robbing the bank was madness. I can see that now, but by the time we got to London most of us were half crazy. It made even less sense at the time. We all thought the world was at an end and someone, it might have been me, said we should grab the gold and then we'd be the last millionaires on Earth.

Getting to London was a horror we couldn't believe. The infected we'd encountered in the north were, for the most past, newly switched. We called them Romeos, I'm not sure where that name came from. In London, the Romeos we met had been sick for months. There were far more of them and they looked like something out of a horror movie. There were other things we saw in London too. Things I'm still having nightmares about. Please, Vi, if you don't believe anything else I write, please believe this: YOU CANNOT TRUST THE OFFICIAL ACCOUNTS OF WHAT WAS GOING ON DURING THE OUTBREAK.

Robbing the bank did one good thing, it gave us a mission. Once we got involved with that, the training took over and at least that gave us a sense of purpose. We set up containment areas and weapons posts and organised ourselves to defend the site. When I think about it now, and I think about it a lot, I believe we latched onto something familiar that we could understand. Being soldiers again, in that city, was the only thing that made sense.

They're saying now the Romeos were drawn by the noise of us breaking into the bank. We didn't appreciate that at the time. All we knew was, the things (I use the word things here because in the case of the Romeos they were no longer human) kept coming. We took to shooting at anything that moved. The streets around the bank were deep with bodies.

When the gang of the survivors, Miller's Crows, came up the road that day, we opened fire. They didn't react like humans. There was something not right with them, something wrong, deep down. Now, now that it's too late, I can see they were as messed up by everything as us. They'd been living in that hell hole of a place for over a year. It doesn't excuse the fact that we fired on people without good cause, or that we deserted our posts, or a million other things. But, Vi, please believe me when I tell you that the people we were then, the person I was then, they are no longer alive. The world was insane and, for a time, so was I. I am sending this to you via Jimmy and his brother. The official mail here is censored and if they get hold of this, they will use it against me in the court martial.

If you choose not to contact me, I understand. Please know I love you, and whatever you do, or how you decide to judge me, I wish you a happy life.

Love,

Thomas Welsh

Extract from the screenplay of Year of the Crow. Lithograph Studios, California (2026)

INT. HOSPITAL WARD - DAY.
White screen. All the viewer can see is white light.

ROBERTSON
(Voice over)
Sometimes, you see things that don't make sense. Things that get in your head and ask to be sorted out. Ask to have a little light shone on them.

As Robertson speaks, blurred shapes begin to appear on the field of white.

ROBERTSON
(Voice-over)
And a lot of those times, you wish those things had stayed in the dark.

The shapes and the white screen pull into focus. We see a white tiled wall; the shapes are revealed to be splatters of gore. We hear animal-like grunting and the sound of furniture crashing. The camera slowly pans left, appearing to follow the noise. The panning shot moves across a large room with white tiles on the walls. The room is very bright and this highlights the amount of splattered blood.

The floor is littered with smashed chairs, desks and medical equipment.

The panning shot stops as the source of the noise comes into frame. We see the rear view of a huge zombie. It is hunched over an examination table it is in the process of smashing. As if aware it is being watched, it freezes for a moment, still clutching the table.

Close-up, still from the rear, on the shoulders and head of the zombie. The zombie turns to camera; as it does so it begins to straighten. We see it has a second, malformed face growing from its chest. When the zombie has finished turning and is facing the viewer square on, the camera pulls back to show it in full. There is a brief moment of stillness allowing the viewer to see that the creature's second face is complemented by a second pair of arms. With a scream, the creature launches itself toward the camera.

About the time we were ready to start shooting, a lot of rumours began to circulate about mutations that had been spotted during the Lockdown. It was a new element to the story, and we wanted to include it.

The writers came up with this scene where Miller and Robertson raid an abandoned hospital, looking for supplies. They encounter one of these mutations. The writers were very keen on the idea of everything taking place in a clinical environment. It dovetailed with some of the conspiracy theories that claimed the mutations were the result of genetic experiments. The FX team were tearing their hair out over the idea. In the end they made a suit, they called it Octo-zombie, that needed two people to wear it. Mark Philmore, who plays Octo-zombie, was a professional defensive tackle back in the day. He's six foot nine and four-hundred pounds. Sonya Yap, who works the extra arms, was strapped to Mark's back during filming. I don't think he even noticed. She's four-ten and less than ninety pounds. They dressed her in blue and CGI'ed her out of the finished takes.

We filmed two versions of the Octo-zombie scene. In one, Miller and Robertson are caught unawares by it and have to kill it to escape. In the other, Robertson, alone, sees Octo-zombie but can't bring himself to speak of it. In that version he just watches it from hiding. Later he guides the group away from the hospital, saying the risk of infection is too great.

In the end, we decided the mutation angle was straying too far from Robertson's account. Both versions wound up on the cutting-room floor.

Chapter 46. The Hectic Fear Machine

I handed the forms back to the acting consulate and was told to check in one week later. Until then I was given a space in a disused house with two other women. One of them had a painfully underweight baby that didn't cry much. It had its mother's eyes; they were the same shade of hollow.

I suppose the town was under a form of martial law but that wasn't how it felt. There was a quartermaster's store set up in the shell of an old supermarket; a chit was handed to me when I left the consulate. It was really nothing more than a list of goods with my name on it and a date of issue. It listed what I could draw from the quartermaster's each week. Each item resulted in a cross on the page. When you hit a certain number of crosses the chit became useless.

"Don't lose the chit," I was told with a gravity that got the message across.

When I went back to the consulate seven days later I was told I wouldn't be going home in the 'immediate future'. I was also told the US Government might have gainful employment for me.

Herb Shackly was blunt concerning my options.

"Getting home isn't possible right now. Homeland Security has got its hands full keeping the borders closed. The French Flu appears to have reached Mexico and there have been rumours about cases in Canada. At the moment getting into the US is very difficult."

He left the words hanging there. I was to hear the same line again and again over the years. It was the official story from the fear machine that the American government had become. The stories of gondii landing in South America were never confirmed. Instead footage of rioting along the Mexico wall was circulated on repeat, providing scapegoats for all those second amendment gun sights.

"What am I meant to do then? Learn the words to 'God Save the Queen' and cultivate a taste for tea?"

"The current government, UK Government, is situated about seven hundred miles north. Half the original cabinet died in the Outbreak. Another chunk of them refused to leave their families behind when the seat of power moved. What was left had no choice but to form a coalition with the

Opposition parties and the Scottish Government."

He sounded like he was reading from a script and had no idea what anything he'd said actually meant. It was a reaction I'd seen before in people facing awkward questions.

"Which means what?"

"The UK as it stands isn't an international player and, because of the troubles back at home, aid is meagre at best."

"You're telling me the US isn't going to do anything to help me, or you for that matter. And the UK isn't in a position to force a deportation."

He squared his shoulders, because that was about all he had the authority to do.

"Our government is doing all it can to protect its citizens overseas." Before I could ask what exactly, he waved the form at me. "According to this, you were an investigative auditor for Finley and Wintercrown Bank."

"Yeah, that's what I was doing in Paris. I was there for work."

Shackly flipped through the forms again and nodded to himself, as if they had new meaning in light of what I'd just said.

"So, you've got experience of finance," he said finally. The chair he was sat in wasn't fancy enough to swivel or tilt. If it had been, he'd have swung around and put his feet on the desk. "Our government has an agreement with the Limeys. They extend what's called privilege of nationality to US citizens in return for those citizens working in an official capacity within the UK. In short, you work for the Brits and the US pays your wages."

There was another flurry of stop-start action when I was taken for an interview. The interview took place via a Skype connection, but the erosion of infrastructure meant a fifty-mile journey to access a computer with the necessary connections and security. It was situated on an old airbase. Shackly told me the name and I forgot it instantly.

Base Forgettable had been a small-scale installation at the start of the Outbreak. The rapid withdrawal of personnel had left it all but empty. It was now being repopulated with a mix of different Brit services and a gathering of medical personnel.

After the routing of doctors' surgeries and hospitals, medical staff and equipment had become scarce.

The journey took the better part of a morning. The roads were clear of traffic, but the quality of the fuel was an issue. Good petrol was almost impossible to find, and diesel was getting the same way. I assumed the reserves had been used up by survivors. My driver shook her head.

"Fuel has a shelf life. I don't know the chemistry but after a year or so petrol goes bad and clogs the works. Diesel's a bit more durable, but it's beginning to go."

Maybe to emphasise the point she blipped the throttle. Orders were to keep the speed down to conserve the juice.

At the base, I was dropped at an unguarded gate and followed a cluster of hand-painted signs. None of them advertised what I was looking for, but they all pointed in the same direction.

The base held more people than I'd seen in one place since the quarantine in Paris. There was a PA system up and running and somebody was playing music over it. Occasionally the music would break and there'd be an announcement I couldn't make out. To my ear, the garbled messages were an improvement. The open concrete of the empty airfields bounced the amplified music back and forth. The echo and re-echo made the songs sound lost and haunted.

When I couldn't find a site map or see a sign that told me what I needed to know, I asked a man in a dirty blue uniform where I'd find Chief Master Sergeant King. More accurately, I started to ask. As soon as he heard my accent, he waved his hand at me to stop talking.

"Uncle Sam's over there. One in the middle."

The waving hand jabbed impatiently at a collection of low wooden buildings sitting in the shadow of an aircraft hangar. He turned away from me before I had a chance to not bother thanking him. One of the people he'd been speaking to said something that sounded like, 'another poxy hectic'.

The middle hut – there were five in total, all supported on low tiers of bricks – was the biggest of the collection. Like the others, it looked to have been erected as a temporary measure and then left to stand for a decade.

The sign on the door read, C M S King. The sign looked more temporary than the cluster of huts.

King had been a big man in his past, if the way his uniform flapped around him was any indication. His skin was doing the same trick but had a lot less colour to it. There was a lot of paper on his desk and a cup containing a scant inch of coffee wearing a film of cold oil.

"Ms Voss, I assume."

His accent was Midwest.

"Cross, not Voss, and it's Mrs." I stumbled slightly on the word Mrs. I hadn't seen David in over a year, hadn't been able yet to even call him. Other than filling in the forms and requesting he was notified of my survival, David hadn't taken part in my existence since I'd waved to him from the back of the cab.

King apologised and pointed to a seat. When I'd sat down, he drained the inch of old coffee and looked wistfully at the empty cup.

"I'd offer you something to drink, but I have literally nothing to offer. I understand you're here to talk to home?"

"That's what I'm told. I'm being screened for a job as far as I can tell. Getting home …"

He made a gesture similar to the man who pointed me to the huts.

"Don't even go there. I thought, once the situation with the disease had abated, I'd be relieved." He barked a laugh, equal parts bitterness and exhaustion, and shook his head. "I'm officially the base commander here. Technically this is American soil and I'm the highest rank here."

The edge he put on the words officially and technically told a different story. He left a pause, where I was supposed to ask what the unofficial version of events was. When I didn't, he told me anyway.

"Unofficially the Brits have taken over this base because it's one of the cleanest pieces of infrastructure left. I'm very aware that the chain of command here is stretched real thin. Less than three months ago, this whole region was outlaw territory. The local town was nine-tenths destroyed in rioting. There is a lot of anti-American feeling here at the moment. This base was stripped of ninety percent of its personnel in the first stages of the pandemic. The locals' attitude is, we abandoned them."

I thought about the exchange with the man in the dirty uniform. I told King about the muttering of 'poxy hectic'. He rolled his eyes.

"You misheard. The word is septic. It's rhyming slang, Septic Tank: Yank."

King walked me across the base to an ugly grey tower with a rooftop made of radar dishes and antennae. It was situated at the corner of a concrete runway. Weeds had begun to take hold on the cracked slabs. Somehow that was more shocking than the fire and brimstone destruction I'd seen in France. Nature it seemed was just biding its time, waiting for us all to die out so it could cover our passing.

The conning tower was deserted and dark. King had to locate a fuse box and throw switches to bring the power on. The Skype-enabled computer was on the first floor, buried in a room with no external windows. The ceiling was low enough to give the impression it was underground, and I wondered why someone would design a tower with low ceilings. It may have been a bunker-type structure designed for some combat scenario, but I'm only guessing. About twenty feet by thirty, the room was stark white and lit with banks of LEDs that cancelled each other's shadows. When King switched them on, I had a few moments of snow blindness. Three rows of benches lined the floor, each of them heavy with equipment concealed under pale nylon dust sheets.

King pulled out a chair near one of the bulky shapes and pulled its cover aside. It should have been a disappointment, finding all the sheet covered was a perfectly normal HP desktop. The model was even a few years behind the one I'd used at the bank. When King hit the 'on' button and it beeped to show us it was waking up, I horrified myself by crying.

The silence was awkward but short-lived. The screen announced it was ready for a password and King busied himself with entering a string of characters that he had written down in a notebook. By the time he'd finished I had myself back under control.

He hit the call button and the speakers provided us with a ring tone to listen to. Now I'd dried my eyes, King spared me a glance.

"We get planes go over, time to time. Very high altitude, not our equipment; it makes my stomach drop. We've lost so much."

I was about to tell him I understood, not that I did, when the Skype call was answered and saved us any more soul-baring. King patted me on the shoulder and left, telling me he'd wait outside. I wondered if he'd have laid his hand on me if I'd been a man.

I'd expected the call to connect to a government office or another military base. Instead the image on the screen was of a well-fed man with a face the colour of a tomato, sitting in front of a wall adorned with pictures of men and women in police uniform. In case the point wasn't made, directly above the bright red face I could make out the blue and white logo of the Metropolitan Police.

In the bottom corner of the screen there was a gaunt-faced woman with deep set, suspicious eyes. Under the LED light, her pale scalp gleamed through a no-colour scrub of hair. It was a reduced version of what was appearing on a screen 3000 miles away. Unconsciously I edged sideways, and the skeletal face began to slip out of shot.

"Mrs Cross?" The tomato sounded concerned, or at least confused. "Miranda Cross? I don't have visual on you. Can you hear me. Hello?"

"Yes, yes I can hear you." I leaned forward at an uncomfortable angle, so I could put my hand over the corner of the screen. "I can hear and see you."

"Good. I'm Deputy Chief Copeland, from the MPD, financial fraud division. How are you?"

I told him I was fine, and he jumped when I burst out laughing.

Chapter 47. The Stuff of Legends

From Kings of Crows: Life on the Wrong Side of the Lockdown

A lot of people are surprised that I'm not angry at the soldiers who opened fire at the beginning of the Lockdown. Those men I can almost sympathise with. They were scared, panicked. It was a new and completely different paradigm for them. And they probably thought, in some recessed part of their mind, that they were doing the right thing.

I don't know if it's true, but there has been a lot of talk about the men on the bridges that day being brought in from northern regiments. So there'd be less chance of them having family in the south. If that's true, it makes sense of what they did. They weren't shooting innocent people. They considered the people crossing those bridges as a threat to what lay beyond them. In their minds they were soldiers doing a hard job.

Billings and his men, on the other hand, they were just scum. Self-serving scum. I hate the term 'Billings boyz'. They weren't boys, they weren't children who were just playing with real guns. They were adults, men, trained soldiers. They knew what they were doing, better than any of us did. I'll never forgive them. Never.

March 8th, 2021

The chanting woke him. It was light outside, but he couldn't gauge what time of day it was. The room's tiny window looked out onto the blank wall of the building next door. It felt early. On Johnno's insistence he'd slept through the night. Untrusting of the group, now so much of it was made up of Crows, he'd been sleeping less and less, pulling more than his share of guard duties and checks. Johnno had taken him to one side and, choosing words carefully, told him he was getting close to burning out. It was the big Scouser's kid-glove handling that persuaded Robertson to rest. He knew how he'd take care of someone who appeared to be unstable. After finding a room with a door he could wedge shut, he surprised himself by collapsing into a deep sleep.

They'd set up camp for the night in the shell of an up-market shopping street. Situated on the borders of extreme wealth, the businesses had all offered expensive consumer durables. The shopfronts were all topped with high Victorian town houses, most converted into tiny but luxurious flats. Robertson had settled into a top floor box room.

The chanting, the basic chorus of, *Leave them be*, was coming from somewhere below. Dismissing the words, he listened instead to the tone and tried to make out how many voices were in song. It sounded like most of the Crow people were involved.

His mouth tasted foul, but he found he was too dry to spit. Fully clothed he pulled his boots on slowly, trying not to make any noise. He did the same when unjamming the door, then kept his tread soft as he padded along the landing.

The floor below looked deserted, but he listened intently to the chanting to be sure it wasn't coming from directly beneath him. He was less cautious as he made his way down the stairs, though he still didn't rush to announce his presence.

As he stepped onto the next landing a door cracked open, making him start and pull the axe up in readiness. Sol regarded him from the doorway, head cocked to one side. Although he was attempting to look unconcerned, his eyes were wide and the pupils dilated. He stepped away from the door, backing into the room by way of invite.

Robertson pushed the door shut behind him. The room was larger than the one he'd commandeered and had once been a living room. The far wall was comprised of bookshelves. Water had been getting in somewhere and the library was a swollen ruin.

Sol sat on an overstuffed sofa that had his bedding spread over it. There was another bedroll spread out on the floor and Robertson recognised Johnno's backpack and the indent from his head.

"Something going on?" Robertson said. He pointed at the floor and the noise of the chanting.

Sol rolled his eyes.

"They started with the singing at first light. Johnno's gone to see what it's all in aid of."

"What time is it now?"

Sol consulted his wristwatch.

"Almost eight. He's been gone two hours."

Robertson felt a knot of unease beginning to coil into his stomach. He ignored it and listened to the chanting again. It was measured and calm. There was no suggestion of anger to it. He shook off the feeling of menace.

"I expect he's sniffing around Ally, trying for a chorus of morning glory."

Sol almost smiled.

"In that case, I wish him luck."

"Wait here, I'll go and see what all the fuss is about."

The Crows were gathered on the ground floor in the remains of the cramped showroom. The shopfront had housed a small collection of contemporary furniture. The display had been largely untouched although at some point the cash register at the back of the room had been levered open.

The Crows stood in three rows, like a church congregation. Without the filter of the carpeted floors the chanting sounded less sinister and became simply monotonous. At the head of the row, a middle-aged man was lying on his back, stretched along an enormous sofa displayed in the window.

At first glance Robertson thought he was dead but when he got closer he could see his chest rising and falling. The movement was highlighted by his hands, crossed just below his throat. He was smiling benignly and when he saw Robertson was looking at him, he lifted one of his hands. It was only then that Robertson saw the bite mark on his cheek. The man touched the wound and offered his blooded fingers to Robertson.

Behind him he heard Johnno call to him, "Boss."

The word was softly spoken but there was a note of warning to it. He turned and saw the big man, near to the entrance to the shop. He beckoned Robertson towards him, the movements of his shovel-like hand small and measured.

Robertson went to him, and as he did he was aware that some of the congregation had eyes on him. He noticed too that most of the chanting Crows had double smears of blood across their lips.

Johnno moved them away from the front of the shop so they weren't visible to the gathering.

"We back to the shit that went down in the sickbay again?"

Johnno nodded.

"Ally was on lookout last night. A load of them followed her out …"

"Why?"

Johnno rolled his eyes.

"Like you said, she's like the high priestess. There's a lot of them follow her around like kids."

"More like fucking sheep. What happened?"

"As far as I can make out, about ten of them were stood on the corner." He waved distractedly at the end of the street; the junction was marked by the gutted remains of a delicatessen. The stripped-out display counters in the window had been restocked with dismembered Gonzos. Three empty torsos swung from butcher's hooks. "From what I understand some Gonzos appeared. They cut them down pretty quick but before they took out the last one, Bernie offered himself up to it."

"Bernie's the prick on the sofa?"

"Yeah."

"What's with …" Robertson brushed his fingers across his lips.

Johnno didn't answer, other than to shift his weight from foot to foot.

"Fuck's sake. Where's Ally?"

"She's with Miller, Boss."

"So where the fuck's Miller?"

"In the deli."

Johnno pointed at the corner again, and its display of butchery.

"Oh Christ. Look, get upstairs and keep an eye on Sol, okay?"

He found Miller by following the sound of blades being sharpened. He was sitting at a table in the back of the delicatessen, focused on his collection of knives. Ally was standing at his back. Robertson thought she was watching Miller work but as his vision adjusted to the gloom of the shop he saw her eyes were closed. She wasn't even facing Miller. Her attention was on a long chill cabinet that had once held overpriced sandwiches. Something was moving in the bottom of the structure. Sounds, wet and thick, drifted over the low muttering that was coming from Ally. She had a layer of cloth tied around her face. He assumed the smell was bad.

A Gonzo had been stuffed into the cabinet. Both its knees had been shattered and bent the wrong the way to make it fit. Belts, tightly cinched around its upper arms, acted as tourniquets. The stumps, just below the elbows, were cleanly cut. It looked like Miller's work. Writhing in a puddle of brackish fluid, the Gonzo was trying to get at Ally. As Robertson stared down at it, its attention switched to him.

"What the fuck is wrong with you people?"

Ally, eyes still shut, wasn't startled by his voice. She let the rhythm of her muttered chant draw to a natural close before smiling, benignly – like the fool on the sofa offering his infected blood.

"Listen," she instructed and put her hands out in a gesture of offering.

The Gonzo was babbling. Robertson, unable not to, turned his head to hear. Wrecked by the disease and the brutality wrought upon it, the thing's voice was all but extinguished. Occasionally the slur of sounds resolved themselves into a word that might have been haven or raven.

Ally, still smiling, still with her eyes closed.

"It's a sign."

Robertson ignored her and turned to Miller. As Robertson watched, he sheathed the knife he'd been sharpening and began work on the next one. Like Ally, he was at peace.

Robertson found a chair and sat with him at the table, positioning himself so he could keep Ally in sight. She'd started mumbling to herself again.

"Hey, Miller. Miller."

Miller raised his eyes from the blade and met Robertson's gaze. His hands carried on working. He didn't speak.

"We ought to move out. Go to where the army fellas are camped out. There'll be loads of Gonzos there. Party time you know?"

He watched Miller closely for any reaction. At the same time he kept an ear tuned into the steady rise and fall of Ally's mumbling.

Miller appeared to think, or at least took a while to process what he'd just heard. Then he nodded and gave Robertson a tight-lipped smile.

"Okay. Let's go."

He gathered the knives still on the table in front of him and was fitting them into the various sheaths and loops of webbing as he followed Robertson to the door.

Has anyone seen the photos of the mutant Grippies? Shit man, that proves the virus was a bio weapon. Nothing like that would come out of nature.
Username: MRShip
Posts: 98

****

If you mean those photographs of the two headed man Someone posted on the Gondii Express site, they're obviously photo-shopped.
Username: ZedBomb
Posts: 991

****

They're not photo-shopped. That's a genuine example of a stage five/epsilon infection. There's been sightings of mutations exactly like that all over Mexico.
Username: A2Child
Posts: 34

****

I've seen the pictures of the two headed man. I don't know if it's a fake but it's definitely not in Mexico. If you can find a copy of the full photo you can make out a street sign in top left corner that reads Lombard St. That's in London. Anyway it's a poor quality picture. It's hard to say what it is.
Username: David_K
Posts: 99

****

David, the photograph that has been posted on the Gondii Express site is a digitally enhanced version of the picture U R talking about. That's why it looks like it has been photo-shopped.
It clearly shows a male, Caucasian, Gondii with a second head growing directly behind the 'normal' head, if you look carefully you can also see a second pair of arms,

although they are not fully formed and appear to be useless.
The photo was reportedly taken in London shortly before the disease's progress was stopped.
Username: BoneDaddy
Posts: 790

Advert from the Gondii Experience Tour website. Posted on November 20th, 2027, removed on December 9th, 2027, following multiple complaints of false advertising

FOR A LIMITED TIME ONLY AT THE NATION'S PRIMARY GONDII EXPERIENCE TOUR
THE LEGENDARY DOUBLE-HEADED GONDII. PRESERVED CORPSE OF THE GENUINE MUTANT HV-TG SUFFERER BROUGHT FROM THE LONDON MUSEUM FOR EXCLUSIVE TOUR OF THE TRI-STATE COUNTY AREA
LIMITED TICKETS AVAILABLE

March 8th, 2021

"I think we should leave them to it," Johnno said for the dozenth time.

He was standing at the back of the room, as far from the window as he could get. In contrast, Sol was almost pressing his face into the glass, unable to look away from the street below.

"Can we rely on them anymore?" he asked.

There was no reply and Maccallan, who was trying to pace in the confines of the room, asked the same question. Robertson, seeing the question was being asked of him, laughed in his face.

"I thought you were the one with all the answers."

Maccallan stopped pacing.

"You think scoring points off me is going to help?"

Robertson laughed again.

"You think this is funny?" Maccallan demanded.

"Yeah," Robertson told him, "I do. What do you think, Miller? You up for a laugh?"

Miller was sitting on the floor by the window, though he had his back to it. As usual he was honing his knives. The heavy butcher's knife he was running along the steel was noticeably thinner than it had been when he first acquired it. Robertson picked up one of the smaller blades Miller had laid out on the floor. He tested its edge on a section of net curtain blackened by mould. The material parted with practically no effort.

"This fella knows how to put an edge on something," he said and put the knife back where it had been. Miller acknowledged the words with a nod. He adjusted Robertson's placement of the blade before returning to his butcher's knife.

The chanting in the street was getting softer. Robertson ripped the curtain away from the window, making Sol jump. No one in the street seemed aware they were being watched.

The storefront sofa, with Bernie still lying on it, had been carried out into the middle of the road. The choir of Crow people had drifted around him, unsure how they wanted the ritual to take shape. They settled on a semicircle in two rows, heads bowed. The Gonzo that had been writhing in the chiller cabinet had been dragged out into the street. Surrounded by so much noise and activity its efforts to attack had redoubled. Its broken knees and the stubs of its arms glistened wetly where it had struggled to lift itself from the tarmac.

Ally came into view. Robertson couldn't see her face. Her hood was pulled forward like a cowl, but he recognised her by the way she carried herself. She held a cleaver, darkened with use.

She made for the Gonzo and there was another break in the ritual-like atmosphere, as it was decided who would hold the thing in place. Lacking the brute strength of Miller, she struggled to hack through the Gonzo's thighs. There was another improvised moment when it became clear the first tourniquet wasn't tight enough to stem the blood loss. There was a desperate thrash of movement, as the four men holding the Gonzo all tried to act at once.

The second amputation went more smoothly.

"I say we leave them to it," Johnno said again.

Maccallan, who'd stopped his pacing to watch the ceremony, let out a shaky breath and looked away from the window.

"I think he's right. That bunch have flipped out, we can't rely on them." He looked at Robertson. "Oh, you think that's funny too?"

Robertson turned his back on the window. Behind him the congregation was busy strapping the limbless Gonzo onto the back of Bernie.

"What's funny is you. You've been giving it all the fucking yap about what we should be doing and how fucking clever you are. Swanning about with your machete and its little notches." He rapped the window with his knuckles. "Now it's all getting a bit imminent, your bottle's gone. Or has it?"

"What's that supposed to mean?"

Robertson moved away from the window and sat down on the big sofa. It still had Sol's bedding spread over it.

"You were holed up in your little flat for how long?" When Maccallan didn't answer, Robertson waved his own question away. "You were in there for fucking months. Then you see us passing by and come out to join in. Looking up an old friend, were you? Missed me, had you?"

"I came out to get across the river so I could get to the banking sector. Same place you were headed. Only I'm not dumb enough to think the government left the bullion there." He kicked the end of the sofa and jabbed his finger in Robertson's face. "You need me. You better remember that."

"Or what exactly? You plan on leaving us to our fate, and carrying on heroically alone?"

"We need each other," Sol said. He'd pulled himself away from the scene in the street. "If the government did leave the bullion, those bastards have beaten us to it. And without Maccallan's know-how, just having access to the power isn't going to do us a scrap of good." He went to the sofa and shooed Robertson off his bedding.

"We've only got his word for it that he can do any of it."

Sol waved his hand at him again.

"If you remember, you're the one who vouched for him."

Robertson regarded him coldly as he vacated the sofa.

"All I said was, the cunt was good with IT. I think my exact words were, 'He can run a computer with one hand and never take the other one out the till.'"

Sol laughed, "And we wanted moral fibre? Good with IT and honest we can do without."

"And when I had my hand in the till, what did I find?" Maccallan pointed at Robertson, "I found your hand was already there."

Robertson ignored the remark.

"Okay, Sol, let's say wonderboy here can walk the talk, what good does that do any of us if you're all too scared to carry on?"

"Boss, it ain't about being scared, it's about who we can rely on. Right now …" – he looked at the window but didn't make any effort to see what was happening in the street – "… right now, they're out of control."

"Where Miller goes, they follow," Robertson said.

"For how much longer, Boss?"

Robertson nodded and dry-scrubbed his face with his hands. He used the motion to cover his eyes and watched Maccallan. He was still pacing and being careful to keep Johnno as a buffer between him and Robertson.

"Okay, Johnno, I take your point. How's it standing between you and Ally?"

The bigger man shrugged.

"I don't know. We're still together but she's …" He put a finger to his temple and drew circles.

"What about Patrick?"

"He's solid, Boss. He's only hanging around with them 'cos … y'know."

"'Cos he's getting his dick wet, I know."

Robertson went back to the window.

Whatever had been going on outside was over. The sofa was still standing in the middle of the road but the Crows had dispersed.

"I say we press on. We can't be sure what's happening with the army boys, or the lights. We wait for them to go and for all we know the power goes out again once they've left."

"Now you're just guessing," Sol said.

"And you ain't?" Robertson snapped. He was losing patience with the conversation. "If you want to go back across the river and wait it out with the others, then piss off and do it. If you seriously think the boy wonder over there can set us all in clover then we need to move." He rapped the window again. "Those wankers are trying to get themselves infected. We don't have long before we lose our muscle."

Now Maccallan laughed, "Our muscle. You think those maniacs are on our side?"

Robertson tilted his head in the direction of Miller.

"His side, our side. Same thing."

Miller, oblivious to the voices, was arranging the collection of knives in complex patterns. Maccallan looked at him for a long moment.

"That's the insurance, is it? We all follow Crow-Headed Jesus."

"Best chance I'd say."

Johnno let out a long hissing sigh.

"You might want to bear in mind, Boss, they crucified Jesus."

I was talking to someone online, who was in London toward the end of the Lockdown. He saw mutant, two headed zombies.
Username:SlipperE
Posts:9

****
Zombies? Whoever U were talking to is full of s**t. No one who was involved in the Outbreak for real uses the zee word. That's just Hollywood BS.
This forum is about sharing information not fairy-tales. Go and sign up with the Zombie-Hunt site if that's what you want.
Username:FaxBoy
Posts:56

****
The dude I was speaking with was in the English Army. He didn't use 'the zee word' (I just went back to the site where he posts and rechecked his statement) that was my phrasing, a term I use because MOST people understand it.
He refers to the zombies (that's victims of HV-Tg induced psychosis, in case you don't know) as Romeos.
He maintains that he saw at least three 'Romeos' with two heads during the last months of the Lockdown. He also maintains that the picture of the two headed Romeo was taken by him.
FYI, FaxBoy, this wasn't posted on the Zombie-Hunt site, it was posted on a site that can only be accessed on the dark-web.
Username:SlipperE
Posts:10

Chapter 48. Getting Back

I didn't want the job. Being a cop had never been on my list of childhood dreams. Any more than being thousands of miles away from my friends and family had been.

What I wanted was to get home.

That was the crux of the matter.

Copeland, with his overfed tomato-coloured face and full head of lice-free hair, knew that. He may even have sympathised; he delivered the harsh truth of the matter in a roundabout way that, in the right light, might have been considered gentle.

If I wanted a shot at getting home, I'd need Uncle Sam's good grace and help. Failing that, money to mount a legal battle. If I wasn't going to play ball I could more or less kiss goodbye to either.

"Look, Mrs Cross, from my understanding of how things are out there, what we're offering isn't that bad a deal. You'll be paid, by us, via the …" he looked down to something out of shot that must have had the details on it, "… Metropolitan Police. As you'll be acting as an official member of the British force you'll be entitled to full rations. But here's the thing, as you'll be working under the authority of the US you'll also be entitled to accommodation and your salary will be in excess of that of your British colleagues." He paused and looked directly at his computer screen, and I assumed directly at the image of me staring out of it. "That can be helpful." The word 'helpful' came with the tiniest of nods.

I didn't ask what kind of help he was talking about.

"What options do I have? I mean if I don't take the deal?"

"From what I understand you'll be entitled to apply for an emergency ration book, and there are food banks in some of the less … damaged towns, and shelters too. But realistically, unless you want to go underground and risk being shot as a looter, then you'll probably end up being thrown back into France. From what I hear about …"

"I get it."

I took the deal.

The process of becoming a cop, start to finish, took less than twenty-four hours. I was told I had a day to think about it and a second Skype call was scheduled for the next day to hear my answer. It was stressed this was a one-time offer. For the second call, King stayed to witness my swearing in and to coax the software to accept my digital signature. The position didn't come with a badge, but I was gifted an impressive amount of documentation to showboat with instead.

I'd expected my life as a cop to involve long hours sitting in a damp office looking for ramped-up expenses claims and overtime payments. Copeland took a certain delight in telling me I was going to be assigned to a homicide squad.

I suspect my wasted features didn't permit the comic reaction he'd hoped for. The slightly jerky image coming in from across the Atlantic waited a fraction of a second before explaining.

"Someone's been mining Double Cees in huge numbers, and not spending them."

He made the statement as if it would mean something to me. I don't know if that was another attempt to coax a reaction from me or just an example of the belief, held by many of my countrymen, that America's problems were automatically forefront in the world's mind.

"Double Cees?" I said, too tired by the process going on around me to even pretend interest.

"Double Cees," Copeland repeated slowly. "Cryptocurrency."

"Like Bitcoin?"

"Same kind of thing, only it's semi-official, so there's a degree of centralisation. Whatever that means." He tried to laugh off his own lack of knowledge. "Bitcoin, along with most of the other cyber currencies, went under. I won't try to bluff you, Cross ..." – I'd lost the honorific 'Mrs', when I'd become a cop – "... I don't know enough about the tech stuff to explain why, but when the French flu took out Europe, it devalued Bitcoin to the point that no one could use it."

I understood, or at least could make an informed guess. The loss of power and access to the internet made accessing cryptocurrency next to impossible. Because the whole idea of cryptocurrency was to have decentralised banking, the tallies of coins were kept logged in a thousand servers worldwide. When the lights came on again in Europe, a huge number of those digital accounts had no owners. So, the money sat there, inaccessible. With so much coin held out of circulation and no one knowing how long it might stay that way, there was no way of assessing its value. The market drifted.

The bottom line: the coins were devalued to the point of being worthless.

"And if someone's holding on to a vast reserve of this Double Cee it'll cause problems." I wasn't really asking. Copeland told me I was right anyway. "If this is about a semi-centralised American currency, why am I being told to play cops and robbers in homicide?"

"According to the tech boys, it's practically impossible to trace where all the coins are coming from. They've only managed to narrow it down as far as the UK because there was a massive data dump registered from …" – he consulted a sheet of paper – "… Lands End." He shrugged and looked helpless. "That's the main connection between them and us in terms of the fibre optic. That's what I'm told."

I nodded and left him to his ignorance. The internet isn't some ethereal world, floating in the air around our heads. It's a system of data banks linked via miles and miles of optic cables. Few people know that because they don't think about it in the first place.

"Look, I've been in the police less than two hours. How the hell am I meant to find out who's been doing this?"

Copeland gave me an indulgent smile and held his hands up.

"Calm down, we've got a lead on that already. We just want you to gather some evidence and give us your opinion on it. If we can find our man and persuade the Limeys to let us have him, we can find out who he's working with and release the coin."

"I still don't know why I'm in homicide."

Copeland smiled some more. It was a man-dealing-with-hysterical-woman type smile and I dearly wanted to punch it.

"Relax. The boys upstairs are going on the basis that putting you in as a homicide detective gives you extra muscle. And since anything taking place during the Outbreak would have involved bloodshed, you've got an automatic right to flex that muscle." He took the patronising smile up another notch. "Relax, okay? All you're going to do is crunch numbers and count beans. You can handle it."

April 15th, 2028

"You show me a passport, what do you expect me to do, stamp it maybe?"

Solomon folded his arms and looked away from me, as if offended by my stupidity.

"Recognise it?"

Solomon did his squinting act again.

"Looks like Robertson?"

I turned the passport briefly towards Winslow, so he had a fleeting glance at it before I put it in my pocket again.

"Where did you get that?"

"Maccallan's flat. It was in the suitcase, the one with the money hidden in the lining."

"Why didn't you tell me that, for Christ's sake? They place Robertson at that block. We can connect him to that trail of bodies."

Solomon turned to meet my eye again, and laughed at Winslow.

From Kings of Crows: Life on the Wrong Side of the Lockdown

By the spring of 2021, the group was on its last legs. About a third of them had split from us when we crossed the Thames. With the numbers down we lost people to infection victims. The Gonzos we encountered in North London were further gone than those south of the river, but there were more of them. It's been said that in the north, post-Lockdown, there was a false sense of security. Something the government was complicit in, while at the same time hightailing it to the borders. People carried on as normal and went into denial when the symptoms appeared. And after the failure of the first Lockdown there were no others. No places to run.

It's not a view many people will share, but the more I think about it, the more I think being on the Lockdown side of the city was a lucky break. Sure, all hell broke loose but at least we had our eyes open.

Until we crossed back that is.

Then we headed back to 'civilisation'. And were mown down.

Chapter 49. What Did You Do Before?

March 10th, 2021

It had taken two days to move what remained of the group to the banking district. Covering the ground wasn't so hard. The number of Gonzos they found along the way had increased but most of them were close to death and posed little threat. What took the time were the increasingly elaborate rituals of the Crow people.

Miller was indifferent to the ceremonies; he carried on with his own practice of filleting Gonzos as the mood took him and throwing offal to the ever-present hordes of crows. Robertson had made the decision to join him in his madness. Although he still stuck rigidly to his disinfectant and bleach routine. The abandoned houses they settled in for the nights usually had central heating systems and smashing radiators produced brackish water. It was good enough to wash in.

On the second night, Johnno stood in the doorway watching him soak dried blood off his hands. Robertson could hear the floor creaking as the big man shifted his weight from foot to foot.

"Another one got bit today, Boss."

"Another offering?"

"Yeah, dozy bastard put one on its back, put his arm in front of it. Snap." The creaking of the boards changed tempo slightly. "They're all billeted in a place across the road. Ally told me they'll be performing the rites at first light tomorrow."

Robertson finished washing and, with nothing to use as a towel, began swinging his arms back and forth to get dry. He could tell Johnno had something else to say.

"And?"

"She's asked me to attend."

Robertson laughed, catching himself by surprise.

"Attend? You make it sound like you've been invited to a fucking wedding. Is it black tie?"

Johnno had been surprised by the laughter too and had taken a step back. As the moment of humour passed, Robertson saw the big man's stance was in readiness for an attack. There was a beat of silence before Johnno said:

"Nah, Boss. Dress code is smart casual." He forced a laugh at his own response but didn't change his position. "You alright if I go? It don't mean I'm part of that bollocks, you know? It's just …"

"Yeah, yeah, I know. None of that shit though." Robertson wiped his fingertips across his lips, mimicking the Crow's anointment.

"No worries, I ain't looking to go Gonzo. I want to get through this. If we can pull off this shit Maccallan's on about, it's a bonus, but I'm with you, I just want to get back to normal." When Robertson didn't comment, Johnno put his head to one side. "You alright, Boss?"

"What did you do, before it all went to shit?"

"I was a roofer."

Robertson nodded but still didn't comment. What did you do, before? It wasn't a question people asked much anymore. If they did, the response was always the same: a job description. No one seemed comfortable admitting they had something worth losing. Or maybe they were uncomfortable admitting they'd lost nothing.

"What about you, Boss?"

"I took shit off cunts like Maccallan and paid taxes for the privilege."

March 11th, 2021

Again, he was woken by the chanting. It was barely light. The street outside was a narrow mews, a living space grudgingly allowed in the narrow gaps between financial machines. A pair of cars had been wedged into the mouth of the cobbled lane. Burned out and rusting, one of them was serving as an altar with the bitten man laid on its roof.

The Crows knew their places now and the ritual was smoother. Robertson caught the first few minutes but dismissed the spectacle. He noted Johnno's presence, stood to one side like a lower tier wedding guest. Robertson took a spiteful pleasure in seeing Maccallan standing in the same line. The tension was written across his face like a tattoo.

Bernie seemed to have attained some rank in the proceedings. He was standing to one side of Ally as she officiated. He was hunched forward, adjusting his balance to the weight of the limbless Gonzo still strapped on his back.

Another broken-limbed Gonzo rocked pointlessly on the cobbles, tourniquets already in place. It snapped at the men stationed around it.

"What's your rush?" Sol asked him.

The old man had taken the room directly above his. Robertson ignored the question and started packing his rucksack. The word possessions didn't seem to fit anymore; the things he carried were just supplies.

"There's no point hurrying. Those fools outside are having a religious experience."

"What do you want, Sol?"

"I want to know what we're all doing."

Robertson pulled the backpack on and adjusted the straps until it sat comfortably. Angry without knowing why, he picked his axe up and deliberately got too close to Sol. Sol, for his part, didn't back away.

"What we're going to do is head over to the bank and make a fucking withdrawal. Then you and Maccallan can sit and hold hands until the cavalry arrives." Sol didn't reply. After a few seconds Robertson smiled at him. "Now, do you want to get out of my fucking way?"

Miller was watching as the mutilated Gonzo was carried to the bitten man on the car roof. The volume of the chanting was muted, and Robertson could hear the Gonzo's jaws snapping shut. He cocked an ear to it, listening for any sign of coherent speech. Satisfied there was none, he walked up to Miller and slapped him on the shoulder.

"Come on Miller, let's go find a few live ones, eh?" Happy he had his attention, he laughed and slapped his shoulder again. "You feeling sharp, eh? You up for it?"

He was aware that at his back the chanting had changed. Some people had stopped; others had redoubled their efforts. There was a new undertone of muttered complaint.

"Johnno, Patrick." The two men both looked uncomfortable to be singled out. "Come on, enough of this shit. The crows need feeding."

He turned away but was careful to keep half an eye on his lieutenants. They broke ranks with the congregation, but he saw Johnno flick a questioning look towards Maccallan.

Miller reached the mouth of the mews first and climbed over the shells of the two cars without glancing to see who was behind him.

The man who'd been laying on the roof and was now being tied to the snapping torso, offered his blood-stained fingers in anointment. Miller ignored him. Robertson told him to fuck off.

For the first time, Miller began to scare him. Robertson had worked him into a frenzy. Luck had been with him for once and minutes after leaving the mews they'd crossed paths with a pack of Gonzos. About twenty in number, they were in bad shape. Wasted and thin they shuffled slowly in the same direction, strung out into a decaying line of stick figures.

Robertson, like Johnno and Patrick, approached them with habitual caution but knew they presented easy targets and little threat.

Miller ran at them, a knife in each hand. Where they intercepted the pack, at a junction choked with the remains of a jackknifed lorry, he met the first one head on and hacked at it. Before it had fallen, he was away to the next one. He'd taken seven of them down before Robertson had got close. Robertson didn't intervene until Miller began his butchery act.

The remaining Gonzos fell easily. Robertson, Johnno and Patrick were slow and methodical. When they were done, Robertson went to the seated figure of Miller and told him there would be more. There was work to do.

By the time they were in sight of Threadneedle Street Miller had abandoned the careful fileting routine and was simply hacking the fallen Gonzos into shapeless piles of meat and bone. He was slick with sweat and his clothing was black with blood.

Robertson had an inkling of how the Crow people reacted to him. There was a force of will to his actions that was almost hypnotic. He wondered aloud where Miller was getting the energy from.

"He's fucking mad," Johnno answered.

He sounded slightly awed.

"Can you rein him in?" Patrick said.

"I'll let him wind down for a bit," Robertson told him. "Can you get those dumb fuckers to do something useful, like look for supplies?"

He jerked his thumb over his shoulder. The rest of the group had caught them up at the junction marked with Miller's first killing spree. They'd begun work on the corpses and the road had echoed to their chanting. The rhythmic sound had become disjointed when they realised Miller wasn't waiting for them.

The group settled into a pattern, Miller following Robertson's promises of more Gonzos, and the Crows following Miller. Fearful of losing their icon, they abandoned their elaborate rituals of mutilation; instead they kicked or hacked their kills into pulp. Every one of them was splattered with gore.

"I'll find Ally, tell her we're taking a break." Johnno said.

"Tell her Miller's stopping to sharpen his blades," Robertson told him. "I'll get the mad bastard to take a breather."

Half the Crows had been dispatched to find food. The other half sat in a loose circle, chanting and watching Miller sharpen his knives. The chant held time with the rhythm of his blades.

Ally was wiping him down with disinfectant.

Sol watched the gathering with clear disgust. When he turned to look at Robertson his expression barely changed. Robertson returned his scrutiny with his blank stare. He was sitting on the bonnet of a police car. There were three of them positioned at a set of traffic lights. One had been rolled onto its side and hung at an odd angle, caught against a crumpled section of safety barrier.

"Prefer the view from the tenth floor?"

Sol ignored the question and issued one of his own.

"Do you have any sort of plan?"

Robertson shrugged.

"I told you, we're all going to the bank."

"And if Maccallan and I don't?"

"Have you not noticed, Sol? This …" he spread his arms wide, encompassed the abandoned cars, the emptied and burned buildings and the shattered bodies of the Gonzos, "… is a free country." He smiled. "You can do what you fucking want. But if you think me and Miller are waiting for you, you have got another thing coming."

"Colin, listen, we're all under a lot of strain, but this …" he made a similar gesture to Robertson's own, "… this is madness. If we just walk these fools up to the bank, it'll be a massacre."

He could see, over Sol's shoulder, Maccallan approaching them. He carried nothing other than the machete, but the wax cotton coat he wore was bulky and misshapen, his few possessions stuffed into pockets.

He waited until Maccallan had joined them before responding to Sol.

"These fuckers are already dead. Look at them." Neither of the men moved. Robertson got off the car and grabbed Sol's arm, spun him to look at the people gathered around Miller and his blades. "Look at them," he hissed the words low, directly into the old man's ear. "They're trying to get infected. They wipe infected blood on each other and let themselves get bitten. They … are … dead."

"You're as mad as they are," Maccallan said.

Robertson turned to look at him and carefully let his gaze drop to the distance Maccallan kept between them.

"Well, what do you suggest? You're the one with the hard-on for the Bank of England."

"We should wait. Let the army do whatever they're doing and move in when they're gone."

"You still have that option. Me and Miller, and his merry band of fuckwits, we're going to Threadneedle Street."

"Colin, listen to me." Sol had freed himself from Robertson's grip and, like Maccallan, had put himself at a safe distance. "Maccallan's right, we should wait a little while. See if the army does move on."

"And what if they torch the place before they go, or once they go the lights go out again? Wonderboy here needs the grid, remember?"

"If you get us all killed it won't matter, will it?" Maccallan's face was flushed but Robertson could see that the knuckles on the hand gripping the machete were white. "Whatever we do, we need to be alive once everything's back to normal, or it's all bloody pointless."

Robertson lifted his axe and studied its edge before stepping nearer to Maccallan. He waited, daring him to make a move.

"Normal? It's never going to get normal again, you fuckwit, don't you get it? It's a brave new fucking world."

There was scuffle of noise on the other side of the junction. A pair of Gonzos wandered into sight. Miller, satiated or just exhausted by his morning's spree, didn't seem to notice. His collection of followers, unsure whether to act or not, lost the rhythm of their chanting.

"Why don't you go and put another little notch on your machete?" Robertson said.

Maccallan turned and made towards the pair of Gonzos; using Robertson's challenge as an excuse to get away from him.

Robertson rested the axe on his shoulder and stared at Sol until the old man looked away, choosing to watch Maccallan instead.

"You and the boy-fucking-wonder can wait around for things to get normal again, if you want. Me, I'm going to work with the status quo. You understand?"

Sol glanced at him, "Yeah, I understand."

From Once They Were Heroes. Interviews with the Billings Boyz (Part 1). Posted on YouTube by Pirate-Documentaries-Channel

The video is 25 minutes and 48 seconds in duration. It consists of an interview with an anonymous individual purporting to be a member of the British armed forces, currently AWOL. The individual is introduced as a man who deserted his post and joined the rogue battalion led by Captain Clark-Billings.

The interview is interspersed with stock footage of urban unrest taken during the Outbreak. None of the footage used is directly related to the individual being interviewed or to the events he relates.

The video starts with a 10-second still of a logo. The logo consists of a white caricature of a human skull that has been sprayed onto a black-painted brick wall. Above the skull are stencilled the words Pirate-Documentaries.

The logo is replaced by aerial footage of a burning building. The footage has been identified as a news broadcast, first transmitted on the BBC News Channel on April 26th, 2021. It was filmed in Lincoln and documents the arson attack on the Lincoln County Hospital. The audio used on the original report has been replaced by the narration quoted below. The voice of the narrator is that of an adult male with a faint Edinburgh accent. The narrator does not identify himself and does not appear on screen during the video.

Narrator - Michael (not his real name) meets me in a lay-by and, before he will speak, insists on searching me. He has no objections to my recording devices but claims he is checking for transmitters. Though we meet long after the mobile blackout, I have to leave my phone in the lay-by. The interview is conducted in the back of Michael's van, but only after he has driven several miles from the original rendezvous.

At the time the precautions seemed to border on paranoia. However, since filming this interview the army has successfully court-martialled another member of the so-called Billings Boyz and issued a twenty-year sentence. A move welcomed by Colin Robertson, one of the few survivors of Billings' actions in North London.

Miller, the celebrated father of the Takeback, famously survived the hail of bullets, only to take his own life in the days immediately after the official ending of the national emergency.

Michael refuses to give details of his regiment or, with few exceptions, to refer to individuals by name.

The news footage is replaced by the image of a backlit head and shoulders. The sound quality is poor with a great deal of ambient noise, including a constant metallic clinking. Later in the video the narrator will explain this is made by a bunch of keys that Michael plays with throughout the interview.

At 2 minutes 11 seconds:

Michael - I wasn't a member of Billings' company. He was never my commander. My own company was stationed at Peterborough before Billings arrived. There were twenty-three of us unloaded at the base and within six weeks, seventeen of them were dead from Toxo. I don't know what happened to the five I left behind.

Narrator - The video continues with Michael giving details of seeing Billings' men, led he claims, not by Billings but by Sergeant Joseph Paxman. This is the only name he will give during the interview. He says he saw Sergeant Paxman die during the incident at the Bank of London. He denies any involvement in the hijacking of two Chinook helicopters and claims not to have witnessed the deaths of Airmen H. Coleman, R. Barker or S. Shackleton.

At 6 minutes 37 seconds:

Michael - People talk about Miller and the Crows as if they're big heroes, and that makes us the villains for opening fire. But I'll tell you this, if you weren't there that day, then you don't know what the [sound deleted at this point presumably to mask an obscenity] you're talking about. Those [sound deleted] were into something strange. Some of the things that came at us that day weren't human, they weren't even regular Romeos.

They came at us out of the rain and you could see the ground around them running red. Some of the things I saw had two heads. People don't believe that, they think I was high or something, like we had drugs lying around. We didn't even have any bloody fags. I know what I saw. Things with two heads, one of them was growing out of its back, looking behind it. I put a round straight through it, took the top of its skull off, clean off, I saw its brain spray out … splat. It didn't miss a step, carried on coming at us like nothing had happened. I had to empty the rest of the clip into the thing. And the whole time this was going on, those [sound deleted] freaks were singing.

Chapter 50. Comfort Zones

April 15th, 2028

Winslow looked at the old man, who had laughed at him. He tapped out one of his look-at-me-look-at-me rhythms. When Solomon deigned to turn, Winslow played what he thought was his winning hand.

"For a man sitting in the dark you own a lot of lights." He swivelled the magnifying light with all the LEDs, so it faced the old man. When he flicked it on, Solomon had to squint against the glare.

"Is this the third degree?"

Winslow angled the lamp, so it puddled light on the bench it was sitting on. He picked up what appeared to be a hi-tech pen, all machined metal and showy precision.

"I don't imagine these are easy to come by these days."

From his little island of light, he spared me a glance and saw I was in the dark. He didn't attempt to enlighten me.

Solomon wasn't interested in either of us; he had eyes only for the tool Winslow was holding.

"My father made most of those tools. I carried them next to me all through the Outbreak and the lockdown. I would be obliged if you'd not handle them."

Winslow put the pen thing back from where he'd taken it. I didn't credit him with the strength of character to be generous and assumed he considered he'd already won. What he'd won, I had no idea.

"Forgery a family business is it?"

Solomon observed a moment's contempt before replying.

"I'd ask you the same about police work, if I'd ever met a copper with a father."

"You keep hold of that sense of humour, old man. It'll keep you warm in your cell at night."

"Family heirlooms are a criminal offence now?"

"Producing fake ration books is an offence."

"I thought you were the big boys. CID, murder investigations, no less. Now you're worried about an old man eking out his pension with a few off-the-ticket extras?"

Winslow gave him a thin smile.

"We're not talking about a few extras though, are we? Not a man of your obvious skill. Those coupons you gave to PC Haddan were good enough to fool the boys in the fraud squad. Only mistake was the date. They weren't due to be issued for another two weeks. Which makes me think you've got a regular supply chain going. What happened, you give Haddan the wrong book when he called?" Winslow let his smile fade with predatory slowness. "They'll throw the book at you. People are going to wonder how an old codger like you could produce coupons good enough to fool the experts. Then they start asking if maybe they weren't fooled, maybe they were complicit. You think policemen are bastards? You don't know the half of it, you wait until you see them covering their backs. They'll throw you to the wolves, big time."

Solomon threw another laugh at him, but it was thinner than the last one. The old man, tough as he might be, was still an old man sitting in a room with two cops and a table full of incrimination. I wondered what a search would yield.

"So, tell me, what do you want?" he asked Winslow.

"I want to know where Robertson's involved, so I can throw that arrogant little shit to the wolves, and not you. And I want to know why a few hours after hearing an old friend has turned up at the station, Robertson decides to contact you. And why that old friend turns up with a hole in his chest." Winslow leaned forward in the big office chair. "But what I really want is to know why he killed Maccallan. You see, that's what I've been told to find out. Call me old-fashioned but I pride myself on getting the job done."

He was staring at Solomon, trying to drive his hard-eyed stare into the back of the old man's skull.

Solomon met his stare for a few seconds, then dismissed him with a flick of his hand. He turned to me.

"Well, now we've established this fool doesn't know his arse from his elbow … what do you want?"

Winslow was about speak again but I held up a rank-pulling hand.

"Where is Robertson?"

"Robertson? He fed the crows."

"Why don't we take this conversation back to the station?" Winslow said. "See if a few hours in a cell makes him talk sense."

I glanced at Solomon to gauge his reaction. If Winslow was thinking he could scare the old man with the threat of a night in the cells, he'd be disappointed. Before I could think up a reasonable excuse for not arresting him, someone knocked on the door.

March 11th, 2021

The wind that had blown in from the east, bringing the rain, had an edge of cold to it. What little warmth the day had held, it was losing as night fell. Johnno was shivering as he washed. The blood had long since gone but he made no move to get out of the rain. In the middle of the road, naked and down on his haunches, he'd already worked his way through an entire bar of soap. His discarded clothes marked a trail from the door of the bank.

"Is he going to be alright, you think?" Sol asked.

He'd lost the quality of quiet superiority he usually spoke with.

"He'll get over it or he won't," Robertson said.

Sol sucked a breath as though he'd just caught his fingers in a drawer.

"The boy did the right thing," he said.

Robertson turned his back on the view of the street. Glass crunched under his boots.

"Who you trying to convince?"

"I'm not trying to convince anyone. They deserved what they got."

The heat had come back to his voice and, not wanting to, Robertson smiled.

"Where's Maccallan?"

"In the bank," Sol said. "He got straight to work."

He inflected the words with a degree of contempt. But you're not going anywhere, are you? Robertson thought.

"I'm going to see if he needs any help. Go and see if you can persuade that dozy fucker to get inside. Won't matter what state his conscience is in if he gets a dose of pneumonia."

"He was right next to Ally when she was hit, did you know that?"

Robertson lifted his axe onto his shoulder.

"No. I didn't. And if I had, what difference would it make?" He surprised himself by being ashamed of Sol's scrutiny. "It's better she went out like that than with a dose of fucking gondii. She was trying to get infected. They all were."

Sol, still watching Johnno trying to clean himself, didn't answer. But as Robertson walked away, he heard the old man spit loudly.

The doors were open and, with the lights on in the main atrium, there was an illusion of warmth. Johnno's boots and trousers were draped over the steps of the entrance. In the fading light, the stains being washed out by the rain looked black.

The bodies of the five soldiers were on the marble floor. The light was brighter here, and the stains were shown up for what they were. One of the men had been dragged to the centre of the entrance hall. The insignia on his arm identified him as a sergeant.

Johnno's baseball bat lay beside the body; it had cracked halfway along its length and was holding together by a broken curve of splinters. The man's head was twisted at an impossible angle. Robertson was grateful it was facing away from him.

The other four, their hands bound behind their backs, were slumped, or maybe propped, against the long run of a counter. One had the same neck-broke posture of the body in the centre of the floor. The three others appeared to be staring intently at the loops of their intestines.

The door marked STAFF ONLY was ornate, the toughened glass and heavy security locks disguised so customers and tourists could be spared the crass brutality of financial security. The locks had been shot away.

The hall and stairway that lay behind were more utilitarian, but they still had the soft shimmer of money. As Robertson climbed the steps, he gouged chunks from the expensive walls with his axe.

Maccallan had his back to the door and didn't hear him coming. The floors were carpeted richly, and silence had become a habit for Robertson. He felt a wave of contempt for the man hunched over the keyboard. It was a mixture of the other's sloppy lack of attention and a revision of feeling from the days they'd worked together in the Redman and Green offices. It was a long time since he'd seen anyone sitting in the glare of an electric light and the flicker of a computer screen.

He had the urge to pull Maccallan's head back and punch him. Not kill him maybe, just drive his fist into his smug little face a few dozen times. The way he'd fantasised about doing. He satisfied himself with slamming the door and making him jump.

"Jesus Christ, what's wrong with you?"

"Is this scheme of yours working?"

Robertson tapped the computer screen. It was showing a desktop with scores of shortcut icons and a box requesting, ADMINISTRATOR USERNAME AND PASSWORD.

"The computers and the hard drives are all intact. That was my biggest worry. I'm just waiting for this to let me in."

'This' was a USB stick. It was plugged into a port and a blue LED set into its side was blinking rapidly. Another half dozen computers were similarly set up.

"After that?"

"Then I go through them one by one and set up the blockchain code. Then I can start mining."

"And then we'll all be rich, so long as we stay in this fucking room."

The screen flashed a message that was gone before it could be read and displayed a business-like menu with a glut of folders and files. Robertson whispered something under his breath. It sounded like, *Come to daddy*. He unplugged the flashing USB and reached inside his jacket. He pulled out a block about the size of a large calculator and began unpeeling the layers of plastic it had been wrapped in.

"Checked that already," Maccallan said and leaned across to an adjacent desk. He hit the keyboard that was resting on it. The blank screen on the desk popped into life, it was displaying the UGOV website. Stark in its simplicity the page listed precautions to be taken against HV-Tg. It looked identical to the last time Robertson had seen it, more than a year before.

"The internet's back up?"

"Yeah. At the moment it's just the government sites, but the infrastructure's survived, at least it has in this part of town."

"But if it's only the government site you can access …"

"I can get around that. Somewhere there's a big block of servers. Once I get the blockchains fired up and start mining I just send them out to the servers. When it all gets back to normal and the servers worldwide start talking to each other – and they might be doing that now for all I know – my blockchain connects with all the others and, bingo, we can drown ourselves in cryptocurrency."

While Maccallan was gazing at his screen and running his mouth, Robertson moved to a window. A loose pack of Gonzos was drifting around in the street outside. He did a rapid count and, even with the group's reduced numbers, dismissed the threat.

"When this happens, when that happens. When it's all back to normal. Don't suppose it's fucking occurred to you that this is the new normal?"

"When did you last see someone switch?" Maccallan answered without looking away from the screen.

"I don't give them the chance to switch."

"Fair point. But when did you last see a Gonzo that wasn't on its last legs? I haven't seen a fresh one in months."

"So?"

"Toxo's run its course, or mutated, or whatever. Anyway, look around you. Light, power." He flicked a hand at the computer screen displaying the UGOV site. "Somewhere, the powers that be are transmitting this crap. That means there must be someone to transmit it to." While he'd been talking, he'd been hitting the keys of the computer in front of him. With a flourish, he hit one last key and whispered in a pantomime cackle, *Fly my pretties, fly*. He spun around in the chair and Robertson was reminded again of when they worked together. Back then Maccallan would have worn a suit and tie to match the expensive office furniture. And worn both with the air of a leader of men. The clothes were dirty and torn but the posture was the same.

"The big problem with mining cryptocurrency is the power. It costs a fortune to run enough code to generate blockchain in significant amounts. It would cost more in electricity than you'd generate. But now ..." – he gestured to the computers he'd set in motion – "... we're getting the electricity as a gift."

"And what if you and Sol ain't as clever as you think you fucking are? What happens if all this cryptocurrency turns out to be worthless?"

Maccallan laughed. The man was in genuinely high spirits. Even in the torn and dirty clothes, he was back in his comfort zone.

"What was it they used to say on those adverts for hedge funds? The value of your investment may fall as well as rise. Sorry pal, it's not the end of the world just yet, terms and conditions still apply. This is all a gamble, it's all a calculated risk."

Out in the street the Gonzos were beginning to group together. Robertson watched them stumble around the debris-strewn pavement for a while. The diggers the soldiers had been using, to try to break into the vault, had been abandoned in the depths of their own earthworks. As he watched, one of the Gonzos mounted one of the banks of soil and hardcore only to topple and fall.

"In case you hadn't noticed," he said, turning back to Maccallan, "the costs of your calculated risk are lying all over the road out there, with a load of bullet holes in them."

Maccallan laughed again. The joy was gone now; this time it was a spiritless bark of disgust.

"Oh, and I suppose you're racked with sorrow and pain about that. If you're looking for someone to blame for what went on out there today, find a mirror. You led Miller here and that gang of freaks followed him, the way they always do. And you knew they would. You fed them all into a meat grinder. So, don't come it with me, pal."

His hand found the arms of the chair he was in and Robertson saw his shoulders brace, as if he was about to launch himself to standing with dramatic flair. He'd seen him do it before.

Different time, different world.

Maccallan's movement faltered and stalled. Robertson saw his eyes flicker across the room, towards the doorway. There was another chair by the door with his backpack sitting in it and his wax cotton coat thrown across its back. His machete was propped against it.

Robertson leaned forward slightly, getting close to Maccallan's face. He used his axe to support his body weight.

"You think you'd get there in time?" he asked, his voice not much above a whisper. When Maccallan didn't give him an answer he stepped back and, moving with exaggerated care, rested the axe on one of the computer desks. Then he folded his arms. "Go on, go fetch it, you cunt. I'll wait, then you can have another go at sacking me."

Maccallan sat further back in the chair and made an effort to look unconcerned. He pushed himself further from the grinning figure of Robertson.

"Shit. Is that what all this is about, me firing you? What choice did I have? You were on the fiddle. You were lucky it was me that spotted it and not someone from head office."

"You fired me for being on the fiddle? You two-faced piece of shit. We both had our hands in the till, don't try to deny it."

Maccallan made let's-calm-down gestures with both hands.

"If I hadn't sacked you, you'd have been caught."

"Says you."

"Yeah, says me. You were not covering your tracks properly. I couldn't give a toss what you were doing, but I didn't want to get pulled into the fallout when you were caught. And you would have been. What did you make on your little deals, go on be honest …" – he looked around the room and dropped his voice – "… no one's listening."

Robertson let the silence hang and didn't answer until he could see it was unnerving Maccallan.

"About nine k, maybe ten."

"Over, what, three or four years?"

Robertson nodded.

"Alright, let me tell you what I had to lose. I'd been stuck in that place for just three years. I'd taken over two hundred and thirty thousand out of it. I had over ninety grand sitting under my bed. The way I had it working I had another year until I was set for life. Pack my bags, buy a nice little place somewhere with no extradition treaty and …" – he pointed at some distanct spot beyond the window and gave a sharp whistle – "… gone." Hand in front of his face, he laced his fingers together. It was his sincere-and-concerned stance. Another set piece Robertson had been familiar with when Maccallan had been his boss. "Now I'm sorry, but I wasn't willing to risk all that, not for the sake of your piddling little con. I wanted you out of the way with no questions asked, and no reason for head office to be sending auditors in. Now, look me in the eye and tell me you wouldn't have done the same."

Robertson closed the gap between them. He'd picked up the axe again first and was gratified to see a flash of panic in Maccallan's face. He was looming over the man before he had the opportunity to get up from his seat.

"I'd have done the same. And that's what fucking burns me. You and me are just the same, we're both animals looking to fill our bellies. Difference is, with me everyone fucking knows it."

Maccallan managed a rictus grin in Robertson's face.

"No, I'll tell you the difference. We're both thieves and right here, right now, we're both animals. But I want to see this world go back to how it was so I can stop being an animal. That's what this is all about …" – he tapped on the desk next to him, where the computer was showing a screen of rapidly changing figures and characters – "… but you, you're telling me you think killing Gonzos and living hand to mouth is it, no going back. Bullshit, you don't think that any more than I do, you're scared it'll stop being this way, because you … you've found your niche. You like being an animal."

He eased himself out of the chair. Pinned between the desk and Robertson he had to twist to get to his feet, bringing their faces within inches of each other.

Before the man could put any space between them, Robertson brought the top of the axe head up to the underside of his chin, he pushed Maccallan's head back until he was facing the ceiling.

"Okay, let's say you're right, Toxo's on the way out and civilisation's on the way in. And let's say you're right again and your little box of tricks there is producing an endless supply of currency. Why should one animal trust another?"

"You don't need to trust me," Maccallan said. "I don't need to trust you. I'll set each of us up with a purse, set it up so no one person can make withdrawals, there'll have to be a majority decision. That way everyone has to pull together, at least until we're all sitting pretty. Then we can split if we want. And everyone's got an incentive to play nice."

He took Robertson's silence and inaction as a sign of consent. Gingerly he put a hand on the axe head and pushed it away from his neck. Robertson let him do it.

"Don't try to cross me Maccallan, alright? Just fucking don't."

Chapter 51. Looking Out, Looking In

END OF AN ERA
START OF A NEW AGE
Mother Ally
Phil Brown
Magpie
Black Wing
Lucy Hancox
Eddie Tyrrell
Blessed Bernie
Blessed Ian
Ann-Marie Carter
Black Bird
Patrick Davies
FLYING WITH THE BONE CROW
CROW NATION FOREVER, FOREVER CROW NATION

Medium: Oil-based black paint, applied by brush.
Location: First floor frontage of the Bank of England.
Date: The piece is not dated.
Note: This is the largest piece of graffiti attributed to Miller's group, or the Crow Nation, as it was then identifying itself. The quality of the lettering and the scale of the undertaking suggests this represents several days' work. It is the final such piece known to have been produced.

From The Writing on the Wall

March 11th, 2021

It had stopped raining, but the wind rattled down the road stealing heat. He found Johnno, still naked, just inside the entrance to the bank. Down on his haunches, he had his arms wrapped round his knees.

"You need to get some clothes on," Robertson said.

He hadn't expected Johnno to acknowledge his presence and was surprised when he spoke.

"Everything's wet."

"You …" He was about say, you okay? but it was evident the man was a long way from okay. "You need to get some sleep."

"Keeping watch. Bastards might come back."

"They won't be back," Robertson assured him. Johnno didn't move, other than to turn his gaze back to the road. "Okay, I'll go and find you some dry clothes."

"No uniforms."

"No uniforms," he agreed.

Sol was in a ground-floor room that had been a makeshift barracks. It bore a loose resemblance to a military encampment, but the cracks in discipline could be traced by the trail of bottles. In a far corner a figure was sprawled on a neat collection of improvised bedding. The bottle that had finally defeated him was resting between the fork of his legs. He'd passed out without letting go of it and his grip had survived death. The eye that hadn't had a bullet put through it looked startled.

Three of the surviving Crows were going through the collection of belongings, stacked beside army issue sleeping bags. They wore the same near-death expression as Johnno but were unconcerned with the blood and dirt that clung to them. Sol was carefully keeping his distance.

"Where's Miller?" He addressed no one in particular and was ignored until he bellowed the question. Everyone, himself included, was startled by the outburst.

"He's upstairs," one of the Crows said and returned to the camo-pattern rucksack he was searching.

"Sol, see if you can find some fresh kit for Johnno. Civvies if you can manage it."

"Okay, is he still out there?"

"I left him in the doorway of the bank. He's not good, see if you can get him dressed and bring him back here for the night."

"He won't want to sleep here. We'll need to set up somewhere else."

"Fine, pick a room. As long as everyone gets some rest."

Sol straightened his posture slightly, "What's everyone? There's hardly any of us left."

"You as well, eh? Go swap notes with Maccallan. Then the pair of you can tell me about the view from the moral high ground. You three," the last was addressed at the trio of Crows, "stop fucking around with the bits and pieces and get that body out of here, got it?"

The three nodded their agreement, or at least understanding. Robertson turned and left without waiting to see if anyone would do as he'd said.

The floor above was another staff-only area, not intended for viewing by tourists or casual visitors. The lights were all on. The expanse of bright corridors and clean space highlighted the lack of noise. He had to strain to pick up the sounds of Miller and the rest of the Crows.

They had gathered in a meeting room of some sort. There were several filing cabinets sitting behind the door, half a dozen columns of plastic chairs stacked along one wall and a pair of easels, still with flip charts sitting on them.

Miller was at the far end of the room, cross-legged with his knives spread in front of him. Still splattered with blood, he was moving with the same methodical rhythm he always used. In the harsh lighting his clothes appeared black.

Five people lay on the floor. There was no reasoning to their positions; they might have collapsed on the spots they occupied. Robertson wouldn't have put money on any of them being alive by morning.

Two other Crows, both uninjured, were sitting on the floor in front of the filing cabinets. One of them was curled forward hugging her knees, in a similar manner to Johnno. She was rocking back and forth, mumbling to herself. Barely awake, her words were too soft to be made out, but Robertson recognised the rhythm. She was reciting, *Leave them be* as if it was a lullaby.

The second one, a man who looked impossibly young, had his back against the filing cabinets. At some point he had pierced both ear lobes with crows feathers and his left ear was swollen and crusted with an infection. He was struggling to stay awake.

"Hey." He kicked the sole of the man's boot, jolting him fully awake. "Go downstairs get some fucking sleep. You can't do anything here."

The man blinked several times and shook his head. He nodded at the huddled forms on the floor, "They will change."

The woman spoke up, "Leave them be, they will change."

Robertson looked at the nearest figure. He couldn't tell the gender of the form buried under the layers of bloodied clothing. The slow gurgling breathing suggested the question was moot.

"Have it your way," he told them. The woman's voice dropped back to a mumble and there was a catch in the rhythm as she started to weep.

Miller's steady honing regime didn't miss a step, but he registered Robertson with a glance.

"You alright, mate?"

Miller seemed to consider the question.

"End of an era," he said, just as Robertson had decided he wasn't going to answer. "End of an era."

He sounded wistful.

"I think it is," Robertson said, then felt stupid for saying it. Miller's occasional utterances made no more sense than the Toxo-damaged gibberish of the Gonzos. "Let's get you cleaned up."

He loosened the straps on his pack and let it fall. There were rags inside and the last of his bleach solution. Miller didn't object as he eased the blood-soaked jacket over his shoulders. At the other end of the room the two uninjured Crows found a new enthusiasm for their chant.

When he'd finished washing Miller, he used the last of the solution to cleanse his hands. It was fully dark in the street now and the windows he and Miller were positioned by had turned into mirrors, reflecting the room at their backs.

Robertson stepped nearer the glass, but all it showed him was his own face.

He'd preferred the views from the other side of the river. There, the dark rooms let the landscape through and let him look out. Here, where everyone kept the lights on, he could only look in.

The woman, who'd been mumbling the chant when he'd first come into the room, had roused herself and was coaxing one of the injured to drink water from a plastic bottle. She insisted, *It'll be alright*, repeating the phrase over and over. Without the self-conscious tone of the chant, she had a northern accent.

The man had fallen asleep slumped against the filing cabinets.

Before he left, Robertson asked the woman her name.

"Janice."

"Okay, Janice. I'm going to keep watch, downstairs. I want you and …" he indicated the sleeping man.

"Jackdaw."

"I want you and Jackdaw to stay with Miller. Make sure he's safe. Okay?"

"I'll look after him, of course."

"Thank you."

The three Crows in the barracks were snoring. One of them had chosen to sleep on the bedding the dead soldier had been on. Sol, a distance away from the sleeping men, was eating a tin of corned beef without any sign of enthusiasm.

"Did you sort Johnno out?"

Sol finished chewing and grimaced as he swallowed.

"I found him some clothes, found his boots for him. I couldn't persuade him to leave his post."

He gave Robertson a mocking salute. Unsure how he was expected to react, Robertson ignored the gesture and walked out.

Johnno was dressed again. The clothes Sol had found were reasonably clean, except for the heavy coat, which was stained and torn. The shoulders had been dressed with feathers. Johnno had replaced the broken baseball bat with a machete. Robertson noted it was Maccallan's.

"You okay, Johnno?"

The big man nodded, pulled in a deep shaking breath and repeated the gesture.

"I'm getting there."

"Maccallan still up there?" Another nod. "Any trouble?"

Johnno pointed at the steps Robertson had just ascended. It took him a moment to see that there were additional corpses there.

"Just Gonzos? No sign of the army?"

"No, just the Gonzos. Poor bastards."

Robertson put his back to the doorframe and let himself slide down into a squat. He rested his axe across his knees.

"I guess the lights are drawing them in."

Johnno nodded again and sighed. His fatigue was catching up with him.

"That and the smell, maybe."

"Smell?"

"Fresh blood. Living blood." Johnno cast a glance behind him, into the atrium of the bank and the bodies of the executed soldiers. "Maybe they can smell it. I don't know."

"I got no sense of smell," Robertson said. "Got my nose broken a few years back. Since then, nothing."

"You're not missing much."

"Get to bed Johnno. Go on, I've got this covered."

Johnno nodded and put the machete beside Robertson.

"Okay, give that back to Maccallan for me."

"Sure. Johnno, I'm sorry about Ally."

As he said it, he realised it was true. Ally, Patrick, the people he couldn't put names to. Even the ones he considered too far gone to really count: Bernie, Raven.

Johnno, who'd been turning to leave, paused and looked into the atrium again.

"It's what she would have wanted." He spat in the direction of the broken sergeant. "That's her tribute."

He walked away and Robertson thought he heard him murmuring, *Leave them be*, as he went.

Robertson waited for half an hour after Johnno had left before moving. At the edge of the cones of light thrown by the streetlamps he could see movement.

As he approached it the Gonzo stumbled and fell. It was still flailing and trying to lift itself when he reached it. He smacked the flat side of the axe head against its ear to make sure it was aware of him. He stepped back and watched it struggling to get to him. In falling it had pinned one of its arms under its flank and couldn't work out why it was unable to use it. Robertson stepped behind the thing and used the axe to roll it off its side. With slow painful movements the thing began to lever itself up. Robertson gave it another smack on the side of the head and walked back towards the bank.

Another flurry of movement caught his eye. Nearer the doorway was an upright Gonzo. Bigger than the one he'd just righted; it was singing. Two notes that might have been words at one time; up and down, up and down. Two Tone was in better shape than the one he'd just allowed to right itself. Without breaking rhythm, it lurched towards him. He sidestepped, backed away a few paces and used his axe on the first Gonzo. He whistled a few times, high and shrill to keep Two Tone with him, led him back into the bank. It followed, its movements smoothing as it gained pace.

Inside the building, surrounded by the viscera of Johnno's tribute to Ally, Two Tone became confused. Robertson, who'd crossed to the door leading to the floor with the IT suite, watched its progress. He kept his head tilted, listening to the high-low note it kept repeating. There was a hard edge to the high note, the remains of a syllable.

Two Tone staggered about in the puddles of congealing fluid and tangles of viscera. In the harsh light of the atrium it was clear the thing was nearly blind. Most of its upper face was crusted with sores. Robertson gave it another volley of sharp whistles. It made him think of a dog walker and that struck him as funny. He laughed and slapped his thighs.

"Here, boy, come on, boy. Come on."

Two Tone picked up on the sound or the movement and started towards him. When it came within striking distance, Robertson hit its head with the flat of the axe. He repeated the motion each time it started to right itself, corralled it into the stairwell. He stepped behind and delivered another blunt strike between its shoulder blades. The soles of its feet slick with the offal from the floor, it fell forward onto the stairs. Something cracked wetly and the two notes stopped. For a moment Robertson thought the fall had killed it, but it pushed itself up and began swinging its head, trying to get its bearings.

As he was pushing the door shut, to trap it in the stairwell, it coughed and a clot of something wet broke past its newly broken teeth. Robertson waited, ready to slam the door but curious to see if it would resume its simple song.

"Tock ..." – it coughed again and vomited black tar-like muck over itself and the floor – "... locks the keys have broken the locks the, tick tock the keys have broken the locks."

Robertson froze and felt his stomach knotting with fear and then something he couldn't place.

Awe.

Two Tone, having found his voice, repeated the phrase again. When the words had been interrupted by the retching they had taken on an almost choral quality. Now the repetition quickly blended into monotony. Robertson listened to another three rounds of it before shutting the door. He pressed his weight against it, expecting Two Tone to try to get to him. When there was no pressure from the other side, he pulled the door open a crack and listened. He could hear the 'song' and, after a few minutes, the stumbling footfalls as the singer found its way up the stairs. Up to the IT suite where Maccallan was lost in the programs he was implementing.

He found a chair lying on its side against a wall with a display of photos, outlining the history of the bank. The chair was surprisingly cheap. Chrome tubes with fake leather covers over thin padding. He set it against the door and sat down to wait.

Noises filtered down the stairwell. He listened for the words of the song but couldn't make them out. What he did hear was the steady thump of fists beating against another door.

He listened to the noises but watched the open doors leading onto the flagstoned walkway outside. It wasn't long before the lights attracted more Gonzos. He killed three before giving up on the idea of finding another that was singing. After that – if they could make their way up the entrance steps – he herded them up the stairs to the IT suite.

It got easier by the fourth and fifth, as the commotion on the upper floor gave them a point of contact to focus on.

He set the chair against the door again and decided five was enough. The pounding noise from upstairs hadn't let up.

He took the file he used to keep his axe sharp and cut a final notch in the back of Maccallan's machete.

Chapter 52. Another Day at the Bank

April 15th, 2028

"You expecting someone?" I asked Solomon.

"Probably Johnno."

"And who's Johnno?" Winslow said.

Solomon rolled his eyes, letting us know he was sick of stupid questions.

"Why doesn't one of you answer the door? That way you'd find out."

Right on cue there was another round of knocking. Winslow made a flicking motion with his hand, aimed towards the door.

"Go and answer it," he said.

"You bloody well go and answer it," Solomon replied. He underlined the comment by settling deeper into the corner of the sofa. "Best hurry up before he goes. Go on, chop, chop."

Winslow wanted to argue the point but there were two heavy knocks on the door that sounded like they were made in frustration. I could picture someone giving up and walking away. Winslow made an awkward exit from the room, trying to hurry without looking like he'd just been bested.

Solomon caught my eye. I expected him to claim his little victory by smirking at me, but he just stared levelly, and I could see him weighing me up. I felt some subtle shift in the balance of power but didn't know to whose advantage.

We heard Winslow open the front door and say, "Who are you?"

"Who the fuck are you? Where's Sol?"

"DC Winslow, Metropolitan Police and I want …"

"Out the way, soft lad."

There was the sound of Winslow being pushed aside in the narrow hallway.

"It's alright Johnno," Sol called out, "I'm in here."

Johnno appeared in the doorway of the room and I saw his attention moving rapidly from place to place. It was a quick scan but obviously a practiced one. He took my presence in with a double take that could have been fitted into the blink of an eye.

Not huge, he was still a big man by the underfed standards of the day. The heavy leather coat he was wearing wasn't new, but it didn't look as if it had too many miles on it. Well fed, well dressed. And checking in on a bargain-bucket flat that was a cover for a slum drinking den.

"You alright, Sol?"

He sounded like one of the Beatles.

"Nothing a year in the tropics wouldn't fix. If her ID's to be believed, this is Detective Sergeant Cross. I believe you've already met Detective Constable Winslow."

Sol nodded to indicate that Winslow was now standing behind the man in the doorway. The tone of the exchange was light. But the contrast with the old man's surliness told me he was trying to put the newcomer on his guard. He kept up the eye contact a shade too long.

The big man surprised me by picking up on the subtlety. He took a long breath and took the remaining seat on the sofa. Winslow came in behind him and stayed standing.

"And who are you?" he demanded.

Johnno looked him up and down very slowly, then waited until Winslow was about to ask him again, before telling him.

"John Downs."

"You got any ID?"

"Have you?"

Winslow did his flipping-the-warrant-card-out routine and Johnno made him stand there with the card on his hip while he carefully examined it. Finally, he nodded.

"I'll ask again … sir. Have you got any ID?"

"No."

Winslow didn't know what to do with the answer and it showed. Sol laughed again.

"So, what are you doing here?"

"I'm dropping in on an old friend. What the fuck are you doing here?"

"I'm about to arrest your old friend."

Winslow picked up one of the tools from the bench and held it in front of Johnno's face. What point he thought it proved, or won, I had no idea.

"For what? Owning a pen?"

"Forgery."

Sol didn't laugh this time. He looked at Winslow, then me.

"Then why aren't I being handcuffed?"

"We told you. We want to know about Robertson," I said.

"And I told you he fed the crows."

Johnno shifted uncomfortably and I could see the answer annoying Winslow again.

"I say we take him in," he said. "Sling him in a cell, see if he starts talking sense."

Sol laughed again but I could see the humour was lost on Johnno.

"Robertson's dead," I told Winslow.

I meant it to shut him up rather than enlighten him. It was a mistake in many ways. Winslow, who'd been leaning his weight against the workbench stood bolt upright. I think the reaction was all about him being out of the loop. As he moved, so did Johnno. In that horrible slow motion that comes with an adrenaline hit, I saw him reach for the inside of his long leather coat as he leapt to stand. He found what he was searching for ahead of me and began drawing the gun. My motions felt even slower than the loop of film he was caught in.

The pistol I'd carried with me from Paris was deep in my coat pocket. My hand found it, but the folds of quilted material wouldn't let it go and I ended up pulling my coat half off attempting to outdraw Johnno.

I was lucky. Johnno's gun was a shotgun with the stock and the barrels cut back. What the Brits call a sawn-off. Shortened though it was, it was still longer than my pistol. And Johnno had his expensive coat to think of. As he struggled to pull the barrels free of the slit in the lining, I fired through the bottom of my pocket.

The bullet passed in front of Johnno and lodged into the skirting board. It had come as close to hitting Winslow as it had Johnno. Both were frozen in place, Johnno with the last two or three inches of barrel pulling at his coat.

I had a vision of Dog Boy, face down on a sidewalk. I allowed myself the luxury of shaking my head free of the picture before speaking.

"Put the gun down, now."

Johnno nodded slowly and changed his grip, so his finger was clearly away from the trigger. He moved slow. And that was fine by me. He bent at the knee, his eyes on the smoking hole I'd blown in my jacket. When the gun was on the floor, I brought my own out into the light. It was painfully easy now I had the upper hand.

I said, "Pick it up." No one moved. "Winslow, pick it up. You …" I nudged my gun in Johnno's direction, "… sit."

"Okay, okay just …"

"Shut up."

Winslow had the shotgun. He was holding it out to me.

"Cover them," I told him, hoping he wouldn't accidentally pull the trigger and kill someone.

There was a strange pause where no one said anything. It took me a moment to remember I was in charge.

"Cuffs," I told Winslow, and there was another point of confusion when he tried to hold a gun and fish out his handcuffs. Then I had to get Johnno to put his hands behind his back and that entailed getting him to stand up again.

I found I was fighting the urge to laugh.

The farce of getting the big man, who sounded like Ringo Starr, into handcuffs and then sitting him down again, gave me time to put my thoughts in order.

Winslow kept the shotgun on the big man. I could see him going down the path that little men with big guns always travel.

I'm God. I'm holding a gun and I'm scared.

I'm holding a gun and someone else is scared.

I'm holding a gun!

I thought, Welcome to America. Winslow looked confused and I realised I'd spoken out loud. I waved him away. He didn't want to risk his new stature by sitting down, so I took the seat in front of the workbench, trying hard not to fall into it.

"Okay. I think we can all agree that this has gone way past suspicion of forgery," I said.

Sol cast a sideways look at Johnno who was now perched on the edge of the sofa with his hands locked behind him.

"I could argue I'm just an innocent bystander."

"So much for honour among thieves," Winslow said. "Is this the gun that killed York?"

Sol laughed at him again, and I suspect he came damn close to getting shot.

"Did you kill Robertson too?" Winslow was talking to Johnno. He jabbed the gun towards him.

Johnno looked at Winslow with an expression that displayed both their histories. He was a veteran of a hundred battles and had seen more than most people would ever dream of. I felt a shiver of regret that we were on different sides, but it didn't last. People like Johnno, and maybe by extension me, didn't really have sides.

"You know something soft lad, if she was holding that gun, I might be frightened."

"Why did you kill Robertson?"

"Fuck off."

Winslow I could see was struggling with the lesson most men with guns struggle with. They're not worth a damn if you don't pull the trigger.

"I think Maccallan killed Robertson. Is that right, Sol?"

Sol smiled and it seemed like genuine humour rather than a point scored. I saw he was looking at Winslow.

Winslow's face was pure confusion. I took pity on him and pulled out the passport. I handed it to him. He flipped it open and glanced at the picture.

"Robertson's passport. So what?"

The edge on his voice was high and ragged.

"Not Robertson," I said.

The photo was Robertson, more accurately the man we'd been interviewing and calling Robertson. The name and details printed next to the photo were Maccallan's.

March 12th, 2021

The sound of Miller's knives woke him. The dull wet sound they made as they struck home. He blinked in the daylight, amazed to find he'd slept. Behind him, up the stairs he could make out other sounds: scraping and gibbering about keys and locks. There was a Gonzo inside the bank with him, tangled in the entrails that were looping around the slaughtered soldiers. He stood and stretched, his back clicked somewhere between his shoulder blades and the sound put him at ease. It was normal, the start of a working day. Another day at the bank. He laughed and picked up the axe, swung it in slow arcs, easing the stiffness from his limbs.

He lined the swing to the back of the Gonzo's head and felt it connect with a pleasing crack. He walked out into the street and joined Miller among the infected.

The remaining Crows were there. There were about a dozen Gonzos staggering and tripping on the debris of the previous day. Blank-faced, blank-eyed, the Crows dispatched them automatically, leaving them where they fell. He made his way over to Miller, who didn't register his presence. The Gonzos, maybe drawn to the noise and the commotion, seemed to be gravitating to him.

Robertson selected one, a badly-stooped woman, young when she'd switched. He lined the swing up carefully and almost succeeded in cleaving her head in two.

He realised there was a thin mist rising as the dampness was warmed away. The sun had come out. He laughed.

He saw Johnno. The big man was scanning the street and picking his way between the shuffling Gonzos. His expression when he reached Robertson was hard to read.

"Where's Maccallan?"

"I haven't seen him," Robertson said. "I fell asleep in the bank. The fucker must have walked out and just left me."

He hadn't thought of the story beyond that point and busied himself with another Gonzo, deliberately misplacing the swing so he'd be occupied with another attempt.

The good mood began to evaporate as he watched Johnno climb the steps. He put the axe through another skull and left Miller to it.

Sol was in the barracks trying to make a habitable space out of it. He glanced up as Robertson entered the room.

"We need to get organised," he said.

"And good morning to you, too."

Sol waved his hand impatiently.

"If we're staying here for any length of time, we need to clear the bodies away or we'll all be dead of cholera. And we need to take the lights out, stop the Gonzos drifting over …"

"Miller's got the Gonzos covered. They give him something to do."

Robertson stretched out on one of the vacant bed rolls and wolf-whistled the ceiling. The space directly above his head had been decorated with pages from a pornographic magazine. He heard Sol throw something down on the floor.

"You think this is funny? There is hardly anyone left. The ones that are …" He finished the sentence with a noise of disgust. "And Miller. My God we should rely on him? The man's …"

"The man's the future, you old bastard. Don't you get it? This is it." He jumped up from the bed, suddenly sick of Sol's voice, the counselling, the planning, the hectoring. He didn't trust himself to get near the man but couldn't bear to keep still. He paced a tight circuit of the bed space with the erotic ceiling. "Don't you get it? This … is … it. One way or another, this is the end of fucking days, Sol. Finito, over. End-fucking-of."

"No, no it isn't. That's why we did this, why you did this." Sol didn't sound scared, but his tone had changed, lost its edge of impatience. "All we need to do is sit tight. We let Maccallan do his tricks and when all this is done and dusted and the world's back on an even keel …" he made a soaring motion with his hand, "… an airborne escape."

"Back on an even keel?" Robertson said. "What if you're the one out of balance, eh? You ever think of that?"

He burst out laughing and saw the old man register real fear. It brought him up short and he forced himself to lie down on the bedding again. He tried to rekindle his interest in the display of flesh he was looking at. When he was calm enough to speak without laughing, he lifted his head and looked directly at Sol. Sol hadn't moved. He still had one hand lifted, as if moving might tip Robertson into some act of complete insanity.

"You know the smartest thing I've heard anyone say for a while, Sol?"

"No, no I don't."

"The locks have broken the keys."

Robertson rolled onto his side and tried to get back to sleep.

"Wake up, you piece of shit."

He opened his eyes to find Johnno standing over him. There was a moment of confusion when he wondered why the big Liverpudlian had lost his accent. Then the big man rammed something blunt into his groin. His body pulled into a ball, he rolled onto his side and felt his stomach muscles spasm.

"You piece of shit."

Maccallan's voice, not Johnno's.

Robertson tried to straighten but his stomach spasmed again and he only succeeded in retching. There was nothing in his gut to come out. He could make out the dark shapes of booted feet and little else; his eyes were watering to the point it was hard to see. A disconnected part of his mind registered surprise. He'd always thought the comments about eyes watering were for comic effect. Someone grabbed the collar of his coat and dragged him upright. Hauled backwards, he felt a wall behind him. He wiped his hand across his face, trying to clear his vision.

Johnno, expressionless, was standing directly in front of him, holding a pickaxe handle. Behind him Maccallan, holding an axe, his axe.

"You piece of shit," Maccallan said again.

Robertson tried to laugh at him, but another muscle spasm turned it into a cough.

"What's going on?" A new voice: Sol's.

"He tried to bloody kill me," Maccallan said.

Robertson still couldn't laugh, but he managed to pull his face into a stiff grin.

"If I'd tried to kill you, you'd be fucking dead. You can't even handle a couple of half-rotted Gonzos? We've been carrying you for months, about time you started pulling your weight." He finally managed a laugh. "I even cut the notch on your little machete for you."

"You piece of shit," Maccallan said again.

The last thing Robertson saw was his own axe coming down.

Chapter 53. A Short Period of Negotiation

Item posted on the Resist News Dot Com website (29/08/2023)

DRUMPH ADMINISTRATION DENY PAY-TO-PLAY IMMIGRATION POLICY

The White House issued a rebut to claims that entrance visas and requests for repatriation are effectively being sold. It follows a report, from Resist's Joanna Scott, that successful applications for US visas, residency permits, or repatriation are almost wholly dependent on donations being made to party funds.

President Drumph's press secretary, Martha Saunders, responded to the allegations of partisan money grabbing, via a pre-recorded statement. In it she maintained that the story was a distortion of the facts, suggesting the negative spin was a move to undermine President Drumph's policy to protect Americans from the very real threat of HV-Tg.

The last clinically diagnosed case of HV-Tg was recorded in Valencia, Spain, in June 2022.

The policy she is referring to concerns the requirement – instigated quietly in 2021 – that anyone wishing entry to the USA, permanent or temporary, must display a "willingness to participate in the democratic process, by donating a minimum sum to a viable political party."

The wording of the requirement has been criticised as "viable" is widely interpreted to mean either of the two main parties. It was further revealed, late last year, that only applicants donating to President Drumph's party were successful.

The controversy was brought to light on the back of another story, also broken on the Resist News website, that the list of approved medical insurers (medical insurance is mandatory for all applicants) are all organisations in which the President's wife and son are both majority shareholders.

April 15th, 2028

"You been making passports as well as ration books?" Winslow said. It was halfway between a question and an accusation. He realised he was not only wrong, but stupidly wrong as the words left his mouth. I could see it on his face.

"I hadn't set eyes on that passport until tonight," Sol told him. There was a pause, into which Sol fitted another point-winning smile. "Is that simple enough for you?"

"I've never even met Robertson, have I?" Winslow said.

I was surprised that he'd admit his gullibility so readily, but he was calculating rather than brooding. His cop's way of thinking had come to him.

"Johnno, best shield your eyes, the lights are coming on," Sol said.

Beside him Johnno made a grunt of contempt. "The boy's a genius."

"Richard York was the only one who'd known Robertson and Maccallan before the Outbreak," Winslow said.

"There may be others, but they didn't show up at the police station shooting their mouths off about knowing the King of the Crows. Leastways, none that Maccallan was told about." Sol said this and then tilted his head slightly, inviting Winslow to make the connection.

He didn't admit it but the way he stiffened showed the old man's latest barb had sunk in. It had been Winslow who'd told the man we'd thought was Robertson that somebody from his past was in custody. Winslow had even given him his name. Effectively he'd put a target on his back.

"That's what was in the letter PC Haddan passed to you. York's name and orders to get rid of him." It wasn't a question. Winslow hefted the gun, nodded at Sol. "I'm guessing you didn't pull the trigger, not without falling over." It was a cheap shot and Sol smiled again, letting us know he'd just won another point without even speaking. "So, I'm guessing you're in the frame." This to Johnno. Johnno told him to fuck off again.

"I say we call it in," Winslow said. "We get a van for big boy here and see how cocky this old bastard is once he's in an interview room, answering questions about aiding and abetting a murder."

I didn't answer him straightaway. I didn't want to call it in. Not at that point. Winslow was too busy giving Johnno the hard-eye treatment to notice my hesitation. Sol was on it like a steel trap.

"You want to know the difference between a bent copper and a straight copper?" he said directly to Winslow, but not before flicking a glance to me. He didn't wait for an answer from either of us. "A short period of negotiation."

Johnno laughed at the comment, but he didn't take his eyes off Winslow. Winslow thought they were in competition to see who'd blink first. I could tell Johnno, even in handcuffs, was watching for an opening.

"Where's Maccallan now?" I asked Sol.

"What does it matter?"

"It matters to the pair of you enough to murder an innocent man on his say-so." Winslow said.

Johnno rolled his eyes and muttered, "Jesus Christ."

Strangely it was this remark that finally pushed Winslow over some internal line. He threw himself out of the chair, nearly losing his balance when it slid away from under him.

"Now I suppose you're going to give me the line about why it doesn't matter. Just one more death."

Johnno, still meeting Winslow's eye, nodded very deliberately.

"That's exactly right, soft lad. We dragged ourselves across this shit-hole of city. I saw people die every day, people I cared about, people who were worth something. You think I care what happens to some fucking junkie grass?"

The tendons in his neck stood proud and his voice was barely more than a snarl. He didn't sound like one of the Beatles anymore. The handcuffs were probably the only reason he didn't go for Winslow, shotgun or no.

There was silence and for a second or so I thought Winslow was about to use the gun and make it permanent. Sol was looking at me. I had the feeling again that I was being measured up. I couldn't be sure for what.

"Where is Maccallan?" Winslow said, finally.

"Why does it matter?" Sol repeated. "I'm being serious. What difference will it make to you if you find him? Okay, he killed Robertson. They had history. Do you really think that was the only score settled that year?" He made a gesture with his hands that managed to sum up the pointlessness of everything. "Robertson was no better than Maccallan and Maccallan was no worse than anyone else."

"Why is he using someone else's name then?" Winslow said.

Sol looked across at me again. Appealing for help.

I told him to answer the question.

"Again, you think he's the only one doing that? You think he's the only one running from a past they'd rather forget?"

"I think he's running from a one-way ticket on a labour gang. Or the noose if I get any say in it. You sanctimonious bastards keep on about how hard you had it, how bad it was and how you did what you had to." Winslow's breathing had slowed now; he was getting himself under control. As if arguing the point with Sol and Johnno had reminded him, he belonged on the moral high ground. "You know what he's running from, do you?"

He took his eyes off Johnno for the last bit. He was asking Sol.

"I don't consider it my business," he said. The tone was prim, a spinster aunt delivering sage wisdom. Except he was lying and we both, he and I, knew it. He considered everything his business.

"Well I'll tell you anyway. That fancy tower block he was holed up in? Well he wasn't the only one. He was the only one to get out alive though. The top three floors had been ransacked, all except his flat."

I was a beat behind Winslow on that score. Once I'd found Maccallan's passport and realised we were trying to pin the man with his own murder, I'd discarded most of what we'd found in the rest of the tower block. Now it was obvious. Maccallan's beautifully-stocked bolthole had been stocked at the expense of his neighbours.

I thought of the first flat Winslow had shown me. Puppy-walking me through the reading of a crime scene. A woman in a flat, letting someone she knew and trusted into her home. Dying in the doorway of the bedroom.

The intimacy of the act belied the story Johnno and Sol wanted to spin, of random acts of survival wiping everyone's soul into a uniform blameless grey.

"That's the problem, is it?" Johnno said. "You're cut up about a couple of boltholers getting it in the neck. Kindred spirits and all that. I should have guessed you spent a couple of years hiding behind the curtains. You got that pasty-faced look about you."

Winslow reacted before any of us had time to blink. He lifted the gun he was holding and brought it down in a backhanded arc across Johnno's head. The stock on the shotgun had been cut down until it was no more than a pistol grip, and the rough-sawn wood lifted a flap of skin from the man's temple. He fell across Sol's lap. He wasn't unconscious but he was close.

Sol cradled the injured man's head and leaned over him, shielding him from Winslow, who, I could see, was as shocked as any of us by what had happened. I'd seen it before, more often before the Outbreak. Men and women who carried an anger in them so deeply hidden it was almost alien to them.

"Okay, that's enough," I said and put myself between Winslow and the sofa. "Sit down and take a moment, okay?"

Winslow sat himself back down again, but not before I saw the look of confusion that crossed his face. It was the usual bewilderment of alpha males when women aren't impressed with their temper tantrums.

I motioned Sol that he could let his friend come up for air again.

Johnno was obviously a tough son of a bitch. He sat himself upright again and muttered half a dozen colourful curses, aimed at the universe in general. There was blood trickling into his right eye and, hands cuffed at his back, he tried to wipe it on the shoulder of his coat. When I tried to look at the damage he pulled away and shook his head impatiently, then doubled over as a wave of nausea hit him.

I noted Sol, who'd been eager to keep him alive, didn't bother trying to comfort him.

"Where's Maccallan?" Winslow repeated, once Johnno had carefully set himself upright again.

Again, Johnno told him to fuck off, his accent turning it into, fook arf.

"Sergeant," Winslow put an edge on the word. "Why aren't we calling this in?"

"Because the difference between a straight copper and a bent copper is a short period of negotiation," I said.

Sol swallowed a smile. I couldn't tell if it was because of what I'd said or because of Winslow's outrage. Winslow was building up to an explosion. I stressed whose side I was on by standing next to him and pointing the pistol in the direction of the sofa.

"Do you know who you can trust in the station? Maccallan arranged a murder for the price of a fake ration book. If we put these two in a cell, how long do you think it'll take for word to reach Maccallan?"

The part of Winslow that was pure cop took the reins again and, angry as he was, he allowed the truth of what I was saying. He'd seen Maccallan's famous flat with its ready-packed case and hidden money. The flat he'd killed three people to stock, then abandoned on a moment's notice when a better deal presented itself. It wasn't that hard to slip through the cracks. The cracks were bigger than they'd once been. And Maccallan had history.

"Then what next?" he said.

"Maccallan's going to come to us."

Johnno laughed, but he was no actor and it was too fast and too loud to be anything other than an attempt to hide his concern. Winslow glanced at the man he'd just pistol-whipped and nodded.

"You, ring Maccallan."

"Fook arf."

I stepped forward and put the barrel of the pistol against the side of his knee.

"Ring Maccallan. Trust me, I will pull this trigger."

"I ain't got his number."

I took a leaf from Winslow's book and brought the grip of the pistol down hard on Johnno's knee. It was a fraction of the pain he'd get from a bullet, but it was enough to bring his head up with a jolt and flick drops of blood into the air.

"I'll do it," Sol said. Johnno tried to say something, but the older man shushed him. "Johnno, they're right. If Maccallan hears we're arrested or he gets spooked, he'll do a runner. If we get him here …" – he gave me another of his measuring looks – "… maybe we can … salvage something from the situation."

I moved a step back from the sofa, keeping the gun in the direction of Sol, while he leaned to one side and reached into his hip pocket. He took out a cell phone that would have looked antiquated before the Outbreak.

"If you tip him off, he'll run. And then we'll cut our losses and bring a case against the pair of you," I told him.

"I know that."

He dialled a number from memory. It took some time, because of the tremor in his fingers. He scowled at his hands as he concentrated on pressing the numbers in. About halfway through the process, Winslow chipped in,

"Put it on loudspeaker."

Sol told him he didn't know how, which neither of us believed. Winslow hauled himself from the chair again. He was still holding the shotgun and might have had another pistol-whipping in mind, but the ringtone cut off as the call was answered. Winslow did nothing worse than narrow his eyes at the old man.

"Robertson? Sol. You better get over here, we got problems." Maybe out of need but more likely out of belligerence, Sol kept the cell phone pressed tightly to his ear. To us the other end of the exchange was just a series of gaps. "A problem you need to deal with … That's the usual solution … Robertson, everybody, everybody, is bent."

He finished the call by throwing the cell phone down in disgust. A fit of pique that broke it. And stopped either Winslow or I from checking the call log to see the number he'd called.

"He'll be a while," Sol told us.

We sat in silence for a few minutes. Downstairs, we could hear the woman who ran the door for the drinking den shuffling about, running water and making the plumbing clank and rattle. The noises sounded peculiarly English to me and I got to thinking about America. The one I'd left and been told I might get back to one day. One day.

Sol might have read my mind.

"You're American?" It wasn't a question. "I take it you were caught on the wrong side of the Atlantic, when it all went wrong."

"Paris."

Sol nodded and pursed his lips, calculating.

"From what I've heard, Europe had it worse than here."

Winslow took the remark as a personal insult and made a tutting sound, here we go again.

"I only know what I saw. It wasn't easy."

"Why didn't you go back? America, I mean. Isn't that home?"

He knew the answer and the question came with one of his measuring looks. It wasn't the same as being undressed with the eyes but there was a feeling of nakedness.

"Chalk it up to my sense of duty."

He didn't laugh.

"I think I'll chalk it up to America's policy of 'Ultra Protectionism'."

"Yeah, God bless America," Johnno said. He did that slow flat voice that the English think is a Yankee drawl.

"Was that your plan?" I asked. "Once everything had calmed down and the economic situation was back on the rails? Head to the land of the free and sit out your days in the sun. Where were you thinking of, Florida, LA?"

"Maybe Texas, fresh air, dry heat, a population that respects money."

"Then Drumph closed up shop and told you you're stuck in the rain with me, waiting on a permission docket to enter US dominion?"

Sol left a moment of silence for me to contemplate my assumption.

"We weren't planning on asking permission, Ms Cross. And we're not stuck, we could cross that forty-eighth parallel any time we choose." He left the statement hanging for a while and took another set of measurements. "It's all in the timing."

I wondered how much he knew about the paperwork spread over the shrine that had once been Maccallan's flat. If I'd read it correctly, Maccallan's timing had been off before.

"Let me guess what you're waiting for – Maccallan's cryptocurrency mine to generate enough." It was my turn to laugh. Sol's open expression of surprise drew the reaction out of me without warning. At the edge of my vision I saw Johnno, who'd still been trying to wipe blood from his eyes, stiffen.

Sol's look of surprise didn't last long. He didn't bother trying to pretend it hadn't happened; instead he gave me an ironic salute and acknowledged I'd blindsided him.

"Indulge an old man, Detective. How did you know?"

"I don't know the exact details but there was a huge amount of internet traffic coming from the UK around the time Miller's group clashed with the Billings Boyz. At that point the only part of the UK that amount of unaccountable data could have been produced in was North London. When the stories about Miller's Crows heading into Threadneedle Street came to light, some bean counter in the US made the connection."

"That's why Maccallan was arrested? The historic murders spiel was just a pretext?"

"Pretty much."

"And why are you assuming that Maccallan is still mining?"

I could see he was fishing now, hoping there were holes in my knowledge. I hadn't believed his helpless old man act when I'd first seen it, and I didn't want to underestimate him.

"We visited 'Robertson's' flat, and then had a look at the one underneath it, a dozen computers and a soundproofed generator. I'm guessing the coupons for all the diesel came from you?"

Sol stole a glance at the workbench where Winslow sat. He tilted his head, not really in an admission of guilt, but more as an artist accepting a compliment.

"That was always the stumbling block apparently. Generating cryptocurrency isn't that hard if you have the know-how and the software Maccallan did. Trouble is, the cost of the electricity was greater than the value of the currency."

"Unless you hijacked a bank of computers that were being powered for free during a national crisis."

"Exactly."

"Surely a couple of diesel generators can't put out the sort of power you'd need? Even if you are getting the diesel for nothing."

Sol didn't answer for a beat or so. I thought he'd decided he'd given enough away but then he shrugged.

"It's slower than is ideal but now we know where to concentrate the efforts. When Maccallan started the process, it was a gamble what currencies would be useful. He's a smart boy, Maccallan. He foresaw the US would adopt the crypto, then try to centralise it so it could be taxed. But even he couldn't know for sure which one. In Threadneedle Street, he was producing six different types of coin. Six different sets of the Blockchain code …" – he said the words with that careful intonation of someone who has no idea what they mean – "… and at that stage four different purses for each of the chains. The idea was me, Maccallan, Johnno here and Robertson would hold a purse each. It's been set up so that all transactions require at least three of those accounts to agree to it. It meant we'd have to stick together."

"The country goes to hell and you're thinking about how to use it to make money," Winslow said.

"And since Robertson's been murdered it's just the three of you left and now you're all bound to each other," I said.

"Yes."

"Sol, for Christ's sake shut up," Johnno hissed.

"I'm telling her nothing she doesn't know. And I suspect she knows more than that."

"Was it Maccallan who suggested heading back into North London. Was that the whole point of it?"

"No, it was just chance that he saw us. We were heading to the lights and the power. And yes, the banks. Maccallan had been holed up for almost a year by then. He'd been trying to build blockchain on his own computers. I don't know enough about IT to say how, but after a year the petrol was getting stale and the generators wouldn't function. We were a huge group by then. I suspect he'd have watched us from behind the curtains and stayed put."

"But he recognised his old friend Robertson," Winslow piped up.

"Exactly. He knew another villain when he saw one."

"Sol, shut it," Johnno pleaded.

Whatever Sol might have replied was interrupted by a knock on the door.

I let Winslow go to the door, telling him to be careful. I heard him pull the door back with too much force and say, "Hello, Mr Maccallan."

He brought Maccallan back in at gunpoint. Both men had deliberately blank expressions, but only Maccallan's was unreadable. Winslow was a powder keg waiting for a spark. I wondered if it was the abrasive smugness of Sol that was pushing his buttons or just the faux power some men seem to draw from firearms.

There was a farcical moment when Maccallan got to the front room and we couldn't decide where to put him. In the end Winslow waved the gun in his face and told him to sit in the chair by the workbench.

"So." He crossed one leg over the other and laced his finger together around his knee. "How are we playing this?"

I felt something close to revulsion. The gesture wasn't one I'd seen him make before and the tone of voice was wrong. The façade of Robertson, the only thing left of the man, had been shed. The whole thing had a reptilian feel to it. I preferred the obnoxious grit of his portrayal of Robertson than his true self-image.

"How about we start with multiple murder charges. Then we can discuss whatever financial fraud you pulled on the American government?" I said.

"We've been here before Detective Cross. Last time you didn't have proof of anything, and I was in a cell."

I took out the passport and showed it to him. He looked at it and sighed. Boredom.

"I've also got the name of the police officer you bribed to pass details of Richard York onto your accomplice. And the gun my colleague is holding will be presented as exhibit A, the murder weapon. There's also the mess you left behind in your flat to be considered. Even with the state the records are in, it shouldn't take too long to find the names of the people you slaughtered. Including what would appear to be an intimate acquaintance."

"And what good will that do you?"

"It's called building a case," Winslow said.

His voice was higher than usual, the muscles in his throat betraying his stress.

"Okay, I'll try again. Last time, when you had not one shred of evidence, I was sitting in a cell, in an excuse for a police station, surrounded by due process and official lines. Now, when you've got me bang to rights, I'm sitting in a very comfortable chair, in a friend's living room having what I would guess are two illegal guns pointed at me. No badges, no uniforms. No back-up." He pretended to pick a piece of thread off the knee of his jeans. "So, I repeat, what good will arresting me do you?" He aimed the question directly at me. "Let's put it another way – what would be good for you?"

It was Sol that answered.

"A new ID, new papers, a ticket back home and a credit balance that allows her in."

Maccallan smiled.

Chapter 54. The Night the Lights Went Out

April 15th, 2028

I felt Winslow's position change. He was behind me. I didn't need to see him to know he'd taken a step back. As much distance as the cramped room allowed. I knew as surely as I knew my own name that I was now in the line of fire from the shotgun.

I fixed Maccallan in the eye. "We'll add that comment to the list. It'll come under the heading of attempted bribery, maybe even perverting the course of justice."

"Justice?" Maccallan said, and there was an edge to his voice that I recognised from the hours in the interview room. It was impossible to tell if it was a crack in the façade or a crack in Maccallan himself. Either way it felt more solid than the sophisticated Bond-villain image he'd been trying for.

I adjusted my grip on Dog Boy's pistol. There was nothing wrong with how it felt in my hand; I wanted to remind Maccallan I was holding it.

"Ms Cross," Sol said to the side of my face – I didn't intend looking away from Maccallan – "you talk about the course of justice. Where was the justice you claim to serve when they closed the bridges, when the army opened fire on civilians and the government fled to safety while telling the plebs to stay in their homes to mitigate the risk of infection spreading? We needed justice four years ago when the French police went into hospitals with machine pistols and the …"

"Shut up," I said. Then to Maccallan, "You, stand up, turn round and put your hands behind your back."

He'd used the cover of Sol's little speech to smooth over the crack again. He didn't move. This time I lifted the pistol, so the threat wasn't veiled in any way.

"I don't think you'll shoot me, Detective Cross."

"Just stand up, turn round and put your hands behind your back. I'm not the only one is this room holding a gun."

He glanced over my shoulder at Winslow and the shotgun. He hadn't got the Bond-villain role as pat as he had the Robertson role, but he made a brave attempt to look suave as he stood up. When his hand flickered briefly out of sight, Winslow stepped forward and put the barrels of the shotgun into his lower back.

"Hands where I can see them. I swear, half an excuse, that's all I'm going to need."

Maccallan put his hands behind him and Winslow used my set of cuffs. I saw his fingers tense before he backed away. I guessed he'd just resisted the urge to clamp them on as tight as possible. Standard cop payback on smart-mouth detainees. He allowed himself a minor vent by spinning Maccallan round and pushing him back down into the chair. The chair rolled and hit the workbench, rattling the tools. Maccallan gave both of us a contemptuous look as he used his heels to push himself upright.

"Good use of justice."

"Sneer all you want," Winslow told him. "You're up to your neck in trouble and wearing handcuffs."

I noticed he'd moved forward again into my field of vision. The stubby barrels of the shotgun were squarely on Maccallan again. The border between me and the bad guys had been reinstated.

"Yeah, law and order in action. Civilisation at its best." He glanced at me and slowly pulled his gaze towards Winslow. "Pull the trigger, Lincoln. Go on, cross that line and join the club, why don't you?"

He waited, and of course nothing happened. His laugh was ice cold but genuine.

"Times have changed, Maccallan. We're passed the days when problems could just be killed," I said.

"Civilisation," he said flatly. "Only we're not quite there yet, are we? Because if we were this would all be taking place in an interview room with a set of rights for me and a deck of recording equipment to record the confession. And like I said already, who would that benefit?"

"Maybe the people you murdered?" Winslow said.

"You think the dead benefit from anything you can do? That's what you tell yourself, is it? I'll make this arrest and it'll make a difference?"

"One less of your sort at large? Yeah, I think that'll make a difference."

"And what's my sort, Lincoln? A killer? Yeah, me and a thousand others. We were living in hell. You think you've got a right to hand out justice to me?"

"Why don't you stop with all the crap about fighting across the Lockdown zone? That was Robertson's story, remember? You spent most of the Lockdown sitting pretty in your bolthole. That's where you did your killing. Who was the woman you butchered, Maccallan? The one who trusted you enough to let you into her flat and was heading towards her bedroom?"

Maccallan tried to sit back in the chair but found he couldn't because the cuffs kept his hand bunched in his lower back. He settled for angling his body so he could rest some of his weight on the edge of the workbench. He didn't look at either me or Winslow.

"Her name was Anthea DeSoto. I'd barely spoken to her before the Outbreak. I'd said good morning once, in a lift. That was it." One side of his mouth pulled into half a smile. "If we had anything in common it was lousy timing. She lost her passport the month before the block was put on international flights. I hung on too long."

"You were waiting for one last payout," I said.

Maccallan nodded, "Only the world economy folded in two."

"Anthea DeSoto?" Winslow said evenly.

"There were four or five of us holed up at the start. Anthea and another fella on her floor. A couple in the flats lower down, they quit pretty soon. And the guy on the top floor, the expensive floor. He cracked up real quick." Maccallan straightened in his seat again and looked Winslow up and down with calculated rudeness. "A lot of people like to make snide remarks about boltholes, talk about people hiding and cowering. Well, I'll tell you something, Lincoln, you think it's the easy way out. You try it. You fucking try it. Sit in a room on your own with nothing to do but eat your supplies and wonder how long you've got. The guy on the top floor didn't last a month. That's how I met Anthea.

"Her flat was directly underneath his. She could hear him pacing backwards and forwards for hours at a time. When he started smashing the place up, she got scared and ran out of her flat. Then she ran down onto my floor and was too scared to go further. I heard her on the landing hammering on the door and screaming for help."

"I'm surprised you answered," Winslow said in the same flat voice.

Maccallan shrugged.

"It was early on. Two months later …" He shrugged again. "Who knows? Maybe I wouldn't. Maybe that would have been better."

"What happened?" I wasn't sure I believed Maccallan's poses of remorse and anyway, I didn't particularly want to watch a melodrama.

"Anthea had convinced herself that the guy on the top floor had a gun. He didn't. I think she'd just heard him smashing bottles and panicked. I brought her into the flat, tried to calm her down. Even in my flat we could hear him stamping about. The block was nearly empty. After a while we went up to see what was happening."

"How very gallant."

"This was early on. None of it felt real. Even when there were still news reports coming in about riots and half of Europe being dead, it was like hearing about something on the other side of the moon. Sitting in my flat listening to a noisy neighbour was acceptable. The idea of an armed man roaming the building was something else that only really happened on the TV. We had a belt of scotch and convinced ourselves he wasn't dangerous."

Maccallan looked puzzled by his own story. Maybe it was the first time he'd told it and hadn't realised how insane it sounded. Maybe he'd been telling Robertson's story for too long and was intrigued by his own.

"We crept up the stairs, calling out to ask if everything was okay. I felt embarrassed. That's the craziest thing, you know? Creeping up the stairs in a deserted block of flats, holed up for the end of the world, and I was wondering if I should be minding my own business. I never found out the guy's name. He was building that stupid barricade at the top of the stairwell, trying to seal off his floor by putting a couple of armchairs at the top. He was a youngish guy, drunk or high. He looked like a trader, you know what I mean?"

The question was addressed to me and I nodded. I knew what he meant. I pictured the man on the top floor, clean-cut veneer and an expensive haircut draped over a coke habit and a moral abyss. It was probably a different picture to the one in Maccallan's head, but we were on a common wavelength.

"He screamed when he saw us at the bottom of the stairs and then he started throwing things. Once we could see him, it wasn't scary anymore. Just pathetic. Sad little city boy building a fort and throwing his toys out of the pram."

"So, you went up to sort him out?" Winslow asked, though it was more an implied insult than a question.

"I went up and did the terribly British thing of asking him to keep the noise down."

Maccallan suddenly roared with laughter and made me jump.

"He ducked out of sight and then came running down the stairs waving a bloody machete. Silly bastard tripped and went down the stairs headfirst."

He blinked as if startled by the farce he'd just recounted.

"I picked up the machete. Anthea and me just watched him for a while as he got his bearings again. Once he could walk straight again, he ran up the stairs and locked himself in his flat. We could hear him shouting but we left him to it. After that Anthea pulled herself together. I think she felt safe."

"With you?" Winslow said.

His voice was expressionless and Maccallan narrowed his eyes, trying to read meaning into the question.

"I don't know about that, to be honest. I think she'd seen the monster upstairs was just another nobody. Scared and confused. We knocked on the door of the other guy on her floor, but he wouldn't come out. We could hear him shuffling around. I called out to ask if he was alright. He just shouted, 'Go away.' I didn't even see his face."

"Until you murdered him."

"Not even then. That night when I got his door open was the night the power had gone off. He was just a shape in the hallway."

"Why? What made you go from asking if he was alright to killing him?" It was Winslow that asked but Maccallan gave his answer to me, with a knowing smile that I dearly wanted to put a bullet through.

"That was the night my world came to a fucking end. You can guess can't you, Detective Cross? You looked through all my paperwork."

"You realised you were poor."

He looked disappointed.

"No, not poor, dead. I realised I didn't fucking exist anymore."

Winslow, who'd been getting more tense with each word Maccallan said, stepped forward and hit him across the face, backhanded. It was nothing compared to the pistol-whipping Johnno had received but it was enough to topple him out of the chair. He landed at Sol's feet and the old man made to lean forward. If he'd been planning to help him sit upright, Winslow beat him to it. He stepped past me and grabbed a handful of Maccallan's hair, dragged him into a sitting position and then pushed him back so he was propped up in the shell of the boarded-over fireplace.

The back of Winslow's hand had split both of Maccallan's lips and his chin was coated with blood. He was conscious though and his expression, through the pain, told me he was about to make some clever remark. Winslow cut it short by forcing the barrels of the shotgun between his teeth.

"Alright, Maccallan, this is how you want it? You don't want justice or law and order? That's fine. We'll sit here and listen to your stories, but you talk sense or I'll blow your lying face off."

"Okay, Winslow, you've made your point. Back off."

Winslow didn't back off. He twisted the gun so the barrels were sideways in Maccallan's mouth, forcing it open and grinding on his teeth.

"We're worried about procedure now are we, Sergeant?"

"I said, back off."

Whatever point he'd been intending to make he considered it made. He yanked the gun out of Maccallan's mouth. Sol pulled in a sharp breath and Maccallan's face clenched in a spasm of pain. Johnno swore at Winslow.

I had to turn my head to see Winslow's reaction because when he'd backed away from the workbench, he'd put himself outside of my sight once again. He wasn't looking at Johnno or watching Maccallan bleed. I met his eye.

"I want this man's confession. If your agenda includes something other than that, I'll happily take you off this case."

"As you like, Sergeant. Should I make him a cup of tea?"

Maccallan made a subtle spitting noise and wiped blood onto the shoulder of his jacket.

"That's the spirit, Lincoln. That's why you became a copper ain't it? Flex a bit of muscle?"

"Shut it, the pair of you. Enough dick waving. You, what do you mean you didn't exist?"

Maccallan tried to smile but stretching his lips caused him too much pain, so he winced instead.

"You know I said everyone's got a sob story? Well, this is mine." He wiped more blood onto his shoulder. He looked away and I thought he was going to tell his story to the floor, but he looked up again, unashamed, or proudly defiant. "I'd spent years in that shitty little agency, me and Robertson. I knew the job inside out and back to front. You're right, I was stealing from the firm for years. Little bits, accounts that could take the hit and not notice. I had nigh on three hundred thou hidden away, cash, offshore accounts. Spread it about you know. Then …" – he shook his head – "… the reports started coming in about the disease, clients started shifting their funds abroad rather than trying to make the housing game pay. I had one big take-down left and then I was ready to go. So, I waited."

"Then the American markets shut you out."

"That was later. The airlines shut before that. Oh, I expect if you had a private jet you could get off the ground. I don't know about landing again." He laughed at his own gallows humour. "I was stuck, in my flat. I bought more groceries than I'd seen in my life and a couple of gennies and I pulled the drawbridge up."

He didn't speak again for a few beats and I could see his eyes slipping out of focus.

"Those were the worst times for me. I had an internet connection via my phone. Do you remember how dark it was after the Lockdown?" He wasn't asking me, and I wasn't even sure he was addressing Sol and Johnno. "If you looked out of the windows there was nothing. I went around to the south side of the building and I swear there wasn't a light to be seen some nights. Not even a fire going sometimes, it was pitch black. There was no horizon, just blackness curving back on itself." His attention flickered between me and Winslow.

Paris had been different, France had been. The fires never stopped there. Some nights I'd pray for darkness. Still, I knew what he was talking about. The end. Writ large. I nodded at him to show I understood. And of course, he laughed in my face.

"My view was 'Who gives a shit?' The lights went out, big deal. Most people were too fucking stupid to turn the lights on before the power went down.

Now the world had gone all shit and most people were just bright enough to sit in the dark. Gosh. What a surprise." The man's humour or malice passed, and he looked thoughtful for a couple of beats. "It was the internet that frightened me. Things began to vanish – sites, newsfeeds, things just stopped being there and what was there was an account of my money shrinking. Dollars and sterling, that was how I spread it. Two of the most stable currencies in the globe. And they were both withering in front of my eyes. Dying. You get that? Money, money was dying."

"Money never dies," Sol muttered.

There was a definite tone of admonishment. Maccallan looked towards him and tilted his head in a salute of sorts.

"I realised that. And I adjusted my mindset to the new economy. Survival was the new wealth. You couldn't keep accounts on a ledger sheet anymore or buy a new car to keep up with the Joneses. All you could do was outlive them."

"By which you mean murder them," Winslow said. The words were barely audible but Maccallan heard.

"Yes. There really is no point denying it. I killed the competition for the building's wealth."

"And that doesn't bother you?" I asked.

"Yeah, it bothers me, I regret it. I have daydreams where Anthea and I both made it through and we both lived lives worth having. But it didn't happen and what did happen can't be changed. I can't make it unhappen. Any more than your sob story can be unmade, Lincoln. Whatever happened to you is history and locking me up or sending me to a labour unit to be worked to death won't change it." He turned and looked squarely at me, "I think we might be able to turn your sob story around."

I ignored the question he wanted asked.

"What happened with Miller's group?" I asked. "Why did you join up with them?"

"That was some time after I'd flipped out."

"After you'd murdered three innocent people. Call it what it is," Winslow said.

"Alright, Lincoln, if it makes you feel better about yourself, after I murdered three innocent people and looted their homes." He turned back to me. "That's when I produced all that paperwork you saw. First I listed my new wealth – tins of soup, bottles of water. It didn't take much time, and it was a one-sided ledger sheet. Every meal was a deduction and I got to sit and watch my stock market get eaten. Mousetraps, good investment." More gallows humour that only he found funny. He looked at me with the same measuring look that Sol had subjected me to.

I tried the male thing of waving the gun around to hurry him along.

"You can't guess what happened next?"

There was no point waving the gun around. If you don't mean to pull the trigger the things ain't worth a damn.

"You beat back the mice and went looking for new markets?"

The answer seemed to please him, and Sol, who made a noise like someone enjoying a good wine.

"Nine out of ten. I saw off the hostile takeover bid from the rodent collective and looked at an up and coming market." He waited for me to fill the gap again but glanced at Winslow, who sounded as if he was about to start dishing out the old school policing again.

"Cryptocurrencies?"

"Exactly. I'd put a few a hundred into Bitcoin in the early days, curious about it. And of course, it was hard to trace back. If it took off, the tax evasion possibilities alone were worth a mint. But it didn't look as if it was going anywhere. I put about seven hundred sterling into it at one point, before the Outbreak. It was too volatile to be worth pursuing. The real-world value was up and down like a yo-yo and it was practically impossible to use it to for real-world transactions. If you wanted to buy software, virtual houses or a couple of grams of coke it was great. If you wanted to buy real-estate …" He flicked a hand dismissively.

"But that changed."

"I was still getting internet connections. Europe wasn't there anymore. China had firewalls so all you'd get was a government website, but America and Japan were still transmitting. The Yanks were trying to hide the fact that their markets and economy were dust and ashes. But crypto started up with force. The Japs were trading it by the middle of 2021, using it on an official basis. The Yanks resisted for a while, but when the income tax rate soared and the US Treasury started printing next-to-worthless banknotes, a market started to develop."

"You said your money was worthless?" Winslow asked, interested despite himself. "What good did it do you?"

"An intelligent question from the floor, who'd have thought it? Before the Outbreak I'd bought the software to build blockchain code. That meant I could generate crypto. It was an impulse buy, literally a way to make money."

And his flat had shown a classic boys and their toys IT addiction.

"You were mining crypto, making your own Bitcoins?"

"I was trying. The problem with crypto – from my point of view – was the cost of making it." I couldn't see Winslow because he was still keeping himself behind me. But he must have looked baffled because Maccallan directed a smug-looking grin in his direction and said, slowly and clearly, "The cost of the electricity was more than the value of the coins it generated."

"Even with looted generators and petrol?"

"Well, effectively the coin was free, but I couldn't get enough gennies or enough fuel to do it quickly, it was all too slow. And then the gennies started to fail. I didn't know it at the time, but the petrol and diesel were going bad. After about nine months the stuff I was finding was stale as hell. Getting the gennies started nearly killed me sometimes."

"By then the power came back on across the river?"

"Yeah, but I'd nearly wound up dead a couple of times out scavenging. And all the bridges had been blown away. And the last time anyone had tried to cross over to the north of the city a bunch of government monkeys cut them down with machine guns. But it was something to cling to. If the power was back on then things weren't over."

"But you didn't want to stay put?" Winslow said.

"No. I'd cracked up once. I knew that, I made it back the first time, but I didn't know if I'd be so lucky again. Then I saw Miller's group coming down the street. I heard them first shouting commands, but carefully. They weren't bringing a shower of trouble down on themselves. They obviously had order. And they were heading north."

"You just left everything and followed?"

"Not until I saw Robertson. A blast from the past."

"Are you saying you two did get on, before the Outbreak? You were friends?"

Sol chuckled and muttered, "Oh, my lord."

"No. We didn't get on. But I knew he was as crooked as me. The mistake I made was overestimating how bright he was. I saw him heading north and assumed he was thinking the same way I was."

"We're not all as clever as you," Sol said. The words came with a definite edge on them but there was respect there too.

"If he was that clever, he wouldn't be sitting on the floor in a pair of handcuffs," Winslow said.

Everyone ignored him.

"Robertson and Sol had seen the lights were on in the financial sector. They were headed that way with the idea of pulling the bullion from the vaults." Maccallan's voice lacked respect but not affection. It was the voice of a teacher pointing out the obvious mistake for the tenth time.

"Gold is still a good investment. Solid," Sol, the bored pupil, said while looking into a corner of the room, addressing the universe that might be listening.

"Which is why the government took it with them when they broke for the border." Maccallan, answering on behalf of the universe.

"It was still …"

"A waste of time," Maccallan said firmly. "Even if the gold had been left in an abandoned city how did you plan on getting into the vault? Digging in like that gobshite Billings and his pack of cunts?"

"Then why head to the bank at all?" Winslow asked.

"The computers," I told him.

"Exactly. Mining the coins isn't like downloading a song. It takes time. And if I teamed up with people, they'd expect a cut. It was going to be divided by six to start with. By the end of the game it was down to three. But that still meant three fortunes to make and the real problem was I couldn't be sure which of the cryptocurrencies was going to flourish. I narrowed it down to seven that had enough mobility to them to keep on working. In effect I needed a minimum of twenty-one mines, all pumping and transmitting like bastards. Then I needed a server big enough to store the stuff." He looked at Winslow again and grinned, looking horrific with the blood starting to dry on his face. "You explain it to him, eh?"

"Cryptocurrencies don't respect borders. They go wherever they're needed, but to make it work every transaction is recorded on a huge network of servers. They can be anywhere in the world. I don't get it fully, but the blockchain codes are updated constantly. It takes a lot of computing power to do it quickly."

Winslow considered it for a while.

"So, your mobile connection to the internet wasn't going to do you any good?"

"Right. Until the internet connection was sure enough to transfer a vast slab of blockchain, I had to keep everything in a holding pattern. I'm guessing it was the transfer that put you on to me?"

"The US Treasury have their own blockchains to keep an eye on. There's a vast amount of stagnant Double Dee that's consistent with an info dump that came out of the UK. The only place that much data could have been unofficially generated in one hit …"

"… was North London."

"It was your book that gave you away," Winslow put in. His voice was higher than normal, stressed, angry, something sour. "I hope stroking your ego was worth going to prison for."

"It wasn't about stroking my ego. It was …" he left the sentence hanging.

"Proof that you existed? Even if it was under an assumed name."

"Spot on, Sergeant. And of course, I get a percentage of the sales. All for chatting to a ghostwriter for a day or two."

"Why did you murder Robertson?"

"I don't call it murder. It was a mercy killing. I saved him what I went through. I knew him before all this shit, worked with the man. He was nothing, a worthless piece of shit with a shit life, a shit job and a shit house to live in. The truest bit of that book – the truest part about him at least – was that description of running along the Thames just after the bridges all went up and the Gonzos got in among the crowds. He told that story again and again and again. I thought he was boasting at first, then I realised it was his epiphany. For the first time in his sad little life the world was the way he wanted it. All his problems, all his worries reduced to a simple equation: kill or be killed. He was a thug, who'd never known it before. A messiah for the maniacs. He loved every minute of it. It's a pity you never met him, Lincoln. You could have swapped stories about horrible it all was and then told each other how far you've come. Best thing that ever happened to either of you."

"You know nothing about me, you smug arsehole, nothing." Winslow's voice was too calm. "You think any promotion I got was worth the shit I've been through? You honestly think I prefer being a detective in London than a PC in Lincoln?"

"Yes, I do, Lincoln. That's exactly what I think. That's the difference between you and me. Everything I did was about getting my life, my way of life, back. Robertson, you, people like you, they revelled in it. Rolled in the blood and the shit and forgot they were just nobodies."

"While people like you just went straight back to making the same mistakes," I said.

The intervention popped the bubble of tension that had been growing. I could feel the puzzled looks of both men on me. Strangely, Johnno was the only one who seemed to get the reference.

He grunted an agreement and said, "Amen."

"You've pulled the same trick you did before, Maccallan," I said. "You ended up sitting in a flat before watching everything you'd worked for turning to ash, because you were greedy, hanging around for just a little more money to come in."

I used the hand that wasn't holding the gun to wave at the dingy walls and ceiling. The new flat he was sitting in, trapped.

He shook his head at my assumption.

"Not quite the same situation, Sergeant. The money's pretty much in and counted. What I'm waiting for this time is somewhere to go. Europe's still in ruins. Japan doesn't really appeal and the communist countries …" He pulled a face. I could see the lack of interest for such a confirmed money man. "America's going to be the place to go. I'll give it another two or three years before the current government collapses, then they'll be throwing their precious borders wide open. Looking for investment in their rebuild policies. You're a money person too, Sergeant. Don't tell me you don't spend some of your internet allowance keeping one eye on the money markets."

I didn't give him the satisfaction of agreeing with him or the satisfaction of making me a liar by denying it. Uncle Sam was presently residing over the only continent untouched by HV-Tg, that was going into a fourth year of recession. The economic rebuild had largely been passed over in favour of a pageant every three months, screaming 'America's number one' and 'God bless the second amendment.'

"And assuming you're right, that's your great plan. Take your celebrity and money and live the American dream. Even if Drumph does lose the next election, if he even holds one, those border controls are going to relax not vanish. Your passport has a dead man's name on it, a famous dead man's name on it."

Maccallan and Sol both snorted laughter. It wasn't at the naivety of my suggestion; it was at the transparency of it.

"Passports, ID cards, health insurance documents, tax returns and social security numbers. Sol here has even got the paperwork saying generous donations have been made to the appropriate political parties. A set for each of the major ones. Just in case there's a shock result somewhere down the line."

"Sure you have, big man," Winslow said.

"Why are you still here then?"

"We could leave anytime we want. Sol here's not that fussed about going, Johnno's doing okay where he is." Maccallan shrugged. "And I could leave tomorrow if I needed to. Or if I had something worth making the journey for." He looked at me and nodded. "Sol here produced the papers I needed, like he produces the coupons and a dozen other items. Before Toxo, the name Solomon Abrahams was legendary in certain circles."

"You're a forger," I said.

Sol laughed.

"I used to be *the* forger." He held up his hands to showcase the tremor playing at his fingertips. "Now I'm merely a talented artist." He found this funny and chuckled to himself before saying, tonelessly, "I can make a new identity, bank accounts with pretty balances and histories, numbers, licenses for trades, titles for properties. In two months, tops, a brand-new person with a lifetime of paper trail could land in a New York airport and start a new life."

"And for so little cost," Maccallan said. "That's the beauty of money. It not only talks, it deals."

"Is that all any of this is to you people," Winslow said, "money?"

He stepped forward, each movement independent, the way a machine moved. He lifted the shotgun and put it in Maccallan's face.

"Was that all any of it boiled down to? Money?"

"I told you, in that poxy interview room. All those fucking hours and you didn't listen. Money is all there fucking is, money is civilisation. Robertson didn't get it. He thought he was living some sort of primal wet dream. Miller? The legend? That didn't exist. He was just some bloody sick freak with a knife. All that crap about him killing himself. He didn't kill himself, he didn't have the sense, he just faded away when there was nothing left to slaughter. You half-bright twat, is that what you want? You have money, you have trust, that's how it works. Even with thieves it's down to trust – if you don't trust the money, we don't bother stealing it."

He was angry, breathing hard.

Winslow didn't have an answer. But he didn't need one. He had a shotgun.

"You are under arrest. For the murder of Colin Robertson, and whoever those poor bastards in your block were. You're going to die in shackles, in a work crew. You can tell them how civilised you are."

"And you really think I don't have the necessary to buy my way out?"

Maccallan addressed this to me.

I could see in Winslow's face he didn't get it. Could see the fury, the image of a burning hospital and the pointlessness of ambitions meet, because London needed coppers.

Could see a bloodless white knuckle tighten on a trigger. That's the thing with guns, it takes one finger to change everything. One finger and even less thought.

Chapter 55. Donna Riley

News report broadcast on BBC Radio London (17/04/2028)

A fire at a private residence, in which one person died, is believed to have started in an illegal drinking venue, operating in an adjacent building. A spokesman for the London Fire Brigade said the speed and ferocity of the blaze was possibly due to spirits being stored on the premises.

The identity of the body, found in the early hours of Sunday morning, is yet to be confirmed, but is thought to be that of Peter Brockfield. Mr Brockfield was lodging in an upstairs flat and was last seen entering the building on Saturday afternoon. The owner of the flat, Mrs Hayling (61), was unaware of the illegal activity taking place in the next-door building.

Police and fire services are treating the incident as an accident.

Memo from the desk of Superintendent Taylor, Metropolitan Police (03/05/2028)

From: Lucas Fielding, Anglo-American joint policing liaison officer, Washington State Police.
To: Oliver Taylor, Superintendent, Met. Police.

As of midnight (EST), April 30, Miranda Cross is officially logged as missing in the course of duty. We currently have no one positioned in the UK who would be able to competently handle the investigation she was undertaking. If we find a suitable replacement you will be informed. In the meantime, we will require any records or documentation relating to Detective Sergeant Cross's investigation. All official paperwork and requests are being compiled and will be with you within the next forty-eight hours.

Movie Madness Forum > General Discussion > Movie Gossip

FanguRobertson
POSTS: 85
Is it true there's going to be a follow up to Year of the Crow? I heard rumours that Hollywood had asked Robertson to star in it.

****

tHATmOVIEgUY
POSTS: 877
I heard something about that too. I also heard that Robertson's flown out to LA start filming.

****

Big_Foot
POSTS: 65
There is another film being made about the Lockdown but it's going to be about the Billings Boyz. I don't think Robertson would want to appear in it, not after what he said about Billings and his men in his book.
I did read that Robertson had left the country.

****

IwinUlooz
POSTS: 98
Robertson's disappeared.

****

QWERTY12
POSTS: 74
I think MI6 took Robertson out because of all the bad mouthing he did about Billings.

****

SeeSawn
POSTS: 43
RIP Robertson.

May 19th, 2028

Among the stack of documents he'd provided, Sol had included a licence to carry a concealed gun. Possibly as a joke. That famous ultra-dry sense of humour the British use to exclude everyone else from the laughter.

In the way Maccallan could only define himself in relation to how well he could acquire and manipulate money, Sol defined himself by how effectively he could scam people. Getting one over, to use his phraseology.

I got to observe him at work, in close quarters for almost six weeks. When he wasn't making fake papers and passes, he'd cheat at chess, cards, checkers and anything else he did. If there was a system or a set of rules, Sol took it as his sacred duty to screw it over.

It had been Sol who'd taken the still smoking gun from me and deftly emptied the cylinder before asking me for the keys to the handcuffs. He didn't need to threaten or coax me with promises. I'd crossed the Rubicon now and left myself no options.

Johnno had reclaimed his shotgun with a blank man-at-work expression.

Maccallan had seen to the fire.

The gun licence didn't raise an eyebrow at the NY airport's check-in desk. The guards didn't give a shit about anything other than the receipts for payments and the colour of my skin.

It was clear that Drumph thought the glories of his new American dream shone brightest when reflected off pale surfaces.

If I hadn't been so nervous about the fake papers being spotted, I would have taken a moment to wonder if coming home was desirable, never mind wise.

The guards nodded, told me everything appeared to be in order. And waited for their bribes.

And I was in.

My new name was Donna Riley. Sol chose it; it was right for my age and the region I was now claiming to come from. I was an orphan of Irish descent. The Irish being liked and disregarded in equal measure, almost universally. On instruction I dyed my hair a dull no-colour and styled it to be unflattering without being ugly and added a pair of glasses, too big and too old for my face. Donna Riley wasn't going to be turning heads as she walked through clearing.

Plain as she was, Donna Riley didn't come without a cost.

"You can't go back to your old job, school, college," Sol told me. "Miranda Cross died the moment you pulled that trigger. Forget her, build someone new."

I hadn't said anything about David and Maria. My plan was simple enough. Maria would barely remember me – I told myself – and David would understand that we'd have to move and start over. Miranda was missing, presumed dead, somewhere in the ruins of the UK. David and his new love, Donna, were moving away to start a new life. David would be able to manage the deception – I told myself.

It started raining as I reached my house. Or what had been someone else's house. Donna Riley didn't have a home yet. I parked across the street and left the engine running, enjoying the luxury of an automobile as opposed to a car. I'd taken Sol's advice and bought rather than hired. One transaction and the delay while the pink slips were processed meant fewer official eyes knowing my movements.

Let it get to be a habit: leave a light footprint, leave as little paper as you can.

I'd had to sit and work out how much I'd paid for it. It had taken me a while to make the adjustments from old world values to new, and another while to adjust to the seemingly random numbers associated with the virtual coin stored in my crypt.

The price had been cheap by any reckoning and I'd patted myself on the back for getting a bargain. Until I did the same set of calculations at the gas station and realised I was driving a white elephant. Drumph's insane foreign policy had put American oil back on the top rung of domestic supply and sent fuel prices rocketing.

The once nondescript sedan I'd picked drew attention as it idled its fuel away.

Across the street I watched alien beings living their alien lives. David still forgot to draw the curtains. Through the big picture window, I watched him and a tall girl, who looked like a woman who'd been her mother, eat popcorn and laugh at something on a flat screen TV.

I checked my watch. In the UK, it was almost nine p.m. and the mobile networks would be shutting down soon. If Miranda was there, she'd only have a few minutes before she missed the window of opportunity to make the call.

Tick tock. The locks have broken the keys.

I thought about Dog Boy and the smell of burning and the feel of a trigger against a finger. And a woman I'd known once who hadn't existed for a long time.

At nine o'clock GMT, I put the shifter into drive and pulled away.

THE END

About the author

Russell Day was born in 1966 and grew up in Harlesden, NW10 – a geographic region searching for an alibi. From an early age it was clear the only things he cared about were motorcycles, tattoos and writing. At a later stage he added family life to his list of interests and now lives with his wife and two children. He's still in London, but has moved south of the river for the milder climate.

Although he only writes crime fiction Russ doesn't consider his work restricted. 'As long as there have been people there has been crime, as long as there are people there will be crime.' That attitude leaves a lot of scope for settings and characters. One of the first short stories he had published, The Second Rat and the Automatic Nun, was a double-cross story set in a world where the church had taken over policing.

In his first novel, Needle Song, an amateur detective employs logic, psychology and a loaded pack of tarot cards to investigate a death.

Russ often tells people he seldom smiles due to nerve damage, sustained when his jaw was broken. In fact, this is a total fabrication and his family will tell you he's always been a miserable bastard.

In 2018, Russell won the Margaret Allingham Short Story Award.

Acknowledgements

Over the years, through a combination of bad luck, poor reflexes and rank stupidity, I've managed to notch up sixteen fractures over ten different bones. I've also collapsed both lungs, having punctured one of them first. I've had concussion, sprained my ankle and been bitten by a mouse. But, strangely, I've never broken my nose .

I was pondering this odd hole in my medical history one day and got to thinking about my sense of smell. This led to a rambling chain of thought that turned into King of the Crows.

Between, I've never broken my nose, and Dear Sir, please find attached a 165,000 word manuscript, there's a lot of gaps to fill. A lot of things I realised I didn't know. Luckily, a lot of good people were willing to help educate me. So, in no particular order, I need to say thanks to the following people:

Ian Patrick, for his advice on writing a believable police report. And his editing of my first attempt.

Jo Perry, who put up with me sending her snippets of random dialogue and asking, does this sound too English?

Kirsty Yeomans (Crowartist), for answering my weird questions about the behaviour of crows. And, on an unrelated matter, for producing the damn fine

Raven decal currently adorning my Harley.

Dr Nicola Parry, who was a tireless source of information on Toxoplasma gondii and Scouse swear words.

Lorraine Mace, for putting my short story about the Lockdown, Keeping Score on a Machete, in Writers' Forum Magazine. Knowing someone thought my oddball tale was worth reading, finally kicked me into developing it into a novel.

William Baginsky, for proofing my manuscript and getting it to a standard where I was able to submit it. Given that I can misspell my own initials, that was no small task.

And finally, I need to thank Chris McVeigh, the main man at Fahrenheit Press. Offer most publishers a zombie heist novel and they'll politely decline. Try and sweeten the deal by pointing out it's packed with quotes from books that don't exist, online rants that have never been posted and pages from a screenplay that gets the facts wrong, and they'll probably call security. Offer it to McVeigh and the mad fucker sends you a contract.

Thank you all.

Before he can be laid to rest though, his wife makes an unusual request, one which Yakky fulfils with characteristic stoicism.

The funeral is a particularly tense affair and it becomes clear to Doc that there's more going on than initially meets the eye.

All is clearly not well within the ranks of The Handsome London Boys and when Doc starts asking questions about the circumstances of Dago's accident and the disappearance of a young pledger, he and Yakky find themselves being dragged into the secretive and potentially dangerous world of the 'one-percenters'.

Doc & Yakky need to tread very carefully if they're going to ensure the truth is revealed, justice is served - and they both get out of this alive.

Dead Is Better by Jo Perry

Charles Stone has just woken up dead. Well he's pretty sure he's dead, what with the bullet holes in his chest and all. He also appears to be totally alone in the after-life except for the ghostly dog who seems to be his new companion.

Unable to interact with the world of the living other than watching and listening, he and the dead dog (whom he names Rose) have nothing to do and all the time in the world to do it.

When Charles and Rose try to unravel the circumstances of Charles's death, they uncover a criminal who is raking in millions of dollars by cruelly exploiting, and sometimes killing, his victims.

But what difference can a ghost make?

And what does the damn dog have to do with any of this?

Rubicon by Ian Patrick

Two cops, both on different sides of the law – both with the same gangland boss in their sights.

Sam Batford is an undercover officer with the Metropolitan Police who will stop at nothing to get his hands on fearsome crime-lord Vincenzo Guardino's drug supply.

DCI Klara Winter runs a team on the National Crime Agency, she's also chasing down Guardino, but unlike Sam Batford she's determined to bring the gangster to justice and get his drugs off the streets.

Set in a time of austerity and police cuts where opportunities for corruption are rife, Rubicon is a tense, dark thriller that is definitely not for the faint hearted.

Printed in Poland
by Amazon Fulfillment
Poland Sp. z o.o., Wrocław